"I sometimes forget the colo

"I sometimes forget that I am hated of man and remember that I
am loved of God."

Frederick Douglass

"...and Remember that I Am a Man."

The Life of Moses Grandy

A historical novel by John Bushore

"...And Remember that I Am a Man."

...and Remember that I Am a Man © 2010 by John Bushore

A MonkeyJohn Books Production

First Edition: January, 2011

The cover art is a depiction of the Lake Drummond Hotel, built in 1829 on the bank of the Dismal Swamp Canal, straddling the border between North Carolina and Virginia

To order additional copies of this book, visit the author's website at:
http://www.johnbushore.com

ISBN-13: 978-1453653807

ISBN-10: 1453653805

"…And Remember that I Am a Man."

This novel is dedicated to the memory of Moses Grandy

Acknowledgements

I would like to thank the following persons for their help, advice and encouragement in writing this novel:

Juanita Alexander
Betsy Davis Boling
Jacquelyn Bushore
Jeff and Jacqueline Falkenham
Steve Horton
Ingrid Parker
Richard Rowand
John Rosenman
Melissa Solzenberg
David Weimer
Tom Wright

I hope you enjoy

John B.

"…And Remember that I Am a Man."

A Slave in the Dismal Swamp
by Henry W. Longfellow

In the dark fens of Dismal Swamp,
The hunted Negro lay;
He saw the fire of the midnight camp,
And heard at times a horse's tramp,
And bloodhound's distant bay.

Where will-o-wisps and glow worms
Shine in bulrush and brake,
Where waving mosses shroud the pine,
And the cedar grows and the poisonous vine,
Is spotted like the snake.

Where hardly a human foot could pass
Or human heart would dare,
On the quaking turf of the green morass
He crouched in the rank and tangled grass
Like a wild beast in his lair

A poor old slave, infirm and lame,
Great scars deformed his face.
On his forehead he bore the brand of shame,
And wild birds filled the echoing air
With songs of liberty.

On him alone was the doom of pain,
From the morning of his birth.
On him alone the curse of Cain
Fell like a flail on the garnered grain,
And struck him to the earth.

"…And Remember that I Am a Man."

Part One

The Pharaoh's House

Chapter One

In the Great Dismal—1792 A.D.

My name is Moses Grandy: I was born in Camden County, North Carolina. I believe I am fifty-six years old. Slaves seldom know exactly how old they are: neither they nor their masters set down the time of a birth; the slaves, because they are not allowed to write or read; and the masters, because they only care to know what slaves belong to them.

The master, Billy Grandy, whose slave I was born, was a hard-drinking man: he sold away many slaves. I remember four sisters and four brothers; my mother had more children, but they were dead or sold away before I can remember. I was the youngest. I remember well my mother often hid us all in the woods, to prevent master selling us.

The Life of Moses Grandy—1843 A.D.

Rebecca looked nervously over her shoulder. Last year, the first time she'd run to the swamp with her children, he'd let her get away with it, but he'd warned her not to try it again, threatening the whip.

A scrawny black woman with close-cut, wiry hair, Rebecca had no idea how old she was, but she'd born thirteen children, counting the two who'd not lived. Her drab, faded dress was of rough hemp. Her feet were bare. She carried a bundle, wrapped in an old blanket.

The Great Dismal Swamp surrounded Rebecca and her family like a damp, steamy section of Hell. The day was growing hot for early summer. As they walked, juniper, gum, and maple trees towered above. Sunlight streamed down on a vast, nearby marsh pond. Baldcypress trees grew directly out of the pond, spaced out like they couldn't stand being close to one another. At the base of each tree, roots jutted from the water like jagged teeth set to protect its privacy. Many were old trees, dead and leafless, their branches emerging like skeletal fingers from behind curtains of hanging moss.

The surface of the water rippled as fish fed on floating insects, causing expanding circles of tiny waves. Near the middle of the pool, the v-shaped wake of a swimming water moccasin moved along, only the snake's head visible. Large turtles watched from fallen logs as the humans passed. Every once in a while, Rebecca would see small birds flitting about in the bushes, but the birds never chirped, as though pleasant sounds were forbidden in the swamp. The world under the trees was eerily silent except for the sucking sounds of footsteps as she and the children followed a faint path through the mire. The dank smell of a primeval world rose about them.

She had awakened the children in the middle of the night and got them started well before dawn. They'd sneaked silently out of the Grandy slave quarters. By daybreak, they'd crossed the fields and entered the swamp.

Benjamin, the oldest child, led the way. He carefully kept to the faint trail they'd used last year when hiding out. Behind him, from oldest to youngest, came Mary, Tamar, Malachai, June, Jebediah and little Moses.

Shortly after entering the swamp, Rebecca had rubbed pawpaw leaves over the children to keep mosquitoes off. It had worked for long enough. By the time the protective coating had been washed off by sweat, the mosquitoes had disappeared, gone into the shady leaves to wait out the heat of the day. But then the biting flies had showed up and she didn't know of any plant remedy to keep those pests away. Soon the children were swatting at piercing bites, ten times worse than the puny stings of mosquitoes. Each puncture mark soon swelled to a lump the size of a half-penny.

The older children didn't complain. Slave children learned to suffer silently. Not the two littlest ones, though, not yet.

Jebby and Moses swatted and cried and screeched so loud she thought they'd bring the patrollers on them for sure. Finally she broke off a leafy branch and waved it over their heads, keeping the insects away. The screeching stopped, but the young ones didn't shut up entirely.

"Are we there yet?"

"I'm thirsty."

"Will there be anybody to play with when we get there?"

"I'm hungry."

"Mosey pushed me."

"Did not."

"Why are we in this stinky old swamp, anyway?"

She smiled, despite the noise. These were her babies.

Moses, a bright-eyed, lively four-year-old, was her youngest. He wasn't used to being outdoors. He spent a lot of time inside the Grandy house, playing with young Master James. The two children, black and white, had been born two days apart and Mistress Grandy had taken a shine to Moses. He didn't know how lucky he was. Other slave babies went to the fields with their mothers every day, carried in slings. Children were made to pluck worms off the tobacco leaves and squish them.

Jebby, although a year older, acted younger than Moses. He wasn't quite right and had to be coddled. In the fields, when Jebby was supposed to be plucking worms or making holes for tobacco seedlings, he'd forget and wander off. The overseer, had given up, and let Jebby stay with the little ones in the shade at the edge of the field, where they played with corncob dolls, sticks, feathers, or whatnot.

Rebecca and her family came to a fallen tree, its uprooted bottom standing sideways like a gigantic spider. Rebecca took another look

7

behind and then called a halt. The little ones were about tuckered out.

The hole at the base of the tree had filled with rain. Unlike the water in marsh ponds, scummy and full of dead leaves, this puddle was clear. It was deep brown, but then all water in the swamp had that color. It had something to do with sap from the juniper roots, folks said. The older children quickly gathered around and began scooping water up with their hands and drinking it. Moses stood back.

"What's the matter with you, boy?" she asked.

"I can't drink that water, Mama," he said. "Somebody went potty in it."

"Hush, boy," she said. "There ain't nothin' bad in that water. It's as good as the farm pond."

"Why's it brown, then?"

Rebecca sighed. None of her other children held a candle to this one. Moses had a mind that never let up.

"All the water in the swamp is like that," she told him. "Brown don't hurt nothin'."

Moses peered closely. "There's bugs in it, too."

She shook her head. Moses would have to learn slaves couldn't be picky about the water they drank. White folks might drink well water, but a slave working the hot fields would be glad to get stagnant ditch water.

"Them are only tadpoles," she said. "You know, baby frogs. They don't hurt nothin'. But I'll get 'em out for you."

She eased her herself down on her knees and took out a scrap of fabric, turning to the child nearest her.

"Mary, you dip out some of that water and pour it through this here cloth."

Mary, a skinny-legged, somber child, scooped up water and poured it through the cloth in Rebecca's left hand. The small bugs and tadpoles were unable to pass through the thin fabric, and clear water dripped down into her cupped right hand. Rebecca showed the water to Moses and then drank it. "Yes indeedy-do, mighty fine."

"I still ain't drinking it," Moses said.

8

"I ain't drinkin' it neither," said Jebediah. It was a silly thing to say, because the boy had been drinking from the puddle moments before. But Jebby often relied on Moses for signs of how to behave.

"Pretend it's coffee," Mary told her younger brothers as she slurped water. "That's what I do."

"Why, you ain't never tasted no real coffee, Mary," Moses told her. "Best you ever had is chicory coffee."

That's Moses for you, Rebecca thought. *Boy never quits arguin'.*

"Just drink it," said Benjamin. He'd started doing man's work in the fields last year and was beginning to fill out with muscles. His voice was also growing deeper. "You drank swamp water last year, remember?"

"I did not," Moses argued.

"This water is good for you," said Tamar, a wide-eyed, light-skinned girl who considered herself an authority on everything. "I heard tell sailors come here and load this water in barrels to carry on their ships, 'cause it don't go stale. Folks who drinks Dismal Swamp water don't never get sick."

Moses pouted and squinted at her. "You ain't foolin' me, Tamar. That water prob'ly tastes same as poop."

"Suit yourself, then." Rebecca snapped. "The good Lord put this water here for you to drink. If you won't have it, then you'll go thirsty."

Benjamin had finished drinking. He stood and wiped water from his chin. "You oughta' be glad for this water," he told Moses. "It's better to drink water with bugs than get sold."

"Ain't nobody gonna sell me." Moses stuck his chin out. "Mama says Master promised he ain't never gonna sell me. He's gonna give me to Master James when we grows up, because we plays together, and Master James likes me."

"He didn't make no promises about your brothers and sisters." Rebecca spat on the ground. "And white folks ain't too good about keeping promises, noways. Help me up, Benjamin. Mama's joints went and got all stiff with the cold."

They set off again, skins glistening with sweat as they followed Benjamin like baby ducks waddling in a line. Again, Rebecca kept a lookout behind her.

"…And Remember that I Am a Man."

When she'd heard a slave dealer was making his way through the county, she had lit out into the swamp with her young ones. If she and her brood could stay away for a few days, the slaver would be gone, and she would face no more than a few harsh words. Master Billy Grandy was a hard man, but Rebecca figured she knew how to handle him.

A while later, Jebediah whined, "I thirsty, Mama."

She took a deep breath. Darn that Moses! "Wait a bit, Jebby," she said. "I'll stop as soon as we find a good place."

"I'm thirstier than Jebby," Moses stated. "I'm so thirsty, I could drink a whole river, I bet."

Rebecca snorted. "You're the one what wouldn't drink."

When they came across another puddle, she stopped. This water wasn't as clear as the last, but beggars couldn't be choosers.

Moses knelt down and peered into the water. "Will you scoop it for me, Mama?"

"Why, of course, Moses," she said, sweet as maple syrup. "I wouldn't want you to fall in and drown, would I?"

"He's such a baby," Benjamin said, "the tadpoles would probably eat him." He let out a guffaw.

Moses stuck his tongue out. "I ain't no baby."

"Hush, y'all," Rebecca said. She knelt and scooped up water, then held it out for Moses. He looked to be sure she hadn't missed any bugs or tadpoles and then drank.

When everyone had drunk enough, she said, "Let's go sit on that hummock. We can have a mite to eat."

She found a log to sit on. The children crowded around. She opened her bundle and broke a piece of cornbread into small pieces. Moses gobbled his down. He picked up crumbs putting them in his mouth. "I'm still hungry, Mama."

"There ain't no more," Rebecca said.

"Are we goin' to stay here, Mama?" Malachai asked. "Is this where we're fixing to hide?"

"Lordy, no, boy," she said. "Ezekiel's shack is a mite farther up the trail." Ezekiel, a friend of Rebecca, was a shingle cutter who hired out to a lumbering company.

Mary popped a last crumb into her mouth and wiped her lips. "Will there be enough to eat while we're there?"

Rebecca nodded her head. "Shore 'nough. I'll sneak out into the fields at night and find us some tucker.

"I don't wanna stay in no swamp." Moses had tears running down his cheeks. "I wanna go home."

"Not 'til that slave buyer has left," Rebecca said.

Tamar asked, "How long do you figure, Mama?"

"I'm thinkin' three days. "

"Won't Master Billy be mad?" asked Mary. "He said last year that he'd whip you if you was to run again."

Rebecca gave a quick shake of her head. "I don't care. I'd druther take a lashin' than lose any more of my babies. 'Sides that, I don't think the Mistress would let him whip me."

"Master Grandy prob'ly wouldn't sell me," Benjamin boasted. "I work hard in the fields."

Rebecca whirled on him. "You get this straight, boy-child. Billy Grandy owns you, body an' soul. If he gets the right price, he'll sell you."

"Would he sell you, Mama?" Moses asked.

She looked down at her son and knew, one day, her heart would break for him. As it had been broken for others of her children when they'd been sold away. "Even me, baby."

*

Moses felt sick to his stomach at the idea. Mama would go away and never come back. Tears flooded down his cheeks. He'd never thought about Mama being sold. He'd once heard Master say to a neighboring farmer, "I'll never get rid of that one. Rebecca's a decent cook, works real hard and she's had a dozen or so whelps. And she's one smart nigger, too."

Thinking of that made Moses feel better. Master would never sell Mama. Moses was proud she was so smart.

Mama pulled herself to her feet and led off. Moses stayed close behind her, followed by his sisters and brothers, Benjamin at the rear. Mama said they didn't have to keep quiet anymore; they were deep in the swamp now.

The ground was soggy and Moses often stepped into shallow puddles, muck seeping between bare toes. It was fun. They went around the bogs when they could, but sometimes had to wade. That

11

was even more fun. Even so, Moses wished he could be home, playing with Master James. Master James had lots of toys, and sometimes let Moses play with them.

While wading, Moses kept his eyes on the water for snakes. Except then he remembered there were other dangerous critters in the swamp, so he began watching all around.

"Look out," Benjamin suddenly shouted. "Gator!"

Moses, his heart in his throat, leaped for dry land, along with all the children. Except Benjamin, who laughed.

Mary put her hands on her hips. "That was mean, Benjamin."

"Y'all hush up," Mama said. "There ain't never been no gators seen in the Great Dismal. You chil'ren know that."

"You can't be sure, Mama," said Benjamin. "Maybe them folks what seen a gator, never lived to tell about it."

"You hush up," Mama said. "There ain't no gators."

Moses kept his eyes out, after that. What if Mama was wrong? What if a gator was to come up out of the brown water, big mouth snapping? Why did they have to come into this scary, stupid old swamp, anyway?

Before long, he began sweating. Not a breeze stirred to disturb the smell of mud and rotting leaves. Mama seemed to be following a trail, but how could she be sure they weren't lost? Every tree looked like every other to Moses. Every bog looked alike and every hummock seemed exactly the same.

When they came to the shack, Moses' heart sank lower than a skunk in a hole. It was a lean-to, made of juniper poles with the spaces filled with mud. Built on a hummock of dry land, it was about big enough for two grown men to lie down. To his horror, it was open on one side.

Mama didn't seem bothered. She put her bundle in the shed and said, "You young-uns stay here. I'm gonna go find us somethin' to eat. Y'all mind Benjamin, now, y'hear?"

Once she had gone off, Moses had nothing to do. Benjamin began messing with the shack, chinking holes with mud. Jebediah and Malachai went off in search of frogs, or turtles, or whatnot, but Moses decided to stay on dry land. It was warmer now and gators, he figured, would be looking for something to eat. And Moses had seen a few snakes, although none close enough to scare him. Snakes were terrifying creatures; there was something evil about a thing that slithered around. The water moccasins were the worstest, some so big and fat Moses figured they could eat a little boy's leg off.

From somewhere inside her clothing, Tamar pulled a corncob doll, and June came up with another one. The dolls had crude faces and wore scraps of cloth. The girls made up things for the dolls to do, such as cooking or sewing.

Moses sat down, pulled up his pants legs, and began plucking off slimy leeches. Some of them, bloated with blood, had been sucking on him for a while. He put them on the ground and stomped them, but then his feet were sticky.

Benjamin looked up from his work. "Why ain't you playin' with Malachai and Jebby?"

"Don't feel like it."

Benjamin laughed. "Scared o' gators, more like it."

"Am not," Moses said. "Just don't feel like playin'."

"Scaredy cat." Benjamin went back to work.

Moses wandered around a bit, then went back to the shack and asked, "There ain't really no gators, is they, Ben?"

"Course there's gators." Ben said, all serious-like. "But there's even worser things than gators, y'know."

Moses felt a chill. "Worser? What could be worser?"

"Pattyrollers." Benjamin nodded his head for emphasis. "That's what's you really better watch out for."

"What's a pattyroller?"

Benjamin leaned down and lowered his voice. "They's white devils, whiter than Miz Grandy's sheets, as white as haunts. They's got red eyes and yellow fangs and they's got long swords to chop off heads, that's what." He drew a finger across his neck. "And they ride fire-breathing horses that stomp little boys to death."

Moses gulped. "You're joshin' me, ain't you, Ben?"

"Nope. You'll see for yourself, sooner or later."

Moses, trying to act unconcerned, went and sat inside the shack, where nothing could get to him.

Mama was gone for a long time, returning just before dark. Moses and everybody jumped up and ran to greet her.

"What did you find, Mama?" Mary asked.

"…And Remember that I Am a Man."

"I didn't get nothin', chil'ren," Mama said. "There was men riding the road and I didn't dast go out into the fields."

"Then what we gonna eat?" Moses asked.

Mama said, "I'm sorry, honey-child. We'll try again in the morning. I'm sure we'll have better luck."

That evening, Moses remained awake long after the others slept, sure his belly had got stuck to his backbone, it ached so bad. He and Jebediah slept with the girls in the shack; Mama and the older boys stayed outside. As the youngest, Moses had the place fartherest from the open side of the hut, but that didn't make him feel safer. If a bear was to come lumbering along, he reckoned it could easily reach past his older sisters to grab the most tenderest meat, which happened to be him. And an alligator would probably start at the front and then eat its way back to Moses with a mouth as big as a bushel basket.

But he wasn't worried about pattyrollers, he told himself. Ben was making them up. So Moses laid there and pretended to be a swamper. A swamper wouldn't be afraid.

The night outside was black and moonless. He couldn't see a thing, but from the noise, there was lots going on out there. Tree frogs peeped in numbers so large that they made an awful ruckus. Water frogs, which were larger, made a flat, long, rasping sound. Every few seconds, the deep, mournful croak of a bullfrog broke through.

After a while, Moses' ears grew used to the commotion and he began to fall asleep. Then a splashing sound brought him fully awake. Something was out there, just outside the shack. He heard another splash, then another. It sounded like something walking in shallow water. A Pattyroller, maybe? He put his arms around sleeping Jebediah, tucked in tight, and tried not to listen.

Chapter Two

Slaver—1792 A.D.

1st # free white males 16 year upwards and head of families
2nd # free white males under 16 years
3rd # free white females
4th # all other free persons
5th # slaves
      Grandy, William......................1-1-3-0-18

Excerpt from Microcopy No. T-498 Roll 2
1790 Census, North Carolina
Camden Co, Edenton District

Rebecca got up before dawn, as always. She had spent most of the night shivering and dozing. She rose to her feet, stretching and moving her arms and legs about to warm her trembling frame.

The first thing to worry about was food. The children had eaten nearly nothing the day before. They had to have something this morning. She didn't want them to get like they did in late winter, after most of the food had run out, all bony and lazy-like, with rounded little bellies.

She knew about a stand of pawpaw trees, but it was too soon for the fruit to be ripe. She'd have to find something else. After looking to see that all the children were all right, she set off. After she'd gotten out of sight of the camp, she squatted, relieved herself, and went on.

"...And Remember that I Am a Man."

She found some blackberry bushes shortly after the sun rose. She took the cloth she'd used to wrap the cornbread, and began filling it with the large glossy, berries to surprise the children when they woke up. They might get the trots from so much fruit, but that was better than starvation.

On her return trip, she knew there was trouble before she got in sight of the camp. Jebby was bawling his head off. As she drew near, she heard the murmur of her other children's voices and then heard the snorting of a horse.

She crept forward and saw her family clustered together. Two white men sat atop horses, staring down at the children. There were rifles and whips attached to the saddles.

Rebecca stopped for a moment. She could slip back into the swamp with them being none the wiser. But what good would that do? She squared her shoulders and stepped into view.

The two men reached for their rifles, but relaxed when they saw an old slave woman. They watched as she came up, their eyes cold and mean. She walked to the horses and stared up at the men, returning their cold looks with ice. She knew what they were. Patrollers. Pattyrollers.

The largest of the men, a gangly, sallow-faced man on a handsome roan, asked, "You Rebecca?"

"'Course, I'm Rebecca," she snapped, angry at herself for being found. "Who else might you be expectin?"

"Watch your mouth, nigger," said the man. "I ain't in no mood for no sass. I got better things to do than ride around all goddamned night lookin' for runaways. I didn't ask no goddamned court to appoint me to no goddamned patrol."

Jebby broke loose from the others and ran to her. He wrapped his arms around one of her legs, sniffling.

"We got the right to whip you," said the other man, shabbily dressed, with a pointed jaw and a mean face. He was so small that his stirrups were raised almost to the bottom of the saddle. "They's laws about runaways, y'know."

"That's right," the skinny man agreed. "Fifteen goddamned lashes, on the spot."

"…And Remember that I Am a Man."

Mama stuck her chin out, one hand holding Jebby's head to her thigh. "That's what you gotta do, then go right on ahead an' do it," she said. "You jus' leave my chil'ren alone."

"Hoo," the whip man blew out a breath. "You sure are an uppity bitch, ain't ya? You're jus' lucky I don't want to have to drag you out of this goddamned swamp with your back all tore up. Now you gitcher goddamned pickaninnies together and march their goddamned little asses back home before I change my goddamned mind, y'hear?"

It took all morning to walk back to the Grandy farm. When they arrived, Master Grandy waited. He gave Rebecca a nasty look, then went over to talk with the two men. He gave each of the patrollers a greenback, and they left.

Master Grandy walked back to her, all angry-looking. "'Becca," he growled, "you know better. I warned you last year that you'd better not try none o' your shines again."

She bowed her head. "Yassuh, Massuh Billy."

"I'll deal with you later. For now, send little Moses up to the house to play with Jimmy and then get yourself and the others out to the fields. You've cost me more than a day's labor, and two dollars, to boot."

Master Grandy strode off. Rebecca looked down at Moses and said, "You heard the master. Get on up there." She hurried off, the rest of the children behind her. She tried not to let them see her crying.

*

"I heard you and your Mama ran away," was the first thing Master James said to Moses.

Moses nodded, looking around. Sometimes Mistress Grandy would leave out some scraps from the family meal for him to eat. He didn't see anything today, though.

"Well, it was a stupid thing to do." Master James showed an evil smile. "Papa said your stupid-nigger Mama is going to catch it."

Not wanting to show his anger at his mother being called stupid. Moses only nodded.

Master James dropped the subject. "We're going to play jackstraws today," he said.

17

"…And Remember that I Am a Man."

There was no need to wonder who'd throw the straws down first.
After he threw them down, Master James managed to pick up
several straws without moving any others, but then made a wrong
move. It was Moses' turn. He picked the straws up in a bundle and
dropped them again. It was a good throw.

Moses saw a chance to pick up the black straw. If he could get it
without moving any other straw, he'd have the edge. He would be
allowed to pick up straws with the black one, which was easier. He
started easing the black straw free.

Master James made sure he always won, and Moses had always
gone along with it. But this time, Master James had called his
mother stupid. Moses wanted that black straw.

"You know," said Master James. "Papa says he's gonna have your
stupid mama whipped."

Tears of anger flooded Moses' eyes, but he kept his head down so
Master James couldn't see. His vision blurred, he moved a straw
next to the black one and lost his turn.

*

The morning after they'd been brought back from the swamp,
Rebecca's eyes flew open. Someone was banging on the outside of
their shack.

"Rebecca," a voice called. It was the overseer, Mister Riddick.
"Rebecca, wake up."

"Yassuh?" She answered cautiously.

"Y'all are to stay indoors this morning."

She sprang off the corn husk mattress on the floor. "Oh, no,
Mister Riddick. Not today." And then she realized it didn't matter. If
not today, then some other day.

"And just to make sure," said Mister Riddick, as metal rattled.
"I'm locking you in."

She heard him leave. After a bit, she tried the door. It didn't
move. She leaned against the door frame and lowered her head.
"What am I to do? What am I to do, Lord?"

"What is it, Mama?" Moses asked. "What's wrong?"

She didn't answer, but Benjamin's quavering voice came from the
corner. "They must be a buyer coming."

"…And Remember that I Am a Man."

It was a good thing they had a jar of water to drink from and a rusty old pan for the other thing, because they waited for hours.

Finally, Mister Riddick, a short, burly white man with a bald crown and thick black beard, came and ordered Rebecca to line the children up outside the shack, and then go back in. She did as she was told, and watched from inside the doorway as the sun beat down on her brood. Their dark skin glistened with sweat, but they knew better than to complain. Mister Riddick waited in the shade of a nearby peach tree, a short whip in one hand, the one he used out in the fields. She wondered who was watching the workers while he was here.

Today, she'd rather be toiling in the hot sun than waiting for the slaver. She and the other adults and the older children would be hoeing weeds out of the cotton fields. Children too young to hoe, but old enough to work, would be plucking tobacco worms. Children too young, like Jebby, would be left to play at the edge of the field. Infants either rode at their mothers' hips or lay in blankets out of the way.

But Rebecca *wasn't* in the fields, not this day. After a time, a wagon came down the lane. A small, rat-faced white man held the reins. A handful of black men walked behind the wagon, strung on a chain. Master Grandy came from the main house to meet him and brought him to where Mister Riddick waited. The slaver had a set of manacles attached to his belt.

"Here they are." Master Grandy waved towards Rebecca's children. "All fine, healthy whelps."

The slaver stood off a bit, hands on hips, and looked them over. He walked over to Mary. Master Grandy followed, while Mister Riddick stayed under the tree.

Grinning, Rat-Face felt Mary's scalp through her thick hair, ran his hands over her breasts and haunches, then reached inside 0her skirt and touched her there. She closed her eyes and set her teeth. Rebecca felt her bile rise, but there was nothing she could do.

"Don't like a white man touching you down there, gal?" the rat-faced man asked. "I bet you give plenty of this to the bucks on the farm."

He must have squeezed, because she winced in pain.

19

The slaver pulled his hand out and laughed. "She's a prize this one. I might buy her for myself next trip."

Rat-Face and Master Grandy started down the line. Benjamin was next. The slaver looked him over. "Too old."

Master Grandy's jaw fell open. "Too old? He's not even full-growed. He's got many a year of field work in him."

The slaver gestured toward the wagon. "I don't need any more field workers this trip. Got enough already."

"Then what are you after?"

"I've got a client who wants a male for a house-nigger. She ain't concerned if he's old enough, just yet. She wants a little one that ain't picked up too many bad habits."

A slight hiss escaped Rebecca. If the rat-faced bastard was looking for a young male, why did he have to stick his hand in Mary's crotch?

The master nodded. "Ah, so that's why you asked to see Rebecca's whelps."

Rat-Face nodded. He paid no notice to Tamar, or June, but when he came to Malachai, he stopped. "Open your mouth, boy."

Malachai obeyed and the slaver looked in his mouth.

"Shut it." Rat-Face reached out with both hands and pulled down the skin beneath Malachai's eyes. "Seems healthy enough. Turn 'round, boy."

Malachai did as he was told.

"No scars," said Rat-Face. "A mite too old, though."

He stepped past Tamar and June, coming to Jebediah.

"This is more the age I'm looking for," he said.

Jebediah squirmed and looked back at Rebecca. She motioned for him to turn around, afraid he might be slapped if the slaver took his confusion for disrespect or disobedience.

The slaver examined Jebediah. "He might do."

Then he went to Moses. It made Rebecca proud that Moses held his head high and looked the slaver in the eye.

"Open your mouth, boy."

He looked into Moses' mouth, checked his eyes and then checked his back. As he did, Rebecca waited for Master Grandy to say he wasn't for sale, but the words never came.

Then the slaver said, "This one's too young," and she breathed a sigh of relief, even though she knew *one* of her children would be taken away.

Rat-Face stepped back in front of Jebediah, who again turned around to look at Mama, fear and puzzlement in his eyes.

"What's your name, boy?" asked the slaver.

Jebby turned back around. "J-J-Jebby."

"What kind of name is that?"

Master Grandy cleared his throat. "His name is Jebediah." He sounded nervous. Rebecca knew why. Jebby could never be a house slave; he wasn't smart enough.

"Well, Jebediah," Rat-Face said, "Are you so dumb you don't know to call a white man 'master?'"

Jebediah looked back at Mama again and she heard him whimper.

"I'm talkin' to you, boy. Answer my question."

Again Jebby turned, a rat in a corner, not knowing which way to go. His lower lip quivered. "Wa-wa-wa?" A dark stain began to spread on his pants. He had wet himself.

Rat-face started, then bent down and looked deeply into Jebediah's eyes. "What are you trying to sell me, Grandy? This one is a half-wit."

"He's not as dumb as he pretends," Master Grandy said. "He…"

But Rat-Face was back in front of Moses. "What's your name, boy?"

"M-my name is Moses, Master."

Rat-Face nodded and smiled. "I'll take this one. How much you want for him?"

"…And Remember that I Am a Man."

"…And Remember that I Am a Man."

Chapter Three

Peach Tree—1792 A.D.

"Now, then," inquired one of Tibeats' companions, "where shall we hang the nigger?"

One proposed such a limb, extending from the body of a peach tree, near the spot where we were standing. His comrade objected to it, alleging it would break, and proposed another. Finally they fixed upon the latter.

Twelve Years a Slave, Narrative of Solomon Northup, a Citizen of New York, Kidnapped in Washington City in 1841, and Rescued in 1853—1853 A.D.

Rebecca slumped against the doorway and closed her eyes. *Not Moses, Lord,* she prayed. *Not my baby.*

"Well, I don't know," she heard Master Grandy say. "I hadn't figured on selling this one."

She felt the aching sensation inside her chest ease. *Thank you, Lord,* she thought. The master had remembered his promise.

"I'll give you a hundred for him," the slaver said. "That's a lot for one this age."

Master Grandy said, "This is a smart little nigger, here. Make it one-fifty."

A giant, invisible hand squeezed Rebecca's chest.

23

"A hundred twenty-five," offered Rat-Face.

The master nodded. "Done."

"Put your hands out, boy." The slaver took the manacles from his belt.

Rebecca watched in astonishment and grief. This wasn't supposed to be happening. Moses began to cry.

"I said put your hands out, boy."

Moses sobbed, but put his arms straight out.

"Stupid niggers," the slaver said to Master Grandy as he put the first cuff on. "Why do you have to tell them everything twice?"

Rebecca bolted from the doorway, rage boiling inside her. "Not Moses," she screamed. "Not my baby."

The slaver looked up, but it was too late. She was upon him. She pulled on his arm.

"Get away from me, woman." Rat-Face tried to shove her away. She began to claw at him, determined to kill him.

Rebecca and Rat-Face whirled around, each pulling on Moses. She scratched like a wildcat as the sound of Moses' bawling tore at her insides. The slaver kept hitting her with his free hand, but she didn't feel it. She tucked her head down and kept fighting as blows rained down on her head and shoulders.

Suddenly, someone grabbed her by the waist and pulled her away. Master Grandy! He spun her around and threw her on the ground. She landed on her back and the breath left her body in a grunt.

The slaver shoved Moses to the ground, and then started kicking Rebecca. He wore boots. Each kick felt like a sledgehammer as it connected with her sides, chest or stomach. She curled up in a ball and heard herself begging, "Not my baby. Please, not my baby."

From the corner of her eye, she saw someone rushing up fast and thought someone was coming to help kick her. But it was Benjamin! Fury on his face, he reached for the slaver.

"Go back," she screamed. "Stay out of this."

Suddenly, Benjamin's head snapped forward, his eyes went blank and he crashed into the dirt as if pole-axed, not five feet from where she lay curled. Mister Riddick came into view behind her son, the heavy whip-handle in his fist.

The slaver continued kicking her. Each blow felt like it broke bone as the punishment slowed, then stopped.

Rat-Face stood over her, gasping. She couldn't see him, but she sensed him. Drops of wetness fell on her cheeks and, with satisfaction, she realized it was the slaver's blood.

"Damn your eyes," he said, breathlessly. "Damn your worthless, nigger eyes."

"Are you all right, Mister Talbot?" asked Master Grandy.

"That she-wolf scratched the hell out of me."

"I'm sorry, Mister Talbot," Master Grandy said. "She was upset"

Her vision returned and she saw the slaver using a dirty bandana to wipe blood from his arms. His skin had been marked by long, deep gouges from elbow to wrist.

"Upset?" The slaver's voice rose "I don't give a damn if she was upset, Grandy. Can't you control your niggers?"

Master Grandy spun around. "Mister Riddick, lock that boy up, then go on up to the house. Get Samantha down here. Tell her to bring her medicines."

Rebecca wondered which boy they were locking up, then realized he must mean Benjamin. He'd attacked a white. Even though he hadn't actually touched Rat-Face, it probably meant a whipping.

"First things first," the slaver said. "Let's get the little nigger over to my wagon and hook him on."

Rebecca eased her tucked position and turned to watch. Rat-Face stepped over to Moses. "Get up."

Moses bawled as the slaver yanked him up and began dragging him away. Looking around, Rebecca saw Mister Riddick taking Benjamin off someplace. Jebby was on the ground, curled up. The other children stood in a group, crying.

The white man dragged Moses over to his wagon, adding him onto the chain of slaves. He looked tiny among the group of black men, who were nothing but blurs to Rebecca. Those men didn't matter; they were outside her world.

Rat-Face walked back to Master Grandy. Samantha, who bound up cuts, removed splinters, cut hair and otherwise tended to those on the farm, came running up with her basket of medicines.

"…And Remember that I Am a Man."

Mistress Grandy ran behind her, holding her skirt up out of the dust. Her harsh, high voice filled the air. "William Grandy, what is the meaning of all this

Master Grandy turned to his wife, his face red. "Why, er, nothing to concern yourself with, my dear. We were merely conducting a business transaction, when one of the slaves…" he gestured toward Rebecca. "…went amok and attacked poor Mister Talbot, here."

Mistress Grandy turned and looked. "'Becca? I can't believe it. Why would that sweet woman turn vicious?"

"I have no idea," Master Grandy said. "You know how niggers are. Can't trust any of them."

Rebecca couldn't see Mistress Grandy's face but when the mistress put her hands on her hips and cocked her head, her eyes had probably narrowed. "You sold one of her children, didn't you, Billy?"

Master Grandy began to sputter something, but his wife pressed on. "That's it, isn't it?"

"Why, it's nothing to concern yourself, my dear," the master said.

Mistress Grandy ignored him and looked over to Rebecca's teary-eyed children, obviously taking stock.

"Where is little Moses?" she asked.

"Now, Selma…"

"Don't 'now, Selma' me, William. Where is Moses?"

"He's tied onto my wagon, Missus," Rat-Face said. "I done bought him fair and square."

Mistress Grandy turned and looked toward the group by the wagon. She must have noticed them when she walked down from the house, but little Moses was hard to see through the legs of the grown men around him. Rebecca saw the mistress's lips set into a thin line.

She whirled back. "I don't care what you two have been up to. That one is not for sale."

"I done bought him fair and square," Rat-Face repeated. A whine had come into his voice.

Mistress Grandy's voice went cold as the river in January. "Have you paid the money for him, yet?"

Master Grandy and the slaver looked at each other, then Master said, "Well, no, but…"

"That's it then," Mrs. Grandy snapped. "William, you know very well that little Jimmy will cry his eyes out if you sell his playmate. You tell this gentleman to let Moses loose."

Anger appeared in Rat-Face's eyes. "Is that what you want, Grandy?"

Master Grandy nodded. "I guess I sort of forgot I'd promised not to sell that one. Turn him loose and we'll find another one to suit you."

"All right, then, have it your way," the slaver said. He jerked his arms away from Samantha, who had begun to tend his wounds. Stomping over to the wagon, he unhooked Moses. As soon as he was free, Moses ran back to his brothers and sisters, who welcomed him with open arms. Rebecca smiled. The beating she had taken had been worthwhile.

But that was not to be the end of it. As Mistress Grandy and Samantha returned to the big house, Master Grandy and the slaver went at each other in low voices. Rebecca couldn't hear most of what they were saying, but could tell the slaver wanted a "deal," after what he'd been through. Then both men nodded and approached the frightened young ones.

"You!" Master Grandy said, pointing at Malachai. "Come here."

Malachai went stiff, his eyes like those of a frightened deer. He made no move toward his master. Rebecca lost all hope. Stopping them from selling Moses had only forced them to choose another.

Master Grandy didn't bother to repeat himself. He stepped forward and pulled Malachai away from the others. The slaver took out manacles again.

Within minutes, money had changed hands and the slaver's wagon departed down the lane. Rebecca sat up to watch. Malachai looked back, tears running down his face, until he passed out of sight.

Master Grandy turned to Mister Riddick. "Get the field hands in. I want every God-damned buck and wench back in the quarter."

Mister Riddick nodded and left. Master Grandy looked down at Rebecca and she turned her head, unable to face that merciless glare. She heard footsteps as he stalked off toward the main house.

The children gathered around and helped her up. With her family supporting her, she managed to get back inside. She sat down on their plank bench, cuddling the children as they gathered to her. Moses grabbed her lower leg and squeezed, crying harder than he'd ever done. Jebby attached himself to her other leg and bawled just as loudly.

*

Rebecca prayed. She had not been born a Christian, had not even heard of God until, as a young girl pregnant with her first child, she had listened to a wandering free black preacher from the north. who had held a secret meeting in the nearby woods. Once she'd heard that God would keep a place in Heaven for her, where she would be free, she had accepted Jesus as her savior. After a long while, Mister Riddick's voice sounded from outside the walls of the shack. "Rebecca, you and your young ones get out here."

Jebby began to wail. He might not be smart enough to know what was going to happen, but he had enough sense to know it wouldn't be good. Even as an infant, he'd seemed unusually sensitive to the moods of those around him.

"Hush, Jebby," she said. "We're going to go out there with our heads held high."

Painfully, she pulled herself off the bench, shuffled to the door, then stepped outside. She sensed her children behind her.

She looked around in the dazzling sunlight. It was well past noon now and even hotter. Every slave on the farm, including the hired hands, had been gathered. Mister Riddick stood waiting, a length of rope in one hand. Beyond him, Master Grandy waited by the old peach tree, slapping a whip against his leg. He didn't look like he'd settled down any. To her surprise, young Master James stood beside his father.

"Come with me, Rebecca," said Mister Riddick.

She turned back to her young ones, who had tears running down their cheeks. "It'll be all right, children."

She followed Mister Riddick to the peach tree, the oldest fruit tree on the farm. Quite a few branches had died back, but undersized peaches still hung from surviving limbs. They were ripening early, as fruit does when it's shriveling or full of worms. The peaches had borers in them; she could tell from the holes where sap leaked out. The children had been looking forward to eating these particular

28

peaches because Master Grandy wouldn't bother harvesting wormy fruit.

When they reached the tree, Mister Riddick lifted one of her hands and tied a rope around her wrist. He put the rope over the lowest branch of the peach tree, then tied her other hand so that her arms were above her head. She noticed big, new bruises on her arms.

He stepped behind Rebecca and grabbed her thin dress with both hands. With one motion, he ripped it from her body, the old, thin cloth parting easily.

She heard gasps as the dress fell away. She lowered her head and looked down upon sagging breasts, stretch-marked belly and protruding ribs. Surprised, she saw deep purple and black discolorations all over her torso. The other slaves hadn't gasped because of her nudity, but because they'd seen the bruises.

Rebecca normally didn't mind that her children gazed on her nakedness. They'd seen their mother's body before, many times. It couldn't be helped when everyone lived in one room. The boys had seen all their sisters naked, and the other way around, but nobody gave it a thought. They were family.

This was different, though. Somehow, being forced to be exposed turned it into a bad thing.

She turned her head to the left, seeing the slaves who had been gathered. Her children had joined them, still crying. She scanned the crowd for a sight of Benjamin, but didn't see him. Had they locked him in one of the sheds, waiting for his turn under the whip?

Looking to the right, she saw Master Grandy and his son, James, a few feet away. Master Grandy looked right through her and addressed his slaves, his face still red and angry. He spoke in a loud voice

"This woman, Rebecca, attacked a white man today. I have gathered y'all here to witness her punishment. Since she's not given any trouble before this, I shall be merciful today and only ten lashes will be given. But each and every one of y'all, take note that disobedience or disrespect will not be tolerated." He held out the whip. "Mister Riddick, you may carry on."

Mister Riddick went over and took the whip. Most whips were fashioned with a thin strip at the end, for driving oxen or horses.

"…And Remember that I Am a Man."

They would be snapped above a team of animals or used lightly on the rumps of more stubborn creatures. This whip was different. The end had been knotted several times. It would do more than make noise.

The overseer went behind Rebecca, where she couldn't see him. An overwhelming silence came over the slave quarter, but she wasn't sure if it had truly become that quiet or if she couldn't hear anything for the roaring in her ears. Numbness overtook her and time seemed to have lost meaning.

It was like a dream she had once had. She had fallen in the river and drowned. All feeling had stopped and time stood still. *Is this what it's like to be at peace, to not suffer or worry?* she had wondered. It seemed the same, now.

She was jolted out of her reverie by searing pain, accompanied by the slap of leather on flesh—her own flesh. She screeched. Cursing herself for daydreaming and not preparing herself for lash of the whip, she was still screaming when the next blow fell. It took her breath away, breaking off her cry.

She whimpered, "Oh, please, Jesus, plea…"

The lash came again before she could finish her prayer. Again she screamed.

In the moment before the whip struck again, she tried to regain control of her emotions. She'd seen several whippings over the years and the victims had reacted in different ways. Some had blubbered for mercy, others had screamed but a precious few had borne the lash in silence, glaring at their masters. She had always believed she would be one of the strong ones.

But when the knotted whip struck again, her mouth opened wide and she screamed so loudly her throat burned. It felt as though the whip had traveled all the way through her body.

With every bit of concentration she could muster, she broke off her wail and turned toward her children. They huddled together, with their eyes covered by hands, or their heads turned away. Except Moses. His eyes were on Master Grandy and they spoke hatred.

The sight of her children reminded her that Benjamin was not with them. Would he be the next to endure the whip? If so, it would be harder to bear than taking the punishment on her own skin.

Make me strong, Lord.

When the whip hit again, she managed to keep her response to a grunt. Tears rolled down her cheeks, but they were not for her. They were for Benjamin.

The whip fell again, and again she managed to stifle the scream that wanted to erupt from her lungs. How many lashes had she taken? Five? Six? She had lost count.

Turning to her right, she saw Master Grandy through her tears. The anger had left his face, and his lips were set in determination.

He'd always been a fair man. Would he stop if she begged him? Perhaps. But if she took all her lashes, he might listen later, when she begged mercy for Benjamin. He had a son of his own. Maybe he'd be kind

She looked down at Master Grandy's son. James stood with one hand holding a crease of his daddy's pants, leaning forward to watch. His face had a rapt expression she might have expected of someone watching a cockfight. He was enjoying the event.

"…And Remember that I Am a Man."

"…And Remember that I Am a Man."

Part Two

The Wilderness

Chapter Four

Auction—1800 A.D.

The first time I was separated from my mother, I was young and small. I knew nothing of my condition then as a slave. I was living with Mr. White, whose wife died and left him a widower with one little girl, who was said to be the legitimate owner of my mother, and all her children. This girl was also my playmate when we were children.

I was taken away from my mother, and hired out to labor for various persons, eight or ten years in succession; and all my wages were expended for the education of Harriet White, my playmate. It was then my sorrows and sufferings commenced. It was then I first commenced seeing and feeling that I was a wretched slave, compelled to work under the lash without wages and often, without clothes enough to hide my nakedness.

Narrative of the Life of Henry Bibb—1849 A.D.

"…And Remember that I Am a Man."

When Moses started up the steps to the auction block, the chain between his ankles caught and he nearly fell. Large hands grabbed him from behind and yanked him upright.

"Watch your step, boy," a gruff voice said. "You won't fetch much with your head busted open."

Moses looked up the steps. Taking a deep breath, he drew in the sweet, spicy, tang of cured tobacco. He saw the roof beams high above, where bundles of tobacco leaf hung every fall. But the New Year had come and the latest crop was gone, barged down the Pasquotank River to the Albemarle Sound for shipment across the ocean. The rafters were bare.

Shafts of brilliant sunlight pierced the wide chinks in walls, illuminating the interior of the large building. Dust motes sparkled as they danced in the air currents like moths in firelight. Moses had the sensation of standing in dense woods, sunbeams dappling through rustling leaves. He almost expected to hear the trilling of birds as he started up the steps.

Numb from sleeping on the cold ground, and light-headed from not having had anything to eat that morning, nothing seemed real to Moses. The smell of tobacco leaf—the smell of home—made him feel safe, as though he were truly in that pleasant grove of dancing sunbeams.

His head came up level with the platform. Wispy white clouds rose from the other side. He heard a soothing murmur, like rain on the roof of Mama's shack. Another step, and he saw the heads of many white men. The murmur of falling water turned out to be their low-voiced conversation. The clouds were cigar and pipe smoke, rising in the cool air.

The men milled about in front of the auction block, talking, gesturing, spitting, and smoking. Most wore the sturdy clothing and floppy hats of farmers, but a few wore coats and ties. Moses went up the last two stair treads and stepped off.

A small, gangly boy with chestnut-colored skin, Moses was the last of the slaves put on the block today. He stared at his feet, as he always did in front of whites, but someone reached up from behind the block and popped his pants leg with a switch. "Keep your head up, boy."

"…And Remember that I Am a Man."

At the sound, many of the men turned and looked up at Moses. Most seemed disinterested, but some stared appraisingly.

Moses was being put up "for hire." The hiring-out auction was always held at the beginning of the year. The year 1800 had started the day before, Moses knew. All the whites had been talking about the new century for weeks beforehand. It was supposed to be important for some reason.

Moses took small comfort that they weren't selling him "down the river," to join the slave gangs in the deep south, where cotton plantations needed more slaves because of some new invention called a "cotton gin." Being sold away to the Deep South was akin to going to Hell, the older slaves said, because no one would ever come back from either place.

But even though he was only going to be hired out, just being on the block was enough to scare the begeesus out of him. Not to mention having shackles on his legs, the sheriff's way of making sure he didn't run. Moses couldn't help but think of older brothers and sisters, sold in years past.

Moses had hoped never to be on the auction block at all, but old Master Grandy had died a couple of years back. Moses had been left to Master James. Since Master James was a minor, he wasn't judged fit to handle slaves, so the state had taken over.

North Carolina law required that any slaves of a minor must be hired out, year-by-year, until the young master reached adulthood. The white men of Camden County had gathered here today to hire slaves for a one-year term; the money would be paid to the young masters—minus the state's auction tax.

Not all the slaves belonged to minor masters, though. Some belonged to adults who wanted cash money from hiring their workers out, rather than supervise the slaves themselves.

The auctioneer, a bald, portly man with a gray goatee, brought himself to the business at hand.

"Gentlemen, may I have your attention please," he called out to the men. When they'd grown quiet, he continued. "Last on the block, we have a slave belonging to young James Grandy. This is his first hiring-out, but you can see he's a sturdy lad, sure to give good measure for the your money. Who'll give forty dollars to get a year's work out of him?"

No one spoke up. Some of the white men smirked and raised their eyebrows to show that they considered forty dollars too steep for a boy. Moses noticed that several of the men were walking away, not interested in a scrawny boy.

"Come now," the auctioneer said. "I realize this slave is on the young side, but he's strong and hearty. He's from the Grandy farm and you know they take care of their slaves."

"Mollycoddle them, you mean," a man called. Laughter ran through the crowd.

"Be that as it may," the auctioneer answered, "this boy stands before you without a lash mark on his hide, sound in body and ready to work. Who'll start us out with a bid of thirty-five dollars a year?"

No one spoke and Moses began to hope. What if nobody wanted him? Would he be allowed to go home?

"Hell, I'll bid thirty," a man said. "He's not worth a cent more."

The words cut into Moses like a knife. He glanced down to see who had bid on him and his stomach curdled. Jemmy Coates! A farmer who was said to be quick with a boot, fist, or whip.

"Thank you, Mister Coates," the auctioneer said. "I have a bid of thirty, who'll give me thirty-five?"

With a screech, one side of the big double doors of the warehouse swung outward and several men walked out, leaving the door ajar.

"Come, gentlemen," the auctioneer said. "Surely this boy is worth thirty-five dollars."

Over the crowd of white men, through the partially open door, Moses could see a line of trees to the northwest. Beyond, he knew, was the Great Dismal Swamp. Moses wished he could run away to the swamp, like Mama had used to do when Master Grandy wanted to sell one of her children.

"Come now." The auctioneer's impatient voice brought Moses back to the auction. "Who'll give me thirty-five for the services of this fine young buck? Let's hear from someone who can use such a boy. Step forward, if you wish and check his teeth, feel his muscles."

Moses didn't like to be reminded of how the men had come to the outside pen earlier, inspecting the merchandise. He had been poked and prodded every which way.

"Tarnation, Luther," a well-dressed, weasel-like man called out. He scratched the crotch of his trousers and grinned. "I'll bid thirty-five just to shut you up."

Everyone in the crowd laughed and someone clapped the speaker on the shoulder.

"It'll take a mite more than thirty-five dollars to shut me up, Enoch Sawyer," the auctioneer said.

Again there was laughter and the auctioneer, Luther, swung right back to the same pitch, this time asking for forty dollars.

Moses had heard of Enoch Sawyer, another hard man—the worst of the lot, according to rumors.

His Mama had taught him to pray to Jesus for strength at times like these, so he lowered his head and asked God to see him through.

Time and misery dragged on and nobody else bid. The auctioneer said, "Going once!" He paused. "Going twice!" A lump grew in Moses' throat. He would end up going to Enoch Sawyer, it appeared. But, at the last minute, a graying, heavy-set man with a thick beard said, "I'll pay thee thirty-eight, Luther. He's small, but I have use for him."

The man looked odd, wearing a black frock coat over a gray shirt with a white collar. He also wore a round, broad-brimmed hat. Moses wondered why the man dressed so differently.

Luther acknowledged the bid and then went back into his spiel, asking for forty dollars. No one was willing to go that high. He banged a hammer down and said, "Hired out for thirty-eight dollars to Mister Joshua Kemp."

As Moses climbed down from the block, he found himself trembling. He'd never seen nor heard of this man who'd bought his services for a year. Was he lucky? Or damned?

After paying the clerk, Moses' new owner walked up and appraised him with flashing green eyes that took the harshness from his face. "Dost thou have a name, boy?"

"Moses, Master," he mumbled. Why was the man talking so funny?

The man's eyes went cold and he drew back as though Moses had insulted him. "I am *Mister* Kemp. Thou art never to call me 'master,' for the Society of Friends disapproves of slavery and I would never own a slave. Hiring a slave is different, however, in my opinion. I could do with an extra hand at my place, and have decided to take thee on."

Moses nodded to show he understood. He felt like he should say something, but had never had the chance to talk to white folks other than the Grandys, and didn't quite know what to say. Especially since he was confused about Mister Kemp's funny way of talking.

Mister Kemp gave a fleeting, thin-lipped smile. "Good. Thou wilt do."

Then he looked down at Moses' legs and his eyes went hard again. He turned to the nearby deputy and said, "Remove this boy's shackles." Moses noticed that Mister Kemp's fists were clenched as though he was mad about something.

The deputy gestured to a nearby white man, who came toward Moses with a large key. Spitting a stream of tobacco on the dirt floor, the deputy turned and walked away, muttering, "Damn nigger lover."

After the shackles were off, Mister Kemp led Moses from the warehouse and took him to the town's only store. He went in and came back out with a small, paper-wrapped package, topped off with a pair of shoes. He handed it all to Moses, saying, "Go around back, boy, and put these on. Thou art about to bust out of thy pants and thou art too old to be going about where ladyfolks might see."

It took Moses a moment to realize what was happening, since no one had ever given him anything before. Then he remembered that, when a white man hired a slave for the year, he was required to buy clothing for the slave.

On unsteady legs, Moses hurried around to the rear of the store and ripped open the bundle. He found two new shirts, new brown pants, and a soft, floppy hat. He stripped and donned the only new clothing he'd ever had, and then pulled on the shoes. They were hand-me-downs, but they made him feel grown up, since they were the first shoes he'd ever worn. Being hired out might be a good thing after all. He rolled up his old clothes, though, just in case.

When he got back to the wagon, a white boy stood next to Mister Kemp. He looked to be about two years older than Moses, and a lot bigger, with a body like a solid log. His brown eyes were close-set below heavy brow ridges, his nose large and bulbous above full, pouting lips. He wore farmer's clothes, so Moses figured him to be Mister Kemp's son.

As Moses neared, Mister Kemp gestured toward him.

"Chadwick, this is Moses. I've hired him to help thee with the mules."

Chadwick's jaw dropped. He had been looking at Moses like he was rotting meat, but now he whirled to look at Mister Kemp. "You hired a nigger?"

Mister Kemp raised a finger. "I have told thee not to use that word. Thou should say, 'colored,' or, 'Negro.'"

Chadwick ignored the rebuke. "I don't need any help. Not somebody like him."

"Never thou mind, Chadwick," said Mister Kemp. "I have hired him and that is the end of the matter."

Minutes later, Moses walked behind Mister Kemp's wagon as it rolled out of town. Chadwick rode up on the seat with Mister Kemp, looking back every now and then with contempt clear on his face.

They went in the opposite direction from the Grandy farm, so the rutted dirt track was foreign to Moses, even though it didn't look much different from any other road. He'd never been farther than town—gracious, he'd only been to town twice before and he'd never been in any of the stores, though he'd looked in the windows. He'd seen piles of fancy goods, stuff only rich people could afford. Mister Kemp must be rich; he'd not flinched about the cost of dressing his new worker. Besides, his loaded wagon was drawn by two matching brown mules, two of the finest animals Moses had ever seen. Mules were new to the county, and cost more than most horses, he had heard.

By the time they'd gone a mile or so, Moses' feet hurt. The shoes were too big and rubbed below his anklebones with every step, where the shackles had dug in earlier. It chafed him something terrible. He would have liked to take them off and go barefoot for a while, but wondered if that might be disrespectful of Mister Kemp, him having bought these shoes. And Mister Kemp had said to show respect at all times.

So he trudged along, wincing at every step, hoping Mister Kemp would feed him when they reached wherever they were going.

"…And Remember that I Am a Man."

"…And Remember that I Am a Man."

Chapter Five

Jack-Ass—1800 A.D.

The Deacon had declared that I should not only suffer for the crime of attending a prayer meeting without his permission, and for running away, but for the awful crime of stealing a jackass, which was death by the law when committed by a Negro.

But I well knew that I was regarded as property, and so was the ass; and I thought if one piece of property took off another, there could be no law violated in the act; no more sin committed in this, than if one jackass had rode off another.

But after consultation with my wife I concluded to take her and my little daughter with me and they would be guilty of the same crime that I was, so far as running away was concerned; and if the Deacon sold one he might sell us all, and perhaps to the same person.

Narrative of the Life of Henry Bibb—1849 A.D.

The wagon stopped and Moses came to a surprised halt. He hadn't been paying attention. He looked up to see Mister Kemp's eyes on him.

"Is something wrong with thy feet, boy?"

Moses looked down and then back up. "Yes, sir."

"…And Remember that I Am a Man."

Mister Kemp tied off the reins and dismounted from the wagon. He came around back. "I should have known. Thou hast never worn shoes before?"

Moses shook his head.

"Climbest thou onto the wagon. Thou may ride atop the goods for the remainder of the journey."

He took Moses by the elbow and led him forward. There was a step attached to the side of the wagon and he helped Moses climb up. "Get in back," he said.

Moses did as he was told. Chadwick grudgingly slid over to let him pass. Then Mister Kemp got back in and sat down. He turned to Moses.

"Takest off thy shoes. I should have purchased stockings for thee, but I was not thinking."

When Moses removed his shoes and set them nearby, Mister Kemp leaned over and looked. "Thou hast broken blisters. I'll have Mrs. Kemp give thee a pair of my old stockings." He pointed at a raw area above the anklebone. "What is this here? This is not from the shoes."

"Them chains was too small for me, Mister Kemp. They rubbed me something awful."

Mister Kemp made a clucking noise, shaking his head. He picked up the reins. "Thou will not be wearing chains again anytime soon."

Moses would have preferred "never" to "not anytime soon," but the hurt in his feet was letting up and that was the important thing. The bags were soft and made a comfortable bed. He snuggled down into the goods on the wagon.

"Giddap," Mister Kemp said, and the mules stepped out smartly.

The wagon had no springs and bounced a bit, but the road was not badly rutted. Moses squirmed around until he'd made a bit of nest and let his head loll.

"Hast thou ever laid eyes on a prettier brace of mules, Moses?"

Moses glanced ahead and down. They didn't look so intimidating from up here. "No, Mister Kemp. I ain't seen all that many mules, though."

"Just like I figured," Chadwick muttered.

"Mules are new to these parts," Mister Kemp said. "General Washington started breeding them, back when North Carolina was a colony. I acquired a herd of donkeys eight years ago and moved here to Camden County. Mules are going to make me rich."

What donkeys—whatever they were—had to do with mules, Moses had no idea. But it was nice to talk with a grown-up white man in a pleasant way; it made him feel important. Talking about General Washington—the first president and most famous man in the union—gave them something in common. "How you figure to make money off mules?" he asked.

"Why, the Grand Canal, of course."

"What's that?"

Mister Kemp glanced back. "Thou hast not heard of the new canal?"

"Yes, sir. I guess so. Don't know much about it, though."

"The Dismal Swamp Company is digging a canal between the Albemarle Sound, here in Carolina, and the Elizabeth River in Virginia," Mister Kemp explained. They began digging from both ends in the Year of The Lord 1790 and will come together in five years or so."

Moses wondered if he'd ever understand a single word Mister Kemp said. When they spoke of mules, he talked of "donkeys." When Moses asked about getting rich off mules, the talk turned to "canals."

"What's a canal?" Moses asked.

Mister Kemp sighed. "Ah, the vicissitudes of slavery! I forgot that thou hast not had the advantage of an education. Dost thou know what a ditch is?"

Moses nodded.

Mister Kemp said, "A canal is nothing more than a big ditch. It will allow shipping of goods between north and south. It will also drain much of the swamp, clearing rich land for farming."

Mister Kemp went quiet, as though thinking of something, and Moses began to doze.

He awakened as the wagon turned in at a farm. Moses guessed they'd arrived at their destination. The Kemp property looked nothing like the Grandy tobacco farm. He saw no curing barns or storehouses. There were no vast fields of tobacco. Instead, the property had been divided into many pastures and paddocks, which held horses, mules and some smaller horse-like animals with rounded bellies and huge, hanging ears. Chickens scratched around in the yard.

A woman came out of the house. When they drew near, she looked pointedly at Moses and said, "Well now, Joshua, what do we have here?"

The woman, who must be Mrs. Kemp, was a thin, big-nosed, narrow-lipped woman, wearing a black bonnet and a long, gray dress along with a white apron.

"Whoa." Mister Kemp halted the mules. He looked down at his wife. "Well, Dorothea, when I got to town, I found it was hiring-out day." He tied off the reins and climbed down from the wagon. "This boy was on the block. I couldn't let it happen. I had to mind the light."

As Mister Kemp talked, Chadwick climbed down on the other side and walked away, headed toward a nearby necessary shed.

Moses wondered if he'd ever understand this way of talking. What was minding the light?

"Nevertheless, thou well knoweth we are not to buy slaves," Mrs. Kemp said.

"I didn't buy him. I hired him for the year." Mister Kemp put out a hand and touched his wife's arm. "Enoch Sawyer was going to hire the boy."

"Oh." Mrs. Kemp gave Moses a pitying glance and put a hand to her mouth. "Well, I suppose…"

Mister Kemp put his hand on her shoulder. "I've already signed the papers and paid the money. We have him for a year, in any case. Thou preparest a bit extra this eve, so the boy will have something to eat. I shall begin to instruct him in his duties."

He turned and gestured for Moses to come over, while his wife hurried inside. Moses shuffled over, trying not to hurt his ankles any more. He noticed the skinny faces of two white girls peeking out from inside the doorway, both with brown hair in braids. The older one, probably a couple of years older than Moses, had unusual green eyes, while the younger one's eyes were brown. She looked to be about Moses' age. He turned away from them as Mister Kemp spoke.

"Dost thou know how to get mules out of harness, Moses?" He asked.

Moses shook his head. The closest he had ever been to a mule was right now.

Mister Kemp looked around. "Where has that boy gotten off to? The mules are *his* responsibility."

Moses realized Mister Kemp was talking about Chadwick. He could have said where the white boy had gone, but decided to keep mum.

Pointing, Mister Kemp said, "Thou goest to the shed over there and openest the doors. I will drive the wagon over and show thee how it is done." He began to climb into the wagon.

Moses set out for the low, narrow building, which had large double-doors on each short side. The wagon soon passed him, the mules eager to get there, so Mister Kemp had to wait until Moses arrived to open the door. Mister Kemp began to back the wagon, shouting a combination of sounds, "Back," "Gee," "Haw," "Walk up" and "Whoa."

Mister Kemp used the reins sparingly; the mules seemed not to need them. Soon the wagon had been backed into the shed, with the mules standing in their traces. Moses went in, but stayed in a corner, where his bare feet weren't in danger of being stomped.

"Do not stand there gawping, Moses," Mister Kemp called as he again got down off the wagon. "Comest thou and help me get the mules put up."

Moses was soon helping Mister Kemp unbuckle and untie all the buckles and doo-dads that connected the mules to the wagon. He wasn't much help, far as he could tell.

Mister Kemp held out a set of reins. Moses hesitated. At the other end of those lines was one of the mules, which had turned out to be even larger than expected, now that he was close up.

"Go ahead," Mister Kemp urged. "Takest him into the large barn and put him in the second stall on the right."

Still Moses did not take the reins. The mule seemed had an evil glare. "Does he bite?"

"No, this one does not bite." He took Moses' hand and closed it around the rope. "Thou must not be afraid. It will be thy job to taketh care of my mules."

His job? He'd thought he'd be helping Chadwick, who probably knew all about mules. Moses looked at the mule on the other end of the line. Mister Kemp had said, "*This one* does not bite." Did that mean other mules *did* bite?

"Go ahead, lead him," Mister Kemp said.

Moses walked as far as away he could and gave a gentle tug. The mule didn't move. Moses pulled harder. The mule didn't move. Moses looked over at Mister Kemp. If he didn't do it right, what would the man do? Most white men rewarded failure with a cuff or a kick. Mister Kemp was smiling, though. Moses put both hands on the rope, set his feet and put his weight into it. The mule didn't even seem to notice.

"Do not fight him," Mister Kemp said. "Goliath loveth a fight, and will surely win out over thee."

Moses looked over. Mister Kemp smiled now.

"Whatever you say, Mister Kemp," Moses said. "But he won't budge. What should I do?"

"Never argue with a mule. Let him know which of thee art boss. Watch now." Mister Kemp took the line attached to the other mule, which had been standing placidly. "Just turn around and walk away. If thou wouldst encourage the mule to follow, he will do so."

The white man turned, took a step and said, "Walk up, Samson," in a stern tone. The mule followed, although Mister Kemp had not pulled. In fact, the line was slack.

Mister Kemp led Samson a few feet away and then turned to look back. "Put thy back to Goliath. Ease up on the line and calmly walk away.

Moses slackened his rope, and then took a deep breath. He turned and began to move away. "Walk… walk up, Goliath." When he'd got two steps away, the lead line went taut and jerked him back. The mule hadn't budged a smidgeon.

He faced the mule and joined battle with the beast again, pulling with all his might. "Walk up," he said, grunting with the effort. "Walk up, you old jack-ass, for Christ's sake."

Something grabbed his arm and spun him around. Mister Kemp held him in one hand and had the other hand clenched above him, ready to bring his fist down on Moses. Fury distorted his red face and veins stood out on his large nose.

"Thou shalt not use the name of The Lord in vain," he growled.

46

"…And Remember that I Am a Man."

Moses fought back tears. As Mister Kemp shook him, Moses wondered what he'd done wrong. He'd often heard Master Grandy say, "Christ," or "Jesus Christ," when he'd been upset about something. Moses had used the word in an attempt to appear "grown up."

Mister Kemp said, "And don't use that other word, either."

"What word?"

Tight-lipped, Mister Kemp said, "Jack-ass."

What was wrong with, "jack-ass?" Master Grandy had used that word often when mad at some slave or other. But it was Mister Kemp's farm so…"Yes, Master."

The hand holding his arm tightened like a bear trap. "I told thee never to call me that."

"Yes, Mas… Mister Kemp." It was difficult to remember. He had always been required to call white men "master."

"Yes, sir."

Mister Kemp held out his hand. "Giveth me the reins."

Moses did as he was told and watched, shamed, as Mister Kemp led the two mules into the dirt-floored barn. There were stalls all around the edges. Samson went into the first stall on the right, Goliath into the second.

When the mules had been closed in, Mister Kemp stood before Moses again and looked him in the eye. "I am sorry I chastened thee, Moses. But thou vexed me beyond endurance. Never curse in my presence again."

"No sir." Mister Kemp didn't *sound* sorry, he noticed.

"There is hay in the loft." Mister Kemp nodded his head toward a nearby ladder. "Give both the mules a forkful, then clean all the stalls. There's a wheelbarrow around here somewhere and the manure pile is behind the barn."

"Yes, sir, but…" Moses knew he'd sound stupid, but he had to ask. He knew what a fork was; white folks used them when they ate their meals. "Ain't a forkful awful small for a mule?"

"Small?" Mister Kemp gave him a skeptical look. "Do thou not knowest what a pitchfork is?"

"No, Mister Kemp, I truly don't knowest." Moses wasn't sure if he should try to imitate Mister Kemp's odd way of talking, but maybe he wouldn't come across as quite so stupid if he did.

The white man shook his head. "I can see my work is cut out for me. I'll show thee how to feed, one time only."

Moses followed him up the ladder, where a long-handled tool stood against a wall. "Pitchfork," Mister Kemp explained. Moses watched as he tossed hay down into both occupied stalls. The loft had been designed so that every stall in the barn could be supplied with hay. When they were done, they returned to the main floor.

"Dost thou knowest what a wheelbarrow is, Moses?" Mister Kemp asked.

Moses nodded. "I knowest that, Mister Kemp."

"Thou wilt find one around back, by the manure pile. The manure fork over there is for mucking out the stalls. Thou cleanest all the manure out of them and put it on the manure pile."

"Yes, Mister Kemp."

Mister Kemp stood and looked at him until Moses realized that he was to get busy. He turned and set out to look for the wheelbarrow.

When he got back, Mister Kemp was nowhere to be seen. Moses took up the manure fork and began picking mule droppings out of the straw. He cleaned out the empty stalls, then paused. He didn't look forward to being in a small space with an unpredictable mule.

He decided to tackle Goliath's stall first, since Mister Kemp had said he didn't bite. The beast's rear end was to the door. He cracked the door and eased the wheelbarrow inside, not latching the door behind him, in case he needed to make a quick getaway. The mule, eating its hay, eyed him sideways and put its ears back. It didn't make any hostile moves, though, so Moses took the fork and picked up the only pile in the stall, which was fresh and steaming. He deposited it into the wheelbarrow, then opened the door partway and began pushing his way out.

Something slammed into his rear end, harder than he'd ever been struck in his life, and sent him flying out the door, along with the wheelbarrow. It wobbled and fell, taking Moses and the load of manure to the ground with it. It took him a moment to realize the mule had kicked him.

Someone giggled. He looked up to see Mister Kemp's daughters—the two girls he'd seen in the window—in the loft. They

48

must have sneaked up there while he was working. The green-eyed one pointed at him while they sniggered.

Ashamed, Moses got to his feet and tried to wipe the manure off his brand new pants. It smeared. Not looking up toward the loft, he closed the stall door and peered in at Goliath, again eating hay. As he slid the latch shut, the mule turned, looked wide-eyed at Moses, and brayed. "Hee-haw, hee-haw."

Samson joined in from the next stall. "Hee-haw." In the loft above, the Kemp girls burst into laughter again.

"…And Remember that I Am a Man."

Chapter Six

Cheap Labor—1800 A.D.

There is a saying that we shall doe (sic) to all men like as we will be done ourselves; making no difference of what generation, descent or colour they are. And those who steal or rob men, and those who buy or purchase them, are they not alike?

Quaker Protest against Slavery, Germantown Pennsylvania—1688 A.D.

Moses cleaned up the fallen mess and wheeled it to the manure pile. He learned that keeping a moving wheelbarrow upright took more skill that he possessed, but managed to finish the job. Maybe he should tell Mister Kemp that hadn't done any work back at the Grandy Farm, since he'd spent so much time playing with Master James. He decided against letting Mister Kemp know. If he couldn't do the job, he might end up working some other place—like Enoch Sawyer's farm.

By the time he went back into the barn the Kemp girls had gone, to his relief. He still had Samson's stall to clean and that mule scared him even more than Goliath did.

It turned out, however, that Samson had not yet made any messes in his stall. Moses put the wheelbarrow away and wondered what to do next. He looked over to the house and wondered how long it would be before Mister Kemp returned. And when did they feed around here?

"…And Remember that I Am a Man."

After a while, Moses decided to look for a pond or trough to wash the mule dung from his hands and clothing. There must be a source of water nearby, for the mules.

He went around to the other side of the barn. Sure enough, he found a hand pump there and washed his hands. The manure wouldn't come out of his new britches, though, without scrubbing, and he wasn't about to take his pants off with two girls sneaking about.

He wandered back over to the building where Mister Kemp had parked the wagon, and looked in. Why did Mister Kemp have so many different types of wagons? He went inside. Plows and other farming tools were spaced along the walls and there were spare wagon wheels, metal bars, wooden poles, and all sorts of other unidentifiable items. A lot of other stuff hung from the rafters. Moses wondered why Mister Kemp needed all these things for when he didn't cultivate his fields. He climbed up on a wagon to look it over.

"What you doing here, boy? Where you come from?"

Moses turned to see a scrawny, old, light-colored, Negro man with a ring of tight, white curls around a patch of shiny yellow scalp. He stood well under five feet tall, almost childlike in stature. In fact, he was a bit shorter than Moses. His clothing was ragged and torn, but not so much more than other folks' that you'd take notice. He wore a pair of old lace-up work boots.

The man also wore a suspicious look. Was Moses not supposed to be in here? He wondered if he should make a run for it, but decided to stick it out.

"I'm Moses," he said. "Mister Kemp hired me today.

"Oh, deed he now?" The distrust left the man's face, replaced by curiosity. "Come down here off dat wagon."

When Moses stood on the ground, the man asked, "What means dat name, Mooses?"

Moses shrugged. "It's just my name. It comes from the bible but it don't mean nothing."

"Nah." The old man shook his head. "Names mean sumting. "You should find out what eet means."

Moses looked over at the machinery he'd been inspecting. "What's all this stuff for?"

The man ignored his question, and puffed out his chest. "I am Keentoon. An anaké of the Angare clan of the Kikuyu people."

Even his name sounded funny, "Keentoon," with a puff of air bursting out with the "T" sound. And there were a lot of words Moses couldn't even begin to pronounce. He sure talked different."

"What's a nanocky?" Moses asked.

"Anaké means warrior in de Kikuyu language."

Moses peered at him. "You can't be a warrior. You're a slave."

"Noo, not slave," Keentoon said. "I am free man, now. So I can be warrior again."

"How did you get to be a warrior in the first place?"

"When I am boy, day cut my man-part, den I become warrior."

Moses made a face at the thought of being cut down there. Had they cut this man's *thing* off?

"Was this in Africa?"

"Yes, Afreeca." Keentoon nodded his head up and down. "When I am young warrior, I goo to guard oover women who trade witt Kemba tribe, including my mudder. Dey trick us and sell us to white man. White man bring Keentoon one place, take mudder anudder place."

Since the man had said names mean something, Moses was about to ask what Keentoon meant, but he noticed the older Kemp girl coming out of the back door of the house with a tray. All thought left his mind at the sight of food.

The girl walked over to a plank table and benches beneath a tree. She set the tray down and waved for them to come over.

"Come, Mooses," Keentoon said. "We eat."

The girl smiled as they walked up. "Good evening, John."

"Eefening, Meesy Hannah," Keentoon answered. He sat down on one of the benches and gestured for Moses to take the other one.

Moses sat, wondering why Missy Hannah had called his new friend, "John." His name was Keentoon, wasn't it? Was everybody crazy around here? But then the tray caught his attention. There were two bowls of stew, along with a plate of bread, two cracked mugs and a pitcher of what he assumed to be water. The aroma rising from the bowls was mouth-watering. Moreover, the stew included some sort of meat. As Missy Hannah began placing food in front of him, he wondered what kind of meat it was. Maybe rabbit? He loved rabbit.

Then he realized Hannah Kemp had said something to him, but he had no idea what. He looked down at his feet. "Yes'm," he mumbled, not daring to ask her to repeat what she'd said.

"Well, art thou not going to say, 'Thank you?'" she asked.

"Yes'm," he said. "Thank you."

"Tank you, Meesy Hannah," he heard Keentoon say.

"Thou art quite welcome." Missy Hannah turned and walked back toward the house, putting her hand to her mouth. Moses guessed she was trying not to laugh at him, but forgot about it as he eyed the feast.

Keentoon grabbed the pitcher and poured white liquid into Moses' mug. Milk! They served their slaves milk here? And then it hit him. Missy Hannah had *served* him. He'd never heard of a white person serving a slave.

As Keentoon poured his own milk, Moses ignored the spoon and picked up his bowl. He sipped. Chicken! Even better than rabbit. At the Grandy farm, he'd been lucky to get chicken wings or rump once or twice a year, when there were a few scraps left over from the Master's table. This was the most tender and delicious meat he'd ever eaten, he decided.

He was halfway through the stew when he felt eyes on him. Looking up, he saw Keentoon, a stew-soaked hunk of bread in his hands, staring.

Keentoon smiled. "I guess dey don't haff food where you come from, eh?"

Moses felt shame. He put the bowl down. "They do, but I have to fight my brothers and sisters for it."

Keentoon nodded and gestured at Moses' mug. "Haff some mikk and wash dat down."

Moses complied. The warm milk was rich as honey stolen from a bee tree. "They sure feed you good, here."

"Yah. Meester Kemp, he a good man."

"Why does he talk so funny?" Oops. Keentoon might take offense, seeing as how he talked funny too.

The old man didn't seem to mind, though. He laughed. "you neffer meet a Quaker before dis time?"

54

"What's a Quaker?"

"It is a *releegion.*" He pronounced the word with care and solemnity. "Dese Quakers are good people."

"What's so good about them?" Moses knew what religion was—worshipping God and Jesus like Mama had taught him to do—so this didn't tell him anything about Quakers.

Keentoon wiped juice from his chin. "Dey don't beleef in slafery, dat's what's good about dem."

Moses choked on his bread. White people who didn't believe in slavery? He shook his head, trying to take in such an incredible concept.

"Close you mout' before de bugs flies in." Keentoon said. "I tell you fact. Summa dem Quakers, day help safes escape to ad north."

Moses chewed on a bit of gristle while soaking up the dregs of his stew with bread. Quakers helped slaves escape? Was that why Mister Kemp had bid on him? Dare he ask?

He swallowed and said, "Mister Kemp, he helps slaves escape to the north?"

Keentoon looked off into the distance as if composing his thoughts, then said, "He don't do dat, not deeps Quaker. He say he don't beleef een slafery, but beef God don't want slafery to happen, den God would stop eet."

"He sure gets mad if someone curses."

Keentoon smiled. "Meester Kemp, he not born a Quaker. He become Quaker when he marry Missus Kemp. He steel have trouble wit' temper, sometime."

"If he doesn't believe in slavery," asked Moses. "Why did he hire me?"

"Most Quakers have lots of boys. But he don't have boy cheeldren, only girls. He not allowed to oon slaves, so he hire people he don't have to pay much money for, like you and me."

"What do you mean he doesn't have boys? There's Chadwick."

Keentoon laughed long and hard, then said, "Meester Kemp hire Chadweek, too." His voice dropped to a whisper. "Chadweek so dumb dat he don't cost much to hire, same as us."

Again Moses considered. He'd finished his milk, so he hefted the pitcher by its handle. Still some left. He poured it into his mug.

"What about you?" he asked. "You're a free man. Why don't you go work for somebody who pays better?"

Keentoon chuckled, as though to himself. He leaned forward again and whispered. "I be free because I runner away, many summers ago. I stay in de swamp for years, come here two years ago. Meester Kemp pay me wiff food and stuff to wear and don't tell on me. I go into de swamp at night."

Moses' milk suddenly tasted sour. So Keentoon wasn't free; he was merely another runaway slave. But if he lived in the swamp, he was a maroon, and that was interesting.

Moses started to ask about maroons when the back door slammed and Mister Kemp appeared, heading out at a fast pace. "Keentoon, Moses, there is still time before sunset for work." Chadwick came out the door behind him, still wiping his lips. He ate inside with the other white folks, of course.

Moses jumped up and started to go after him, but stopped to watch Keentoon, who gathered everything back on the tray, carried it to the back door, and set it on the step. When he bent over, the shirt rode up on his back and Moses saw scars from a whip. Then Keentoon straightened, nodded to Moses, and the two of them took off after their boss.

"…And Remember that I Am a Man."

Chapter Seven

Lion Killer—1800 A.D.

Rearing, the lion struck the man, bearing down the shield, his back arched; and for a moment he slaked his fury with fang and talon. But on the instant I saw another spear driven clear through his body from side to side; and as the lion turned again the bright spear blades darting toward him were flashes of white flame. The end had come. He seized another man, who stabbed him and wrenched loose. As he fell he gripped a spear head in his jaws with such tremendous force that he bent it double. Then the warriors were round and over him, stabbing and shouting, wild with furious exultation.

African Game Trails, Theodore Roosevelt—1919 A.D.

"Come over here, niggah boy." Chadwick had appeared in the barn, just outside the stall where Moses combed Goliath's mane.

Dutifully, Moses put down the brush and left the stall, closing the latch behind. He'd already learned that mules were smart enough to push out of an unlocked door.

He went and stood before Chadwick, not saying anything, mostly because he wasn't sure what to call the white boy. Normally, he'd just call him master, like any other white male, but Mister Kemp didn't like that word.

Chadwick leaned forward with his jaw out. "What's your name, boy?"

"Moses, sir." Sir seemed the safest word to use.

"Let's get one thing straight, Moses.

"What's that, sir?"

The words were barely out of his mouth when a roundhouse punch connected with Moses' cheek, knocking him to the ground. He leaped back up, fists clenched, ready to fight. But he knew he wouldn't dare. He could try to block Chadwick's blows, though.

The white boy grinned, obviously not afraid of being hit back. "I'm the master of this place, as far as you're concerned, nigger. And if you go running to Kemp, I'll beat holy bejeezus out of you." He turned and walked away.

*

Moses soon learned that, along with being stupid, the stocky white boy was lazy. Once shown what to do, Moses did most of the work while Chadwick put on a show of being busy. Moses wondered how work had gotten done before he'd been hired, and soon learned many things had been left undone, such as fixing fences, cleaning water troughs and keeping food bins covered to keep rats out. Also tools were left out in the rain to rust, and there was a general disorderliness to the barn. He tried to catch everything up, but it was hard work, especially since Chadwick did all in his power to make Moses' life miserable.

Moses loved working with the mules, however. He mucked manure, fed the animals, cleaned their hooves, brushed them, whatever it took. It didn't take him long to learn the animals' individual traits, which ones did whatever you asked, which were stubborn, and which ones you didn't turn your back on.

Moses discovered how much he *didn't* know about horses, mules, and donkeys.

The average mule was stronger, nearly as fast, had more endurance and required less feed than a horse. And, surprisingly, mules were better jumpers. They were smarter, too, in his opinion. Males, no matter what their individual names, were called "Johns," and the females were "Mollies." A mule resulted when a male donkey mated with a female horse.

Male mules were naturally sterile—which meant they couldn't father babies—but they still tried to mate the Mollies. At six months or so, they were gelded to curb aggressive behavior, which made Moses wonder how mean they'd be if they hadn't been "fixed."

Donkeys were the smallest animals in the pasture, like little furry horses with long, floppy ears. Some people called them "asses," which was the old, English word for the animals. "Jackass" was a slang term for a male ass, and a somewhat crude word at that, Jack being English slang for a man's private parts, which was why Mr. Kemp had been upset that first day. He preferred the more modern term, "donkey," for a male and, "Jenny," for a female.

Most of the time, when Moses worked with the mules, he could feel Chadwick watching him. Chadwick was the slyest person Moses had ever known. He was cruel, too. He wasn't supposed to hit Moses and Mr. Kemp didn't like anyone using the word "nigger," so Chadwick made up for it by calling Moses "monkey-brain," "spear-chucker," "tar-baby," and any other insult he could think of.

Moses didn't really care; he knew he was none of those things and it *was* better than being called "nigger." It did gall him, however, when Chadwick called him "stupid." Chadwick was dumber than a rock.

There was generally free time for Moses in the evening. After enjoying one of Mrs. Kemp's delicious meals, he and Keentoon would talk for a while before the older man went away to sleep in the swamp.

Keentoon, who the Kemps called John, his former slave name, liked to talk about Africa. Sometimes he sat with knife and needle in hand while he fashioned new pieces of harness from strips of leather, or cleaned and oiled leather to keep it from drying out. Harness-making was his job at the Kemps, and he was very good at it.

He told tales of men hunting lions and chasing gazelles—they were sort of like deer, Keentoon explained, and lions were like bobcats, but much bigger and meaner.

"Have you ever killed a lion, Keentoon?" Moses asked.

The man's eyes grew dreamy, and he smiled. "One time. To shoo I am brave enough to become <u>anaké</u>."

59

"…And Remember that I Am a Man."

"What happened?"

Keentoon rose from his place on the bench. He looked around, warily, as though he expected a lion to come from behind a bush at any moment. Crouching slightly, he began to circle around the tree and the table as he spoke, shading his eyes from an imaginary sun with one hand. "I sneak eento jungle, look for lion." He made his other hand into a fist and shook it, as though holding something. A spear, Moses imagined. "I look for many days." He continued stalking around, peering intently.

Moses looked around, too. It wouldn't have surprised him if a lion *had* appeared.

Suddenly, Keentoon stopped and put a hand to his ear. "Den, I hear lion." He made grunting noises deep in his throat. "I see heem. Lion sleep een beeg bush. I call udders. We sneak up and get all around him." He suddenly rushed two paces forward and drove his imaginary spear down. "Den we run up and stab heem weeth spears."

Moses felt his eyes go wide. "You killed him?"

Keentoon continued to fight the imaginary beast. "Beeg fight. Lion fight hard." He whirled and suddenly turned into a crouching, snarling, slashing lion. Then he roared and clutched his chest, as if he'd been stabbed, and fell over. He remained "dead" for several seconds, then opened his eyes. "And dat is how I keel lion."

Moses wanted to feel proud of his friend, but he had to ask. "*You* killed the lion?"

Keentoon rose, puffed out his chest and nodded. "Yes. That is how."

"Then who were all those others with you?"

"Other young men who want to become anaké," Keentoon said, coming to stand in front of Moses. "We all shoo how brave we are."

Keentoon still looked proud, but Moses hadn't expected this turn of events. He looked at the man suspiciously. "Why didn't you kill him all by yourself?"

Keentoon looked puzzled. "Why would I do dat?"

"To show how brave you were."

The man's eyes went wide. "One man – one lion? Man would die. Dat would be foolish. I weeshed to become anaké, not become dead."

"If I was showing how brave I was," Moses found himself saying, "I'd have kilt that lion all by myself."

"Den you would be dead. See dis?" Keentoon pointed out a long scar on his leg. "Lion had me, anudder man pull me away. It is much brave for many men to hunt lion. One man did die dat day." He made a quick slashing motion across Moses' face with his fingernails and Moses drew back, but not quickly enough. "Could have been *me* dat died," Keentoon said solemnly.

Moses rubbed his face where Keentoon had lightly scratched him. "Still. . .," he said, "wouldn't you be even braver if you'd done it yourself?"

"Hmmm." Keentoon resumed his seat on the bench. He rubbed the side of his neck, considering. After a moment, he looked around to see if anyone might be looking, and said, "Den, eef what you say is true, eet would be much brave for me to fight against white man who make me eento slave, eh?"

Moses couldn't see what fighting lions had to do with fighting white men, but he nodded cautiously.

"Dat would be foolish, same thing. Too many white men and all haff guns. Anaké waits to fight unteel he has chance to win."

Moses could figure out where this was going now. "But you might be waiting forever."

Keentoon shook his head. "No. Lions go to sleep, sooner or later. When white men catched me, I wait my chance. Many years go by. I runned away. Dey catch me and beat me. Again I runned. Dey catch me again. I runned away third time, now I leeve here. Someday come, I weel run to de north and find my way back to Afreeca."

"But that's not fighting. That's running!"

Keentoon smiled. "Eef dey come to Afreeca and try catch me again, den I fight. Not soo many white men een Afreeca."

Moses would have none of it. "But you keep saying a warrior is brave. It's not brave to run away."

The old man sighed. "Sometimes, eet is brave to run away. To run is to risk de whip." He looked around again. "Mooses, black man who fight white man weel get dead. White man weel just go Afreeca and catch 'nother black man." He thumped himself in the chest and sat up straight. "Keentoon ees brave. But Keentoon ees not fooleesh."

"…And Remember that I Am a Man."

Moses began to reply, but the back door opened and Missy Hannah appeared. She usually brought out their food and left them alone, but maybe she wanted to gather the dishes since Keentoon and Moses had let their talk go on much later than usual. Keentoon muttered something and walked away, heading for the swamp as usual.

Moses stood and waited for the oldest Kemp girl to approach. He thanked her for the supper.

"Thou art welcome" she answered. He expected her to pick up the empty containers, but she stood looking at him. Her gaze was steady, but he noticed her face seemed redder than usual. She licked her lips. "Moses, I want to ask thee a question."

He nodded. "Yes, Missy?"

She hesitated so long, he wondered if she'd ever speak, but then she blurted out, "Doest thou know Jesus?"

Moses was taken aback. Her question seemed to have come out of nowhere. "No, Missy Hannah. Mama told me about him, but I never set eyes on him."

Missy Hannah's eyes went wide. "Do you know about the Bible?"

"What's that, Missy?"

"It's a book. It's the story of God."

She looked uncertain for a moment. Then she took a deep breath. "Mama sayeth it would be proper for me to instruct thee about The Lord. I have felt the call to teach His way and thou wilt be my first convert."

He nodded. "Yes, Missy." What else was there to say?

She smiled. "Fine. Tomorrow, before thou eatest thy first meal, I will teach thee how to bless thy food. And then each evening, I shall instruct thee in the ways of The Father."

"Yes, Missy."

"...And Remember that I Am a Man."

Chapter Eight

Muleskinner—1800 A.D.

I could see the jail full of coloured people, and even the whipping post, at which they were constantly enduring the lash.

The Life of Moses Grandy—1843 A.D.

In the morning, as promised, Missy Hannah began Moses' religious instruction by teaching him a simple blessing. Keentoon ignored the goings-on and dug into his food.

The delay of memorizing the prayer kept Moses from finishing his meal before Keentoon stood and headed off toward the barn. Moses jumped up and went after him, stuffing a small piece of biscuit in his pocket. He would give it to Goliath, first chance he got.

As the weeks went on, Moses had learned to like Goliath more than any other animal on the farm, despite being kicked by him at their first meeting. Goliath was the smartest mule. He liked to play jokes. If Moses had his back to him and wasn't paying attention, the mule would sneak up and push him with his head, just enough to throw him off balance. When Moses set down a curry brush or hoof pick, Goliath would pick it up and run off. Moses would chase after him and a game of "keep-away" was on.

That summer, after he'd memorized a few prayers, Missy Hannah began reading to Moses from the Bible. She read about how God had created the world and everything in it. Moses didn't understand a lot of it. Especially when Missy Hannah got to the part about the first man and woman living in a garden. The only gardens he knew about were vegetable gardens and it didn't make sense to live there instead of in a house.

"Did Eve really talk to a snake?" Moses asked.

"It says so in the Bible and that makes it so," said Missy Hannah. "You see, Moses…"

"Why are you telling that black boy about the Bible?"

Moses whirled to see that Chadwick had come up.

"I am to become a preacher of the word," Missy Hannah said. "Moses is my first convert."

"He's just a dumb nigger," Chadwick said. "He can't learn anything."

Missy Hannah frowned. "Thou mustn't use that word, Chadwick. Thou knowest better."

Chadwick shrugged. "Your grandfather always said it, until he died last year. Quakers could own slaves in his time, remember. Anyway, your mother sent me to tell you to come in now." He walked back to the house.

Moses turned to Missy Hannah. "You're gonna be a preacher?"

She nodded enthusiastically. "I have heard the calling. I shall spread the word of The Lord."

"But you're a girl."

Missy Hannah nodded. "Yes. Many preachers in the Society of Friends are women."

*

As the days went on, Moses learned more and more about mules. His days were full, and caring for the animals was interesting. The evenings were even more fulfilling. Keentoon taught him how to be a warrior. Not fighting with spears or anything like that, but how to act when things went against you and how to keep courage from failing when facing danger. And how to work hard to get what you wanted.

After Keentoon went back into the swamp in the evening, Missy Hannah continued his religious instruction. He learned about Cain and Abel, David and Goliath, and Moses, who had led the Israelite slaves out of Egypt. He had much to think about at night as he lay in the straw of the stable, under his old blanket, for those few minutes before sleep overtook him. He had been homesick for a few weeks after coming here, but now he felt at home.

After a few weeks, he asked Missy Hannah if he could learn to read the Bible. She shook her head.

"I asked mother about that," she said. "Thou art quite intelligent and I knew thou wouldst want to learn."

"Then why won't you teach me?" asked Moses.

Missy Hannah looked at him sadly. "It is against the law to teach a slave to read.

*

After they'd finished breakfast one day in the fall, Keentoon said Mister Kemp wanted them in the barn.

When they got there, Mister Kemp held out a loop of coiled leather in his hand. "Dost thou know what this is, Moses?" he asked. He shook it out.

Moses nodded, unable to tear his eyes away from the uncoiling length of leather. Only two things in the world frightened Moses to the point where his muscles went rigid: snakes and whips. He swallowed hard. "That's a whip, Mister Kemp."

"And thou knowest what a whip is used for, dost thou not?"

"Yes, sir," he said weakly. Had he done something wrong?

"It's used to teach a lazy animal how to put his back into his work," Mister Kemp said. "This particular type of whip..." His right hand came back and the whip curled into the air behind him. Then he moved his arm forward and the entire length of the whip flew along with it. His wrist flicked and a loud cracking noise erupted, causing Moses to jump. "...is called a muleskinner," Mister Kemp continued.

"A... a muleskinner?"

"A skilled mule driver can be gentle enough to snap a fly off a mule's rump without touching the mule. But he can also rip a strip of skin off without harming the muscles beneath. A good mule-handler is often called a muleskinner, after his whip."

"…And Remember that I Am a Man."

Moses had seen whips used. They went deeper than skin; they tore through muscle; they drank blood and ripped dignity to threads. His own mama had…

He felt a hand on his shoulder. "Meester Kemp talking to you, Moses."

Blinking, Moses looked about. Mister Kemp looked at him with concern. "Moses? Art thou all right?"

Moses managed to nod. "Yes, I'm good."

"Take this." Mister Kemp held out one of the whips. "Learn to use it, for I will teach thee how to drive mules."

Moses wanted to say he didn't want to drive mules; he wanted to go home and live with his mama. He'd have rather laid hold of a squirming water moccasin, but reached out and took the whip.

"Now thou watchest me." Mister walked several steps away and shook his longer whip free of its coil. "The skill is all in the wrist." As earlier, the whip floated back and then came forward so fast it disappeared. CRACK!

Despite expecting the noise, Moses jumped.

"Watch again," Mister Kemp cried. CRACK! exploded the muleskinner. "Again." CRACK! "Again." CRACK!

Keentoon stood rigid beside Moses. Moses looked more closely and realized he was trembling slightly. Keentoon was afraid of whips, too, and was trying not to show it.

"Thou tryest thy whip now," Mister Kemp said, gesturing toward Moses.

"What do I do first?"

"Shaketh it out in front of thee, as I did."

Moses tossed the whip out. Keentoon said, "I weel goo do somet'eeng else, now." He walked away.

With his right hand, Moses tried to use the whip, but the lash didn't go far. He backed up two paces to straighten it.

"Takest a good look at the whip. The part in thy hand is the 'handle.' Thy whip is about five feet long, a good length for a beginner. At the other end is a single, narrow strip of leather, called the 'fall,' with a piece of unraveled thread at the end. That thread is the 'popper.'"

Moses stared at the snake-like thing stretched out in front of him. It was old and well-used, the leather scuffed and cracking in places.

"With thine arm bent," Mister Kemp continued, "bring it back above thy head and then quickly to the front again. Do not try to pop it yet." Mister Kemp backed away.

Moses did as he was told. His arm went back and the whip followed, but it didn't go over his head. It snaked by him, on the ground.

"Too slow," called Mister Kemp.

Moses tried again, jerking his arm forward and the whip went over his head, landing on the ground before him.

"Try again."

"I'll never be able to do this," Moses complained.

Mister Kemp's whip lashed out. Moses tried to jump out of the way, but he had barely begun to move when the whip popped five feet away from him. Mister Kemp did something with his hand, the whip whirled in mid-air, and the tip came to rest at Moses' feet.

"Look at it," Mister Kemp said. "This is a mule-skinner, slender and capable of a loud noise. If it was a bullwhip, it would have a thicker fall on the end, and no popper, so would make little sound. It is heavier so an ox can feel it through its thick hide. Noise does not affect a dumb ox's behavior. It must be controlled with brute force."

Moses wondered if they had a special name and type of whip to use on slaves. "How do... how doest thou make noise with it?"

"When the whip is moving forward as fast as thou canst manage, pullest thy wrist back sharply to stop its motion. Now thou pop it." Mister Kemp walked a few steps away, out of the reach of Moses' whip.

It took a dozen tries before he managed a weak "pop." After that, he managed to crack the whip nearly every time.

"Thou wilt get better," said Mister Kemp. "Continue your lesson. I will come back in a bit and see how you fare."

Moses kept at it. The crack of the whip hit only air, but it sounded to him like skin being flayed.

"…And Remember that I Am a Man."

"…And Remember that I Am a Man."

Chapter Nine

Reliable Mule—1801 A.D.

In my early days there were no schools for those of my class; for it was under penalty of death for any one to be caught teaching the Bible. The poor whites were in as bad condition, as far as education was concerned, excepting the penalty.
I can just remember, one summer, way down in my neighborhood in a meadow, there was an Englishman teaching four boys the alphabet, and the slaveholders came on top of the hill and discovered him, took their guns, crept down upon him and shot him dead. The authorities applauded them for so doing, said they did right.

The Life of George Henry—1894 A.D.

Mister Kemp hired Moses again that January. Missy Hannah continued to teach him about Christianity. Not allowed to teach Moses to read, she decided to teach him how to "cipher." She used money to teach him about numbers, having him work out sums in the currency of the new nation, dollars and cents, for America had abandoned the old British system of pounds and shillings.

He learned about copper cents and half-cents, silver dismes, half-dismes, quarter and half dollars. In gold, there were dollars, half-eagles worth five dollars and eagles worth ten dollars. Four dollars was worth about one British pound.

Moses took to the subject and enjoyed any kind of counting. He soon took pride in knowing how many of each type of animal lived on the farm, right down to the chickens. Once he had counting mastered, Missy Hannah taught him addition, subtraction, multiplication and division.

One spring morning, Mister Kemp appeared in the barn door. "Get thy whip," he said. "Comest thou with me."

He had Moses get in the same wagon he'd first ridden to the Kemp place. Mister Kemp and Keentoon rode in front. Moses shared the cargo area with a large, wooden crate. He sat in the back, on the tailgate, facing the rear and holding ropes leading to four almost full-grown mules. They dutifully walked behind.

They drove to a deserted pasture, where Mister Kemp told him to tie the extra mules to the fence. Moses did as he was told, knowing enough to tie the animals far enough apart that they wouldn't fight.

By the time he'd finished, the two men had got the crate torn apart. Moses put a foot on a wheel spoke and rose up to watch. As the top of the box lifted free, Mister Kemp said, "Ah, she's a beauty, all right."

Moses could hardly wait to see the "beauty" but was disappointed when the crate's sides dropped away. It was a plow. New, shiny and more sturdy-looking than any he'd ever seen, but still only a plow.

Mister Kemp and Keentoon went to the rear of the wagon and dragged the plow to its edge. "Takest thou the plow handles and ease it down, Moses," Mister Kemp said as the two men pulled it down so the handles could be reached.

Then, grunting with the effort, they all lifted the heavy plow off the wagon. It came down fast, hitting the ground with a thump.

Moses saw why Mister Kemp had called the plow a beauty. Instead of the crudely-carved handles of most plows, which were fitted together with wood pegs and screws, on this one brass straps and metal fittings locked heavy, well-made handles together. The wooden frame, shiny with shellac, had been bolted to a plow unlike Moses had ever before seen, bluish-black and shiny.

"It's made all out of metal," he said. Every other plow blade he'd seen had been wooden, with an iron blade, or plowshare, attached in front.

Mister Kemp dropped to one knee and ran his fingers over the leading edge. "First all-iron plow in the area. I've agreed to represent the firm that makes these plows, here in the county. This is much better than a strip of metal nailed onto a wooden plow. Once the other farmers see how many more acres a man can plow in a day, they'll beat a path to my door."

There was an eager tone to Mister Kemp's voice and Moses noticed he wasn't using "Quaker-talk." Then he remembered Keentoon saying Mister Kemp hadn't been a Quaker all his life. He talked like other people sometimes.

Chadwick picked this time, after all the hard work had been done, to show up. He strutted up to the wagon, carrying a whip. Moses knew the white boy well enough that the whip was meant to show he was a muleskinner, far from the truth as that might be.

"I'm here," he said to Mister Kemp.

Mister Kemp eyed him, as though considering rebuking him for his tardiness, but said, "Hitch the mules to the plow, Chadwick. Moses will be learning how to handle them."

Chadwick, a mocking look on his face, threw a thumb in Moses' direction. "The darkie? He's too dumb to learn mule handling."

Mister Kemp sighed. "Just harness the mules, Chadwick."

Moses had learned that Chadwick was the son of one of Mister Kemp's wife's relatives. It looked to him like Mister Kemp would like to get rid of Chadwick. Was Chadwick smart enough to guess that Moses had been hired to do the work he wouldn't or couldn't handle?

When Chadwick had finished, Keentoon went behind the plow and grabbed the handles, muscles in his small, but powerful, shoulders and arms bunching. Mister Kemp stood a couple of paces behind Keentoon.

"Moses, stand aside. Watch what we do and learn from it. These mules are halfway trained. We traine them with a whip now so they will later answer to commands without a whip. A man handling a plow can't let go of the handles, so the mules must obey without hesitation."

Moses nodded, backing away.

Keentoon grabbed the handles. "Geettup," he said in a clear, loud voice. The mules began to walk forward. Keentoon followed, keeping the plow blade raised so it didn't dig in yet. Mister Kemp followed behind him.

"I am ready," Mister Kemp said softly.

Keentoon lifted the handles and the front of the plow dug in. Moses smelled the rich dirt and crushed grass as the plowshare turned up a line of dark earth. He became aware he was being left behind and wouldn't be able to watch, so he ran and caught up.

Nothing happened until they reached the end of the pasture. "Gee," called Keentoon. Mister Kemp, who had moved to the left and allowed his whip to trail behind him, lashed out and the whip cracked beside the mules opposite the direction of the ordered turn.

The mules' ears flicked as they turned to the right. Moses couldn't tell if they'd turned due to the crack of the whip or Keentoon's rein directions. They came around until the plow moved in the opposite direction, digging a furrow beside the first.

When they'd almost come back to the wagon, where Chadwick now perched on the seat watching, the same routine happened. The team made a turn to the right, but without use of the whip. Several more times Keentoon commanded, "Gee," and a portion of the grassy pasture became a plowed field.

Then he said, "Haw," and Mister Kemp cracked the muleskinner on the other side. The mules performed the turn, Keentoon using the reins to bring the plow's travel back alongside the original furrow. Keentoon took them through several more left turns and then began shifting directions at random.

Mister Kemp broke off and came to stand beside Moses.

"The mules must respond to either reins or voice," he said. "This pair is doing well, and need but little guidance. Once they are more experienced, they will not need reins to guide them back onto the furrow-lines. A truly reliable mule will turn at the end of the pasture without any command at all. You see that even a small man like John, here, who doesn't really know mules, can guide the plow, while the beasts do the work."

"They're that smart?"

"In my opinion, mules are smarter than most Negroes. They know their job and they do it. But some of them need a touch of the whip to keep them steady."

Mister Kemp didn't seem to realize how cruel his words were. Moses tried to maintain a blank expression. Mister Kemp turned and called out. "John, thou canst stop. We shall do the other pair now."

Moses fumed as he helped Keentoon hitch the other team to the plow. This time Mister Kemp stepped up behind the plow. "Moses, thou followest close behind me. If I sayeth, "Gee," thou poppest the whip on the left side of the mules so they know to turn right. If I sayeth, "Haw," pop the whip on the right side."

Moses nodded and took a deep breath. He walked over and took the position Mister Kemp had used with the first team.

"Giddap," Mister Kemp said. Instead of the smooth start Moses had seen with the first team, the mules seemed to move their legs aimlessly.

"Poppest the whip, Moses," Mister Kemp cried.

Moses cracked his whip; Mister Kemp shouted commands and the team broke into an uneven walk. They soon steadied out, however as Mister Kemp let the plowshare drag behind them. Apparently satisfied, he let the plow dig in.

As they neared the end of the pasture, he said, "We'll go right first. Art thou ready, Moses?"

"Yes, sir." Moses moved to the left and readied himself.

"Gee!"

Even though he expected it, Moses was a beat late bringing the whip forward. The feet of the mules worked to cross-purposes, it appeared. The plow wobbled and the whole affair ground to a stop.

"I'm sorry, Mister Kemp." Moses figured he'd be in for a tongue lashing, at the least. Chadwick, atop the wagon, grinned from ear to ear.

"Not thy fault, Moses," said Mister Kemp. "I gave the command and used the reins, the mules should have turned without the whip." He raised his voice, "Giddap!"

Hauling the mules around with brute force applied to the reins, the man soon had them going in a straight line again. "We'll go left this time," he said.

"Haw!"

Moses cracked the whip and, to his relief, the mules managed to make an awkward left turn. Maybe he was getting the hang of it and the hard-headed animals would wise up.

However the pattern for the rest of the morning had been set. The mules could not make a decent right turn, even though the whip kept cracking.

"The mule on the right is too hard-headed," Mister Kemp said. "This time, I want thee to makest him feel the whip, Moses."

Moses gulped. They started out again and he wondered what he'd do when the team got to the end of the field. He didn't want to whip the mule, but how could he not? Mister Kemp had saved him from being hired by a harsh master, treated him decently, and fed him better than he'd ever eaten before. *Help me, Jesus,* he prayed. *Help me to do the right thing.*

He looked back and saw Keentoon watching intently, a look of worry on his face. Moses had never seen the African warrior use a whip, and had no idea what Keentoon would have done in his place. Was this a test? Would Mister Kemp take him, Moses, back to town and leave him there for someone else to hire? When Mister Kemp called, "Haw," Moses struck out with the whip. It caught the mule on the rump and he brayed pitifully, lunging in the traces.

"Again," called Mister Kemp, struggling to keep the plowshare in the ground as it bucked.

Moses could see a wide stripe on the mule where he had whipped it—harder than he'd meant to. Still, he lashed the mule again. It turned away from Moses' torments and joined the other mule in turning to the right.

He hoped this would be the last time he'd need to use the whip, but it was not to be so. Twice more he had to whip the stubborn mule through right turns until it got the idea.

To Moses' surprise, nothing bad happened, except to the mule. On the wagon ride back to the barn, he looked at his dark-skinned hand and it had not changed. Whipping a mule was not like whipping a person, he told himself. Still, he felt ashamed.

"…And Remember that I Am a Man."

Chapter Ten

African God—1802 A.D.

The enemies of Africa wish to persuade the world that five out of the six thousand years that the world has existed, Africa has always been sunk in barbarism, and that ignorance is essential to the nature of her inhabitants. Have they forgotten that Africa was the cradle of the arts and sciences? If they pretend to forget this, it becomes our duty to remind them of it.

Réflexions Politiques sur quelques Ouvrages et Journaux Français Concernant Haïti (English: Political Remarks upon Certain French Publications and Journals Concerning Haiti), Baron De Vastey, African Haitian—1817 A.D.

Moses began his third year with the Kemps, the nicest people he'd ever known. Although slavery would always keep a certain distance between them, they treated him almost like family. Missy Hannah, especially.

He enjoyed learning about numbers and Christianity. He didn't see how knowing numbers would ever be of any use, but Christianity gave immediate rewards. The best part was observing Sabbath, which was something they'd never done on the Grandy farm. On that day, Mister Kemp allowed both Moses and Keentoon freedom to do what they pleased—as long as the animals were fed and watered, of course. Since Keentoon worked mostly with making or repairing harnesses and other implements, his work could be left off for a day.

Mister Kemp provided the time for leisure. Mrs. Kemp and the girls provided lengths of thread and old, bent or dull pins from their sewing supplies. The woods provided cane poles and bits of bark to use as floats. Moses poked about in the soft earth and provided worms and grubs for bait. Keentoon assembled all these things into fishing poles that provided magical, lazy afternoons. And, according to Keentoon, Ngai, the creator, provided the fish. Moses gave credit to Jesus, instead, since these were American fish rather than African.

While the Kemp family attended meeting for a good part of the day, the old man and the boy would wander along Sawyer's Creek. They learned the best places to angle for sunfish, perch, bluegills, and Moses' favorite meal, catfish.

Using their crude, hand-bent hooks, they lost as many fish as they landed, but it didn't matter. Just having the time to relax and talk was the best thing.

Keentoon often spoke of Africa as they leaned back against trees and watched the floats for nibbles. Ngai, he said, was the only god. He suspected that the god of the white people was the same one, but that they worshipped him in a different way.

When Moses learned more about Ngai, he had to agree. The Kikuyu didn't have a Jesus, but they had a god much like the Christian God.

Like the white god, Ngai was all-powerful and could do all things. He could not be seen but was manifest in the sun, the moon, thunderstorms, stars, comets, rainbows and in the great fig trees of Africa under which the Kikuyu had roamed from the beginning of creation. Ngai had given birth to all people and had created the land, the plants, and the animals. Yet Ngai was not the distant god of the whites. He had human characteristics and would sometimes come to earth to inspect his realm, to bestow blessings, and to give out just punishment.

"If Ngai can do anything for us, why do we have to pray for freedom from slavery?" Moses once asked, as he held his pole ready over a wiggling bobber, made from a piece of bark. "Why doesn't he just end slavery?"

"…And Remember that I Am a Man."

"He ees a long ways away, een Afreeca and does not knoo about white man's slavery. We must pray loud for heem to hear us. Eef we lived in my land, de land of the Kikuyu, we might pray for rain, or de birth of a male-child, or to make beegger de size of de cattle herd, but what good would dat be here? More rain would bring better crops and de white man would buy more slaves to work de land and more Kikuyu would be brought on de slave ships. A male child who was taken could noo longer help hees fameely with de herds or hunt for meat. And only whites can own cattle here, een dees evil country."

"But we could pray for guns and swords and spears," Moses argued, jiggling his bait slightly. "We could ask Ngai for victory over the whites, because there are more of us, at least around here, on the farms."

Keentoon shook his head. "Noo, Mooses. A hunter might pray to keel de lion, but who say dat de lion not be praying to de god of de lions for a bite of man-meat. We do not ask Ngai to put down de whites, oonly to take care of hees own people."

Moses thought for a moment. "Maybe it's like Mister Kemp says. Maybe God doesn't have a problem with slavery. After all, being a slave isn't all that bad, I guess."

"What!" Keentoon jumped to his feet and pulled the pole away from Moses, grabbing him by the arm. The line went flying through the air so fast that the worm came off the hook and disappeared into the nearby bushes. "Don't you ever say dat."

Moses tried to squirm away. "But it's not so bad here. The Kemps feed us up and treat us good."

"Dat doon't matter. We are steel slaves."

"But we're not like the field hands or the work gangs digging the canal." Moses had once seen the canal workers coming out of the swamp,, most of them big, burly brutes, covered in muck to their armpits or even their necks. He'd never seen a sorrier group of men.

Keentoon shook Moses. "A slave ees a slave. Mister Kemp treat us noo better than hees mules. He feed us, geev us a place to sleep— for you, anyway—and lets us have a short time each week to rest up. Dat's all we get."

"What more is there?"

"…And Remember that I Am a Man."

"You tinking like a slave. Eef you was free, you would get money for you work and you could oon tings."

"But I'm black." Moses wrenched his arm away and sat down by his usual tree, crossing his arms. "I can't have those things."

Keentoon threw Moses' fishing pole down. "De color of your skeen have notting to do weeth eet. Dere are free blacks in de north, free blacks een Afreeca, blacks who have run away to de west to leeve with de savage eendians, maroons who hide een de swamp."

Moses forgot his anger at the mention of the maroons. "You live in the swamp, Keentoon. What's it like to be free?"

Keentoon hung his head as if ashamed, and his hands dropped to his sides. He flopped to the ground to sit beside Moses. "I am not maroon. I am too scared of de snakes and de monsters in de swamp to stay een dere. I oonly sleep een a hut I build, on de edge of de Dismal."

"But you're free."

"No," Keentoon said. "I am only runned away. Somewhere dere ees a beeg book of de whites dat say I am a slave. As long as eet say soo een dat book, I am a slave."

"But the maroons, they're free, aren't they."

Keentoon shook his head. "No, dey are runned away, too. Dey hide een de swamp hooping to find a way to de north. In de north, de whites have a different book, one dat does not say dey are slaves."

"Why don't you go to the north, then, Keentoon?"

"I am too oold," he said, sadly looking into Moses' face. "And also, I am scared of de slave catchers who would catch me and wheep me. Besides, I would steel be leeving among de whites. And even eef I find a way to get back to Kikuyu land, my mudder is gone, my fadder ees surely dead by now, and I would have noo cattle or goats."

Moses thought a moment and nodded. "So you've given up on being free."

Keentoon's eyes flashed with anger. He started to reply, but no words came out. Finally, he lowered his head and said, "You are right. I have become an oold man who seets outside his hut and talk-talk-talks. I am too oold to run far." His shoulders slumped and he sighed. "Running away ees noo good. De only way for a slave to become truly free ees to earn his freedom."

But then Keentoon's head came up again, a bit of fire returning to his eyes. "But you must not geev up on freedom, Mooses, my son. You have never been to Afreeca, so you cannot goo dere, but you can go to de north, or you can go to de west. But you must fight to be free."

Moses did not answer. When Keentoon had called him, "my son," he had begun to wonder what it would be like if he'd had a father around while growing up. Once Benjamin and Jebediah had been sold off, he'd been the only male in the family, and had been babied by his sisters.

"Mooses," Keentoon broke into Moses' daydreaming.

"Hmmm?"

"You must promise me dat you weel work for your freedom. Promise me dat."

Moses nodded. If that's what Keentoon wanted. "I promise."

"Good," said Keentoon. "I leeved my whole life with my woman and thought dat was good enough, even soo we was slaves. Eet was only after she died dat I runned away de first time. Do not spend your whole life and end up an oold man like me, steel a slave."

"Maybe Master James will free me after he grows up."

"Dat noo good, eeder. White man can make you a slave, but oonly you can make you free." He tapped his chest above his heart. "Here."

"…And Remember that I Am a Man."

Chapter Eleven

Slave-catcher—1802 A.D.

30 Dollars Reward
Runaway from a subscriber in Fredericksburg, a Negro slave named John Day, a sadler (sic) and harness maker by trade, he is also a good hand at shoe making; about four feet seven inches high, well made, of a yellow complexion and good countenance, about forty years of age, and gray headed; had a drab coloured cloth coat on, brown linen shirt and trowsers,(sic) and may have better clothes with him. Whoever takes him up and secures him, or brings him to me, shall receive twenty dollars reward, if taken in this state, and if out of this state Thirty Dollars Reward, paid on delivery by me
William Smock, Fredericksburg, August 3, 1790

Fredericksburg Herald—1790 A.D.

The last of the leaves had fallen from the trees and the air was brisk. As Moses went to fetch a mule from one of the pastures, out of the corner of his eye, he noticed an armed rider come out of the woods from the direction of the swamp. He didn't think much of it. Hunters often passed by the Kemp farm this time of year, looking for deer or wild turkey. When two other white riders appeared, spaced out from the first, however, he began to wonder what might be happening. Especially since all of the men seemed to be taking up positions, rifles at the ready. Moses hadn't heard any hounds baying, as if dogs were running a stag. But the men were waiting for something.

"…And Remember that I Am a Man."

Keeping an eye on the men, he put a rope around the mule's neck and led him back to the big barn in time to see a skinny white man riding up the lane. Moses put the animal in a stall and peeked out from the edge of the barn door.

The man rode an old swaybacked, short-legged, piebald horse, mostly brown, but mottled with white specks all over its rump. The horse had one white ear. That was it—one ear. Where the other should have been was a ragged tuft of skin and hair, as though it had been bitten or cut off.

The gaunt rider seemed even mangier than the mount, with greasy, ragged gray hair trailing like snakes down his neck. He wore a too-small greatcoat over a dirty, torn white shirt and fawn-colored breeches. His eyes, set above a narrow nose, were small and piggy beneath thick black eyebrows. His mouth hung open like a dying trout. An old, faded tricorner hat had been jammed down over his head, pushing down the tops of his jug-handle ears.

What most caught Moses' attention, though, was the ornate flintlock pistol tucked into a black leather belt about the thin man's waist. The gun, with its fancy silver metalwork, did not match the rest of the man's appearance and Moses wondered if it had been stolen. Besides the gun, Moses noticed a coiled, well-worn whip hanging from the man's saddle.

Mister Kemp appeared from behind one of the sheds and walked out to greet the visitor. The gaunt man halted his horse a step away, but failed to dismount and shake hands, as did most visitors to the farm. Instead, he stared down at Mister Kemp as if looking at something unpleasant.

Mister Kemp looked up at the visitor without a hint of welcome on his face. "Good day, stranger. Is there something I can do for thee?"

The rider on the ugly horse spat to the side, shooting out a stream of brown juice. "Ye be Mister Kemp, I take it." A thin trail of tobacco juice ran down his chin.

Mister Kemp nodded. "That is my name. Do I knoweth thee?"

"Not yet," said the man. He looked around with a slow, searching gaze. "This your farm?"

Drawing himself up in obvious annoyance, Mister Kemp said, "It is. May I again inquire as to thy business here?"

"Where's the nigger?"

Moses felt his throat go tight.

"Who… what dost thou mean?" Mister Kemp took a deep breath. "I own no slaves."

"Didn't say you did." The man's dull gaze began sweeping the farm, as though looking for something—or someone. "I'm talkin' about the runaway you been hidin'. Name of John Day."

Runaway! Those riders by the trees…they were looking for Keentoon, Moses realized.

Mister Kemp shook his head. "Why, I hath not been keeping…"

"Don't quibble with me, Quaker." The man stopped and chewed a few times. "A little birdie told me. You been feedin' him an' workin' him. It's the same thing."

Mister Kemp drew himself up even further, his face turning red. "Thou hast no business being on my property. I commandest thee to leave."

The man grinned, showing brown, scummy teeth. "Leave is it? Ye want me to leave, Quaker; I'll just do that. And I'll be back with the sheriff."

"Then be on thy way." Mister Kemp pointed down the lane.

"And what do you suppose the sheriff will say?" The thin man edged his horse a step forward, forcing Mister Kemp back. "I'm Quentin Henholer and I have a paper from Mister William Smock of Fredricksburg, Virginia, authorizin' me to capture his escaped nigger. If I show your blasted sheriff that you've been obstructin' my lawful rights and harborin' a fugitive slave, where does that leave you, mister?"

The door of the house opened, and Henholer's head swiveled toward the sound. Mrs. Kemp stepped out. She held an old, rusty-looking musket in her hands.

Henholer's hand went to the butt of his pistol and he rose in his stirrups. "Tell your woman to put that gun down, Kemp. I have the law on my side."

Mister Kemp glanced over at Mrs. Kemp and the fight seemed to go out of him. "Put the gun down, Dorothea."

"I'll not let them take John," she said, raising the firearm slightly. Henholer started to pull his pistol.

"...And Remember that I Am a Man."

From the corner of his eye, Moses saw a dark figure step out from behind the corner of the house. Keentoon! He was bent over, creeping away. No one except Moses could see him, because the house blocked the view of the others. Keentoon must think he could get away, but he didn't know about the riders over toward the swamp. Moses drew his breath in sharply.

Henholer's head whipped around at the slight sound, saw where Moses was looking and realized what was happening. He kicked his heels into the horse and began edging over to where he could see around the house.

Moses stepped out of the stable. "Run, Keentoon, run."

At Moses' warning, Keentoon veered and made for the swamp. In a few strides, he came out from the cover of the house and ran for his life.

"There he goes," shouted Henholer. "Get him." He spurred his horse.

A loud crashing sounded as two more riders pushed their way out of the brush beside the lane and galloped forward. They went straight through the farmyard, causing Mister Kemp to dodge, and lit out after Henholer, who was fast gaining on Keentoon.

Mrs. Kemp pointed the old musket in the air and pulled the trigger but nothing happened. "Run, John," she cried. "Run for your life."

Keentoon was running to put a younger man to shame. His short legs propelled him forward so that he bounded like a rabbit.

But Moses could see the old man had no chance against a horse, even an old plug like the piebald, ridden by an old man who could barely stay in the saddle. Henholer had put away his pistol and now brandished the whip above his head. "Run, you scalawag, run," he roared. "It'll do ye no good."

Keentoon had reached the corner of the nearest pasture fence and he ran alongside it, heading for the swamp. Henholer was a few paces behind by this time and his two henchmen—on younger, healthier horses—followed close after.

Without thinking, Moses lit out after the whole bunch. Even though he had no idea how to help, he couldn't abandon the man who had become his friend and teacher.

84

Keentoon looked over his shoulder and saw Henholer preparing to use the whip. He turned his head back around, angled toward the fence and launched himself into the air. Legs spread wide in front and back, he cleared the top rail and came down running on the other side. He'd cleared a fence nearly as tall as he was.

"You little son of a black-eyed raccoon," Henholer cried, spurring his horse at the fence. "You won't get away." At the last instant, the piebald set his front feet firmly on the ground and stopped dead. Henholer flew off the horse and over the fence.

Moses, who had reached the front of the pasture, squeezed between two rails and ran after Keentoon. By the time Moses had taken several strides, he became aware he was gaining on the old black man. The dash from the house and the vault over the fence had sapped Keentoon's energy.

Far out beyond Keentoon, Moses could see the three riders from earlier rushing to intercept. No way would Keentoon make the swamp. One of the two men who'd been following Henholer jumped his horse over the fence and resumed the chase from behind. He guided the horse with his left hand and held a thick club in his right.

Keentoon looked behind him again and Moses was close enough to see the naked fear in his eyes. The old slave would have done better to have turned himself in, but the scars on his back must have been flaming in anticipation of the punishment for escape, which he would surely receive.

Rhythmic noises filled the air, the hoarse rasping of Keentoon as his lungs labored, the bellowing breath of the galloping horse merging with the thunderous pounding of hooves, the lesser sound of Moses panting with anxiety and the voice of the slave-catcher urging the horse on. "Get 'em, get 'em, get 'em, get 'em." Because all these reverberations repeated again and again, they seemed to cancel out when they reached Moses' ears. They seemed much quieter than his thoughts, which also echoed. *Please, Jesus. Please, Jesus. Please Jesus.*

Moses felt, more than heard, the vibrations as the horse came up alongside Keentoon, who was running ragged by now. The club went up in silence, then came down with a swoosh. Then came a hollow thud, as though someone had smashed a pumpkin into the solid trunk of a tree.

"…And Remember that I Am a Man."

Keentoon's arms, legs, body, even his neck went limp, as though all his bones had exploded into soft powder. He tumbled over and thudded, face-first, onto the ground.

"…And Remember that I Am a Man."

Chapter Twelve

Less than a Man—1802 A.D.

*Representatives and direct taxes shall be apportioned among the
several states which may be included within this Union, according
to their respective numbers, which shall be determined by adding
the whole number of free persons, including those bound to service
for a term of years, and excluding Indians not taxed, three-fifths of
all other persons.*

*Article 1, Section 2, Paragraph 3 of the United States
Constitution—1787 A.D*

None of the riders bothered to dismount and check the man who had
been clubbed down, so Moses reached Keentoon first. Hardly able
to see past the tears in his eyes, Moses pulled at the old African,
trying to get him up so he could run again. Maybe he could make it
to the swamp if Moses helped. "Please, Keentoon, get up," he
sobbed. "You can still get away."

Keentoon did not respond at all. Then claw-like hands yanked
Moses up. "Get off him, you young whelp," Henholer's voice
bellowed in his ear. The back of a hairy hand hit the side of Moses'
head and sent him sprawling.

"Did I kill the nigger?" someone asked.

"How in Hades would I know?" Henholer answered. He gasped
for breath, his fat face red from running across the pasture. In one

hand, he held a coil of rope. "Why'd you hit him so hard? He's not worth a half-cent, dead."

Moses rose to his knees and saw Henholer reach down, take Keentoon by an arm, and flip him over.

Keentoon didn't stir. *Oh, no*, Moses thought. *He's dead for sure.* They'd hit him so hard and he was too old. But then Henholer kicked the old man in the ribs. Keentoon moaned.

"Naw, he ain't dead," said Henholer. "But he'll wish he was, by the time Smock gets done whippin' him."

"Please, Master, don't kick him no more," Moses heard himself say. "He's an old man."

But Henholer pulled his foot back and kicked Keentoon once more—viciously this time. "Get up, stupid. I ain't got time for you to be layin' around all day."

Keentoon stirred and tried to rise from the ground. He managed to get to his knees, but didn't seem able to gain his feet. Putting a hand to the back of his head, he felt his wound. When he brought his hand back around, it was covered in blood. He stared at the red smear, seemingly fascinated by it. Then he shook his head, lurched to his feet and stood swaying.

Two men—one the man with the club—got off their horses. They came up behind the old slave and Moses worried they'd hit Keentoon again.

Instead, one man yanked Keentoon's elbows back, like grabbing a chicken by its wings. The other slave-catcher thrust his long club between Keentoon's elbows and his back. Henholer drew his hands in front of his stomach and tied his wrists together, pinning his arms. Then the old slave became aware of his situation again, and his eyes darted about, looking for a place to run or hide.

But he made no attempt to escape as Henholer threw another rope around his neck and led him back toward the Kemp farmhouse. Moses followed, walking behind the horse of the man who'd downed Keentoon. The rest of the slave-catchers waited on the other side of a gate, joking and laughing. One held the reins of Henholer's piebald.

The slave-catcher took Keentoon into the farmyard, where Mister and Mrs. Kemp stood waiting, side-by-side. The musket was no longer to be seen. Moses felt sorry for that, because Mrs. Kemp looked like she wanted to shoot Henholer about now, and Moses wouldn't have minded watching. That musket had probably belonged to Mrs. Kemp's father, though, and no longer worked.

Henholer ignored the Kemps. He handed Keentoon's lead-rope to one of his men and swung awkwardly up onto the piebald horse, which grunted when the slave-catcher's bony buttocks settled into the saddle.

Mister Kemp stepped forward, drawing his wife along.

"I sayeth unto thee again, Henholer," he said, "thou hast no right to come upon my property and taketh this man."

Henholer looked down with obvious contempt. "Quaker man, any more lip out of you, and I'll run you and your wife in for interferin' with my lawful duties under the Refugee Slave Act. This nigger's from out of state and it's a federal crime to help him, y'know, not just North Carolina law."

While Henholer spoke, Moses crept close to Keentoon, who stood with his head down. A line of blood ran down one cheek and dripped from his chin.

Moses could hear Mrs. Kemp talking now, giving Henholer a piece of her mind. None of the white people paid any attention to him or Keentoon.

"Are you hurt bad?" Moses whispered.

Keentoon didn't raise his head, but turned and regarded Moses from one eye. "Dey going to wheep me again, Mooses."

Moses put a hand on his shoulder. "They won't whip you. You're too old." But in his heart, he knew better. They'd whipped his scrawny old mother for trying to protect her own son, and they'd beat the hell out of this old man for daring to want freedom.

"You a good boy, Mooses." Keentoon took a deep breath and then straightened, looking Moses in the eye. "Doon't you worry 'bout me. I been whipped before. I'll be runnin' away again before you knoos it."

"But Keentoon…"

"Listen," hissed Keentoon. "Doon't matter 'bout me. I am oold. You run—run while your legs still be strong. Doon't die a slave, Mooses. Die free. Promise me."

Tears filling his eyes, Moses found he couldn't speak. He nodded and squeezed Keentoon's shoulder.

"…And Remember that I Am a Man."

"You there, boy," someone shouted. "You get away from that nigger." A horse sidestepped near.

Keentoon shrugged away from Moses' grip. "Goo now," he whispered. "Ngai weell watch out for you."

"I've listened to enough Quaker nonsense," Henholer cried loudly. "Let's go."

Horses moved and the line around Keentoon's neck tightened. He stumbled, then shuffled forward to keep up with the slow trot as the slave-catchers rode off.

Moses watched them until they disappeared around a bend in the lane. Little Keentoon followed behind like an ox being led to slaughter.

When he turned around, Moses saw something that filled his heart with hatred. Chadwick peeked out from the hayloft door of the barn, a smirk on his face. Had he somehow got word to slavers that the Kemps harbored a runaway?

*

From then on, the days grew lonely. Moses worked hard all day, now doing Keentoon's work and most of Chadwick's, as well as his own. Evenings were the worst. Moses would eat alone at the table beneath the tree and then wait for Missy Hannah to arrive for his nightly lesson. His arithmetic had improved to the point where he could figure just about any problem out in his head. Even Missy Hannah was amazed. She had to use a slate board to do her ciphering.

Nevertheless, she was the smartest person Moses had ever known. Not only could she quote most of the Bible from memory, she seemed to know most everything else, too. Mama had taught him a little about Jesus, but Missy Hannah knew all about him and how he had lived. And she was easier to understand than the other Kemps. When she was with him, she didn't use "thees" and "thous," at least not all the time. She thought them old-fashioned, but didn't want her parents to know.

He asked her why, when he'd prayed for Keentoon's safety, Jesus had allowed the slavers to strike him down and return him to slavery.

"I don't know, Moses," she said. "Only God knows why he does things. Sometimes, to us, it might not seem to be the right thing but we must trust him. He knows what is best for us."

Moses continued to pay close attention to his religion lessons, but his faith had been shaken. Maybe he was wrong to worship Jesus, a white god. Maybe he should pray to Keentoon's god, Ngai.

As the wind blew colder and the nights grew longer, a chance remark led her to instruct Moses in something else: politics.

While talking about the lands of the bible, she happened to mention the United States was at war with an African country over piracy. President Jefferson had sent ships to stop the pirates from looting American ships. "Do you know what pirates are?" she had asked.

Moses nodded. "Like Blackbeard." He'd heard stories about pirates who had often hidden their ships in the sounds, bays and rivers of North Carolina, years ago. "But I thought General Washington was president."

Missy Hannah looked at him oddly. "He was—for eight years. But Mister John Adams of Massachusetts was then president for four years and Thomas Jefferson of Virginia is now president. Did you not know that?"

He shook his head. "Where's Virginia?

"Virginia is the state just north of North Carolina," she said, "only a few miles from here."

"What happened to General Washington?"

Missy Hannah looked at him quizzically. "You don't know? He died three years ago, just before you came to live with us."

Moses nodded. "So that's why he's not president anymore. He died. Mama will be sorry to hear about it. She thought a lot of him."

"No, Moses, he died after giving up the presidency. President Washington stepped down because he didn't want one man to hold power for too long."

"So now Mister Jefferson is president?"

"Yes, he's been president for two years. He won the last federal election."

Moses wished she'd begin the Bible study, which would be followed by arithmetic problems on a slate board. This president stuff was beyond him. "What's an eleckashun?" he asked.

"That's how people—well, the men really—choose who will run the government."

"Why did they pick Mister Jefferson?"

"Because he's a southerner. Most of the representatives in the federal government are southerners and they control the electoral college."

Moses frowned He had no idea what the electoral college was. "Why are there more southerners?"

She shook her head. "Because free persons are counted as one person for representation and taxes, but slaves are counted as three-fifths of a person. Since there are so many slaves in the south, we have more representatives to congress."

Just when Moses had begun to think he somewhat understood, he became lost. How could he, a slave, be three-fifths of a person? He knew about fractions; Missy Hannah had taught him. But how could a *person* be divided? You'd have to cut off his legs or something. He didn't want to think about it.

"How come you know all these things, Missy Hannah?" he asked.

She beamed. "I read all the papers from Philadelphia," she said. "Mister McBride, our neighbor, gets them by post, only a few days after they're printed. He gives them to me when he's finished with them, so I keep up to date on the world's affairs."

"Why, Missy?" asked Moses.

"Why what?" She looked puzzled.

Moses hoped he wasn't being "uppity," but plunged on ahead. "They won't even let you vote, even after you grow up, because you're a female. Why do you bother to learn all this?"

She sighed. "There is that gender problem that you mention. But in the Society of Friends, a female is considered the equal of a man. I'm sure it will soon become that way in all the states, too." She squared her shoulders. "I shall fight for a woman's right to vote."

Moses had learned that "Society of Friends" was another way of saying "Quaker." For some reason, being a Quaker made all the difference in the world to Missy Hannah. Moses would have liked to be one, too, but knew it couldn't happen.

"But let's see how well you're doing in your figuring, Moses," Missy Hannah said. She often used real-life situations to bring home arithmetic uses.

92

"If a slave-owner has six and four-tenths persons on his farm, how many men does he own?"

It was a trick question, Moses realized. You had to remember the owner had to counted, too..

And, with sudden clarity, he realized the question was rigged in another way. The slaves weren't three-fifths of a man, but only represented three-fifths of an imaginary person. They couldn't vote and weren't considered men at all.

"…And Remember that I Am a Man."

"…And Remember that I Am a Man."

Chapter Thirteen

Betrayal—1803 A.D.

The Slaves Complaint

Am I sadly cast aside,
On misfortune's rugged tide?
Will the world my pains deride
For ever?

Must I dwell in Slavery's night,
And all pleasure take its flight,
Far beyond my feeble sight,
For ever?

Worst of all, must Hope grow dim,
And withhold her cheering beam?
Rather let me sleep and dream
For ever!

Poems by a Slave, George Moses Horton, 1829 A.D.

Once again, it was time for hiring out. Mister Kemp had brought
Moses to town in the wagon early that morning. His ankles were

shackled, but that was done every year. He didn't like it, but at least he knew he'd be going back home to the Kemp place when all was said and done.

Moses looked around the tobacco warehouse, but couldn't see Mister Kemp anywhere. Where could he be? The bidding was about to start.

Luther, the same auctioneer as every year, spoke up. "This here's Moses, owned by young Master Grandy. As y'all can see he's a fine, strappin' young buck. He's been hired out to Mister Joshua Kemp for the last three years and has proven himself to be a hard worker, I'm told. He is well-behaved and doesn't have a scar on his back. What do I hear for a year's labor from this lad?"

Someone came in the main doors and Moses looked over quickly, expecting to see Mister Kemp. It turned out to be some other white man, though. Once more, Moses looked around, but couldn't find the Quaker he sought.

"Forty dollars," cried someone. Moses' eyes darted in that direction. Not Mister Kemp. Where was he? He had dropped Moses off at the auction house early, and Moses hadn't seen him since.

"I have forty," intoned Luther. "Who'll go forty-five?"

"Here," hollered someone else. This time Moses recognized Jemmy Coates and terror rose in his throat. It was as if the years at the Kemps had been a pleasant dream—something that had never happened and he was again on the block for the first time. His heart went into his throat at the thought of being hired out by Master Coates.

"I'll go fifty," yelled a man. Moses' head spun that way. It was the same man who'd bid forty.

"Fifty-five," responded Coates, a large man with a ponderous belly.

"Fifty-six." Men laughed. Moses looked in the direction the bid had come from. Enoch Sawyer. He was said to be even meaner than Jemmy Coates. Moses had learned that most of the whites who hired blacks by the year were hard-scrabble farmers that couldn't afford to own slaves. In order to make their farms pay, they had to get every half-cent's work out of a hired slave to make the situation pay off. It didn't matter much to these farmers if they needed a whip to make a field hand work hard.

Moses looked again at the door, willing Mister Kemp to appear. *Please, Jesus. Please let me see Mister Kemp walk through that door.*

"Just like you to try to skin the government out of four bucks, Enoch," said Luther. "Will you go sixty?"

Moses looked back at Sawyer, who shook his head from side to side.

"Sixty then," Jemmy Coates said.

"Sixty-one," said Sawyer, with an off-hand wave.

"Damn you, Enoch," answered Coates. "You're only trying to rile me. Sixty-five!"

"Sixty-six," said Sawyer. Men laughed again.

Coates scowled and pursed his lips. "Seventy, then."

"Seventy-one." Sawyer grinned. "I told my wife yesterday that I'd bring home a young buck to work in the house. I've got my eye on this one."

Moses' gaze darted around the room as men nudged each other and grinned. This couldn't be happening. Where was Mister Kemp?

Jemmy Coates' face lost its scowl and he grinned. "In that case," he said, "I'll go eighty dollars, Sawyer. You go ahead and bid a dollar more if your wife needs him that bad."

Sawyer grinned back and waved the offer away. "He's all yours, Jemmy. I merely wanted to see how bad you wanted him."

Master Coates went red as the men in the barn laughed loudly.

"You'd better work the boy's ass off for eighty dollars, Coates," someone said.

"I've got eighty dollars for the boy Moses," said Luther. "Are there any other bids?"

There weren't. Moses stood on the block, looking all about for Mister Kemp, until hands pulled him down off the auction block. He was shoved into a group of men, also shackled, who had already had their turn on the block and now waited for their new masters to claim them.

Moses didn't hear a thing as the auction went on. Something had gone wrong. Would Mister Kemp, when he showed up, be willing to pay such a high amount to buy his services back from Master Coates?

"…And Remember that I Am a Man."

*

Moses sat on the frozen ground of the slave-holding pen, in the pitch darkness. The sun had set hours before and all the slaves had been taken away except him and five men. All of them had been hired by Jemmy Coates. All were young men, muscular and fit from years of labor, but lean as snakes from meager food.

Like Moses, each of the men had been hooked to a fence post by a chain leading to a strap on one wrist. Two of them had worked for Master Coates before and they said it was a rough life. They both agreed that Master Coates had gone to the tavern, as he had done other years, and would not be back to collect his new workers until the tavern closed.

Moses paid little attention. He sat, shivered, and tried to figure out what he might have done wrong that Mister Kemp hadn't hired him for another year. Hadn't he worked hard enough?

He also worried about the mules, especially Goliath. Chadwick wouldn't treat them right.

The thought of Chadwick brought a surge of anger, as it always did. Ever since Keentoon had been taken, Moses couldn't look at Chadwick without wanting to hit him with a fist. It had been pure misery to work for the stupid clod.

Moses must have dozed, because the next thing he knew, the slave pen had erupted into a hubbub. Master Coates had returned and was shouting orders as another white man unlocked the slaves. One slave was slow to get up and Master Coates kicked him until he rose.

When the chains came off, Moses tried to get to his feet quickly, to avoid being kicked, but his legs had gone numb and he wasn't able to. Before he knew it, Master Coates towered over him, kicking him into action. He didn't kick hard. He couldn't or he'd have fallen over from drunkenness.

Once the blacks were up, Master Coates addressed them.

"All right, you lazy boogers," Master Coates said, slurring his words, "you've laid around long enough. You won't be lollygaggin' around once I get you home, I guaran-damn-tee you."

He looked around, trying to focus his eyes in the dim moonlight. "You, boy," he said, pointing to Moses. "I hear tell you can drive a team of mules."

Moses gulped and nodded. "Y-yes, Master. Mister Kemp taught me how."

Master Coates drew his head back in a great show of indignation. "Mister Kemp? You'd better learn to keep a civil tongue in that ugly face of yours, boy."

Feeling like a simpleton, Moses bobbed his head up and down. "Yes sir, Master Coates. You won't hear no sass out of me, no sir."

"What they call you, boy?"

"Moses, Master."

Master Coates laughed, although Moses had no idea what might be funny. "Moses, huh? Well, Moses, you get your ass up on that wagon seat and drive me home to the promised land. You prove to me you can drive."

"Yes, sir." Moses ran out of the pen and climbed up onto the wagon, which had been parked there all evening, with the mules still harnessed to it. They'd been standing all afternoon and evening, without a drop of water or food, other than what brown grass they could nibble from where they stood. Moses wondered why Master Coates didn't take better care of his mules; they were valuable animals.

Moses knew this particular pair of mules. Plato and Socrates. Master Coates had bought them from Mister—no, Master Kemp— nearly two years ago.

Master Coates put his foot on the step and then had two of the slaves boost him up onto the wagon. To Moses' surprise, the white man didn't sit on the seat, but climbed over it and into the back, which was loaded with bags of supplies and several large jugs. Moses got a good look at him as he clambered by, his breath foul and reeking of alcohol. He also had a sour smell to him, as though he'd thrown up on his clothes at some time and had never changed or washed them.

He seemed to be in his fifties or sixties, hair mostly gray and quite thin. He wore a full beard, but it couldn't cover all the pock marks on his cheeks and forehead. His eyes were small and close set—or maybe it was that his nose was so beefy that it appeared that way. Moses couldn't tell the color of his eyes, dull and lackluster from drunkenness.

"…And Remember that I Am a Man."

Once he'd gotten in the back, Master Coates gestured at the other slaves, waving them toward the back of the wagon. "You other niggers follow along. And don't fall behind." He sat back down and turned to Moses. "Let's go."

"Yes, sir," Moses said. He faced forward, flicked the reins and said "Giddap, mules."

The mules started off, but the wagon lurched on its springs, then rebounded. The mules stopped, confused. Moses felt a hard blow to his back.

"Take the brake off, you stupid ass."

Moses grabbed the wooden brake handle and pushed it forward until it no longer pressed against the front wheel. He felt about as stupid as Master Coates had called him. So far he hadn't made a good impression on his new master. First falling asleep while waiting, and now this!

He shook the reins again and got the mules moving, but then realized he had another problem. He didn't know whether to keep going south, the way the wagon had been facing or to turn around and go through town. He glanced back at Master Coates, who had put a sack of flour or some such soft substance behind his head and closed his eyes.

"Um, excuse me, Master Coates, sir," Moses said.

The drunken man didn't open his eyes. "What do you want, boy?"

"Um, I don't know where your plantation is, Master. Do I go north or south?"

One eye popped open and regarded Moses. "Keep on south 'til the road meets the river, then turn left. One of them boys marchin' along back there'll tell you when you've arrived at my 'plantation'."

Master Coates closed his eyes and wiggled around, looking for a comfortable spot. "Plantation! That's a good one," he said.

The man snored within seconds and Moses drove along, wondering again what had happened that Mister Kemp hadn't hired him out. He shivered and wished he was walking with the other slaves; at least the exercise would have kept him warm. Besides, he was the only nigger wearing shoes. Might as well call himself a nigger and a slave. He reckoned that's all he was and all he'd ever be. There was no hope for him. He had prayed and Jesus had let him down again.

"…And Remember that I Am a Man."

Chapter Fourteen

The Stump—1803 A.D.

In being hired out, sometimes the slave gets a good home, and sometimes a bad one: when he gets a good one, he dreads to see January come; when he has a bad one, the year seems five times as long as it is.

The Life of Moses Grandy—1843 A.D.

The Coates farm turned out to be little more than a collection of shacks. The slaves' quarters were poorly-built log structures, the chinks filled with mud. The master's hovel had more than one room and more fireplaces than any of the other buildings, but it was still a shack.

Master Coates wasn't married. A toothless, scrawny white woman named Petunia, who seemed to do nothing but drink corn liquor and argue, lived with him. She didn't cook, didn't wash and didn't clean, as far as Moses could tell, and he wondered why Master Coates kept her around.

Moses was assigned to live in a small shed with a burly youth named Levi, the youngest of the slaves who'd walked behind the wagon on the trip out from town. The other four men from the auction slept together in a larger shack.

The only other person on the farm, the sole slave that Master Coates owned, was an old woman called Fanny. She did the cooking in the Coates house. Fanny was an ancient woman who had once been fat, but now had shrunken inside large flabby masses of loose skin. Her eyes were sharp and piercing.

She only cooked for Master Coates and Petunia, however. The half-dozen field hands had to prepare their own meals with vegetables from the winter stores, often bruised and beginning to rot. But there were always plenty. These were stewed, along with any wild game that could be snared or downed with a thrown rock. The older men took turns cooking by the fire in the larger of the quarters, using only a pot, a skillet, a knife and a spoon.

Once a week, Master gave each slave a bag of corn meal, a twist of salt, and some slivers of bacon or salt-herring. Fanny would give the men a pitcher of milk every evening and a couple of the men knew how to make pan cornbread. Moses, the youngest, was sent to gather eggs from the half-wild chickens that nested all over the property and Fanny would give them a pinch of baking soda. If Moses found eggs, they'd make johnny-cake or Carolina skillet bread, both of which were thicker and tastier than regular cornbread. Moses would generally stuff himself with stew and save anything else for breakfast and dinner, the mid-day meal.

Each of the slaves was given one thin blanket and slept on a rough slab of lumber. The nights were cold. Most of them slept in every stitch of clothing they owned. Master Coates had bought them each a decent pair of pants and a shirt, along with rough, canvas foot coverings, as required by law.

There was a fire-pit in the dirt floor of the shed that Levi and Moses shared, with a hole in the ceiling above that didn't do much to get rid of the smoke from the fire. It was always hard to breathe in the place and the flames didn't do much to warm them, either, because too large a fire would have probably burned the wooden building to the ground.

Their work began early each morning. By sunrise they were on their way to wherever Master Coates wanted work done. They munched on cornbread as they marched.

It was too early in the year to work the soil, so they felled trees to clear more land for planting. This turned out to be harder work than Moses had thought he was capable of doing. Not only did the trees have to be chopped down, the branches needed to be taken off and the logs dragged away. Next, the bark would be removed. Finally the men would grunt and groan and lift the wood into loose piles where it could dry for a few months before being split into fence poles and posts.

The hardest part—and it couldn't have been done without the mules—was pulling the stumps. The slaves, three with adzes and three with axes, would dig and chop all around in an attempt to loosen the roots. Every quarter-hour or so, Master Coates would harness the two beasts, Plato and Socrates, and wrap a chain around the stump. He'd slap the reins and holler for the mules to pull their best. If the stump came up, the crew would move to another. If it didn't, they'd hack and jab some more. This was dangerous work. Toes were at serious risk here, especially because Levi, big and strong, proved clumsy at wielding an axe.

As soon as Master Coates became convinced his new, young slave knew how to harness mules, Moses had the job every morning. He was glad for that, because Master Coates didn't know much about mules and always cinched the straps too tight. When Moses took over, Plato and Socrates had rubs and scrapes where the leather bit in. But he saved bits of his bacon fat to rub on the wounds until they healed from better harnessing.

One late-winter afternoon, when the weather had grown unseasonably warm, the crew struggled for hours over a huge stump. Even the callused hands of the slaves were becoming chafed and raw. The workers had stripped off their shirts, all of them sweated like horses in a long race.

Master Coates, standing behind and to the side, would haul the reins this way and that, slapping the long, leather straps up and down on the mules' rumps to urge them on. "Giddap," he'd say, making his command a threat. "Giddap." The team would hunker down and pull, but the large tree's base wouldn't budge.

When Master had allowed for a short breather, Moses summoned his courage. "Master Coates?"

"What?" Master snapped, turning toward Moses from his seat on the stump.

"D-don't you think them mules might need a taste of the whip?"

Master Coates studied him for a long moment, his eyes mean. "And just how am I supposed to whip them, with both hands on the reins? Because if you think I'll let you stand aside and whip them, just to lollygag about instead of chopping roots, you got another think coming, boy."

Knowing he was treading on dangerous ground if he made it sound like Master Coates didn't know what he was doing with the mules, Moses said, "You don't need the reins, Master, sir. Them mules can feel which way to pull a load, they just need to be prodded a mite."

The white man seemed to consider. "What do you mean, 'they can feel?'"

"Well, sir, them two have pulled a heap of stumps in the last few days. They'll have learned to tug here and tug there, then haul like blazes when they feel a weakness. But you need to let them know it's important to pull with all they got, when they do bear down."

Master Coates glowered. "Don't tell me what I need, boy. I don't like sass."

Moses knew when to shut up.

But Master must have realized Moses had a point, because he sighed and said, "I left the whip back in the barn, anyway. Damn this heat."

It was risky, but Moses was sure enough tired of swinging an adze while avoiding Levi's axe blade. "You could use a limber sapling, 'stead of a whip."

A smirk suddenly spread over the farm-owner's face. "Okay, boy, if you're such a smart little bastard, let's see you and them mules pull this stump."

"Yes, sir!" Moses leapt to his feet, but an emerging smile went dead as Master continued.

"And if you can't clear that stump," the white man said, "I'll use that sapling on your sassy nigger ass."

Moses briefly regretted having spoken out, but then brightened. He knew the mules would pull harder for him, and probably Master Coates was bluffing.

He grabbed a nearby hatchet and found a sapling tree in the underbrush. He cut through the base with three or four blows and then he swung the hatchet to cut off the small branches. When he finished, he had an eight-foot-long, supple pole that tapered to a point.

104

He took it over by the mules and laid it on the ground. Walking over to the wagon that carried their tools and gear, he grabbed a canvas bucket and dipped it into their barrel of drinking water, then headed back toward the animals.

"What you think you're doing, boy?" Coates yelled. "It's time to get back to work."

"These mules will work harder after they've had a drink of water, Master," Moses said. "Only take a minute." He had often noticed how Master Coates neglected caring for the mules, and was now glad he could do something for Plato and Socrates. Slurping and slobbering, one after the other, they took in water like bees sucking nectar.

When the mules had finished, Moses put the bucket away, grabbed up the make-shift whip and took the reins. He shook them out to be sure they weren't tangled.

"All set, Master."

The white man got off the stump. The other slaves began to rise, but Master gestured for them to sit back down.

"No need to chop the roots, boys," he said. "Young Moses and them mules are going to show us how it's done. He don't need no help."

He walked a few feet away and turned to watch Moses. Crossing his arms on his chest, he balanced himself on spread legs and smiled like he was about to watch a cockfight or a horse race.

"You go ahead, boy. Don't let us get in your way."

Moses could see that the man was looking forward to giving a whipping, and that didn't surprise him all that much. But the looks on the faces of the other slaves did give him a jolt. They were grinning and nudging each other, seemingly every bit as eager for the whipping as the master. What had he ever done to them?

A cold, hollow feeling seeped into Moses' stomach. He'd have never spoken up if he'd known he wasn't going to get a fair chance. Now he was looking forward to his first whipping, probably with a sapling he'd cut himself. He began to ask Jesus for help, then stopped himself. Praying never did any good.

Fighting down panic, he took a firm grip of the reins in his left hand and pulled them taut. The mules didn't need the reins for commands, but they needed to feel a pair of sure hands on the other

105

end. And, somehow, he could feel a sense of confidence in the mules; they knew their strength. All they needed was someone who had faith in them.

He swallowed his fear. "Giddap."

The mules didn't rush to their task; they knew they weren't going anywhere until the stump did. They inched forward until the chains went tight. Then they set their feet and began to haul. Their hooves dug deep into the soft earth and found traction.

"Pull!"

Muscles strained, bulging beneath the mules' sweaty coats. Moses looked down at the stump, watching for any sign of give. He glanced back at the mules and saw they were angling a bit away from each other, minimizing their force.

"Gee up, Plato."

Plato moved over slightly.

"Pull!"

The stump stayed solid as the sun in the sky.

"Pull! Giddap!"

No movement. Moses looked at the ground carefully. Were the roots chopped more deeply on that one side?

"Haw, mules, haw!"

The chain veered as the mules moved left. They were pulling off center now, and it would probably be better to stop and shift the chain, but now was the time to push, right after the mules had enjoyed a rest and a drink.

"Pull! Giddap!"

The mules set their hindquarters and pushed their rear legs into the ground. Did the stump shift a little?

He slashed the sapling through the air, making a hissing noise above the mules. He wished for a mule-skinner, with its popper to crack the air with authority, but the sapling was all he had. Inwardly, he cursed his big mouth.

Moses became aware of voices. Emboldened by Master's leniency in allowing them to sit and watch, the other workers began calling out. "Whip them mules, Moses."

"Give 'em what's for, boy."

"Put the fear o' God in them mules."

Were they being encouraging or were they making fun of him? Moses couldn't tell.

He didn't want to use the hand-fashioned whip, except maybe to hit the animals enough that they realized how important their effort had become to him. He'd long ago decided that if you whipped a mule mercilessly, the beast would be spending more energy cringing than pulling. The only time he'd actually hit a mule was to correct him, like spanking a child. Mules learned quickly.

He slashed the air again. "Pull, Plato. Pull Socrates. Giddap!"

Plato and Socrates strained and moved forward slightly. A moan came from deep down in the ground. The stump came up a fraction, then settled back down, pulling the mules back slightly.

"Once more," Moses called. "Pull!"

Again they put their backs into it. The stump began to come up. The chain went tight as a fiddle wire and began to make popping noises.

"Pull."

The stump was loosening, but only a bit. The mules had pushed their legs all the way back and would have to step forward to gain leverage.

"Giddap!" The sapling sliced the air.

Together, Plato and Socrates both lifted a foot and planted it a few inches farther on. The stump settled back. The mules shifted the other foot. The stump came up again.

"Pull!" Swish. "Giddap!" Swish. "Pull, mules, pull!"

The stump began to rise again and then Moses heard Master Coates yell.

"Get up, you other niggers. Grab your tools and cut."

The five men jumped up, grabbed axes and adzes, and attacked the roots that had begun to rise from the ground. Thank you, Lord, Moses thought to himself.

"Pull!" Swish.

The mules were gaining now, giving it their all. Their breathing sounded loud and raspy, soughing in and out like a blacksmith's bellows. Thudding sounds arose as the workers assaulted the clinging roots with sharp metal. The chain popped. Leather harness straps hummed. A groan arose from Mother Earth.

"Pull, mules, pull," Moses called.

"…And Remember that I Am a Man."

"Dig, you lazy bastards, dig," came Master Coates' voice, like a warped echo.

There was a space between one side of the stump and the ground now. It tilted and quivered, holding on to the hard, rich earth that had lifted a mighty tree high into the air, until Master Coates had decided to chop it down.

"Giddap!" Moses didn't need the sound of the whip now; the mules' famed stubbornness came to the surface as they embraced the fight.

He glanced over at Master Coates, who swung his fists in the air as if urging on his champion in a fist fight, hollering at the slaves. The master seemed to have forgotten his threat of a whipping.

For a few moments, they were a team: Moses, Plato, Socrates, the older workers, and their master. All of them had invested a great deal of time and labor in this project and had begun to feel like the stump might win out until Moses had worked the mules up.

The stump suddenly lurched free of the ground and swung all the way over. The mules stumbled forward a step, then stopped, not needing to be told, "Whoa." The axes and adzes went silent. The slaves slumped against their tools, catching a breath.

Moses dropped the reins and rushed to the mules. He hugged Socrates, then Plato around the neck, wishing he had an apple for each of them.

When he stepped back, Moses realized that Master had come up silently and stood regarding his young slave and the mules.

"I'll be a ring-tail, snaggle-tooth varmint," the master said, "if that wasn't the best, damnedest team-handling I ever seen."

Moses lowered his head and looked at the ground, not wanting the man to see the broad smile on his face. He shuffled his feet. "Thank you," he mumbled. It came out sounding like, "Yawwah."

"Guess them mules saved you from a whippin', didn't they?"

"Yawwah." Moses realized, for the first time, why many older slaves answered every white man's command with sounds like "Yassuh" and "Yayboss." A meaningless response was the safest.

Master Coates said, "You take off the chains and hitch up the wagon. Be sure to put the chains in the back and don't let 'em get all tangled."

"Yawwah." Moses ran to do his master's bidding while the other slaves went back to work, chopping through any roots still hanging on to the ground.

Soon, the work crew was on the way back to the farmyard, Moses riding up with Master Coates and driving the mules. The other slaves walked behind.

*

That evening, as he fed the mules, Moses' step was light, despite his tiredness. It was good to work with mules again. From the way things looked, Master Coates had turned the handling of the animals entirely over to Moses.

Plato and Socrates seemed to have quickly recognized the change in their situation. They nuzzled Moses and butted him lightly as he moved around their stalls, caring for them. In turn, he patted their flanks and spoke softly to them, telling them how proud they'd made him.

When Moses finished with the animals, he went to his shack for the rag he used as a towel. He planned to wash off by the pump before supper; he smelled like a dead possum from all the sweating. The sun hung over the western horizon.

Moses stepped up into the dark doorway of the shed. He saw a blur of motion and the side of his head suddenly exploded in pain. Next thing he knew, he was lying in the dust outside the shed, his mind in a daze.

Levi came to stand in the doorway and look down. He had the appearance of a black warrior-god, his bare, muscular torso shining with sweat, fists clenched, eyes blazing with hatred. His nostrils flared.

"Hope that teaches you a lesson, you little smart-ass," he snarled.

Moses raised up on his elbows and shook his head. "What'd I do?"

"You only did that business with the mules to get out of chopping. Now there'll be more for the rest of us to do."

That didn't make sense to Moses. If the mules pulled harder, there'd be less work to do. He'd better explain that to Levi and the others.

"But you…" he began.

109

"…And Remember that I Am a Man."

"Shut up." Levi stepped down from the shed. Moses expected to be hit again, or kicked. Instead, the big youth growled, "If you want to talk to somebody, go kiss the white man's ass some more." He strode off.

"...And Remember that I Am a Man."

Chapter Fifteen

Master's Pet—1803 A.D.

United States, your banner bears
Two symbols—one of fame.
Alas! the other that it bears
Reminds us of your shame.

The white man's liberty in types
Is blazoned by your stars'
But what's the meaning of your stripes?
They mean the Negro's scars.

To the United States of North America, Thomas Campbell

Levi had little to do with Moses after that, other than sleeping in the same room. Levi spent his meager amount of free time with the older men, who seemed to talk of nothing but women. Most farms had both male and female slaves, but not this one. True, there was Fanny, but she was quite old. Some of the men would sneak away in the evenings, walking to nearby farms in search of girls to court. They took the risk of being caught out without a pass. Moses, left out of their talk, spent most of his time with Socrates and Plato.

When he tired of their company, he would clear an area of the barn's floor and scratch number problems into the soft dirt. He had never let anyone know about his ability to reckon sums; they'd surely laugh at him. It was a worthless activity, not something useful like his ability to handle mules.

He enjoyed reckoning with numbers, though, and wondered what reading would be like. Wouldn't it be fine to learn about all those people in the Bible that Missy Hannah talked about? He wondered if there were any books about presidents; he'd never found out if Mister Jefferson had won that war with the pirates.

If he'd had a book, or anything like that, Moses would have tried to figure out what the marks used for reading might mean. Since he could solve number problems, maybe reading problems would become clear if he could study the marks. Did you add them or subtract them to calculate what they said? One thing he did know, there were a lot more reading-marks than number-marks. No use wishing, though, there wasn't a book on the farm, not even a bible, far as Moses knew.

As the weather grew warmer, the work shifted from clearing new land to getting the fields ready to plant. Again, Moses was set apart from the other slaves by his mule-handling abilities. To the others, it looked like he had an easier job. They didn't know how exhausting it was to keep a plow running straight and true, or how jarring it could be when the plowshare hit a root left behind after the stumps had been pulled. And this plow wasn't all metal, like Mister Kemp's. Moses would straighten and sharpen the plowshare, an iron blade nailed to the front of the wooden plow, every morning before daylight, but it would be dull and dented by afternoon, making the work all the harder. Moses would be drained of strength by sundown and still need to care for the mules.

To the older slaves, it looked like Moses had only to walk behind the plow. They didn't consider that he was small, young boy, unused to hard physical labor. They didn't appear to notice that he wrapped his hands in rags every day to hold down the blistering of his fingers and palms. They weren't around when he struggled with bags of grain and bales of hay that weighed half of what he did. To them, he was Master's pet.

He grew stronger every day, though, eating enormous amounts of stew every night. Fanny noticed his appetite and slipped him extra cornbread and even some maple syrup as a treat now and then.

Moses became more skillful with the mules and the plow, as days went on. He also developed strong muscles in his legs and upper torso. The work became easier.

When all the fields had been turned over, Moses was sent to work with the other slaves again. But again he remained apart. He drove the wagon while the other men followed behind, grabbing tobacco seedlings off the wagon and stooping to stick the young plants in the earth. It was repetitive work and the mules went forward only a few steps at a time. To relieve his boredom, Moses counted how many plants Levi planted in one passage through the field. Since each man planted one row, he multiplied Levi's output by that number and then began keeping track of how many times the mules crossed the field.

At the end of the day, when Master Coates came out to check the day's work, he rode back to the farmyard on the wagon with his young mule-driver. Moses, proud of how much he and the other slaves had planted that day, mentioned that he and the other slaves had put "about forty-eight hundred" tobacco plants into the ground.

Master Coates turned and looked at Moses with suspicion. "And how would you know that?"

Moses felt a hollow feeling in his stomach. "Er, I counted them, Master." Better to say that probably, than mention multiplication. He was beginning to think that it might be dangerous to appear too smart.

"You counted them?" Master's eyes went wide in wonder. "I never knew any slave that could count higher than ten. How did you learn to count so high?"

"Um, I just sort of, um, figured it out, Master."

What a fool he was. What if Missy Hannah got in trouble for teaching him? It wasn't illegal, like teaching slaves to read, but it would still be "wrong" in the eyes of most whites.

"Figgered it out, huh?" Master Coates stared at him for long seconds, and then turned his attention to the mules.

"Plato seems to be favoring his right foreleg," he said. "Are you tending their hoofs carefully?"

"Yawwah." Moses could feel the "stupid slave" protection creeping into his voice. "Prob'ly jes' step on somethin' an' bruise it."

The white man's only answer was a grunt.

"…And Remember that I Am a Man."

*

When all the tobacco had been planted, Master Coates stopped working the slaves so hard. The tobacco plants would grow with the oncoming summer's sun and rain. Other things were grown on the farm, but leaf was the farm's cash crop.

The mules were no longer needed once all the fields, along with the vegetable garden for Fanny, had been plowed. Moses spent most days with the other slaves in the fields, hoeing out weeds. While they weeded, they watched the plants around them, picking tobacco worms off the leaves and squishing them, since there were no children on the Coates farm to do the simple job.

Summer came on like a blast from a fireplace. The slaves toiled under the sun. Their skin grew darker as they worked bare-backed in the fields, sweat making them glisten like ebony jewels.

The other slaves, including Levi, accepted him once more. He was careful not to say anything that might set him apart again. The tobacco and corn grew high. The rains sometimes came down so hard that the slaves were allowed to stay indoors. They ate well and they often sang as they worked.

His first indication of something wrong was the sound of someone bellowing his name in the middle of the night. He quickly sat up, sleep leaving him like a quail scared into flight.

"Moses!" Master Coates' voice bawled from outside the shed. "Get your black ass out here."

Moses jumped off the board he used for a bed, hitting his head on the roof rafters. He stepped to the doorway, guided by a thin line of moonlight at the edge of the smoke-smelling blanket they hung in an attempt to keep out the worst of the mosquitoes. Pushing it aside, he stepped down onto the ground.

Master Coates stood ten feet from the shed. He swayed slightly. Moses could smell the liquor on his breath even at a distance. Ominously, he held a wooden switch, a long, flexible length of sapling like Moses had once used on the mules.

The master's horse stood behind him, saddled and tied to a post, so Moses figured Master Coates had been to the tavern in town. Usually he got so drunk that he wouldn't return home until the following afternoon. The slaves liked that because they could work at their own pace when not supervised.

"You called for me, Master?" said Moses.

Master Coates smiled, but it wasn't a nice expression.

"Yes, Moses," he said. "I called you down from Mount Sinai, so that I might have a word with you."

Moses had no idea what that meant, so he said, "Yawwah."

"I thought I told you to hill the corn, today, Moses." The master was drunk, but his words were clear and icy.

Moses nodded. "Yawwah, Master. And I hilled it, yes I did."

As corn grew, the roots grew exposed to the sun and needed to be covered. Moses had pushed soil up into "hills" at the base of the plants.

Master sneered. "I saw what you did. You call that hilling, boy?"

Moses knew he'd done a fine job, but also knew better than to contradict the master.

"No, Massuh," he said. "I sorry, Massuh."

"You know what they were saying at the tavern tonight, boy?"

This confused Moses. He'd never been to the tavern in his life. How could he know what was said there? "Nossuh." He hung his head, fearful of challenging the master with his eyes, which were filling with hatred. This wasn't about the corn.

"They said," Master Coates continued, "that my nigger is better at handling mules than me. They said you're a right smart nigger."

Moses stayed silent, hoping it would keep him safe. Why would white men talk about him? Other white men often visited the farm, but Moses had never thought they took notice of him. Often, the other farmers were accompanied by slaves, who'd pass along news the black part of the local community. Since the whites also shared information, Moses' intelligence must have been passed along the white branches of the county's grapevine. Once again, too smart for his own good.

"Well?" Master Coates said.

"Massuh?"

"Are you a smart nigger, Moses?"

Moses only shook his head, which he kept lowered, watching the master's feet. Smarter than you, he thought.

"That's right, you dumb, black bastard." Master took two steps forward. "Too stupid even to hill corn."

Moses saw the white man's feet set and heard the "swoosh" of the sapling. It hit him even before he could raise his eyes, nicking his left ear and coming down on his shoulder. His skin erupted with flame-like pain.

For an instant, he glared at Master Coates. Then, realizing this would antagonize the man, he turned his back and cowered as the sapling slashed out again. He put his hands up to protect his face.

The whip came down again and again on his naked back. The branch would swish through the air, announcing the pain's arrival. No matter how hard Moses tried to prepare himself, each cruel blow was a surprise to his skin. If this agony came from a wooden imitation of a whip, how painful must a true whipping be?

There was nothing to do but stand and take it. Where would he run to? Any white man in the county would bring him back to Master Coates' farm in chains.

For the while, he cursed his intelligence. He damned himself for learning to manage mules and how to do sums. He condemned Mister Kemp for teaching him a skill and then abandoning him. But he couldn't find it in him to blame Missy Hannah, even though her Quaker compassion seemed to have turned out more of a curse than a blessing. Then rational thought was driven from his mind by the pain and his fear. Would this torture never end?

Master Coates continued yelling as he lashed his slave. It seemed to Moses that every other word was either "stupid" or "nigger." The words burned almost as much as the whipping.

The master's arm was wearing out, apparently, because the branch was not hitting as hard. *Please, Jesus,* he found himself thinking. *Please make this end.* Suddenly the whipping stopped and he dared to hope his torture had ended. But Master Coates had paused only to be sure Moses heard when he spoke.

"Well, that's the lash… the last time you'll make the f-fool o' me, boy," the master said. The labor of whipping must have brought more alcohol to his brain, because he had difficulty speaking.

Again the makeshift whip swished. Moses cringed away and the whip caught him sideways this time. It slashed his side below the ribs. He felt a sharp pain in his stomach as something bit deep into the flesh. As though from afar, he heard Master Coates speak again.

"By firsh… first light tomorrow, you carry your black ass off thish…thish…my property and carry it to Sawyer's Ferry. Your dumb ass hash been sold to Enoch Sawyer."

"...And Remember that I Am a Man."

"…And Remember that I Am a Man."

Chapter Sixteen

African Princess—1803 A.D.

This man's back was not yet well. Many of the gashes made by the lash were yet sore, and those that were healed had left long white stripes across his body. He had no notion of leaving the service of his tyrannical master, and his spirit was so broken and subdued that he was ready to suffer and to bear all his hardships: not, indeed, without complaining, but without attempting to resist his oppressors or to escape from their power. I saw him often whilst I remained at this place, and ventured to tell him once, that if I had a master who would abuse me as he had abused him, I would run away. "Where could I run, or in what place could I conceal myself?" said he. "I have known many slaves who ran away, but they were always caught and treated worse afterwards than they had been before. I have heard that there is a place called Philadelphia, where the black people are all free, but I do not know which way it lies, nor what road I should take to go there; and if I knew the way, how could I hope to get there? Would not the patrol be sure to catch me?"

Fifty Years in Chains, The Life of an American Slave, Charles Ball—1859 A.D.

"...And Remember that I Am a Man."

Moses didn't wait until dawn to "carry his ass." He gathered his shirt, his spare set of clothes, his shoes, and a small pot given to him by Fanny. He left the blanket behind. It had been "given" to him by Master Coates, but he was sure it was only for his time on the Coates farm. If he took it with him, he could be really whipped—for stealing.

Master Coates had not "sold" Moses, since he had never owned him, but it made no difference what you called it. He'd be working for a man said to be even worse than Master Coates in the treatment of slaves.

Nor did it matter that it was against the law to whip a slave who'd been hired out, unless he was caught where he wasn't supposed to be by the patrollers. No one would side with a slave, no matter how badly abused.

He traveled the main road, going north. Occasionally, he caught sight of the Pasquotank River, which paralleled the road, flowing south.

He fingered the sore, bloody hole in his belly as the sky grew brighter. The tip of the branch had gone deep into his belly and broken off. Although he'd pulled it from his stomach muscles, there must still be a sliver of wood in there, because it would stab him when he twisted his body. He couldn't keep himself from probing around inside the wound with his fingernails, hoping to locate the splinter.

The cool morning air felt good on his striped back. The makeshift whip hadn't scored deeply, but a criss-cross of welts had come up. Some blood seeped out, but not that much. He'd never before felt such pain, though.

Moses didn't know exactly where the ferry was, but it had to be on the Pasquotank, and he'd heard it was north of Sawyer's Creek. If he recalled correctly, there was a road leading west. He hoped to reach it early, before the sun scorched his sore back.

He tried not to cry, but tears came anyway. Why didn't he learn to keep his dumb mouth shut? He'd only thought to help Master Coates with the mules, but it had caused him trouble from both sides, white and black.

The creek wasn't as far away as he'd remembered, so he reached it just after sunrise. He turned left at the next road and saw the river ahead. The Pasquotank was the widest water he'd ever seen, broader than any creek. Moses had no idea what lay on the other side. Maybe, since he would be working for the ferry owner, he'd get a chance to cross. Wouldn't that be grand? Mama would be proud of him if she knew he'd traveled so far. That thought caused him to weep some more. He hadn't seen her in more than three years.

He passed a grand, two-story brick house on his right, the front door and wooden shutters painted dark blue. The main structure had chimneys on both ends, but the only smoke drifted up from the flue of a brick outbuilding—the kitchen no doubt, built away from the house in case of fire. There were many other outbuildings, including a small, two-door shack, which must be the privy. A two-holer! The people who owned the place must be rich.

As he came to the river, much narrower here than anywhere else, he observed a short pier constructed on pilings. He saw a matching structure on the other side of the Pasquotank. A flat-bottomed barge with railings—large enough to hold a wagon and team—was tied to the far pier. Slave shacks dotted both sides of the river.

"Watcha gawpin' for?" a high, clear voice said.

Moses turned and saw a girl, about his age. She must have begun following him down the road at some point, but so quietly that he'd not been aware of her.

Her skin was a yellowish brown, her eyes deep brown. Each pupil had a depth like the deepest night, lighted only by the glint of a distant star. Her narrow face, with its high cheekbones, might have been that of an African princess, and her full lips curved up at the tips as though she knew a secret more precious than gold or jewels. Her pretty face was set off by a yellow head-tie that hid most of her black hair. She wore a ragged, but clean blue dress that ended above her knees, showing off her long slender legs. He must have taken too long looking at her, for her nostrils flared and she said, "I asked watcha lookin' at? Aintcha never seen a river before?"

"Huh?" He didn't remember what he'd been looking at a few seconds ago.

Her eyes grew sharp. "You got business here, boy?"

Moses nodded. "Er, I'm looking for Sawyer's Ferry."

"What for?"

"I'm to be working for Master Sawyer. Is his farm nearby?"

"...And Remember that I Am a Man."

"Farm?" She pursed her lips and considered. "Mas' Sawyer don't have no farm."

Moses hadn't considered such a thing. "If he doesn't have a farm," he said carefully, "what's he need slaves for?"

The girl laughed like he'd said something funny. "Oh, he finds lots of things for them to do." There was an edge to her voice.

"Like what?"

"Never you mind. What's your name, boy? Where you from?"

"I'm Moses. I've newly come from the Coates farm, hired out to Master Sawyer."

"Jemmy Coates? He the one who whipped you?"

Moses dropped his chin and nodded. He'd forgotten about his lash-marks while talking to this girl. She'd have seen them, walking behind.

"Figures," she said. "I've seen lots worse that he's done, though."

He felt a surge of anger. "It's bad enough."

Her features changed to show compassion. "I'm sorry," she said. "I'll bet it hurts."

"Not so much," he said roughly, not believing what he heard coming from his own mouth. For some reason, her sympathy angered him as much as her earlier indifference. "Now, you gonna tell me how to get to the Sawyer place?"

The girl's face hardened to match his tone. "You're standin' on it. That's his house you just passed." The girl brushed past him. "Follow me. I'll take you where you need to go."

He watched her walk away, a slave girl so saucy that she had called a white man "Jemmy," instead of "Master." She moved with a sway to her hips that entranced him. After a few seconds of watching, he caught hold of his wandering mind and rushed to catch up.

"Ain't you taking me to see Master Sawyer at his house?"

"Now why would he want to see a no-account like you, boy? I knows where you need to go."

He followed her to the dock, where she reached up and grabbed hold of the clapper string and sounded the bell on the pole. As she stretched, Moses' eyes were drawn by her breasts.

122

"…And Remember that I Am a Man."

On the far dock, a black man appeared and waved, ringing the bell on that side. He then disappeared behind a weathered structure, probably a stable.

Moses looked around, awestruck that he was going to ride a ferryboat. There was another stable on this side that he hadn't noticed and he realized the two ferry stations were identical to each other. Each side had a dock, a shack and a stable with a small pasture.

He considered the ferryboat, a barge with a wide, flat deck. This platform sat almost level with the dock and a ramp of boards connected the two. Moses figured a team could pull a wagon across that ramp, easy as molasses in July.

"Well, come on." The girl stepped off the dock onto the riverside. Two rowboats had been pulled up on the bank.

By the time he caught up, the girl was sliding one of the boats into the river.

"Aren't we taking the ferryboat?" asked Moses.

"Sure, and my auntie's the Queen of England," the girl replied, stepping into the boat. "Come along now. Don't dawdle."

"Why'd you ring the bell, then?" he asked.

"That's to let them know I'm comin' across," she answered. "And so they'll know ain't nobody stealin' this here rowboat."

Moses put his small bundle into the boat and awkwardly climbed in. It swayed under his weight, and he nearly lost his balance. He caught himself, thanking The Lord he hadn't fallen in, since he couldn't swim. He sat down on the rearward of three seats.

The girl took the middle seat, at the widest part of the boat. She pulled two oars off the bottom, and set them each in between pegs set into the side of the boat. Bracing her feet, she pulled on the oar handles, putting her back into it. The boat began to move. Soon they were making headway across the wide, brown waters. The opposite bank looked to be no more than three or four hundred paces away, but Moses hardly noticed, unable to take his eyes off the girl. He felt all funny inside.

As they cleared the trees and got out into the river, Moses attention was drawn to a huge expanse of water to the south. The farther away he looked, the bluer the water. That must be the vast Albemarle Sound he'd heard of. Missy Hannah had said a sea-going ship could go south from here and find passage into the ocean, taking tobacco and other goods to England, wherever that was.

Looking back toward the eastern bank—the one they'd left—he observed docks and warehouses that he'd never imagined to be there. No roads came down to these piers, and he wondered what they were for.

Moses turned and faced the girl, who rowed steadily, paying him no mind. He opened his mouth to ask her about the piers, but realized she hadn't given him her name.

"Hey," he said.

She looked at him. "Huh?"

"What's your name?"

She pursed her lips as though thinking, and he wondered if she didn't want to tell him. But then she said, "Naomi."

"That an African name?"

"Don't know 'bout that. It's my name."

He gestured toward the shore. "What's all them there docks for?"

Naomi looked annoyed, but said, "Barges and boats bring goods downriver. They unload here and keeps the stuff in a warehouse until a schooner come by to take it away."

"What's a schooner?"

She sighed, making it clear she thought him to be thicker than a fence post, but then pointed behind him. "That's a schooner."

Moses looked. Hidden from view by a point of land until now, a ship was leaving a dock. White fabric billowed from high poles, graceful and awe-inspiring.

He turned farther and stood partway up. A twinge of pain shot through his belly. The boat tilted sharply. He fell overboard, into cool water.

Never before had he been in over his head. He sucked in water before he got the notion that he needed to stop breathing. It didn't do him any good to close his mouth, though, because he began to cough up the water he'd sucked in, forcing his mouth back open. Pain wracked his chest as cold water filled his lungs. His arms flailed about, seeking something solid to grab, but there was only water. *Help me, Jesus,* his mind screamed. *Don't let me die!*

Something jabbed him hard in the ribs and he grabbed onto it. Flat, smooth wood. An oar! He clutched it with both hands and it dragged him to the surface. Bumping into the boat, he switched his grip and grabbed the side. There he, hung, retching up water.

When he'd recovered enough, he looked up. Naomi stared down at him with a merciless gaze. "You're lucky you didn't drown, you know."

He nodded and put up an arm for her to help him get back in the boat. She drew back.

"No way," Naomi said. "You don't know how to get in and you'll turn the boat over. They'd have to row out and fetch us and then I'd get me a spankin' for sure."

"How – how do I get to shore?"

"Move around to the back of the boat," she said. "Then you hold on and I'll pull you in." She put the oars back in their holders and waited until Moses had moved to her satisfaction. Then she set herself to rowing again.

Trying to cover his shame at being towed along by a girl, he said, "Why did you say, back then, that you'd get a spanking? Don't they whip slaves around here?" Talk of whipping reminded him of his welts. They were really painful from having thrashed about, but the cool water helped somewhat.

Naomi blushed. "Master Sawyer don't whips no girls. Don't want to mark up their backs."

"Why not?" he asked.

"You ask too many questions," she said, and wouldn't talk anymore.

*

After the crossing, saying the fewest words possible, Naomi turned Moses over to Jonas, the blackest, strongest-looking man he'd ever seen. Jonas wasn't a large man, but his chest, shoulders, and arms bulged with muscles. He wore only a pair of pants, pulled tight by muscular thighs and calves. He was barefoot. When he smiled, the midnight blackness of his face highlighted the red of his lips and the whiteness of his teeth. And he smiled a lot.

"You the new man, eh, Moses?"

Moses swelled with pride, not ever having been called a man before. He looked to see if Naomi had heard, but she had slipped away. "I guess I am," he answered.

125

"…And Remember that I Am a Man."

He had put his shirt on after getting out of the river, to hide the marks of his recent whipping. If Naomi hadn't sneaked up behind him on the road, he wouldn't have let her see his shame, either. At least he didn't have to be embarrassed upon meeting Jonas.

"That's fine," Jonas said, nodding his head. "We been needin' a new hand. Master Sawyer hired you to take the place o' Bartholomew on the ferry."

"What will I do?"

"You take the pole on one side, while Caleb—you be meetin' him shortly—poles on the other side." His smile grew broader. "I takes the sweep."

Moses had no idea what that meant and didn't really care. He looked around, wondering if he was in time for a bite of breakfast. "Bartholomew get sold off?" he asked idly.

"Nope." Jonas's smile never faltered. "He drowned."

"...And Remember that I Am a Man."

Chapter Seventeen

Ferrykeeper—1803 A.D.

An act to Encourage Enoch Sawyer to make a road through Pasquotank River Swamp Opposite to His Plantation.

I. Whereas, a road through Pasquotank River Swamp opposite to Sawyer's ferry would be of great advantage to travelers crossing Pasquotank River; and Enoch Sawyer having agreed to make it at his own expence on condition of having the benefit thereof for the term of twenty-five years;

II. Be it therefore Enacted by the General Assembly of the State of North Carolina, and it is hereby Enacted by the authority of the same. That it shall and may be lawful for the said Enoch Sawyer to make a good and sufficient causeway through the said swamp opposite the said ferry, which shall be at least twenty feet wide, and one foot high above common tides; and after making the road as aforesaid, it shall and may be lawful for he said Enoch Sawyer, his heirs, executors, administrators and assigns, top take and receive from all persons that shall pass through the same and cross his ferry, the following rates and no more, that is to say: For every person six pence, for every horse six pence, for every carriage of two wheels one shilling, for every carriage of four wheels two shillings, for every head of neat cattle

four pence, for every hog or sheep one penny, for and
during the term of twenty-five years and no longer.

<u>State Record of NC</u>—*1790 A.D.*

His belly empty, Moses asked Jonas if he'd arrived too late for breakfast. Jonas's smile faltered.

"Boy," he said, "Don't never miss a meal 'round here. There ain't enough food to go 'round, sometimes." But he found a biscuit for Moses to eat. It wasn't much but it helped.

Later in the morning, the bell on the far side—the eastern shore—sounded. A cart, pulled by a swaybacked mare led by a white boy, had come to be carried across.

Jonas took Moses aboard the ferryboat and led him to the right side of the barge, which he called the starboard side. "Time you started learning to be a ferryman."

He picked up a long, stout pole. "Pushin' with this pole is going to be your job, Moses, but I'm going to show you how to do it this one time. Naomi will run the sweep."

Moses looked around and, sure enough, Naomi stood on the ferryboat. She seemed to have the ability to appear out of thin air.

A tall and skinny scarecrow of a man came a-running and jumped onto the boat. He nodded to Moses.

"Howdy-do."

"That's Caleb," said Jonas.

Caleb went to the other side and picked up a pole. He and Jonas walked to the end of the boat farthest from shore and put their poles, each three times as long as Moses was tall, in the water.

"You ready, Jonas?" Naomi called.

"Cast 'er off," the smiling man answered. Naomi, still on the pier, untied some ropes. She tossed them onto the vessel, and then jumped aboard herself. Moses marveled at her slim legs as her skirt swirled up. Jonas looked over at Caleb and nodded. Both men set poles firmly in the river bottom and began to walk toward the shore, pushing their feet down on the deck. As they shoved against the poles, the boat left the dock.

Naomi picked up an oar, nearly as long as the poles, and set it in some contraption on the edge of what had now become the ferryboat's rear end as it moved out into the gentle current. Moses watched her graceful motions.

"Out of the way, boy."

Moses jumped from the path of Jonas, who strode along the edge of the vessel, propelling it with his pole. He strained and Moses quickly realized where Jonas had gotten his muscular frame. Maybe Caleb hadn't been poling as long?

Jonas nodded toward Naomi as he passed by. "See how she set the sweep in that there brace, Moses? That brace is called an oarlock. Usin' the sweep like that, she'll steer us across."

The two men pushed and the boat moved slowly across the water. Moses noticed that Naomi wasn't going straight across, but upstream, and wondered why.

When they reached the middle of the stream, she changed course to downstream and Moses studied on why she'd done the crossing in that fashion.

The two pole-pushers no longer had to strain to keep the boat in motion, he saw. The river pushed them now. Gazing at the river, he realized that if they'd come straight across, the current would have pushed against the long side of the boat and they'd have gone far downstream. This way, once the current pushed them, they went much faster. It would be easier to steer the vessel straight to the dock.

When they got there, Jonas directed Moses to tie the boat up. He ran to the front and found two ropes, identical to the ones on the stern that Naomi had undone earlier. He picked them up, one at a time, and looped them over some metal fittings on the dock. Before he could finish, Naomi was at his side.

"Not that way, stupid," she said. "Take them around one way and then the other, like this."

Moses, ears burning from being called stupid, said, "I see. A figure-eight."

Naomi looked at him like he'd jumped out of a snake hole. "A what?"

"…And Remember that I Am a Man."

Moses realized she would never understand. Like most slaves, she could probably count, but she'd never seen the actual symbols for the numbers. His learning had betrayed him again.

He couldn't meet her gaze. Lowering his head, he mumbled, "Nuffin." Even as he said it, he wondered why he garbled the word, like he would have done when being careful not to upset a master.

"You crazy, boy," she said.

Then Moses knew why he had slurred his words. He didn't want Naomi to call him stupid again. Even crazy was better than stupid.

She sauntered off toward the master's house and Jonas removed a railing so the horse and cart could drive onto the ferryboat. Moses noted that the horse didn't seem nervous at all, and guessed the animal had made this crossing many times. Jonas put the rail back and they set off back across the river. This time, however, Moses had to use the pole. Jonas took the steering sweep.

They made a rough crossing, both Jonas and Caleb giving Moses instructions at the same time. He pushed hard as he could, but couldn't match Caleb's strength. His performance was made worse by the stiffness of the scabbing skin on his back and the pain from the piece of wood in his belly. Jonas had a tough time adjusting his steering for the unequal forces.

Moses wondered if Caleb and Jonas also thought he was stupid.

*

In the days that followed, Moses' back burned and itched, making his sleep fitful, at best. And it didn't help that every muscle in his body ached from poling back and forth across the river. Worst, though, was the hole in his stomach, just above the rope holding up his trousers. It oozed yellow pus, and the skin around it had turned an unhealthy, orange-purple color. The wound throbbed constantly. Whenever he moved wrong, something sharp stabbed him inside.

One other thing plagued Moses, especially at night. Naomi. She consumed his thoughts. He saw her often, but she rarely even said hello. If they were part of a group of people, she was friendly enough. Otherwise she acted like he was poison.

Moses slept in a crude, dirt-floored cabin with Jonas and Caleb. The three of them were the ferrykeepers—set apart from slaves in other nearby shacks, who worked at other things.

None of the slaves saw their master often. As long as the ferry brought in money everyone did what they were supposed to, he had no interest in them.

Unlike others Moses had worked for, Master Sawyer didn't believe in keeping his slaves fairly well-fed. They were given a daily ration of a pint of cornmeal—half of what most masters provided—and nothing else. This master thought his slaves should provide most of their own food by growing vegetables near their shacks or foraging in the woods and swamplands. They could count on paw-paws, nuts, berries, wild grapes, bullfrog legs and other items, though, since it was summer.

Lucky for Moses, ferrykeeping was an off-and-on job. The ferrymen could tend to their own business as long as they stayed near enough to answer the bell within a few minutes. And they could wander farther at night, when the ferry was closed. Moses didn't have a garden, of course, so he ate off the kindness of others at first. He weeded and hoed in return.

Jonas, who seemed to be the community's leader, pointed out a parcel of dirt that Moses could use to begin his garden. Several folks gave him advice and bits of seed or seedling plants to grow. Moses didn't like grubbing in the dirt, but he knew he'd better work if he wanted to eat any better than he was. He made sure to gather every grub and worm he came across, for fish bait.

Fishing was a popular pastime, since it could be done right by the ferry. Moses quickly learned how the river was different from the creek on the Kemp Farm. As he got better at fishing the river, he ate better. Fishing from a dock was easy, once he got the hang of it. He learned how to "plank" fish. He would gut, skin, and fillet his catch. After that, he'd nail it to a board and set it close to the fire, where it would slowly cook.

There was another bonus to living on the river: blue crabs. They could be caught by tying a fish head onto a piece of string and simply throwing it into the river. When a crab snatched up the bait, Moses would slowly pull in the string. The incredibly stubborn crab, not to be denied his meal, would refuse to let go while the bait was still underwater. When it got near the surface, Moses would scoop it up with a long handled net. Sometimes, he'd get more than one crab at a time.

"…And Remember that I Am a Man."

The crabs were cooked alive, whole in the shell, until they turned bright red. When done, their shells were simply snapped apart, top from bottom, and then the guts and poisonous lungs—called dead man's fingers—were taken out. What remained was tasty, tender, white meat, easily removed from the shell. Gobs of meat came from the back, from the large muscles that powered the crab's swimmers. The claws, cracked open, provided the sweetest treat of all, and even the slender legs had meat to be sucked out. A messy meal, but well worth the bother.

At every opportunity, when the ferry business was slow, Moses napped, because night had become his favorite time. Caleb, a quiet, untalkative man, though friendly enough, began teaching Moses how to forage off the land.

They set snares for rabbits, possums, muskrats, and such. With torches, they traveled the creek banks, gigging dogfish and bullfrogs with sharpened sticks. Turtles were also fair game. Sighting a turtle meant jumping into the water after it, even if it was a large snapping turtle. They were dangerous. But delicious. Almost as good as the frog legs, fried in fat. They didn't worry much about snakes, either, since reptiles didn't come out after dark.

So, although Master Sawyer barely provided for his slaves, Moses ate quite well. He quickly learned to cook for himself, after a few burnt meals. The slaves—the families owned by Master Sawyer, not a hired man like Moses—were allowed to own chickens. Moses could trade some of his foraged food for eggs, which were easy to boil and could be carried in a pocket until lunchtime.

His back healed after a couple of weeks and the scars were fading, since it hadn't been a real whip used on his back. The hole in his stomach got worse, however, and he often found it hard to keep with his ferry work.

*

Moses was on the east side, near Master Sawyer's house, when the ferry bell rang. He'd been napping in the woods, but came instantly awake. He ran for the dock.

A pair of mules, attached to a wagon, was being led onto the ferryboat. With surprise, he recognized Samson and Goliath. A man in Quaker clothing had to be Mister Kemp. And that was Chadwick

132

sitting on the seat of the wagon. As the wagon moved off the dock, it revealed another person, who had been standing behind. Missy Hannah!

When she noticed Moses, her eyes went wide, her cheeks turned rosy, and she broke into a smile. "Moses. How good to see thee."

Moses could feel a grin spreading across his face. "Hello, Missy Hannah."

She looked him up and down and her face grew concerned. Now that his whip-marks had faded, Moses wore only trousers, like the other ferrymen.

"How art thou doing?" she asked.

Moses, for the first time, became aware that he actually didn't know how he was doing—or feeling. Since leaving the Kemp farm, he'd sort of, well, gotten along. He noticed that Missy Hannah's eyes had settled at his waist, where his pants rope held a cloth against his festering injury. He looked down and saw the crude bandage had turned yellow from the pus seeping out of his ugly wound.

He looked back up at Missy Hannah. "I'm fine, Ma'am," he said. He could feel tears welling up in his eyes.

"What happened?" Her green eyes were on his face, but they had lost the sparkle he'd always associated with her.

"I got poked with a stick," he answered, "and the tip done broke off in my belly."

"How long…," she began and then, "Has anyone…"

"Hannah," Mister Kemp's stern voice called from the ferryboat, "come aboard."

Missy Hannah glanced over nervously. Everyone knew that white girls should not talk to male slaves in public. Especially when the slave was only half-clothed.

Hannah's eyes came back to Moses and there were tears there. She gulped and opened her mouth to say something, but her lower lip quivered and nothing came out.

"Hannah," Mister Kemp called again.

Missy Hannah gulped and, in a low, husky voice, said, "Be strong, Moses. The Lord is with thee."

She turned and stepped onto the boat. Once aboard, she walked over to the mules and stroked Goliath, as if to assure the beast there was nothing to fear about crossing the river. Her back was to Moses, but he saw her take out a handkerchief and dab at her eyes.

"Leh's go Moses," Jonas boomed.

Moses looked up. Caleb already held his pole, and Jonas stood ready to cast off. The wheels had been chocked with pieces of wood to the keep the wagon from rolling around during the crossing, which would spook the mules. Moses jumped aboard and grabbed his pole.

During the crossing, Mister Kemp stood in the bow and stared ahead. He acted like he'd never seen Moses before in his life. Up on the wagon, Chadwick sneered, never taking his eyes off Moses. He had affected a "Lord of the Manor," role, it appeared, since Moses had last seen him. He had a pipe between his teeth, and made great flourishes as he smoked it. The idiot must have thought it made him look older or distinguished, or something. The overall effect, however, was that of a country bumpkin chewing on a blade of grass.

When the ferry reached the other side, Caleb jumped to drag the ramp into place while Moses removed the chocks. Jonas stepped up to lead the mules off, but Chadwick, impatient, waved him off.

The ramp wasn't entirely set up when Chadwick snapped the reins and called, "Gettup." Moses had to pull back quickly to avoid getting his fingers crushed as Samson and Goliath moved forward. They crossed the ramp with no problems. But when they pulled the wagon up on the ramp, one of the rear wheels slipped off the edge.

The wagon tipped alarmingly and looked about to go over. Jonas, Caleb and Mister Kemp, on the side of the off-wheel, shouted and ran to grab it. Chadwick dropped his pipe onto the wagon seat and slid off on the other side. Moses couldn't get around the wagon to help. The wagon wheel on his side rose into the air and he suddenly became aware that he could help more from this side, after all.

He leaped up onto the rising wheel and grabbed on. His weight counterbalanced the tipping wagon and kept it from going all the way over. It gave the men on the other side a few extra seconds to bring their strength into play and set the wagon right.

As the wagon settled back down, Moses put his feet into a spoke and rose until he could look into the wagon. His right hand reached out and grabbed Chadwick's pipe from under the seat, where it had fallen. Quicker than a spring robin on a worm, he dragged the mouthpiece of the pipe through a smear of mule dung on the wagon wheel, then placed it back on the wagon seat. He dropped back down.

Mister Kemp, after glaring at Chadwick, led the mules onto solid ground.

Once the ferry toll had been paid, all three of the travelers mounted the wagon, Missy Hannah squeezed between her father and Chadwick, who acted like he'd had nothing to do with the fiasco he had caused. He took the reins, looked around for his pipe and stuck it in his mouth. Moses could hardly contain himself as the white boy made an awful face, then wiped the pipe stem on his pantleg. He rapped the pipe on the side of the wagon to knock out the burned tobacco, and then stuck the thing in his pocket.

As the Kemps drove away, Jonas thanked Moses for his quick thinking. Jonas probably thought the wide grin on Moses' face was because of his praise, and Moses didn't let on otherwise.

As the wagon passed from sight, Moses wished he could have gone over and run his hands through the fur of Samson and Goliath during the crossing. They were old friends.

*

The next day, a black man appeared, asking for Moses. He handed over a stoppered bottle of some salve or unguent. "Missy Hannah say to put this on your hurt, two time a day."

Moses did as instructed and the infection in his stomach dried up after a couple of weeks. The hole didn't close over, however, and he could still feel the stabbing pains of the wood inside him when he moved wrong.

At the time of year when the leaves turn into God's boast of color, he saw Master Sawyer up close for the first time. The master was a lean man with a sharp nose. His dark, close-set eyes gave him the look of a weasel—or a skunk. He wore an expensive-looking suit and carried a walking stick with a silver knob for a handle. Leading a handsome black gelding with a fancy, gleaming saddle, he came from his house and ordered his ferrymen to take him across.

The Sawyer family, Moses had learned, was quite prominent in Camden County. Master Sawyer had nine brothers and sisters and all had either made a name for themselves or married well. The youngest of the lot, Lemuel Sawyer, Jr. had been elected a United States Congressman. It was this brother who had obtained the license to operate the ferry from the commerce department of the new government.

During the crossing, Master Sawyer watched Moses as if he were a cat considering a fat mouse for a meal. Just before they docked, the master walked up to Jonas, on the sweep. Master Sawyer nodded toward Moses.

"How's that new boy doing, Jonas?" he asked. The river breeze carried the words to Moses' ears.

Without meeting Master's eyes, the steersman bobbed his head in approval. "He a good worker, Mas' Sawyer. He quick to learn the river and the currents. He be a right-fine waterman some day."

Master Sawyer pursed his lips and tapped his cane against his trouser leg. "He give you any sass? Coates said he's a troublemaker."

Now Jonas shook his head in utter denial. "No, suh, he be doin' fine."

The master nodded and walked back to the center of the ferryboat. He took the reins from a young black boy who'd been assigned the task of holding the horse and stood, waiting, until the boat docked and the ramp was pulled across. Without another glance, he mounted and rode off.

Moses was finally able to let loose of the fear he'd felt during the crossing. Jonas had given a good report, because Moses had been doing what he should be doing, tending the ferry. He hadn't let anyone know about his talent with mules and horses, or that he knew how to count. Moses wasn't going to act special anymore. He'd learned his lesson.

Things seemed better after that. He'd expected his new master to be like the black-horned devil himself, but he'd been nothing like that. As long as you did your job around here, it appeared, you'd be treated all right.

Over the next few weeks, the fear of his new master lessened, and he went about the task of learning how to read the river currents, the winds, and the weather. He talked and joked with the others, fished, and sometimes enjoyed afternoon naps so he and Caleb could be free to forage at night.

"…And Remember that I Am a Man."

Then the hungry time began.

"…And Remember that I Am a Man."

"...And Remember that I Am a Man."

Chapter Eighteen

Fool—1803 A.D.

Once a year he distributed clothing to his slaves. To the men he gave one pair of shoes, one blanket, one hat, and five yards of coarse, homespun cotton; to the women a corresponding outfit, and enough to make one frock for each of the children. The slaves were obliged to make up their own clothes, after the severe labor of the plantation had been performed. And other clothing, beyond this yearly supply, which they might need, the slaves were compelled to get by extra work, or do without.

The supply of food given out to the slaves was one peck of corn a week, or some equivalent, and nothing besides. They must grind their own corn, after the work of the day was performed, at a mill which stood on the plantation. We had to eat our coarse bread without meat, or butter, or milk. Severe labor alone gave us an appetite for our scanty and unpalatable fare. Many of the slaves were so hungry after their excessive toil, that they were compelled to steal food in addition to this allowance.

The Experience of Rev. Thomas H. Jones, Who Was a Slave for Forty-three Years. *Written by a friend as related to him by Brother Jones—1885 A.D.*

139

"...And Remember that I Am a Man."

The bullfrogs and turtles vanished when the weather went cool. At the first touch of frost, the dogfish stayed away from the banks and the other fish in the river stopped biting. Rabbits stayed in their burrows, possums kept to the trees and muskrats seldom strayed from their creekbank holes.

At the first hard frost, most of the plants in Moses' garden died. From here on in, he'd be able to eat only those foods that could be preserved. He'd arrived at Sawyer's Ferry too late to put in some crops, but he'd managed pole beans, Lima beans, and black-eyed field peas, all of which would dry in the pods and keep. He'd grown cimnells, also called pattypan squash, and pumpkins, which wouldn't spoil quickly. And his small stand of corn had been left mostly unharvested, so the kernels would harden and he could grind extra corn meal for himself. He had a few things that didn't mind the cold, like collards and worm-holey cabbage. And the fish in the river still bit once in a while.

He didn't have enough to get him through the long winter ahead, but that wouldn't matter. Come New Years Day, he'd be hired out to a new master and leave the miserly Enoch Sawyer behind.

Casual travelers became scarce, so traffic on the ferry fell off. There was still commercial traffic, but not enough to keep the ferrymen busy. Moses was faced with long hours of inactivity, which he usually spent with a line in the water, hoping for the rare nibble.

Those slave families with large gardens and flocks of chickens looked at their small stores of foodstuffs for the winter and became less likely to share their fare with him. Nobody knew how long the winter would hold and they didn't want to feed him something now that their children might need before spring.

At night, he and Jonas talked, with Caleb listening silently. Mostly, Jonas told about his life on the river and what he knew of the goings-on in the area. Sometimes he showed Moses how to tie sailor's knots, and taught him to sew, using a few precious needles and thread he had hoarded.

Jonas had been owned by one Sawyer or another all his life, and said he wished he could hire out. Moses thought this odd until the smiling, ebony man said that hiring-out was different for slaves with an adult owner. Some masters, he declared, would make a deal with their slave. The master would say how much he expected the slave to earn over a year's time. The slave would then be free to hire out in any manner he chose: working in the swamp, laboring on the canal or crewing on any of a variety of vessels that plied the waters of the North Carolina sounds. A hard-working slave could manage to pay his master and keep any other money, especially working as a sailor, where the crew was paid a small percentage of the profits.

Some slaves, Jonas declared with a tone of awe in his voice, had saved enough money to approach their masters and ask to buy themselves free. And some of the white men had been kind enough—or greedy enough—to agree to the deal. Jonas didn't know any of these free blacks personally, but he knew others who said they had known someone who did get free.

Moses decided not to believe this claim. It seemed to him that any slave stupid enough to tell his master of possessing hundreds of dollars would soon be penniless—and still enslaved. There were some free black men in the county, he had heard. But they had usually been set free when a master died and put it in his last will and testament.

Still, freedom occupied Moses' mind almost as much as his infatuation with Naomi. Ever since he'd talked to Missy Hannah on the dock, he'd been thinking on what she'd asked him: "How are you doing?" And the only possible answer he could give to himself was: "Not well at all."

As a child, he'd never thought about being a slave. Slavery was all he'd ever known, and he'd expected to be treated harshly. He'd taken all the abuse of white men because he thought he didn't deserve better.

But now Moses was becoming a man. His voice had deepened and hair had grown on his body. He'd been aroused by a pretty girl.

"How far do you have to run before you get free?" he asked Jonas.

The strong man's smile left his face and he thought deeply. "I don't rightly know," he said. "Even if someone made it all the way to the north, they got no way to send word back."

"What about the maroons? They're free, ain't they?"

"I guess so, maybe," Jonas said.

"…And Remember that I Am a Man."

Caleb surprised Moses by speaking up. "They ain't no more free than you or me, Moses. They's just on the run."

Moses considered this. "But they don't have masters. And they've got the whole of the swamp to themselves."

Caleb shook his head. "They only free until the white men goes in after them with horses, guns, and dogs."

"They can't catch the maroons," Moses argued.

"Yay, they can." Caleb nodded solemnly. "They catched me out the swamp, didn't they."

There was no answer to this. Moses had seen the stripes of whip scars on Caleb's back, but had never asked where they'd come from. Nobody ever asked about things like that.

So, Caleb had once been a maroon. No wonder he knew all about finding wild food. The knowledge excited Moses, and also brought a flash of anger for the scars on the man's back.

"If I get free," he said, "they'll never catch me."

Caleb shook his head, but it was Jonas who said, "You be careful, young Moses. You'll gets a worse whippin' than you got with that switch."

The unexpected reminder of his undeserved punishment made his stomach clench and the sliver of wood, still inside, stuck him like a snake's fang.

"How'd you know about that?" he asked suspiciously.

Jonas laughed. "You ought to know by now that they ain't no secrets in Camden County. Besides, your first day here, I seen the blood on the back of your shirt."

Embarrassment made Moses angry. "You just wait," he said. "I'll be free someday."

Caleb nodded solemnly. "Jes' be careful, Moses."

*

Moses grew anxious as the end of the year approached. He was always hungry, and his supply of food had nearly run out. Jonas and Caleb shared, but they didn't have much either, due to Master Sawyer's indifference. Who'd have ever thought that being ignored could be so merciless? Moses consoled himself with the knowledge he'd soon have a new master, instead of the cruelest man in the county.

142

"...And Remember that I Am a Man."

On hiring day, Moses would be free to walk to town and put himself on the auction block for all the white men to bid on him. For those few hours, between leaving Master Sawyer's Ferry and being hired out, Moses would enjoy a sort of freedom. On that day, even Master Sawyer couldn't forbid him.

His only sorrow would be leaving Naomi. True, she never paid him much mind and was often spiteful when she did, but the sight of her made his heart ache. Why was she so put off by him? He'd never done her any wrong.

Moses had no calendar, of course. He couldn't tell one day from the other except Sunday, when the slaves were allowed to hold prayer meeting and did no work unless the ferry was needed. But white folks didn't work or travel on the Sabbath, either, so Moses usually had the entire day off. But he still knew when hiring day was to be, because the Sawyer's were preparing for a New Years Day feast, and word came down from the house slaves. Hiring-day would be the day after that, unless it was the Sabbath.

On the last day of the year, however, Master Sawyer sent word that the auction would be delayed by one day this year. There had been a death in the auctioneer's family, and the funeral was to be held two days after New Year's. He sent word that Moses was to walk into town by himself and turn himself over to the auctioneer.

The day before, though busy with lots of folks wanting to cross the river, seemed to drag on forever. He was lost in his thoughts about leaving Naomi, and paid no mind to what went on around him. When darkness came, Moses ate the few bites that made up his supper and tried to sleep, knowing he needed to rise early. He shivered under the scrap of canvas he used for a blanket. It took a long time, but he finally dozed.

Before the cock crowed, Moses was up and about. He put on both of his ragged shirts against the cold and donned his shoes, which were getting too tight. Then he set out down the road towards the town of Camden.

A heavy frost covered the ground and Moses was glad for his shoes. They were worn and one had a hole in the sole, but they were certainly better than nothing. Maybe his new master would buy him shoes.

"…And Remember that I Am a Man."

He met no one else along the dirt track called Sawyer's Ferry Road, but that didn't surprise him. Of the slaves living at the ferry and the master's house, he was the only one not owned by Master Sawyer. All of the other men hired-out by the master lived and worked in the swamp.

He didn't see anyone on the main road, either. Both the other times, when he'd been marched away from his mother and the last two years, when he'd ridden in Mister Kemp's wagon, there'd been black men heading to town. They joined up in groups to talk and laugh, not wanting to think of where they were headed.

There'd been white men, too, but they didn't walk. Some came on horseback; but most drove wagons. The slaves got off the narrow road in a hurry when wagons came along.

As the sun rose, he began to worry. Something was wrong. Was he late? Surely not, he'd gotten up plenty early, and the auction wouldn't start until hours after sunrise.

He went straight to the tobacco barn, on the edge of town. It stood deserted. The pen, used for slave men and women awaiting their turn on the auction block for the first time and any "uppity" slaves, was also empty. The barn's big doors had been left open a crack and he could see no one inside.

With a sick feeling in his stomach, he walked into Camden, past the courthouse near the tobacco barn. He noticed a slave woman out behind one of the fine houses, carrying something out the back door, and ran to the picket fence.

"Auntie," he called, for she was old and he wanted to show respect. "Can I talk to you?"

The woman turned. She'd gotten farther away, apparently headed for the outhouse, but she nodded, smiled and made her way to him. She was a big woman, wearing a fancy-colored dress that her mistress must have discarded. In her hand, she carried a jar of some sort. When she got close, he knew what was in the jar. It smelled to high heaven. She'd been on her way to empty the white folks' night jar into the outhouse. He didn't think much about it, however. He had more important things on his mind.

"Hello, young man," the auntie said. "What can I do for you?"

Moses pointed back at the tobacco barn. "The auction. Where is everybody?"

"...And Remember that I Am a Man."

The auntie got a troubled look. "What you mean, boy? The auction was yesterday."

"…And Remember that I Am a Man."

"…And Remember that I Am a Man."

Chapter Nineteen

Rope Trick—1804 A.D.

As a preventative against being tricked or hoo-dooed, punch a hole
through a dime, insert a string through the hole, and tie it around the
left ankle.

Doc Quinn, age 92 WPA Slave Narratives—1936 – 1938 A.D.

A month after the auction, on a moonlit night when the air was cold and still, and snowflakes fell like white chicken feathers, Moses walked through the woods. He had checked his snares, like he did every night. And, as usual, they'd been empty.

Near dawn, he came to the edge of the trees and noticed a cow lying on the edge of a field. He looked around, picked up a branch and went over to the beast. He prodded her with the stick.

"Get up," he said. "Get out of here."

The cow's eyes snapped open. She snorted a blast of steaming air from her wide nose and lurched to her feet. He poked her again.

"Go on, cow."

The creature lumbered away, mooing plaintively. As soon as she cleared the spot, Moses went to the middle of the place where she'd been. He lowered his rear end to the ground and pulled over him the ragged piece of cloth that served as both coat and blanket.

Quickly he slipped off the shoes, which were barely holding together, then unwrapped the rags that served for socks. He pressed his bare feet against the warm soil, soaking up the heat left behind by the cow. His toes tingled as blood flowed into skin gone numb from the cold.

Caleb had taught him this trick of stealing warmth from large animals. He huddled beneath his cloth and tried to keep heat from escaping. The ground would stay warm for several minutes, long enough to thaw out his feet.

"Um, 'scuse me," a voice said from nearby. "Is you somebody under that there blanket?"

Moses poked his head out. A small, wiry black man stood there in the false-dawn light, looking on curiously. Dressed better than most slaves, and wearing high-topped shoes that might once have belonged to a woman, he carried a large cloth bundle over one shoulder.

"Oh, hello, Titus," Moses said. It was the same man who'd brought the medicine from Missy Hannah, the summer before.

"Oh, it's you, Moses." Titus grinned. "Here I was fixin' to ask the crazy man under the blanket whereabouts Moses was, but you turns out to be the crazy man."

Moses smiled back and felt his dry, cracked lips break further. "How's Missy Hannah?" he asked.

"She be fine, jus' fine." Titus bobbed his head as he talked. "She sent me along with this here bundle for you."

Moses felt light-headed. The bundle was for him? He'd about given up hope of anything good happening, ever again. His food was nearly gone and he'd taken to going behind a mill nearby, scraping the cobs for bits of corn missed in the milling.

Titus swung the makeshift bundle to the ground and Moses leapt up to open it. The "sack" turned out to be a thick blanket. Inside was a shirt, a pair of pants and a coat that Moses had often seen Mister Kemp wearing when he worked. Also, there were potatoes, carrots, and cornmeal, along with a bag of apples. He also found a small poke of salt. Moses felt tears come to his eyes.

"Missy Hannah give me a message for you, too," Titus said. "She say she'll be lookin' out for you."

"…And Remember that I Am a Man."

*

Early spring turned out to be the worst. Traffic picked up on the ferry and Moses stayed busy rowing walkers across and poling those who had horses or wagons. Some crossings, he barely had the strength to fight the strong current. The lack of food was affecting his thinking, too, making him dull and listless.

The food from Missy Hannah was long gone, and it was too early to plant the garden. It took all of Moses' will power not to eat the seeds he had set aside last fall for planting this year. He had taken to scraping corn cobs again and even ate the spring blossoms off wild fruit trees and blackberry vines.

Weak though Moses was, he worked hard in his garden. One day, as the sun warmed the soil, he found a few worms. Without even bothering to look around to be sure no one would see how low he'd sunk, he brushed off the dirt and ate them, swallowing them whole.

The next morning, he woke feeling stronger. His mind was working for the first time in weeks. He rolled off his sleeping board and walked out into a warm, clear day, the sky the color called Carolina Blue.

He rushed to the garden and began digging with his crude, wooden shovel. Worms abounded, but he didn't eat them. He put them in a bark container and carried them down to the river, grabbing his fishing pole on the way. If the ground was warm enough for worms to be near the surface, the water must be heating up, too. Maybe the fish would be biting again. He threaded a wriggler onto the nail that he'd bent into a hook and tossed it into the water. Saying a quick prayer, he let it sink to the bottom. As though the worms and the fish had some sort of secret agreement about what time of year was proper for fishing, he got a bite almost immediately. Pulling in a catfish as long as his forearm, Moses felt relief. The starving time was over. For this year, at least.

*

One night in the middle of summer, Moses lay on the ground outside the ferrymen's hut. Jonas and Caleb slept nearby. Their shack was built with no windows, to keep heat in during the winter, and so was unbearably hot in summer, without even a hint of breeze coming through.

"…And Remember that I Am a Man."

Outside, the cooling wind blew across brown skin, relaxing the muscles beneath. Nothing disturbed the silence. It was too late in the year for peeping frogs, and the birds had gone quiet for the night. Moses stared up at the millions of stars in the Milky Way, thinking.

In the times between ferry-crossings, he'd had plenty of time to work his garden so there would be enough stores to last the winter. Enough so, he hoped sell some of his vegetables to travelers. If he could do that, he could buy enough salt to cure the fish he caught, so he'd have them for winter, too. Maybe even earn enough money to buy warm clothing and shoes. That was how free men got by, wasn't it?

Someday, maybe, he could escape to the north. Free blacks were allowed to own land there, he'd heard. Why, if he had his own land, what was to stop him from growing enough cash crops to buy a mule? Without laws against it, nobody could stop him from cutting trees on that land to build a house. And he could grow more crops on that cleared land.

Another thing. Moses had watched when white men paid Jonas for crossing on the ferryboat. Some of them cheated by paying too few coins to Jonas, who didn't know how to count and merely put any money given him in a tin lock-box. If Moses was collecting the fares, that wouldn't happen.

If he ever got to be a free man, Moses could even petition the government for a license to keep ferry himself. A ferry-owner would be quite an important man, helping to get goods across the river. Ferries were necessary for the free trading of goods, Missy Hannah had said, and Moses thought he'd pretty much figured out how that worked. Free people got paid for their work, be it hoeing cotton or barging lumber down river to market, or ferrying folks and goods across the river. Labor for money, money for goods or to buy land to labor on and to hire other folks to work that land. If he ever got a chance to…

"Moses," someone hissed.

He sat up. A man stood nearby, having come up quietly. His dark outline was indistinct, but Moses knew him from his voice.

"Titus," Moses said. "What are you doing here?"

"Sssh!" Titus said, as though Jonas and Caleb weren't lying close by. "Come with me."

150

"What for?"

"You find out," said Titus. "Come 'long." He began walking away.

Moses got up and started after him.

"Be careful," Jonas whispered from the ground. "Don't get caught."

"Right." Moses moved off. Why was Jonas worried? Moses often went off at night to tend snares or do some frog-gigging. It wasn't against the law.

But when Titus led him to the road, Moses stopped. Going into the woods was one thing, being caught on the road at night, without a pass, was another.

"Wait," he told Titus. "Where are we going?

Titus stopped and turned. "Missy Hannah want to see you."

"Now?"

"Now. She say come with me."

Titus set off down the road. Moses gulped and followed. He'd never done anything against the law.

They only went a half-mile or so before Titus turned off the road. They went through the branches of a willow tree and into the shadows.

It was like a cave in there. It took Moses' eyes a moment to adjust. He could see only an outline, but could tell it was a woman in a dark dress and shawl.

"Hello, Moses," Missy Hannah said.

Moses took a deep breath and let it out in a long sigh. "It's good to see you, Missy." He'd not realized how much he missed her.

"How are you?" As she usually did when away from her parents, she abandoned the Quaker way of speaking. "Is The Lord taking care of you?"

"I'm gettin' along," said Moses. "Thank you for the things you sent."

"I heard how Sawyer tricked you." Her voice was hard as flint. "I'm so sorry you ended up with him."

Moses shrugged. So was he. "I'm gettin' along."

"I've got some things, some food and clothing for you," she said. "And I've talked to some men in town."

"About what?"

"Getting you away from Sawyer, that's what. All you need to do is get to the auction house in January. Mister George Furley has agreed to hire you, no matter how high Sawyer goes."

Even though this was Missy Hannah, Moses felt suspicion creep over him. "Why would he do that?"

"We took up a collection in the meeting house. Everyone put something in. I told them how smart you are, and how kind. We'd try to buy you free if Jamie Grandy was of age."

"They'd do that for me?" Moses was stunned. Such a thought had never occurred to him. White people, even Quakers, seemed so remote that he'd never guessed any would care a whit about what happened to him. Except Missy Hannah, of course.

"Yes, they would." She stepped forward and put a hand on his forearm. "Even father put in a few dollars."

Now that his vision had adjusted, Moses could see compassion in her green eyes. He found himself wishing that Naomi would look at him that way, just once.

"Moses?" Missy Hannah said hesitantly.

"Yes, Missy?"

"Please don't hate father."

But Moses did hate her father. The hatred had built up in the hard times since the betrayal. Mister Kemp had given him hope, then dashed it without a word.

"Why not?" It was all he could think to say.

She squeezed his arm. "Moses, nobody's perfect. My father got scared that nightriders would come after our family defied that slave catcher. Even though father's a Quaker, and Quakers are supposed to be against slavery, he's not willing to risk trouble with the community we have to live in. After what happened to John, he thought keeping you might bring trouble. I'm sorry."

Moses set his teeth and squeezed his lips together. He took a couple of breaths, and then said, "He could have told me."

"Like I said, nobody's perfect. Father has trouble keeping his temper sometimes, and he's not quite sure how he feels about slavery because his father owned slaves and he grew up with the system. Father only joined the Society of Friends when he married mother. But he tries to overcome his prejudice."

152

"...And Remember that I Am a Man."

"He could have told me," he said again. But Moses knew, deep down, Mister Kemp had good reason for what he had done. What if Missy Hannah had been hurt? But the betrayal still hurt. "He could have told me."

"Moses, father couldn't face you. He's ashamed."

*

Now that Moses knew he wouldn't be working for Master Sawyer forever, his spirit lifted. The rest of summer seemed to zip by. He fished and napped whenever possible during the days, then trapped and gigged with Caleb in the warm nights. His garden produced a bounty of crops and he ate well, putting a bit of money away for when he might be able to go to town and spend it. In the late summer, he planted the fall crops that would carry him through the oncoming winter. Moses didn't shirk his work in that area; he'd learned his lesson the year before, when his belly had shrunk in so far that it made acquaintance with his backbone. There was no such thing as too much food. Once he'd left, Jonas and Caleb would get the food left behind.

On the last day of the year, Moses sat on the dock, looking out on the water. It was a warm day for winter, but the gray skies, and the increasing wind from the north warned of a cold snap. The auction would be the day after tomorrow. Moses had been at Sawyer's Ferry for a year and a half, and that was more than enough.

He had asked ferry passengers, both black and white, about when the auction would be held and was sure it would be the second day in January. Master Sawyer wouldn't trick him this year. Moses planned to sneak off a day ahead of time.

He would not be the least bit sorry to leave Sawyer's Ferry. He'd had enough of starvation and the wearing of rags for clothes, and he wanted to be shut of Naomi. She always seemed to be hanging around the ferry, but anytime Moses had tried to get on her good side, she'd been nastier than a cottonmouth crawling over hot embers.

"Hey, boy," someone said. Moses turned. Abner, who worked at bringing lumber from the swamp, had come up quietly. "Mas' Sawyer say," he said, "fetch a coil of rope from the shed and bring it to him at his house."

153

Moses wondered why Abner couldn't go get the rope. True, Abner didn't come to the ferry much, but he could find things for himself. Well, no problem.

"What size rope you want?" Moses asked.

Abner looked confused. "I dunno. He just say, 'rope.'"

"What's he gonna use it for?"

Abner shrugged. "He don't tell me nothin' 'bout that."

"That's all right, Abner. I'll fetch a middle sized one." Moses got to his feet and set off toward the shed where they kept ropes and rigging. His feet were cracked and sore from walking on the cold ground, his shoes long ago worn out. Along the way, he saw a pig lying against one of the empty corn cribs and considered rousting it up, so as to warm his feet. He decided against it. He'd do best to get the rope to the main house before Master Sawyer got impatient.

Moses had never been called to take anything up to the house before. He wondered if this might be some sort of trick. Maybe Master Sawyer would try to say the auction was delayed, like he'd done last year, or come up with some chore for Moses to do that morning. Moses would have to be on his guard. Master Sawyer was sure to try something. The rope was an excuse to get Moses up there.

As he came up to the shed, Moses noticed a man going behind one of the nearby outbuildings, but thought little of it. Not allowed to use the white man's privy, slaves had to do their business out of doors and a shed provided a bit of privacy. Moses had seen the man around before; like Abner, he worked with the crew cutting lumber in the swamp.

Still thinking about being on his guard when he saw Master Sawyer, Moses unbolted the door and stepped inside the gloomy outbuilding. He looked around. It wasn't a large building, but it was cluttered with all sorts of gear. He began rooting around. The shed door slammed, but he thought little of it, other than cursing the lessened light. Had the wind blown it shut? But then Moses heard an awful sound.

The bolt slammed shut on the outside. Metal scraped on metal and then something clicked. He heard the sound of someone running barefoot across the grass, going away.

"…And Remember that I Am a Man."

Chapter Twenty

Prisoner of Love—1805 A.D.

The pain in my head had subsided in a measure, but I was very faint and weak. I was sitting upon a low bench, made of rough boards, and without coat or hat. I was hand cuffed. Around my ankles also were a pair of heavy fetters. One end of a chain was fastened to a large ring in the floor, the other to the fetters on my ankles. I tried in vain to stand upon my feet. Waking from such a painful trance, it was some time before I could collect my thoughts. Where was I? What was the meaning of these chains? Where were Brown and Hamilton? What had I done to deserve imprisonment in such a dungeon? I could not comprehend. There was a blank of some indefinite period, preceding my awakening in that lonely place, the events of which the utmost stretch of memory was unable to recall. I listened intently for some sign or sound of life, but nothing broke the oppressive silence, save the clinking of my chains, whenever I chanced to move. I spoke aloud, but the sound of my voice startled me. I felt of my pockets, so far as the fetters would allow—far enough, indeed, to ascertain that I had not only been robbed of liberty, but that my money and free papers were also gone! Then did the idea begin to break upon my mind, at first dim and confused, that I had been kidnapped. But that I thought was incredible. There must have been some misapprehension—some unfortunate mistake. It could not be that a free citizen of New-York, who had wronged no man, nor violated any law, should be dealt with thus inhumanly.

"…And Remember that I Am a Man."

Twelve Years a Slave, Narrative of Solomon Northup, a Citizen of New-York, Kidnapped in Washington City in 1841, and Rescued in 1853—1853 A.D.

Moses sat in the cramped space with Mister Kemp's old coat around him, his cold feet stuffed in a pile of canvas. He had tried to kick the boards out during the night, but had given up. The shed was packed with gear. There wasn't enough room to lie down. Cracks between the wall boards allowed the wind through, piercing him like icicles. He had found a jug of water and a small amount of cornbread in one corner. At least they'd given him that.

"Psst, Moses," hissed a voice from outside the wall. "is you in there?"

"Who's that?" Moses asked, though he recognized the voice.

"Naomi. I been searchin' all over for you."

Moses forced his stiff legs to a standing position. "Someone shut me in," he said. "Open the door."

"They's a lock on it. That's how I guessed where you was."

Moses thought about the situation. There had never been a lock on this shed. The only things locked up at Sawyer's Ferry were food and other things the slaves might consider pilfering. What use would a slave have for boat rigging? Use of the lock confirmed that it had been Master Sawyer who'd ordered Moses' confinement.

Naomi's voice broke into the misery Moses was feeling from the certainty of another year at the ferry. "He locked you up to keep you from getting' hired away, didn't he?" she asked.

"Appears so." There was nothing more to be said. No use crying over spilt milk. Not that he'd had milk since coming to work at the ferry.

"Is you thirsty?" Naomi asked, as though hearing his thoughts.

"There's water in here," he answered. "And a bit of food."

Moses wished he could ask her to bring more food, but knew that it couldn't be squeezed through a crack. Well, he'd live through it.

"Can I do anythin' else for you, Moses?" Naomi asked.

"I'm fine," he lied. "But I'd be much obliged if you'd stay and talk to me for a bit."

"I don't mind," she said, "but I'd be beholden if we goes to the other side, out of the wind."

After they'd moved to where it was more comfortable for both, she asked, "Whatcha wanna talk about?"

"Well, for a start," Moses said, "why does Master Sawyer want to keep me around so bad?"

"It's hard to find someone who's good in boats. And everybody say, 'That Moses, he smart.' Most folks, when they crosses the river, they just goes straight across. But, when we watch you, you uses the wind and currents to make the job easier. Nobody learned you that. And you plans out your garden real careful-like. Folks notice stuff like that."

Moses remembered his first trip across the river on the ferry, when Naomi had used the current, giving him the idea. She was smart, too, but it didn't seem to get her in trouble. He pressed his lips together. Even when he tried to lie low, his sharp mind caused grief. Anger washed over him.

"Someday I'm going to be free," he said, before realizing what he was going to say.

"How you gonna do that?"

The next thing Moses knew, he and Naomi were having a pleasant conversation through the wall. He told her how he was figuring to buy himself free, and how he'd like to run a ferry of his own. He even told her about his counting, and how it had gotten him into trouble.

Naomi didn't seem to have any plans of her own. When he told her what he'd like to do, she'd say, "Me, too," or, "I'd like to do that with you," or, "I wish I could do that."

They talked the rest of the day and far into the night.

*

Moses awoke with a start. He had slept fitfully in his sitting position. A sound had awakened him and he listened carefully. He heard a jingling of keys; someone was messing with the lock. Then came the sound of the bolt being drawn back.

Light streamed through the cracks, so it was daylight outside. Hiring day! He tried to leap to his feet, so as to open the door and get a look at who'd taken the lock off. He suspected Abner had done the locking up and if he could find out for sure, he could at least warn others not to trust him.

His cramped muscles wouldn't cooperate, however, and it took him quite a while to gain his feet and make it out of the shed. The sun stood overhead. He had slept far too long because of staying up so late. The auction would be long over by this time. Legs stiff, he made his way back to ferrykeepers' shack.

Jonas and Caleb were off somewhere. Moses went to the corner where he kept his sack of foodstuffs and pulled out a squash to devour. At least nobody had stolen his supplies. Now that he had been betrayed by a fellow slave, he reckoned some folks might steal other folks' food. Maybe he should hide his sack somewhere.

*

When Moses saw Naomi, a few days later, with her little sister, Betsy, in tow, he walked up and smiled. "Hello."

She eyed him as if he were a snake. "What you want?"

Taken aback, he said, "I only wanted to thank you for being nice to me."

"I just talked to you a bit," she answered. "I'd a done the same for anyone."

She stalked off, her sister hurrying to catch up.

Moses stood rooted, staring after her. What about all the dreams they'd shared? What about the warm friendship he'd felt through a solid wall?

In the cold bleak weeks that followed, Moses tried not to think about Naomi. If that's the way she wanted to be, that'd be fine with him. He was busy enough trying to stay warm and find enough to eat, anyway.

In the early summer, however, when the air had turned warm and the crops had grown ripe for the picking, he felt a hunger that had nothing to do with food. Naomi often entered the world of his dreams and he would awaken hot and bothered.

In these dreams, he and Naomi had jumped the broom and were living together. There were no masters in this world. He and Naomi were inseparable. All day long, he would ferry folks across the river, collecting their money. When he returned to their cabin at night, he and his wife would talk, laughing at how they were free. Sometimes he dreamed she was kissing him and he'd awaken excited, dreaming of soft, warm skin against his own.

During the reality of daytime, he rarely got to talk to her. She didn't avoid him so much as she made sure never to be alone with him. She seemed to spend all her time up at the Master's house, but he didn't have any idea what she did in there.

When Moses saw her walk into the woods one day, carrying a basket, he followed her. He used all the skills he'd learned from Caleb to stay quiet. If she heard him coming, he'd never find her.

A warm spring sun beamed down as birds flitted from tree to tree. From above came the sounds of baby birds begging. Several times he scared up gray squirrels with his stealthy travel. He kept on, even though he was getting a little too far from the ferry. If the bell rang, he'd be late getting back.

It didn't take long until he found her. She was in a clearing, down on her knees, digging in the dirt with a large spoon. He crept closer and realized she was gathering goldenseal. Moses remembered his mother forcing him to chew on ground-up goldenseal root when he'd been little. Someone at the house must have an upset stomach.

He watched her from behind for a moment. She had hiked up her skirts to keep them out of the dirt and he admired her light brown legs. When she crawled on her knees to gather another plant, however, he decided she might not appreciate being spied on. Mama had always said the direct approach was best, so Moses walked into the clearing and said, "Hello."

Naomi sprang to her feet, knocking over the basket of dirty roots in the process. Flushing, she tried to brush the dirt and grass from her knees while straightening her skirt at the same time.

"Moses." She looked around as if hoping for someone to keep them from being alone. "Whatchoo doin' here?"

"I saw you go off and I followed."

"Why?"

Moses was taken aback. He hadn't thought about a reason. To stall, he said, "I wanted to talk to you."

"What about?"

"Um…" He looked at her overturned basket, and it gave him an idea. "Um, I know where there's a patch of fiddleheads. I wondered if you might want to go with me to gather some." Fiddleheads were the new, uncurling leaves of ferns that grew in swampy areas. One of the few wild foods available in spring, they were cooked as greens. To people starved for fresh foods after a winter's preserves, they tasted wonderful.

She looked at him suspiciously. "Now why would I wanna go off in the woods with you?" She looked down at the basket, as though she wanted to snatch it up and run away. But the contents had spilled out and it wouldn't be that easy.

Despite all the things to say that he'd practiced in his mind, Moses lowered his gaze and said, "I dunno, I guess."

"You don't know? Well, I knows. I knows why boys try to get girls off by themselves and you ain't pullin' no wool over my eyes."

Resentment flared and he raised his head. "I only want to talk to you. But you never give me the time of day."

To his surprise, tears filled her eyes. But she still bristled.

"And why should I? You ain't nothin' special to me. Now you go away and stop pesterin' me."

She turned her back and crouched down to gather her roots. Feeling like someone had pulled the world out from beneath his feet, Moses stood dumbfounded.

Naomi turned, eyes wet, and snapped, "You heard me. Go on. Get outta here."

He left.

*

"What's been eatin' at you, Moses?" Jonas asked.

Moses whirled his head around. He had been fishing off the edge of the ferry dock and hadn't heard the older man come up behind.

"What do you mean?" Moses said. "I'm just fine."

"That why you ain't moved in all the time your bobber's bein' pulled around by a fish?"

Moses looked back at the river. Sure enough, he had a fish on his hook, the piece of bark he used as a bobber was being tugged this way and that. Now when had that happened?

"It ain't just that, my young friend," Jonas said. "You been mopin' around the place for weeks. You don't pay a bit of attention to what you doin' when we're crossin' the river. Caleb says you quit goin' out with him at night. So what's the problem?"

"Ain't no problem." Moses pulled in his line, along with a small perch. He worked the bent-wire hook out of its mouth, then pulled his stringer out of the water. He threaded the stringer, which already held two fish, through his new catch's gills and out its mouth and slid it down to join the others. He tossed the whole mess back into the river, with one end of the stringer tied to the pier. The fish would stay alive and fresh.

While he was doing this, Jonas sat down next to him. He was chewing, refreshing his breath with a stalk of sweet grass stuck out from his smiling mouth. "How's the fishin'?"

"They ain't bitin' much." Moses worked a wriggling worm onto the hook.

Jonas gave Moses' shoulder a little shove. "They're bitin'. You ain't payin' it no mind."

Moses swung his cane pole out over the river and dropped his bait into the water. The bobber would keep the hook from sinking to the bottom, where fish might have trouble finding the worm. Sure enough, he got a nibble right away. He jerked the pole back too quickly, though, and missed setting the hook. He glanced sideways at Jonas.

Jonas sat quietly, kicking his feet above the river and chewing his grass.

After a while, Moses said, "You know anything about girls, Jonas?"

"Some." Jonas scraped the pulp from the grass stalk with his sharp, white teeth, and tossed the blade into the river. It meandered away in the slow current. "Any gal in partic'lar?"

"Nope."

"What's the question, then?"

Moses pulled the line out of the water to make sure his worm hadn't been stolen. "Why would a girl act nice to you sometimes, and then turn right around and treat you like dirt?"

"Hmmm…" Jonas went quiet for a moment, as though pondering, then he asked, "Somebody doin' that to you?"

"Not me, partic'larly," Moses said.

"Hmmm…we talkin' about gals in general, or Naomi in partic'lar?"

161

"…And Remember that I Am a Man."

Words came out of Moses like Jonas had pulled them out with a rope. "Naomi drives me crazy. She'll talk to me real nice when there's others around, but when I try to get close to her, other times, she's snippy as all get out. What's with her?"

Jonas lost his smile. He stuck out his lower lip and looked up at the sky like he wasn't going to answer, but then he said. "Moses, has you ever thought about what slave gals has to put up with?"

Moses hadn't. "Same as us, I reckon."

"You reckons wrong," Jonas said. He looked around to be sure they were alone and lowered his voice. "A slave gal, 'specially a pretty one, sometimes catches the attention of a white master, if you know what I mean."

"You think…?"

"Shet up and listen. I ain't saying nothing is happening. I'm just saying it do happen, so a slave gal's gotta think about it. And it might be the master is jus' keepin' an eye on the gal, so nothin' happens to her that might lower her price if he decides to sell. A pretty gal, 'specially a high-yaller one, she worth a lot of money."

"I didn't think of that."

Jonas looked straight at Moses, a glint of anger in his eyes.

"Hush, I said. I bet Naomi do like you, but master would whip her hide if she… if she and you got together. Or any other man, for that matter. Either that or he'd sell her for what he could get, while she still young."

Moses felt like his insides had turned to grits. He knew it was possible, even though he had never thought about it.

"And, 'sides all that," Jonas said, "what if she did cotton to you? You be a hired-out man. You'll be movin' on, sooner or later. Then where would she be?"

"I… I never thought about all that."

Jonas's smile came back, but it had lost its pleasant quality. "A man never do. But a gal's gotta. Damnation, boy, she don't dare cozy up to you."

"I see," said Moses, but he didn't. He wanted to stop talking, so he could think about it. This was worse than Naomi not liking him. He stood and the fishing pole dropped from his hand into the river. He didn't care. "I see," he said again, and turned to walk away.

"Moses," Jonas said, "don't go yet. There's somethin' else."

"What?" What else could there be?

Jonas rose and put his hand on Moses' shoulder.

"You ain't gonna like this. But you ain't no good to that gal anyhows. You gots to grow up."

Moses, who had bowed his head, brought it back up with a start. "What?"

"Boy, you jus' drift along like a leaf goin' down this river. 'Bout time you wake up and see what goes on around you."

"What do you mean?" Moses felt like he'd been hit by a brick – a second one. He shrugged out from beneath Jonas's hand.

"You hear me, Moses. Hear me good. Master Sawyer owns every bit of me, 'cept my soul. I'm stuck here. Got no choice. But you can get out and you needs to do it now. Don't count on waitin' round 'til your real master grows up."

"Why not?"

Jonas lowered his head and rubbed his brow as though his head ached. Then he looked back at Moses and sighed.

"I never told you why Bartholomew drowned, did I?"

Moses shook his head.

"The winter afore you came here," Jonas said, "was a hard one. There been a drought that year and not a lot come out of the gardens. Benjamin—hellfire, the whole lot of us—was starvin' to death. One day, on the way 'cross the river, he jus' collapse and fall in."

"Really?" Moses was paying attention now. He'd been really hungry, but he'd never considered that he could die from it.

"Moses, I been here at the ferry a long time. I seen men, women and children starve near to death. I seen a man get his leg crushed 'tween the ferryboat and the dock. He died o' rot because Master Sawyer didn't send for no doctor or no medicine. I seen fever come through and kill every other child. Master don't care. Maybe he think it be cheaper to buy another slave than take care o' the ones he already got."

Swallowing a lump, Moses asked, "But what can I do?"

"You gots to outsmart that old devil. Get yourself to the auction and find some other white man to hire you. This here's the worstest place in the county to be livin' at."

"But how am I going to do that?"

"…And Remember that I Am a Man."

Jonas looked sternly at him. "Tha's what I been talkin' about, boy. You keeps your eyes open, that's how. Think hard on it, and you'll figger a way out."

He turned and began to leave, then looked down into the water. "See them fish down there on that stringer?"

Moses looked down. "Uh-huh?"

"Dat's me down on that stringer. You ain't been strung yet. Swim away, Moses."

"…And Remember that I Am a Man."

Chapter Twenty-one

Piracy—1805 A.D.

On my return down street a watchman hailed me. I sang out with a double oath, "What business is it of yours?" He said it was his orders to take anybody up that was out after dark. So I swore an oath that if he did take me he would have to take me dead. So when the watchman found he had to eat blood pudding before he did take me, he calmed down and talked as pleasant as a man courting a woman. We talked awhile as friendly as could be. He told me about the town, the usages of the town, and what was the law there, and told me not to get angry at what he said to me, he was only doing what he was ordered to do; that the captain of the watch was a nice man, and was always friendly to sailors. So we walked along down the street till we came to the watch house. Now, said he, "just step in and speak to him and that is all that is required." Soon as I got in the key was turned upon me and there I had to stay all night. I swore enough to sink the city, if that would have done it. That was the first and last time a man ever fooled me, for I cut my eye-teeth fully.

The Life of George Henry—1894 A.D.

Moses slipped into the frigid water, upstream and out of sight of the ferry. It would be auction day when the sun rose in a couple of hours. Because the new year had started on a Sunday, the auction had been set for Tuesday, the third, so as to allow bidders a day to travel to the auction house.

"...And Remember that I Am a Man."

He'd snuck away on New Year's Day, when ferry traffic had been slow. He'd slept in the woods. The next morning, when the bell had begun ringing to call him, he'd ignored it. All day the bell rang, because of all the auction traffic. He wondered who they'd found to take his place on the pole, but wasn't about to come near enough to the ferry for a look.

He'd spent a second night in the woods, but had not slept. Now, in the dark hours of the morning, he walked out into the river and began wading downstream, only his head and shoulders showing. He moved slowly, careful not to make the smallest noise.

Moses felt the sandy bottom beneath his bare feet, glad it wasn't slippery mud. If he should slip and fall into deeper water, he'd drown. As it was, he worried that he might step on a catfish and be stabbed by its barbs. No crabs or snakes this time of year, luckily.

When he got to the ferry, he made his way between the dock and the ferryboat. Trying not to think about the man who'd been crushed by the boat, he shinnied up a piling and slipped the mooring line free of its fastening. As the upstream end of the boat moved away from the dock with the currents, he dropped back down into the river. Up another piling, and the second rope was loose. Moses pushed the ferryboat away from the dock with all his strength. Very slowly and without a sound, the vessel moved out into middle of the stream.

Moses waded down the river in the shallows, keeping pace with the slow-moving boat, still not wanting to be seen. When he'd gotten well away from the ferry, he left the river and headed towards town. He grew colder than ever as the breeze blew over his wet body. He shivered, and not entirely from the cold. If Master Sawyer ever figured out that Moses was the one who'd cast off the ferry, and if the plan didn't work... Well, he didn't want to think about it.

By the time he got to town, shortly before dawn, Moses felt numb all over. Except for the slaves in the outside pen, nobody was around the auction house. The whites wouldn't begin to gather until almost noon, he knew. Moses searched around and found a nearby barn unlocked. He slipped in, and settled down in a stall, kept warm by the presence a heat-providing, friendly milk cow.

He'd been up all night, but was too excited to sleep. Ever since he'd talked to Jonas on the dock last summer, Moses had been trying to come up with a plan to get away from Sawyer's Ferry. It wasn't good enough just to get to the auction. Master Sawyer would hire him again, no matter what the cost, for spite. But now Moses had made sure the ferryboat owner would be out on the waters, looking for his missing property.

Moses had done more, during the last months, than plan how to trick Master Sawyer. He'd begun socializing with the grown-ups around the ferry. He listened carefully when they talked of possible routes to the northern states, or discussed using forged passes to travel the roads. None of them could write, so they couldn't forge anything themselves. It was said some Quakers were willing to do it, however, and some would even hide fleeing slaves in their houses.

It seemed every slave had some dream of freedom he or she was willing to share. One slave said that someday he'd run into the swamp and join the maroons. Another talked about buying his freedom, if he could talk his master into a hiring-out deal. A third said she was sure that slavery would soon be abolished by the new government and she would wait for that. Others had decided that it didn't matter, they'd be free when they got to heaven.

Moses didn't know how he was going to get free, but he knew one thing for sure. There was no use praying to a white god for help, he was black and on his own.

The south was no place for him. A free black man in the southern states might as well be enslaved. He wasn't allowed to go into white stores or churches. There were no schools for his children. And he had to watch his mouth. An unwise remark about a white person might get him a beating. Or a lynching.

No, Moses would go to the northern states where he would work hard and save his money. Eventually, when he had enough, he would buy freedom for Naomi and have her come north to join him. But first he had to get free of Sawyer's Ferry.

As the morning wore on, hired-hand slaves drifted in from the surrounding countryside. They gathered behind the tobacco barn and began talking to one another. Old friends greeted each other and caught up on the previous year's goings-on. It seemed more like a festival than a business where men's labor was bought and sold.

Moses mingled. Some of the negros had come by Sawyer's Ferry and had a tale to tell. Seemed that the ferryboat had been stolen in the night and Master Sawyer had galloped off to find a boat to go after it. Meanwhile, the rowboats were kept busy, what with all the nearby folks traveling to the auction. A lot of white men were hopping mad that they'd been forced to leave their horses and wagons on the far side. They'd had to walk to town and, even though it was only a mile or two, white men weren't used to walking.

Late in the morning, the whites began to congregate at the auction house. They stayed out front of the building, away from the blacks. Moses asked around and one of the slaves pointed out Mister George Furley.

Mister Furley stood only a few inches taller than Moses, but their frames couldn't be more different. Mister Furley was a fat man, with a fringe of white hair around a bald dome. His nose and cheeks were red from the cold.

Moses screwed up his courage and went into the white crowd. A few of them gave him sharp looks, but no one stopped him. When he got near Mister Furley, who talked to another man, he stopped a couple of feet to the side. Hard as it was to do, he kept his head up and his eyes on the man, so there'd be no doubt who Moses wanted to talk with.

Mister Furley glanced over, then returned his attention to the conversation. It was only when they'd finished, and the other man walked away, that he turned his attention to Moses. He looked the young slave up and down, appraising him. His face and manner showed none of the suspicion Moses had become accustomed to in white men. Still, Moses ducked his head, as was proper.

"You lookin' for me, boy?"

"Yes, sir." Moses raised his eyes without bringing his head up. He didn't want this man to think him uppity. "If you're Master George Furley, that is."

"I am. Do I know you?"

"No, sir. I'm Moses, sir."

"Moses, eh?" Mister Furley smiled. "Well, what do you want, Moses? Did someone send you with a message?"

"No, sir," Moses said. He decided that wasn't quite right. "Yes, sir. Missy Hannah said she'd talked to you about me."

"About you? I don't recall… Wait. There was something about a young slave. But that was more than a year ago."

168

"Yes, sir, I know. But I was kept away from the hiring last year." Moses looked around to see if anyone was listening. "She said you might help me, if you was of a mind to."

"Yes, I recall." Mister Furley frowned and nodded, his many chins and hanging cheeks wobbling like an old hound dog's. "The Quakers took up a collection. But I doubt their offer still stands."

Moses' heart sank. "'Suppose not, sir," he mumbled, unable to think of anything else to say.

Mister Furley looked at Moses curiously. "You say you were kept away? How so?"

Moses was even more at a loss for words. He couldn't complain about Master Sawyer, a white man, to another white man.

"Come on, boy. Cat got your tongue? Tell me."

"Um, I got locked up in a shed. Sort of by-accident like."

Mister Furley laughed aloud. "An accident named Sawyer, no doubt. I'm surprised the same accident didn't happen this year."

Without meaning to, Moses smiled. The fat man looked at him quizzically, eyebrows raised. "Speaking of accidents, I hear someone made off with Sawyer's ferryboat last night. You know anything about that?"

Moses gulped. "Nawssuh, I doesn't."

Mister Furley regarded him, grinning. "I should hope not. Pirates took it, no doubt. Say, you used to work for Kemp, didn't you?"

Moses nodded.

"You know about mules, then?"

He nodded again.

"You a hard worker?"

Another nod.

To Moses' astonishment, the fat little man's arm came up and a white hand clasped his shoulder. "Young man," he said. "I'm going to hire you and put you in charge of my railroad."

Again Moses found himself tongue-tied. What on God's green earth was a railroad?

"…And Remember that I Am a Man."

"…And Remember that I Am a Man."

Chapter Twenty-two

Railroad Man—1806 A.D.

*Mister George Furley was my next master; he employed me as a
car-boy in the Dismal swamp; I had to drive lumber, &. I had plenty
to eat and plenty of clothes. I was so overjoyed at the change, that I
then thought I would not have left the place to go to heaven.*

The Life of Moses Grandy—1843 A.D.

The day after the auction, Mister Furley took Moses north by horse-
drawn wagon. The early morning was cold and drizzly, but it
couldn't dampen Moses' spirit now that he was free of Master
Sawyer. And he was eager to see this "railroad."

Mister Furley, who was single and lived at a boarding house in
town, had bought Moses new clothing: two linen shirts, two pair of
coarse hemp trousers, an overcoat, stockings, a wool hat, and boots,
which he would need for working in the swamp. It looked like
Mister Furley would be the nicest man Moses had ever worked for.
He'd paid for Moses to be fed out back of the boarding house and
arranged a bed of straw in the barn. Like Mister Kemp had once
done, he had told Moses to address him as, "mister."

Unlike most white men in the county, Mister Furley wasn't a
farmer, but a businessman. He had borrowed money from the bank
and had begun a shingling operation in the Great Dismal. From what
Moses could gather, the shingles were carried out from the swamp
on the railroad he had mentioned.

171

"...And Remember that I Am a Man."

They rode along, catching an occasional glimpse of the Pasquotank on the left, then followed a road beside a creek, which narrowed as they went along

"What's that up ahead?" he asked. "On the creek?"

"It's a barge," Mister Furley said. "We'll catch up to it soon, I imagine."

When they grew closer, Moses saw a vessel not unlike the ferry he'd worked on, but smaller. Two men poled the boat. It seemed to be empty, so they were probably going to pick up some sort of cargo.

Just then, they came to a curious contraption. Two huge wooden gates had been built across the creek, like huge, heavy, barn doors. The gates were closed, and the creek seemed to end, right then and there. On higher ground, above the gates and off to the side, sat a small shack. As the barge approached an old white man came out of the shack and began turning a windlass with ropes that led to the doors. They swung open and the barge floated in, for the level of water inside was the same as the creek. The old man swung the doors shut, hiding the barge from Moses' eyes.

"This is the South Mills lock," Mister Furley explained.

They went up a slight rise and Mister Furley stopped the wagon when they came alongside the lock. Moses looked down. The two polers sat in the motionless barge, with another set of closed doors in front of him. It was as though the boat floated at the bottom of a huge box.

Moses became aware that the water behind the second pair of doors stood a few feet higher. A boy stood on the bank, beyond those doors, holding a mule.

"Watch what happens," Mister Furley.

The old man—the lock-keeper, Mister Furley said—turned a wheel on a shaft that went down into the ground. Moses heard water rushing. There came a roiling in the water beneath the barge, which began to rise. Faster than Moses could have imagined, water lifted the heavy vessel up until it floated even with the higher water outside the second set of doors.

"How in the...?" he began.

"Watch," said Mister Furley

"…And Remember that I Am a Man."

The lock-keeper opened the second set of doors with another handwheel. The boatmen pushed, and the barge floated out of the lock. It had been raised as though light as a feather.

"There are sluice channels under the lock, beneath the gates," Mister Furley explained. "The lock-keeper opens one or the other sluice to let water in or out of the lock. The big gates are angled so the water pressure holds them closed until the levels are even."

Moses shook his head in wonder. "It's amazing."

When the boat got out away from the dock, the boatmen threw a rope to the boy with the mule. The rope was attached to the beast's harness and it began towing the boat, walking down a level path kept clear of trees and bushes along the edge of the canal, the towpath.

Mister Furley gave the lock-keeper a coin to pay the toll for driving along the towpath, then they passed the gimpy-legged boy with the mule, and went on.

The countryside changed. They had entered the swamp. Tall trees rose on their right, next to the towpath. On the other side of the canal, to the left, there was no towpath and trees grew to the edge of the canal. On this side, Moses noticed, the swamp seemed to be drying up. Cypress trees stood with their knees completely out of water and, in some places, there were no pools at all. Many of the trees seemed to by dying.

"The new Dismal Swamp Canal," Mister Furley said. "They started digging it in seventeen-ninety two and it's now open to barge traffic.

"The swamp on this side is disappearing," he continued. "Lake Drummond is in the highest land around and water flows from it to create the swamp. Now that the canal goes through, it diverts much of the water from the lake, drying out vast areas to the east. That's why I decided to set up business here; it's easier to get to the lumber."

Moses stood and swayed with the wagon, looking far ahead to see if he could see the end of the waterway. "How far's it go?"

The brown water, maybe thirty feet across, was contained by two perfectly straight banks that went on to the north as far as the eye could see. The towpath ran close beside it.

"All the way up to the Elizabeth River, nearabouts," Mister Furley answered. "You still have to use Deep Creek, up in Virginia, for a couple of miles, but that's no problem."

"How deep is it?"

"Only four feet. But that's plenty deep for barges."

"Who dug it?" Moses was sure he knew the answer, but couldn't resist confirming it.

"Slaves, of course. They got down in the muck and dug it out, putting the sludge up here on the bank to dry out. They leveled the muck and made the towpath, or road, we're on."

Moses frowned. "They got in with the snakes?"

Mister Furley glanced over and chuckled. "No, they worked mostly in the winter, when they weren't needed on the farms and plantations."

Moses' frown turned into a scowl. It was the slaves who did the work, but the white masters were paid the money. He didn't say anything, though.

He gazed at the canal as they moved along. Moses had become quite used to studying the movements of water and something didn't seem quite right. He couldn't read the currents and movement of this waterway. Other than a slight riffle on the surface from the breeze, the water was dead calm. It should be flowing south into the sound, like all the rivers and creeks.

"Which way does the water flow?" he asked.

Mister Furley laughed. "Ah, young Moses that's what makes this a canal. The water is kept in by locks, which control the water depth. There is a current, but not much of one."

Moses looked at Mister Furley to see if he was fooling. How could you lock up water? Rivers flowed and the waters of the sounds moved with the winds and the tides.

They traveled beside the canal for miles. Mister Furley surprised Moses by talking to him as if they were equals. He told Moses that he didn't believe in slavery, on principle, and owned no slaves himself. Yet economic conditions forced him to take advantage of slave labor. He couldn't run a profitable business hiring white men—most whites wouldn't work in the swamp for any price. And free blacks were scarce.

"…And Remember that I Am a Man."

"I'm only one man," Mister Furley said, "so I can't do anything to stop slavery. I do what I can to lessen the hardships of bondage for those in my employ, however. Someday, perhaps, we'll put an end to slavery. Black men will still do the heavy labor and work for less money than whites, of course, so business will go on as usual, but slavery—which is against Christian principles—will be a thing of the past."

"Why would free blacks work for less money than white folks, Mister Furley?" Moses asked. "Seems to me that work is work, no matter who does it."

"Well, Moses, it stands to reason. A white man is smarter, so he'll figure out ways to do the work better. And white people work harder, since black people seem to lack work ethics."

"What are ethics?"

Mister Furley was quiet for a moment, as though thinking, then he said, "Ethics are the standards that men conduct themselves by. Things like worshipping the Creator, honoring their debts, giving an honest day's work for their wages, that sort of thing."

When he'd been younger, Moses might have accepted such talk. He didn't argue with Mister Furley, of course, but he went silent for a bit and thought about it. Of course whites were smarter. They went to school. They learned how to read and write. They learned…

Moses realized he didn't know what else schools taught besides reading and arithmetic. But, far as "work ethics" went, why did Mister Furley think that black men wouldn't give an honest day's work? They'd work hard for their living, same as anyone; they didn't need to be whipped.

And the other thing, that free blacks would work for less money, seemed ridiculous. In Moses' entire life, he'd never been paid, other than one time when a Quaker woman had given him and Jonas and Caleb a penny apiece for taking her and her buggy across the Pasquotank. What did Mister Furley think free blacks would work for, food and a crude place to sleep, same as slaves?

It was clear, even though he opposed slavery, Mister Furley didn't think blacks were near as good as whites. And if blacks were forced to work for less than whites, wasn't that as bad as slavery?

After a couple of hours, Mister Furley and Moses came to piles of wooden shingles lying in a cleared area beside the towpath, where they could be loaded onto a barge. Moses noticed a mule-drawn wagon on the other side of the pile. A short, wiry black man was unloading shingles and putting them on the stacks. He stopped when he saw Mister Furley and walked to meet the wagon.

"Howdy, Missah Furley," he said. "I's glad to see you's come back to see me again."

Mister Furley stopped the wagon and jumped down. To Moses surprise, he took the black man's hand and shook it.

"Hello, Jim," he said. "You'll be doubly glad to see me when you find out that young Moses here has come to take over the railroad."

"That's a fact?" Jim looked up at Moses with a wide grin on his face. "You's welcome, Moses, climb on down here and meet ol' Jim."

"Hello, Jim." Moses got off the wagon and Jim took his hand pumping it up and down.

"Jim's been running the railroad up to now," Mister Furley said. "But he doesn't get along with Willie."

"Who's Willie?"

"Come along and I'll introduce you." Mister Furley led the two black men around the shingles and stopped in front of the mule hooked to the wagon. "Moses, this is Willie. You'll be taking care of him."

"Meanest ol' cuss of a mule in the Carolinees," said Jim.

The mule brayed, showing broad front teeth as if confirming how mean he was.

Moses stepped forward and patted the animal's neck. "Hello, Willie."

Willie's eyes went wide and his ears flew up in surprise at the unexpected familiarity. By the time he recovered and turned his head to snap, Moses' arm was gone.

"You'll have to do better than that, Willie," Moses said. "You're about to learn some new habits."

Mister Furley laughed. "That's the thing, Moses. Willie has had Jim cowed ever since we bought him."

For a second, Moses thought he meant since buying Jim, but remembered that Mister Furley didn't own slaves, so he meant Willie.

"That mule done kicked me more times than I can 'member," Jim said.

"So what do you think of the railroad, Moses?" Mister Furley gestured toward the mule, the wagon and the swamp behind them.

Moses had been so taken with Willie that he hadn't glanced at his surroundings. He stepped back from the mule and took a look.

The wagon stood on a platform of planks lying atop the muck, set crosswise to the wheels. Nailed on top of the planks, running the other way, were two wooden rails, set inside the wagon wheels. Behind the wagon, the planks and rails ran into the swamp, forming a crude roadbed.

Mister Furley said, "I hired slaves to lay cross-ties down in the bog, sometimes several layers, until they would support the weight of a wagon. Then they put down continuous rails along them. The wagon is kept on the road by the rails, so there's no danger of the wheels slipping off into the bog. Now the crew is cutting the shingles at the other end of the line, where there's a camp. As they cut down more cypress, they just make the railroad longer and move the camp. What do you think?"

"How do you turn the wagon around to go the other way?" he asked. "You'd have to lift it off the rails."

"Look at the back of the wagon."

Moses walked around and looked. The other end of the wagon was outfitted exactly the same as the one Willie pulled. A man could unhitch the harness from one end and move the mule to the other.

"Don't that beat all?" he said. "So this is a railroad."

*

Months later, Moses traveled along the railroad, enjoying the walk. The weather had begun toying with Camden County like a fuzzy kitten growing into a sharp-clawed tomcat, days of warm sun interspersed with bouts of cold winds and frost. The leaves were nearly gone from the trees. Winter was almost upon the swamp. Today, however, the sun beamed down.

When he'd been a child, the Great Dismal Swamp had been a scary place, full of suspected alligators, snakes and bears. Now he knew it was too far north for alligators. As for bears, he'd seen plenty of them, and they seemed harmless enough if you stayed clear. He'd been told they wouldn't mess with a person unless their cubs were threatened.

That left the snakes.

Water moccasins, rattlesnakes and copperheads often sunned themselves atop the rails when the weather was warm enough, but they didn't bother with him unless he came close. They were easy to spot and shoo away with the walking stick he carried for that purpose and, besides, his ankles and shins were covered by his leather boots. But the sight of a snake still gave Moses the shivers.

Moses' job was to move a load of shingles to the canal, unload, and go back again, empty except for the times he carried the weekly food delivery. For each slave's monthly ration, Mister Furley sent a quarter bushel of corn, a quarter bushel of beets, turnips, black-eyed peas, or other long-lasting vegetables, a little molasses and ten pounds of pork or fish—usually salt-herring. And a dozen apples.

The thought of food reminded Moses that he needed to get a move on. This was the last run of the day and he was getting mighty hungry.

"Come on, Willie, shake a leg," he said, stepping out smartly. Willie, walking behind, picked up the pace. No doubt he was as eager for dinner as the young man was. They walked with a carefree rhythm. Both boy and beast had long ago adjusted their strides to come down on the evenly-spaced railroad ties.

They'd also adjusted to each other. Moses had gentled the mule, which had probably been poorly treated in the past. Now Willie always greeted the boy with a friendly hee-haw in the morning. Moses thought a lot of Willie. He could talk to the mule all day and Willie never uttered a word of criticism or bad advice.

Mister Furley's lumbering operation was a small business. The railroad wouldn't support heavy loads of logs with the teams of oxen or mules needed to pull such burdens. On the other, western side of the canal, ditches were dug to transport the logs but, as Mister Furley had mentioned, this side of the canal was drying out. So he had come up with the railroad, as he called it.

Moses whistled as he walked toward the camp he called home. He didn't know what heaven was like, but this was the closest he'd gotten yet. If Moses didn't have his heart set on operating a ferry, he might have considered running a railroad when he got free. Not only did Mister Furley feed and clothe his hired slaves, he gave them an entire day off on the Sabbath, and he allowed them to travel on that day, if they wished. Moses had visited his mother for the first time in years.

Best of all, Mister Furley had promised to buy Moses' labor every year, until his real master came of age. Moses still wasn't free, but not having to fear a cruel master again was the next best thing. If it weren't for Mister Furley, he'd be back at Sawyer's Ferry, scratching for food, along with Jonas and Caleb. And Naomi.

Moses had gone visiting back at Sawyer's Ferry, and she'd changed her attitude toward him now that he wasn't around her all the time. They would sit on the dock and talk for hours. Last time she'd kissed him when he'd left. Maybe next time…

A girl's voice came from the swamp, surprising him.

"Hey, you there."

He turned. A black girl of about twelve plodded toward him, pulling a small boy along. She wore a dress of hemp, which some called Negro cloth, and a light jacket. A scarf was tied around her head. Her legs were covered with mud and Moses knew they must be cold.

The boy looked to be four or five years old. Dressed better than the girl, he wore an overcoat and what looked to be wool trousers beneath the mud that spattered them.

"Hey," Moses shouted back. He brought the mule to a halt and waited for the two to reach him.

They soon stepped up onto the railroad and the girl stuck out her hand. "I'm Ruth."

She was a skinny, hatchet-faced girl with one eye that focused on Moses and a milky eye that looked off to the side somewhere. She had a nice smile, though.

Moses took her hand and shook it. "Moses."

Ruth pulled the boy forward. "And this here's my brother, Nat."

Like his sister, Nat held out his hand. "I'm Nat Turner," he said, with a dignified nod of his head. Unlike most slave children, his face was chubby. Nat's gaze unsettled Moses a bit, for it had an air of authority reserved for white men—or boys too little to know their place in the world, maybe.

179

"…And Remember that I Am a Man."

"Nat!" Ruth chided. "Your name isn't Turner. That's Master's name."

Moses shook Nat's hand. "How do you do?"

"We're from the Turner Farm up in Southampton County, Virginia."

"Where's that?" Moses knew that Virginia was the next state to the north, but he'd never heard of that particular county.

"Other side of the swamp." Ruth pointed in the direction they'd come from.

Moses' jaw dropped. "You walked through the swamp? By yourselves?"

"Sure," Ruth said. "It's not all that hard. Besides…" She reached out and cuffed Nat's arm playfully. "Nat said it wouldn't be hard to do."

"How in the world would he know that?"

"Easy," said Ruth, "He's a prophet."

Now Moses might not be the smartest pig in the sty, but he knew what a prophet was. Moses, his namesake, had been one. But how could a little child be a prophet?

"He's pretty young," Moses said.

"Nat's special," Ruth answered. "He was borned with special marks on his head and, as soon as he learned how to talk, he knowed things what happened before he had even been borned."

Again, it seemed to make no sense. "But prophets predict the future. How does knowing the past make a little boy a prophet?"

Nat puffed out his chest. "Don't call me a 'little boy.' And I am so a prophet. I know how to read, do you?"

Ruth slapped her little brother's face. "Shut up, you ninny. You want to get in real trouble?"

Nat looked about to cry, but Ruth ignored him. She returned her attention to Moses. Her face took on the expression of a begging puppy, but it wasn't appealing with a cloudy, wandering eye.

"You think you could help us?" she asked.

"Help you how?"

Ruth gestured toward the surrounding swamp. "We seen white men on horses a little while back. They was wearing badges. Could be they're after us."

"Why would they be after you?"

180

"Don't know," said Ruth. "Maybe they think we know where our big brother Sam's at. He runned away a couple months ago and he's prob'ly in the swamp."

"Is he a maroon?"

"Don't know. Jus' know he sassed a white man and runned away from a whippin."

Moses looked all around, but saw no one. "I'll try to help," he said. "What can I do?"

"Where you goin'?" Ruth asked.

He nodded down the line. "Lumber camp. I work there."

"Can we go with you? Then if the white men see us, they'll think we belong there, I reckon."

"Sure," said Moses. As they went along, Nat asked dozens of questions about the railroad. But he tired quickly, so Moses lifted him up into the wagon, where he fell asleep. He and Ruth walked along with Willie, watching for white men on horses.

Moses asked about Nat's claim that he could read.

One of Master Turner's sons, Adam, was teaching Nat how to read, she told him. Adam didn't get along with his father, and teaching Nat was a way to get back at him. She asked Moses not to tell because, even though it had been Adam's idea, Nat would be the one punished for his knowledge.

Moses promised.

They walked in silence for a bit, then Ruth said, "I wish Sam had done hit that white man upside the head. I wish he'd killed him."

Moses gulped and looked around. If there were white men nearby, she shouldn't talk so. "Why would you say somethin' like that?"

"Why not?" Ruth ran ahead and kicked a fallen branch off the road, then waited until Moses and the mule caught up. "My mama say all white men be devils. Slavers took her and her mama when Mama was a little-bitty thing, and they both 'bout died in the slaver ship what brought them here. She say we should kill the white devils."

Moses didn't speak. He'd never thought about killing white folks. His mama had told him that killing was against the teachings of Jesus. So had Missy Hannah. But Jesus allowed the whipping, beating and lynchings of blacks, didn't he? So why should a black man follow a white God's rules?

"Nat done had a dream," continued Ruth. "He say all the slaves gonna rise up and slay the white devils in the name of The Lord. An' he gonna be the one to lead us."

Killing in the name of The Lord? Preachers must be preaching a different religion up there in Virginia. Nervousness clutched at Moses' innards with this talk of cold-blooded murder.

"How far north do you figure Virginia is?" he asked. Again he glanced around. Would he get in trouble for helping Ruth and Nat if the white men came?

He kept the conversation on safe subjects until they reached the hummock where the camp stood. The day was drawing to an end and there should have been the bustle of cooking about this time. But the camp was quiet. Something wasn't right.

He brought Willie to a halt and walked toward the large swamper shack where the slaves cooked, followed by a nervous Ruth.

"Hello?" he called when they got close. No one answered. The camp seemed deserted, but then a white man stepped from behind the shack, holding a musket. He wore a badge.

Ruth bolted into the swamp. The white man watched her go, apparently unconcerned.

"Don't try to run, boy," he said. "You're Moses, ain't you?"

Moses nodded, trying to control his urge to run after Ruth. But he'd done nothing wrong, so he was sure things would be all right.

"You're the last of Furley's niggers," the man said. "I'm taking y'all into town."

"But why?" Moses managed to ask. A motion caught his eye. He turned and saw little Nat run for the marsh.

The man brought out a pair of manacles he'd been hiding behind his back and stepped forward.

"Furley couldn't pay back some money he borrowed. So the bank's going to hire you out to somebody else."

Moses' jaw dropped. "They can't do that."

The man grabbed Moses' arm and jerked him around. "They can and they will. I was told to confiscate every bit of Furley's stuff I could lay hands on. That includes you and that miserable mule over there."

"…And Remember that I Am a Man."

Chapter Twenty-three
The Overseer—1806 A.D.

*Indeed Mr. Boylan was regarded as a very kind master to all the
slaves about him, that is, to his house servants, nor did he
personally inflict much cruelty. The overseer on his nearest
plantation (I know but little about the rest) was a very cruel man; in
one instance, as it was said among the slaves, he whipped a man to
death; but of course denied that the man died in consequence of the
whipping.*

The Narrative of Lunsford Lane—1842 A.D.

Moses had wrapped some scraps of cloth around his hands for
protection; they were still too soft to wield a hoe all day long. He'd
been here, at the Micheau tobacco farm, for two weeks now, and his
hands were not entirely healed from the blistering of his first day.
Today the sun stayed behind thick clouds, so at least he wasn't being
roasted.

Dozens of other slaves, both men and women, worked nearby,
each hoeing a different row. It wasn't hard work, lifting the hoe and
chopping the weeds' roots from the ground. It became backbreaking
labor though, when you were forced to keep up a good pace for hour
after hour. Children moved along with the adults, picking bugs off
the leaves and crushing them in their fingers. The white overseer,
Wiley McPherson, watched hawk-like from the shade at the edge of
the field. He liked nothing better than to walk out and lay into a

black back with the riding crop he carried. Since Moses was working in the first row, closest to the overseer, he was nervous.

McPherson, a skinny tobacco-chewer who the slaves called Master even though he owned none of them, scared the begeesus out of Moses. Four days ago, the overseer had come to the slave quarters in the morning and dragged out a man named Old Banjo. McPherson had accused Old Banjo of not completing some assigned task, and tied the gray-haired black man to a post. He pulled Old Banjo's shirt up, exposing a gaunt belly, ribs barely covered by flesh and a back full of scars from previous whippings. McPherson covered the old man's eyes by tying the shirt over his head, and flogged him hard, as the other slaves watched from where they hid in their quarters.

At the end of the whipping, the punishment wasn't over yet. Old Banjo was left tied to the post, his feet barely touching the ground. Yellow flies, mosquitoes, and blowflies in great numbers swarmed to the exposed flesh, biting and sucking. By the time the other slaves had cut him down that evening, Old Banjo had passed out. He had been unable to rise out of bed for three days. Today was his first day back at work, and he was having trouble keeping up.

In being taken from Mister Furley's railroad to this godforsaken tobacco field, Moses had traveled from Heaven to Hell.

As at Sawyer's Ferry, the slaves got little to eat. Since they worked from dawn to dusk, they couldn't keep gardens, and had to get by on the meager food McPherson doled out. Moses was lucky; he was still living on the fat he'd built up while working on the railroad. But the others were boney and weak.

"How are they doing, Mac?"

Moses glanced in the direction of the voice. A man had ridden up, hoof steps hidden by the continual thudding of hoes. It was Master Micheau, who Moses hadn't seen since he'd come to work here. Moses knew the man, though, because Master Micheau had recently married the older sister of James Grandy, his true master. Prior to being hired out to work on his place, Moses had heard that Master Micheau was not that bad to work for. Now he knew better.

Astride a chestnut mare, Master Micheau was a tall, slender, well-dressed man, with long, wavy black hair down to the collar. He wore a full, neatly trimmed beard.

184

"…And Remember that I Am a Man."

Moses kept working, but watched from the corner of his eye and listened closely. McPherson walked over and leaned with one hand against the horse's flank. He wiped his brow with a bandana, as though he'd been working hard enough to sweat.

"They ain't worth a plug of tobaccy, as you well know, Mr. Micheau." He spat out a stream of tobacco juice to help make his point. "Laziest bunch o' niggers I've ever worked."

Master Micheau looked around at his workers, then at the vast fields around them. His eyes narrowed and Moses guessed he must be figuring how far short they'd fall of getting the weeding done on time. "Just a piss-water bunch of workers, eh?" he finally said.

McPherson snorted. "You got that right."

"Do I?" Master Micheau asked, a sudden edge in his voice. "When I hired you this spring, you made a lot of promises about how good you were at getting work out of slaves."

The overseer stepped back two paces and looked up. "I know how to work niggers. Problem is this batch is lazy. I guess I'll just have to whip them a bit more; that'll put fire in their pants."

"You know I don't want a lot of whipping going on, McPherson. Save the whip for when they're causing problems."

"Whatever you say, boss," McPherson said. "But they move like snails. I had to light into one of them last week for not finishing his work."

Moses could hardly believe what he was hearing. Master Micheau didn't want whipping? McPherson had only been hired this year? Less work was being done?"

"Massah," he said.

Master Micheau turned his eyes on Moses, startled. He looked puzzled. "Aren't you Moses? My wife's brother's slave?"

Moses nodded.

Master Micheau turned back to McPherson. "What's this boy doing here, McPherson? He wasn't in the crew I hired this year."

"Well, boss," McPherson said, bobbing his head up and down. His eyes darted sideways toward Moses. "There was a couple of slaves laid up, and I needed another man to make up for that. This one come available, so I hired him."

"Without asking me?" Master Micheau sounded angry.

"I figgered you was too busy to be bothered with such claptrap."

"Claptrap? Why were those slaves laid up? Were they whipped?"

McPherson slapped his leg with the riding crop. He seemed to be getting annoyed. "They needed to be taught a lesson."

Master Micheau's lips set into a tight line. He looked around at the slaves, standing idle and listening. "We'll discuss this in my office tonight."

He turned his attention to Moses. "You wanted to say something?"

Moses gulped, hoping he'd interpreted the relationship between the master and his overseer correctly. If not, he could be in big trouble. He took a moment and decided not to use the submissive "slave" voice he often affected. *Help me, Jesus,* he thought.

"Master Micheau, these folks are too weak to keep up with the work. They're nigh onto starving to death."

The white man's face clouded. He swung down from his horse and stalked over to confront Moses, leading the horse.

"Are you saying I don't treat my slaves in a Christian manner?"

Moses took a deep breath. "I didn't say that. All I'm saying is they need food if they're to be worked so hard."

The master set his jaw and glared at Moses. Behind Master Micheau, Moses could see McPherson gripping his riding crop with white knuckles.

"You look healthy enough to me," Master Micheau said.

"I just got here, Master."

Master Micheau said nothing for a moment, then turned and looked around at his workers. "They do look pretty bony, at that." He summoned the nearest slave, who happened to be Old Banjo. The gray-haired man shuffled over, head bowed.

"Turn around," Master Micheau commanded. Old Banjo turned. His pants hung low, so his jutting hip bones showed also.

The signs of a recent whipping were clear. Pus-leaking ribbons of fresh injuries stood out from a criss-cross pattern of scars long-ago healed.

"That's enough. Turn back around."

Old Banjo shuffled round, keeping his gaze on the ground.

"How long were you laid up because of being whipped?"

The old slave finally raised his face and looked at the master with rheumy eyes clouded by cataracts. "T'ree days, Massuh."

186

"What have you been eating since you got here at the beginning of the year?"

"Jus' beans and corn meal."

"No meat? No fish?"

"No, suh."

"What did you get whipped for?" Master Micheau asked.

Old Banjo gave a puzzled look. "I don't rightly knows, Massuh. De boss say I not workin' fas' enough."

Master's face went red. He whirled.

"Get off my property, McPherson," he snarled. "I gave you plenty of money to provision these slaves, which means you've been stealing from me, as well as whipping old men against my orders."

McPherson glared back, not giving an inch. Then he spat. He gave Moses a venomous glance, turned and walked away through the field. Moses knew he'd made a life-long enemy, but he didn't care much, elated his gamble had paid off.

They all watched until the man passed out of sight, then Master Micheau addressed the slaves. "You all go back to quarters and rest. I'll have the cook fix a hot meal, right away. And there'll be a new overseer in a few days."

He looked at Moses, started to speak, and then thought better of it. He mounted his horse and rode away.

The entire slave population crowded around Moses, patting his shoulder and thanking him. Several women hugged him and one pretty girl kissed him full on the lips. Tears filled the eyes of many. When they finally began walking back to quarters, they sang a joyful hymn. As promised, they were fed well that evening.

Next morning, the slaves went to the field and picked the hoes they had thrown down in their jubilation at the sacking of McPherson. They began weeding with a purpose, to show the master their gratitude. Everyone had a kind word to say to Moses.

At noon, food again arrived for them. Mister Micheau came along. He informed the slaves that their food would be prepared for them now, so that they wouldn't be cheated again.

From then on, the slaves got enough to eat. The other conditions didn't change much, except that whippings weren't crippling affairs. The new overseer, Mister Davis, wasn't needlessly cruel like McPherson had been, but he wasn't kind either.

187

"…And Remember that I Am a Man."

The way Mister Davis worked it, the field hands worked in a line. He put the fastest workers on both edges and required the other slaves to keep up with them. To be sure, he put a man behind the line, a different slave each day, carrying a large paddle with holes in it. From his vantage point atop the horse, Davis would direct this man to use the paddle on any man or woman falling behind.

Moses was never assigned this duty, probably because of his youth, and he was glad. He'd rather take a whipping than give one. Not that he ever fell behind. The hard work and decent meals soon gave him a man's body and muscles.

When winter came and the crops were done for the year, things became a little easier for the workers. The backbreaking labor of the fields was done, and they were assigned easier tasks. Days ran shorter now, and they weren't exhausted every night. They would sing spiritual songs and sometimes Atticus, an old man with an even older fiddle, would play a lively tune and dancing commenced. Moses was very popular and never lacked for a dancing partner. He couldn't stop thinking of Naomi, though. He'd have waded through a bog full of water snakes for a chance to see her face.

On the Sabbath, they would gather in a nearby grove. For the first time in years, Moses felt like part of a family. The slaves had no formal preacher, but did not lack for spiritual leaders. Men and women would stand up and reaffirm their faith in God. The hymns the group sang yearned for freedom, whether in this mortal life or beyond.

When hiring-out day came again, Moses was surprised to see Mister Furley in the crowd, along with a man who looked to be his brother. This man bid on Moses when he came on the block, but Mister Micheau kept raising the price until Mister Furley's brother gave up.

"…And Remember that I Am a Man."

Chapter Twenty-four

Gambling Game—1807 A.D.

A voice within whispered me to fly. To be a wanderer among the swamps, a fugitive and a vagabond on the face of the earth, was preferable to the life that I was leading.

Twelve Years a Slave, Narrative of Solomon Northup, a Citizen of New-York, Kidnapped in Washington City in 1841, and Rescued in 1853—1853 A.D.

Atticus, the fiddler, came out into the fields one day in the fall, which was rare since he worked in the house. He sought out Mister Davis and talked to him. The overseer approached Moses.

"Master wants to talk to you."

Fear struck deep into Moses' innards. Had he done something wrong?

"What about?"

Mister Davis shrugged. "How would I know? Shake a leg, boy, get yourself up to the house."

Moses ran to fetch his shirt, which he'd set aside while he worked. The coarse cloth stuck to his sweaty skin as he pulled the tight garment on. It was too small for him. Moses had grown broad of shoulder and deep of chest.

He ran and caught up to Atticus, who was heading for the house. "What does the master want with me?"

"...And Remember that I Am a Man."

Atticus smiled as Moses fell in step. "I think he needs a new houseboy."

"Me?"

"Looks that way."

Moses knew that Atticus had smiled because being a house servant was considered a soft job. Moses wasn't sure he wanted that position, however. He'd be working around white folks all day and he wasn't used to that.

"Why you walkin' so slow, boy?" Atticus asked. "Don't keep the man waiting. Go on ahead of me."

Moses picked up his pace.

"And when you get there," said Atticus. "Don't knock on the door or make any loud noises. Master got into the corn likker last night, and he's peevish. Just scratch on the door."

Moses set off and soon got to the house. He scratched at the door. One of the cleaning girls, a pretty girl named Junie, who he'd danced with on several occasions, let him in with a smile.

"I hear you're goin' to be working here," she said.

"Don't know about that," Moses said. "Where's Master Micheau?"

"He's in the library, down that hall, second door on the left" Junie said. "Just go stand in the doorway. He'll call you in." She winked. "It'll be real nice to have you working in the house with me."

"Uh, yeah."

Moses made his way the master's library and stood in the open doorway. The white man glanced up with puffy eyes. He put the paper in the top desk drawer and then said, "Come in, Moses."

Moses shuffled in, head down, wishing he could go back to the field.

"As you know, Calvin died last week," Master Micheau said.

A silence followed and Moses realized he was supposed to respond. He nodded. "Yes, sir." Calvin, a frail old codger, had keeled over at Sunday's service while doing some strenuous praising of The Lord.

"I need someone to take over his duties. My wife suggested you, since she remembers you used to be a playmate for her young brother."

190

Moses realized he was acting like a scared turtle and raised his head. "Yes, sir."

"Calvin acted as my butler. Do you know what a butler is?"

Moses shook his head.

"He answers the door, takes the coats of guests, waits on table and the like. I need someone who's bright and can speak fairly well. Do you think you can do that?"

Again Moses shook his head. "No, sir. I don't know how to do any of that." He felt like saying he didn't want to be a butler, but knew better.

"Nonsense. You go see Auntie Rachel. She'll fit you out with a new set of clothing. I'm having a few of my good fellows over for cards next week and I don't want you looking like a ragamuffin."

And that was how Moses ended up on a stool in the corner several days later, yawning as he waited for any of a crowd of gambling men to call on him for service. He fetched drinks, lit cigars, helped Junie bring food from the kitchen, cleared off dirty plates, or anything else anyone told him to do.

He felt like a fool, wearing fawn-colored, tight knee breeches with white, knee-length stockings and uncomfortable shoes with buckles. His shirt was white, with long, billowy sleeves and cuffs. A red waistcoat finished the outfit, two rows of buttons down the front.

He had seen a few of the players at hiring-out auctions over the years. They were a rough bunch, rowdy and crude. Some of the men pawed at Junie as she served them, groping her in places no gentleman should touch. One of the men was Enoch Sawyer. Although Moses had worked for the man three years, Master Sawyer didn't seem to recognize his former ferryman.

The men played a card game called Whist. Moses had no idea of the rules or how the game was scored, but there was a lot of betting going on. And a lot of drinking.

Auntie Rachel had taught Moses how to act as a butler. He knew how to set a table, what side to serve a person from, and what to say when answering the door. And now the lady of the house had gone visiting relatives, which gave the master of the house an opportunity to gamble.

The games had been going on for four days and Moses had hardly slept at all, occasionally dozing on the stool, propped against the wall. He could only leave the corner when the men took an occasional break from card playing. He would dash to the kitchen for food or outdoors to relieve himself, but there wasn't time to take a nap.

Mister Micheau had won at cards for the first two days and had been jovial, laughing and slapping the backs of his fellows as he told lewd jokes. But then the cards had turned against him. As he lost more and more money, he grew sullen and only left the table when others insisted on a breather, a term which seemed fitting to Moses because of the haze of tobacco smoke in the room. The master drank more, too. As the hours wore on, he changed from a jolly man into a red-eyed demon. His language went from lewd to vulgar; he cursed at every losing hand.

Moses wished he knew about card games. If he understood the rules, maybe he could at least take an interest in the play to stave off boredom. As it was, the constant buzz of conversation in the warm room, and the stale air made him sleepy.

To occupy his mind, he set his imagination to work, as he often did. He thought about how he'd one day be free, by whatever means, and the ferry he'd operate. Naomi would be there too, of course, and they'd...

"Wake up, boy!"

Moses awakened to the sight of Master Micheau, his face not a foot away. His blood-shot eyes had large bags beneath them, his normally well-groomed hair and beard were in tangles, and his foul breath reeked of tobacco and liquor. He was furious.

"I'm sorry, Master," Moses said, but the drunkard's bull voice drowned him out.

"Did I say you could go to sleep, you bastard?" The white man roared.

Again, Moses tried to speak, but was over-ridden.

"When I call, you answer, God damn you. Do you understand me, you stupid nigger?"

The master's face grew redder by the second and fear gripped Moses. He'd never seen Mister Micheau upset before.

"Yawwah, Massa," Moses said with a squeaky voice. "I unnerstands."

"No, you don't," Master Micheau screamed. "You need to be taught a lesson."

He jerked away from Moses and took two long strides to the fire place. His hand went out to pick up something and Moses prayed it wouldn't be the poker.

Master Micheau grabbed the shovel and turned back. Moses could only watch him come. He shrunk down in fright. Even if he could somehow get by the man, there was no place to go.

"Give 'im what for, John," cried someone from a nearby card table.

"I'll show you, you stupid piece of shit." Master Micheau raised the shovel.

Without thinking, Moses threw his left arm up to block the shovel coming at his head. The handle of the iron implement slammed into his wrist and pain filled his arm. He brought the injured limb down and cradled his wrist with his other hand as Master Micheau prepared for another swing. Moses could do nothing but crouch down and hope he'd live through this.

He saw the blow coming and managed to duck enough that the blade came down flat on his left shoulder. His whole arm went numb. It was like being kicked by a mule. But this mule would kick more than once.

The next blow came down on the back of his head and the shovel rang like a bell. It knocked him to his knees. He crouched on the floor and hunched his back, trying to keep his head from being struck again.

The skull-ringing had addled his brain and everything seemed to slow down. The master's curses seemed long and drawn out, his breath rasped and he grunted like a boar. Moses heard laughter, as though from far off and realized it was coming from the other gamblers, still sitting at the tables. They were enjoying the show. Some of the men called out encouragement to Moses' attacker.

Moses couldn't raise his eyes to see when the next blows would come, but come they did. The enraged master didn't seem to be trying to hit any specific targets in his drunken state, merely swinging. Mostly they landed on Moses back and buttocks.

A loud clang sounded. The shovel blade had broken off the handle and fallen to the floor beside him. The blows stopped and the laughter died out. The only sound was Master Micheau, gasping for breath.

Moses looked up. The man still held the shovel handle in his hand, but it hung by his side. He stared at the wall as if he had forgotten what he was doing and was trying to remember.

Knowing that Master Micheau might come out of his drunken stupor at any moment, Moses scrabbled on his knees and one good arm. He got a couple of yards away, then stood and staggered into the kitchen.

The black cook stared with wide eyes and a horrified expression as he passed by her and ran out the back door, into darkness and heavy rain. He went straight to his shack in the slave quarter, stripped off the fancy clothing and changed into his old stuff. He grabbed his few possessions, and then began walking northwest, toward the swamp. He'd had enough of being a slave.

"…And Remember that I Am a Man."

Chapter Twenty-five

On the Run—1807 A.D.

"Notice! $500 Reward! Ran away from the subscriber, on the night of June 18th, my Negro man, Simon. He had on, when last seen, a pair of light pants, with a black patch on the seat of the same. He is slue-footed, knock-kneed, and bends over a little when walking. He may be making his way to the Dismal Swamp. I will pay the above reward for his apprehension, or his lodgment in some jail, so that I can get him again.

"JOE JONES."

Early Recollections of the Great Dismal Swamp and Lake Drummond, Robert Arnold—Entered according to act of Congress in the year 1888, by R. Arnold, in the office of the Librarian of Congress at Washington

Moses crossed the road and set out into the woods. Micheau might have men out looking for him already. A couple of hours later, he wondered if he might have entered the swamp without knowing it; it was impossible to know if he was walking through puddles or was crossing a true bog.

Frogs chirped, tweeted, roared, honked and bellowed all around him. The rain and the darkness were their friends. Moses had no friends. Every time something splashed, he flinched. When he did, pain shot through him. His back ached, his shoulder was out of joint and his wrist swollen, sprained or broken. Even his old belly injury twinged as he moved.

When morning came, he was no better off, except that it became warmer and he could tell he was within the Great Dismal Swamp. Now that he'd be able to see snakes before stepping on them, he found a stout stick to protect himself, and went on. He tried to stay to higher ground, but water covered nearly everything. There was no way to know, by looking, whether the dirty brown water might be three inches or three feet deep. Soon the rain stopped and he lost all sense of direction. The sun stayed behind heavy clouds. He tried to find north by checking the moss on trees, but that was no good in the swamp. The thick canopy of leaves overhead kept the swamp in never-ending shadow, so moss grew everywhere. Where there wasn't moss, fungus grew instead.

He sometimes drank when he crossed the deeper pools, remembering how Mama had said the brown water was good for folks. She'd been right. The well-water at the farms tasted bitter and ditch water was foul. Swamp water was sweet-tasting.

The sun appeared, but stood high in the sky and did nothing to help him keep on course. And with the sun, out came the snakes. Long, thick blacksnakes. Fat, stubby water-moccasins. Lean, deadly rattlesnakes. Little, striped garter snakes. Pencil-thin green snakes. Every kind of snake Moses had ever seen and a few he hadn't. And this time he didn't have a railroad to walk on. He shared the swamp with dangerous creatures.

There was nothing to do but to forge on. At least these snakes weren't looking for trouble. They weren't as dangerous as the snakes behind him.

A stand of pawpaw trees provided him with breakfast. He ate several of the brown, ripe, overly sweet fruit, each half the size of a man's fist. They were soft and sweet.

As the day went on, glimpses of the sun through the leaves told him which way the sun was moving. With his sense of direction restored, he put himself back on a northerly route. Most of the time, he walked in water to his knees.

Moses had long been told that the Great Dismal was vast. It would take days to get across. He hoped to find an encampment of maroons, who might help him on his way, but he couldn't count on that. He had no plan, other than to find a Quaker community up in Virginia. They might be able to get him farther north.

The sun sank lower and he began to worry. He was tired and bone-sore. If he didn't find some high ground to sleep on, he'd be walking all night.

Before dark, he came to a railroad. His railroad. He wasn't even in the main part of the swamp yet. Of course! He would have to cross the canal to get into the true swamp.

He'd walked this line so many times; he knew every plank and nail. Since he was coming from the south, he knew to turn right and follow the rails. He could sleep in the old lumbering camp, maybe even have a roof over his head.

When he got near, he slowed and crept forward, listening. Somebody else might be running the operation now, and there could be a crew at the camp. He heard nothing, however, and found the place deserted.

Moses wished for some food, since he'd had nothing since the pawpaws. He cursed himself for not bringing some along, but the need for sleep proved much stronger than hunger, after the days and nights of serving the gamblers. He went to the same swamper shack where he'd lived while working on the railroad, and crawled to a back corner.

He awoke in the afternoon, having slept for nearly twenty-four hours. Or maybe two days, but he doubted it. The gnawing hunger in his belly would not have allowed him to stay asleep for so long.

Stirring, Moses touched a slick meaty mass by his legs and glanced down. A snake! He drew up his feet quick as a bullfrog can jump, and scrambled out of the shelter. It was another cold, damp day and the water moccasin had been tucked up against his legs for the heat. It took him a couple of minutes before the hammering of his heart died down. He'd have run farther away from the shack, but had no idea which way to go.

The whites weren't dumb; they'd look for him in the places he was familiar with. The lumber camp was dangerous, as was the Kemp Farm, the Grandy Farm and Sawyer's ferry. He needed to get far away—fast.

Where to go? He knew that Virginia lay on the other side of the Great Dismal, but how big was Virginia? How many days, traveling at night, would it take him to get across that state and into the north? What was the state on the other side of Virginia? He had no idea. A vague plan formed in his mind. Ruth, the Virginia girl he had once met, had said that many Quakers lived on the northwest side of the swamp. He would find a community of Friends, and throw himself on their mercy.

He'd heard that Quakers would pass slaves along to more northerly brothers and sisters of the same faith. With their aid, Moses might be able to make his way to freedom. Sort of like rails keeping a mule and wagon on course, a fugitive slave might be able to stay safe if he or she kept on a narrow track of friendship.

It was late in the day, however. Rather than trying to get through the swamp in the dark, he'd have to spend another night in the Furley lumbering camp. He foraged in the nearby wilderness, having a good idea where to find pawpaws, blackberries and the like. His shoulder and arm had swelled and now throbbed with every movement, so he made a sling from his spare shirt. One-handed, he ate all the ripe fruit he found, but it wasn't enough.

He slept in the shack again, after making sure the snake had left. With spare lumber that had been set aside to repair the railroad, he made a crude platform to sleep on, out of the reach of reptiles. The following morning, he went to the other end of the railroad. After looking both ways along the tow path, he ran across it and then waded the canal. In the undrained, wetter part of the swamp now, he set out north for the Promised Land.

Moses prayed as he walked, asking God for strength to carry himself to freedom. No longer could he bear living in a place where mothers could be whipped in front of their children, where white men could starve, abuse, beat, and even kill their slaves as they willed. How could God allow such things to happen? White men went to church, same as blacks worshipped in the groves. Were they praying to the same God?

Early that evening, he came to Lake Drummond, the source of all water in the swamp. The sun had stayed behind clouds for all of his time in the swamp, but the air was clear. Near where he stood, baldcypress trees grew out of the lake, sucking up water through their gnarled, spider-like roots and reaching toward the sky. Far off, he could see similar trees on the other side. There was no beach.

Vegetation grew right to the water and some types of plants grew in the lake itself.

Although Moses had been told that the lake never grew deeper than six feet or so, he didn't dare try to wade across. At Moses' height of five-foot-six, a misstep would drown him as surely as if he risked a bottomless sea. He turned left and skirted the western shore.

Moses had found nothing else to eat. Fish lived in the lake, he knew, but he had no string or hook. His wrist throbbed mercilessly and he felt dizzy with fever. He found a dry hummock and fell asleep with his back to a tree.

That night, beside the lake, he dreamed. In his dream, the tides and rivers turned red as blood flowing from the backs of whipped slaves. The herring, menhaden and other fish floated up, dead. The snakes didn't die, though; water moccasins came out of the swamps and bogs, slithering into the houses, barns and stores of the whites.

After that, mosquitoes rose in clouds from the swamps. Since the slaves knew the secret of rubbing pawpaw leaves on the skin, only the whites were affected. Then came yellow flies, and these also ignored the slaves, going after the animals of the masters, instead.

Diseases spread among the livestock. The animals' hides became putrid with sores and boils, and they died by the score.

While all this was still going on, a great hurricane roared in off the ocean, flooding croplands and pastures. When the waters receded, pests invaded the fields: corn worms, tobacco worms, weevils and other plant-devourers.

The whites would not quit. They tasked their slaves with picking off the insects, but the worms teemed in such great numbers, the slaves couldn't keep up. Other masters sent their slaves out in boats to fish, but the fishermen returned with rotted, stinking seafood. Mistresses set their house slaves to setting smoky fires and waving fern branches over their dinner tables, but there were too many flying bugs to keep them off.

Then a great darkness came from the north. Out of this forbidding shadow came a horde of avenging angels in robes of blue, who killed the young sons of the slave owners until the rivers ran red with blood.

"...And Remember that I Am a Man."

Moses came part way out of his sleep, horrified. It was as if the sons were being punished for the sins of their parents and ancestors. Yet how could God stop sin without breaking the chain of sinning?

He was even more alarmed that a part of him enjoyed the revenge being wreaked on behalf of his people. Killing was the worst of all sins, wasn't it? But after generations of suffering at the bottom, wasn't it just for the downtrodden to seek vengeance?

A white-haired, bearded man appeared before Moses in a faded robe. He leaned on a crooked walking stick. Moses wondered if this might be God. "Are you Jesus?" he asked.

The oldster shook his head. "I have the same name as you."

So he was not God. Still, he might be able to help.

"Why does God allow slavery? Can't he stop it?"

"He could. But he won't. Even when his chosen people were enslaved, he did not interfere."

"Why not?"

The old man smiled sadly. "God has decided that men must have the choice of sinning or not. Without sin, there is no redemption."

Moses heart sank. "No redemption?"

"Not from God. Only man can save man."

"What does that mean?"

The man reached out and put his hand atop Moses' head. "Only you can free you. Do not pray to be rescued. Pray for strength." Then he was gone.

He reached out and briefly put his hand atop Moses' head. Then he was gone.

In the morning, Moses thought about his dream. From Missy Hannah, he had learned about Moses of the Bible, and remembered how plagues had been sent against the Egyptians. It was only a dream, maybe brought about by his fever, but it still upset him. He set off for the north.

In mid-afternoon, following a deer trail thought dense brush, Moses burst into a clearing where the trees had been cut. Fifty yards from where he came out, two gangs of slaves worked. One group toiled at clearing stumps; the other men were waist deep in muck, digging a ditch.

"…And Remember that I Am a Man."

A white man stepped into view from behind a huge stump. It was McPherson, the overseer who'd been fired from the Micheau farm. He looked directly at Moses, hard suspicion in his eyes.

Moses leaped back into the brush and ran back the way he had come. His heart hammered and he slogged through the swamp until his side ached from the pace. He slowed, but kept on. After a while, he became sick to the stomach, and his fever seemed worse. He still had no use of his injured arm, which throbbed at each step, despite the sling. Resting often, it took him an entire day to get back to the place where he'd first come upon the lake.

He found a dry spot and lay down to sleep. Exhausted, he slept through the night in a stand of bushes. Near dawn, he awoke shivering and wet. It had turned cold again. A gentle rain drifted down from gray skies. As he stiffly got to his feet, pain lanced through his stomach. He squatted to relieve his troubled bowels.

About to rise, he heard the sound of something moving through water. Something large. He raised himself cautiously.

Not a hundred yards away, a man on horseback rode through the swamp. McPherson? Moses couldn't see the rider clearly through the misty rain, but who else could it be?

"…And Remember that I Am a Man."

"…And Remember that I Am a Man."

Chapter Twenty-six

Returning to Egypt—1807 A.D.

The Lord said, "I have indeed seen the misery of my people in Egypt. I have heard them crying out because of their slave drivers, and I am concerned about their suffering. So I have come down to rescue them from the hands of the Egyptians and to bring them up out of that land into a good and spacious land, a land flowing with mild and honey…

But Moses said to God, "Who am I, that I should go to the pharaoh and bring the Israelites out of Egypt?"
Exodus 3:7,11

Moses dropped back down and stayed motionless. McPherson hadn't been coming straight for the bushes, so he'd probably pass by.

The splashing sounds drew closer, went on, and then faded. Moses waited several minutes longer, and then started on his way again, going the other way around the lake.

By midmorning, he became aware of being followed. The drizzling rain had stopped and silence filled the swamp. He heard the horse splashing along behind him. McPherson had picked up his trail somehow.

There was nothing for Moses to do but go faster. Easier said than done. Injured and weak, he couldn't move fast. Weak and clumsy, he made more noise than normal. The water stood about a foot deep in this part of the swamp and he couldn't help splashing.

"...And Remember that I Am a Man."

The horse stayed behind him, coming closer by the minute. McPherson could take his time; the horse, even walking, would move faster than a man could in this muck.

Moses watched for another stand of bushes—any hiding place—but found none. As his pursuer drew closer, he ducked into the dense roots of a big cypress and scrunched down. Only his head remained above water, concealed by the shadow beneath the tree.

The horse drew closer. Finally, he could see the legs of the animal, sloshing through the water. Moses held his breath. For a moment, he thought it would pass him by, but then it stopped. *Please, Jesus,* he prayed. *Please save me.* Then he remembered his dream and changed his plea. *Give me strength to get through this, Lord.*

"You might as well come out," a voice said. "I know you're in there."

Moses could almost feel the lash of a whip on his back. He remembered how brutally Old Banjo had been whipped by McPherson. Then he realized he recognized that voice. He crawled out and stood.

"Hello, Mister Furley," he said.

Thank The Lord! It was Mister Furley. Moses would be taken back and whipped for running away, but it was his first offense and they wouldn't kill or cripple him, as McPherson might have done.

"Moses," Mister Furley said, a pitying look on his face, "you look half-dead."

"How'd you find me?"

Mister Furley smiled. "Pure luck. I headed toward the lake and hoped I'd get some sign of you. I had about given up, but then I came across a man named McPherson and he put me on your trail."

Panic overtook Moses. "You're not taking me back to him, are you? He'll kill me."

A puzzled expression came over the white man's features. "Now why would he do that?"

"I got him fired from working for Master Micheau. He'll whip me to death if he gets his hands on me."

Mister Furley sighed and shook his head. "Then you ought to be glad he's such a Negro-hater, Moses. He doesn't take notice of slaves except as objects. Unless he's been around one for a while, he can't recognize individual blacks. He only said he'd seen 'a young buck.'"

"You sure?"

"Don't worry." Mister Furley smiled. "I won't let anyone whip you."

The smile reminded Moses how kind this white man had been. Maybe there was still hope.

"You gonna take me back?"

Mister Furley grimaced and shook his head. "No, Moses, I'll not do a slaver's work. I came to make sure you're all right."

"I'm doin' fine. I figure I'll be in Virginia in a couple of days."

"You've been in Virginia for miles, Moses. You're nearly halfway across the swamp."

Mister Furley swung down off his mount and into the water, which was higher than the tops of his riding boots. He waded over to Moses, looked at the crude sling, and put a hand on his good shoulder. "Moses, Micheau is very sorry for what he did. He didn't mean to hurt you; he was drunk."

Moses had never been drunk, but he didn't believe that someone still sober enough to stand wouldn't know that hitting a person with a shovel was hurtful.

"I'm not going back there," he said.

Mister Furley sighed. "I don't blame you. What are your plans?"

"I'm going to the other side of the swamp, where nobody knows me. I hear there's Quakers there who might help me get to the north. If not, I'll come back into the swamp and live with the maroons."

"Moses, do you know how far away the nearest free state is?"

Moses shook his head. "No, sir."

"Why don't we walk on a ways? I'm a bit saddle-sore and need to stretch."

"As long as we walk north," said Moses.

They set off, Mister Furley leading the horse. Both remained silent until they reached higher land, where they could walk rather than wade. Then Mister Furley spoke.

"Moses, to get free, you'd have to get across Virginia, hundreds of miles. The Quakers are trying to set up a route with safe houses all the way. It's not done yet, however, so you'd be on your own.

You'd have to travel in the dark and hide in the day. Odds are you'd be captured or shot before you got twenty miles."

"I'll make it."

"Maybe so," said Mister Furley. "Maybe so. But what about the Fugitive Slave Act?"

"What's that?"

Why, Moses wondered, was this man trying to talk him out of running for freedom? He was the one white man Moses had hoped would understand.

"Congress recently passed a law. Any runaway slave caught in the north can be seized, brought before a magistrate and returned to his master. Believe me, there are plenty of men who make their living collecting rewards for escaped slaves. To be safe, you'd have to go all the way to Canada, more than a thousand miles away."

Moses took the bull by the horns. "Why are you telling me all this? I've already run away. They'll whip me if I go back now. You're just like all the other whites. You don't want me to be free."

They came to the shore of a lake. Since there was only one lake in the Great Dismal, it meant Moses had been walking in a circle. The day had grown brighter, blue sky showing through as white clouds blew in to replace the gray. The lake's calm, flat surface mirrored the sky, as though another, upside down world lay the surface of the water.

Mister Furley again put his hand on Moses' shoulder.

"Moses, I have twenty dollars in my pocket. If you decide to keep going north, I'll give you that money, and wish you all the luck in the world. But hear me out first."

"Go ahead and talk," Moses said. "You won't change my mind." He pulled away from the man's touch and stared out across the false sky.

Mister Furley shook his head, as though weary. "Where to start?" He went silent for a few seconds, then said, "Moses, some of us want to see an end to slavery. We can't help all slaves, but I personally can't bear to see someone so young as you in the hands of cruel men. My brother Richard and I were going to hire you away from Micheau, last auction, but decided not to, because we thought him to be a good man."

206

Moses must have made a face, because Mister Furley put up his hands, palms out. "I know. I know. We were wrong. But Micheau's sorry. You won't be whipped if you come back. Here's what we've come up with. My brother will hire you until young James Grandy comes of age. We've talked to James, and he'll hire you out on your own, if you'll pay him a percentage. Any above that you keep. You can save up your money and buy your freedom. What do you say to that?"

"No."

"Why not?"

Moses took a deep breath. Any other white man and he wouldn't have considered saying what he was about to.

"Whites have been lying to me all my life. If you want me to be free, why don't you just buy me and set me free yourself?"

"I can't Moses. You're "protected" by the state. You can't be sold until young Grandy comes of age."

"You could buy me when that happens."

Mister Furley sighed, then looked away. "Maybe I should. If I've paid off my debts by then." He looked back up and met Moses' eyes. "What if I did? Everyone would know my stance on slavery. I can't fight it in the open. The slavers are powerful, both politically and economically. My house would "accidentally" burn down. Other businessmen would refuse to deal with me."

He was right, Moses knew. The practice of slavery enslaved whites, too, in a way. They weren't free to express their thoughts.

He had done a lot of thinking since the talk on the ferry dock, when Jonas had said, "You gots to grow up." Growing up meant taking responsibility for yourself, rather than relying on others.

Moses recalled standing up to Master Micheau in the field, despite his fear of McPherson, the field boss. There was also the time when he'd showed Master Coates how to handle mules, despite the man's dislike. Then he remembered setting Enoch Sawyer's ferryboat adrift. And he couldn't help smiling about how he'd got even with the bully, Chadwick.

What if he went back? Could he encourage other slaves to resist in small, subtle ways? Moses didn't have the power to end slavery; he was only one man. But he'd do all he could. He owed it to Mama, to Naomi, to Jonas and all the others. And he owed it to himself.

Something else came to mind: Jonas saying something about Enoch Sawyer owning every bit of him except his soul. They could never enslave Moses' soul. And they couldn't defeat him unless they killed him or he gave up and quit. Either way, his soul would remain free.

Moses turned to Mister Furley. "I'm going back."

Without waiting for a reply, he faced south and began walking.

The God of the Biblical Moses had set plagues on the Egyptians and changed the mind of the Pharaoh. What if he and other slaves did all they could to resist giving in, even though enslaved? If they conducted themselves well, could that convince any whites to work toward ending slavery? He had to try.

If Moses and other good people persevered, slavery was doomed. It might not happen in his lifetime. Maybe the best he could do was to buy his freedom, go north, and work for enough money to buy others out of bondage. But he would do his best and put his faith in The Lord, who'd helped the biblical Moses.

That Moses, as a young man, had fled from Egypt and become a shepherd in Midian. He had been free, body and soul, for forty years. In the end, he had gone back to resist the enslavement of the Israelites. He had freed his people from the Pharaoh and led them across a great wilderness to freedom. How had he found the courage to do that?

Maybe, like Moses did now, the Biblical holy man had just kept putting one foot in front of the other. And trusted in God.

"…And Remember that I Am a Man."

Part Three
The Court of the Pharoah

Chapter Twenty-seven

Master James—1809 A.D.

This person was Mister Richard Furley, who after that hired me at the Courthouse every year, till my master came of age. He gave me a pass to work for myself, so I obtained work by the piece where I could, and paid him out of my earnings what we had agreed on; I maintained myself on the rest, and saved what I could. In this way I was not liable to be flogged and ill-used. He paid seventy, eighty, or ninety dollars a year for me, and I paid him twenty or thirty dollars a year more than that.

When my master came of age, he took all his coloured people to himself.

The Life of Moses Grandy—1843 A.D.

On a warm day in late March, Moses walked up the lane to the Grandy farm. He was home. Master James had reached twenty-one years of age and the Commonwealth of North Carolina had returned Moses to his master.

The last few years had turned Moses into a man, in every sense. He stood five-foot-ten, with broad shoulders and a lean waist. His

209

face was narrow, with a wide nose and lips that were thin for a black man, set above a pugnacious jaw. A worn, gray, round-topped hat with a narrow brim perched on his head, a red and white checked kerchief encircled his neck. A bundle, wrapped in his blanket, sat on one shoulder. He kept his hair shorn close and his face shaved. His rich, brown eyes were usually narrowed as if he were brooding, for he was often deep in thought. Already he had become known for his serious approach to life and his business acumen.

He had been to nearly every port on the Albemarle and Pamlico Sounds, from the busy, capital port of Edenton to the Chowan fisheries where fish were dried in the summer and fresh oysters shipped north in the cold of winter. He'd even sailed to Ocracoke Island, where an opening through the Outer Banks allowed ships to sail into the vastness and power of the sea beyond. And many a time he'd encountered white traders who tried to cheat this "young, dumb nigger," when he'd delivered goods for various employers. Little did they know he could do sums quicker with his brain than they could with paper and quill.

Richard Furley, who had managed to hire him for two years by the simple expedient of outbidding any rivals, had given him a pass to work and travel. After a while, many merchants had realized the value of a black man who was willing to work hard without supervision and could also look out for their interests. In addition, once he had expanded his knowledge of vessels, currents and tides, he had occasionally been put in charge of small sailing schooners or fleets of shad boats.

He'd been surprised at the number of black watermen he encountered, working at every maritime profession. Remarkably, many of these had been free blacks. Most white slave-owners did not want their slaves out in boats, where they might be tempted to attempt escape by sailing away.

Wherever he'd gone, slaves talked of freedom when no whites were around. Some schemed to escape on ships bound for the north, as stowaways or relying on the aid of southern abolitionists. Others talked of disappearing into the swamps or lighting out for the wilderness of the west. A reckless few promoted armed insurrection, some even going so far as to suggest American slaves might win their own country, as had happened in San Domingue, which was now called Haiti. Most, however, opted for the safer choice of trusting in God and waiting for abolition, which was sure to happen eventually—hopefully in their lifetimes. Moses had also made the choice to trust in Jesus, but would not wait for Heaven. He would rely on himself. He would try to buy his way free, as Mister Furley had suggested a couple of years ago, in the swamp.

As he neared the slave quarter, he looked for Mama. She wouldn't be expecting him, so she was probably out in the fields. Mistress Grandy had died a couple of years ago, so Mama no longer cleaned the white folks' house, as she had for the last few years. She had been moved out of large shack near the old peach tree, and been assigned to a small hut close to the woods. He had managed to see her a few times lately, since he'd had a pass, but was eager to tell her he'd be living on the farm again.

In his travels, Moses had learned his sister Mary had been sold to a master in Pasquotank County, across the river, but no one had seen her since. He'd also learned the fate of Jebediah, but he'd never tell Mama a word of it. He wouldn't tell anyone. Maybe years from now, when he was an old man, he'd be able to pull his feelings out and look at them, but…

"Moses," someone shouted.

He looked up to see Tamar lumbering toward him, a baby slung on her back and a gaggle of children following her. She was obviously pregnant again. This would be her sixth child, even though she was only a few years older than Moses. For some reason unclear to him, she hadn't been hired out, even though they were owned by the same master. Tamar had been left to fend for herself, so she had cleared a bit of ground in the woods and raised corn and flax. After a while, she had jumped the broom with a man from a nearby farm, but she still lived from hand to mouth. She supported herself and her children by hiring herself out to labor, earning a peck of corn, some herrings, or a piece of meat for a day's work among the neighboring farmers. Her husband could help her but little; he was owned by a master who would let the man visit only once a month or so.

Moses set down his bundle and took her in his arms. She wrapped herself around him, her swollen belly hard, and kissed his cheek. "Oh, Moses, thank The Lord. At last you've done come home."

"It's good to be back," he answered. He could feel the wetness on his sister's cheek and had to keep himself from joining her in silent weeping. "How's Mama?"

"She's passable." Tamar broke free and wiped her eyes on a sleeve. "She can't hoe all day long any more, but she can still earn her keep, I reckon."

Moses nodded. "Good. Where is she now?"

"I expect she's working in the tobacco beds with the other old folks."

"Come walk with me. I can't wait to see Mama's face when she sees me." He reached down and picked up his bundle.

"I'll just do that." Tamar took his hand and they walked past the slave quarters and out toward the fields.

They went along at a slow pace so the children could keep up. Moses looked around. "Where's Talitha?" he asked, not seeing Tamar's oldest child.

He felt his sisters fingers tighten and turned his attention to her face. Her lips were set in a hard line and her eyes were wet again. After a moment, she gulped and said, "Master James done sold her a few days back." She took a deep breath. "He needed money for seed."

"I'm sorry." What else could he say? He squeezed her hand.

When they got to the edge of the fields, they came upon the elderly and infirm slaves who prepared beds for the tobacco seeds. In these raised beds, the young plants would mature, protected by pine boughs until the weather warmed and they could be transplanted to the sunny fields, which were being cleared by able-bodied workers. Tobacco required fresh ground every year, for tobacco moths laid their eggs in the fields each fall and their worms would consume the next year's crop if a farmer was stupid, lazy, or inexperienced enough to put it in the same soil.

As they approached, one of the women working beside Mama poked her and pointed at him.

"Moses," she shrieked and ran to embrace him.

He met her halfway, then picked her slight body up and whirled her around. She kept chattering the whole while, letting the nearby

212

slaves know that her baby had come home. They gathered round, able to take a few minutes to greet Moses since the overseer was nowhere in sight. Once Moses had put Mama down, the old folks patted his back and shook his hands. He recognized almost all of them from his boyhood.

Soon they went back to their work, leaving mother and son to their reunion. Moses could see that Mama's pupils were cloudy and the corners of her eyes were rheumy. She seemed to have trouble focusing on him. After a bit, Tamar drifted away, her face again sad, with her young ones in tow.

"Master James wants to see you up at the house," Mama said after she'd brought Moses up to date with the latest goings on and he'd told her how sorry he was to hear that Tamar had lost Talitha. "Said you're to come as soon as you showed up."

"How'd he know I was coming today?"

"I don't know that he did. He told me a week ago."

Moses nodded somberly. He'd been waiting years for the day he'd see Master James again, and looking forward to it. But now that he'd learned about Talitha, he was having second thoughts. Moses hadn't seen Master James since the first day he was hired out, and still thought of him as a young boy. But the sale of a member of Moses' own family reminded him that, whatever else, his old playmate was now a slaveholder. Would he be like his father? Master Grandy had been a fair master most of the time, but it had been folly to cross him.

There was nothing to do but answer the summons of his master. He kissed Mama on the cheek and set off for the farmhouse. When he got to the back door, he set his bundle down, and knocked.

A few seconds later, a young, light-colored slave girl answered his knock. She appeared to be a few years younger than Moses, not pretty, but attractive with the flush of sexuality brought about by the onset of womanhood. She wore a loose, yellow gingham smock, much finer than a working girl would possess, and it showed her ample physical charms quite clearly. She smelled like a white woman, with some sort of flowery scent about her. He remembered that smell. Master James's mother had used toilet water that smelled of roses.

"...And Remember that I Am a Man."

The girl looked him up and down with an appraising stare. Moses had been sexually evaluated by women before, but never so boldly. When her eyes came up to meet his, she smiled coyly. "Yes?"

"I'm Moses. Master James sent for me." He kept his tone neutral. This girl was far too young to be flirting with a grown man.

"Oh, yes. Moses. Mas' James done talked about you to me before. I'll jes' go let him know." The door closed.

A bit later, she returned. "Mas' James say he see you now. Follow me."

When she turned Moses followed, remembering at the last moment to take off his hat. She set off toward the back of the house, but he stopped. The parlor was nothing like he remembered. As a child, he had marveled at its cleanliness and elegance; now the room was cluttered and dusty, with spider webs hanging from the wall sconces. Rubbish littered the floor and dirty eating utensils were piled on the table.

"You comin' or not?" the girl asked.

Moses set off again, beginning to realize that whatever this girl's job in the house might be, it wasn't cleaning. That accounted for her saucy manner.

Master James received him from behind a desk with piles of ledgers and papers, in the room once used by Master Grandy. He was writing and didn't look up for a moment, giving Moses a chance to study his childhood friend.

His dark-brown, cropped hair was brushed forward in a lively, wind-blown look, coming to a peak above his forehead. This crest of hair accentuated his full sideburns, which ended well below his ears. Master James had his mother's hazel eyes and long lashes, but these features were weighed down by his father's blunt nose and prow-like chin. A thin mustache paralleled a thin upper lip, while his lower lip stretched down as though trying to balance the chin.

He wore clothing the style of young dandies in the cities along the sounds. A long, brown overcoat with wide lapels hung open to reveal a white shirt with high collar and frilly neck. He wore tight, fawn-colored breeches that ended in long black socks. His boots stood empty beside his chair and Moses was glad for the aroma of roses coming from the girl, who stood beside him.

214

"…And Remember that I Am a Man."

Master James made a final flourish, returned the crow-feather quill to its inkpot, and looked up. A tight smile appeared. "Moses, good on." He put a hand out, but did not rise. "I'm quite pleased to see you, my boy."

Moses, who had learned in his travels to recognize dialects from various islands and cultures, noticed that Master James affected an accent not common for Camden County. It sounded like the talk of English naval officers whom Moses had overheard. He put out his hand and shook that of his master.

"It is good to see you well, Master James," he said, trying to talk as "white" as he could. "I was sorry to hear of the passing of your mother."

Moses had long ago lost his shyness when speaking with white men. He knew better than to use overly-familiar language, of course, but he had learned how to be respectful and yet not give way in business dealings. Most whites were so startled to hear him contradict them while carefully *not* contradicting them that they became bemused and disarmed.

"Why, thank you, Moses. Mother thought a lot of you, as I remember." Master James sat back and regarded him. "I've been hearing a few things about you the last few years, I must say."

Moses stood straight and held his hat at his groin with both hands. He smiled and nodded. He'd also learned to keep his mouth shut until he learned which way the wind blew.

"You may leave us now, my dear," Master James said and the girl slid from the room. He put his fingers together in front of his prominent chin and looked up at Moses.

"Yes, the most amazing stories. They say you're a sailor now." He dropped his pose, then pulled out a blank piece of parchment. He picked the quill up again, tapping off a drop of ink. "Is that so?"

Moses nodded, even though Master James no longer looked at him. "Yes, Master James."

Master James began to draw looping spirals that seemed to go nowhere. "And they say you're a savvy dealer when it comes to merchandise."

"Yes, sir."

"...And Remember that I Am a Man."

The young white man looked up and arched an eyebrow. "A black merchant. How uncommon." He smiled and dropped his gaze. "And how did you learn to become a merchant?"

"Mister..., Master Furley taught me, Master. He would tell me how much money certain goods should bring and, when I brought them to market, I'd try to get that much or better."

Master James nodded and continued to doodle. "Where did you learn to count and deal with money, Moses?"

Moses had handled this question more than once. "Why, I certainly don't know, Master James. The only thing I can figure is that The Lord gave me a gift for working with numbers."

The quill dipped back into the inkpot and Master James began to make more careful shapes. "And no one taught you?"

"No, sir."

Master James turned the parchment around so Moses could see it. "Can you give me the answer to this arithmetic problem.?"

It was $11 + 8 = ?$

Moses could feel eyes burning into him as he peered at the paper. He knew what the numbers were, of course; Missy Hannah had taught him that way. And he'd checked shipping invoices and bills often enough. *Guide me, Lord.*

"Are those marks supposed to mean something, Master James? I mean, I can count." He began counting on his fingers, "One, two, three, four, five and such, but you'll have to tell me what the marks mean if you want me to add them up or whatever. Master Furley would tell me numbers to use, but I can't read or nothin' like that." He raised his eyes to those of his young master, trying to look confused.

Master James smiled tightly. "It says to add twelve and nine, Moses. Can you do that."

Liar, thought Moses. "I surely can." He made a show of studying random movements of his fingers, amazed at how Master James continued trying to trick him. Just like he'd cheated as a child.

"That would be twenty-and-one, wouldn't it?" Moses tilted his head until Master James nodded. "And if Mister Furley sent me off with twenty-one bales of shingles and wanted me to get three cents apiece, I could figure that for you, too." He began another round of finger-waving, but Master James waved it aside.

"There's no need, Moses. I can see you truly have a gift. I've never known a black man who knew his numbers higher than ten, slave or free." He turned the paper back around and began to spiral again. "How much did Furley pay to hire you last year, Moses?"

"Eighty-eight dollars."

"And he sent you out to hire yourself out for labor?"

Moses could see where this was going and didn't like it. "Yes, sir, he did."

"And you had to feed and clothe yourself?"

"Yes, Master James."

"And how much did you earn?"

"I paid Mis… Master Furley thirty-four dollars more than he paid out, one hundred and twenty-two dollars."

The white man smiled. "So, if Furley hadn't had to pay the state in the first place, he would have made a hundred and twenty-two dollars pure profit, wouldn't he?"

Moses nodded. "That's right." Maybe he could still turn this around. Work most of the time here on the farm, where he could take care of Mama, and only hire himself out now and then for extra money. After talking to Mister Furley's Quaker friends the last couple of years, he'd been hoping to convince Master James to make a deal so he could eventually buy his own freedom.

Master James stopped drawing and, without looking up, said, "I've been needing cash money for seeds and equipment now that I'm starting Father's leaf business back up. You're my answer, it appears."

The quill pen went back into the inkpot, Master James not noticing that it splashed a dark blotch onto his shirt sleeve, for he stared up at Moses.

"Then here's what we're going to do, old chum. I'm going to allow you the same liberties as Furley; you find merchants who need their goods peddled and are willing to pay for your services. Take what you need to live, then pay the rest to me."

"Yes, sir, Master James, but…"

"But what?"

"I was wanting to talk to you about, if I could save up enough money, maybe buying myself free like others I've heard of."

217

"…And Remember that I Am a Man."

"Ha!" Master James hit the desk with the heel of a hand. "I figured those damned Quakers were putting ideas in your head."

"Yes, sir, but…"

"No buts. Now, I like you, Moses, you know that. But I don't want to hear any more abolitionist clap-trap out of you. Not until you've proved yourself to me, anyway."

Moses clenched his teeth.

"You get yourself out there and start earning money. I expect at least one hundred and fifty dollars out of you this year. You earn that much for me, then I'll talk about you buying freedom. But not before that, you hear?"

Moses nodded, his mind reeling. A hundred and fifty dollars.

"…And Remember that I Am a Man."

Chapter Twenty-eight

A Bucket of Water—1811 A.D.

She was blind and very old, and was living in a little hut, in the woods, after the usual manner of old worn- out slaves.

The Life of Moses Grandy—1843 A.D.

Moses sat on his mule, which he had named Keentoon, and watched the young woman approach up the road. She hadn't seen him, since he and the mule stood behind an old pile of dead trees.

The girl was tall and slender and light of skin. Even at a distance, he could see the beauty of her dark brown eyes. She moved with an unconscious grace, her long, pretty legs striding along the dirt road with bare feet. Her head was covered in a calico head scarf and she wore a drab linsey-woolsey dress. As she came nearer, he could hear her humming one of his favorite hymns.

He kicked Keentoon lightly in the ribs and came out of hiding. "Hello, Naomi."

She stepped back with a gasp, raising a hand to her lips. Then her eyes grew wide with recognition. "Well, if it ain't little Moses, all growed up. And I can see you ain't changed a-tall. Ain't you got nothin' better to do than jump out and scare people?"

"I didn't mean to startle you," he said. "My mule was limping and I got off the road to see if he'd picked up a stone or something. And who should I see coming up the road but a skinny gal I used to know."

He didn't want to tell her that he'd been lying in wait for her. He'd met Jonas a few days back and the former ferryman had mentioned that Naomi had never jumped the broom or taken up with any man in particular. He'd also let out that she walked up the road every Sunday morning to attend services.

It had been obvious that Jonas didn't work on the ferry anymore; his left leg was missing below the knee. When Moses had asked, he said he'd got his leg caught between the ferry and the dock when a wind had come up and moved the boat without warning.

"*Your* mule?" Naomi looked skeptical. "Don't you mean your master's mule?"

"Nope." He slid off the beast's back and faced her. "My master lets me put myself out for hire. I made a little extra money and invested it in a mule." He gestured toward the mule. "Naomi, meet my friend, Keentoon."

He turned to the mule and waved toward Naomi. "Keentoon, this is my old friend, Naomi Sourpuss, of the Camden County Sourpuss family."

Naomi laughed. "I'm not a sourpuss."

"Oh? You've changed, then?"

She waved him off. "Go on, Moses. I haven't changed a bit and I was never a sourpuss. You've changed though."

"Why do you say that?" How long had it been? Six years? Seven? Naomi had changed from a pretty girl into a beautiful woman, with a full figure and generous hips.

She looked him up and down. "You're…, well, you seem…, you act like you own the world, or somethin'. I can't 'zactly put it into words." She pursed her lips and sighed. "If I was to put a finger on it, I'd say you act like a white man. Like you don't have no master."

He laughed and stepped closer. He had grown a bit since the ferry, so he had to look down at her. "I guess you could say that I don't really have a master. Like I said, I hire out. As long as I pay Master James Grandy what he asks, I can keep the rest and live on it."

She eyed him suspiciously. "Where do you stay?"

"I pay rent for a house in South Mills." He didn't want to say it was the usual quarters for a slave, a one-room shack. House sounded better. "But I don't always stay there. I go wherever I can find work."

"And where's that?"

"Mostly out on the water." He breathed her in, a soft musky odor along with an overly sweet, animal smell. She must have washed her hair with tallow soap. "You know, fishing, tonging for oysters, taking crops to market, hauling lumber."

"And you really own that there mule?"

"I surely do." Moses had purchased the creature last fall. Like his namesake, Keentoon was getting on in years. Unlike the original Keentoon, however, the mule was sometimes ornery and stubborn. But Moses could make extra money with an animal strong enough to pull logs. "Are you on your way someplace?"

She nodded. "I'm goin' to prayer meetin'. We meet in a grove off Keeter Barn Road."

"Who leads the service?"

"A man named Joshua, from the Ferebee farm. You heard of him?"

"Yeah, I've listened to him. He's quite a preacher."

She smiled weakly. "Well, speakin' of the meetin', I'd best be on my way."

"Say," Moses said, as though the thought had just occurred to him. "I'd enjoy hearing Joshua preach. Would you mind if I go along with you?"

The smile disappeared. "It's a public road, ain't it? I guess you can walk on it if you want."

As he walked beside her, leading Keentoon, he decided she still *was* a sourpuss.

*

After the prayer meeting, several people told him that his brother, Benjamin, was home, returned a few days ago from a voyage that had lasted two years. He was owned by a man who owned several ships and was now an experienced salt-water sailor. Being away for long periods, however, had not stopped him from jumping the broom with a woman owned by the storekeeper in South Mills, the village growing up around the canal's southern locks. An hour later, Moses had said goodbye to Naomi and was sitting with Benjamin and his wife, Ophelia, at a hand-fashioned table in her shack near the store. She was a small woman who had the misfortune of being born with a hare-lip that caused her to lisp, but her sweet disposition made up for the blemish to her otherwise pretty face. At the moment, she beamed with pleasure at having her husband home.

"I tell you, I was fearful for my life," Benjamin said. "One mast was broken and waves was washing across the decks. The wind was drivin' us towards the rocks and we was tryin' to set the other sail while..."

Moses hung on to every word. Benjamin's ship had been to far ports. Moses had never been out on the actual ocean, but he had weathered his share of storms on the wide sounds and was eager to learn how his brother's ship had come through the nor'easter.

Just then a man's voice called out. "Ophelia, I need you to fetch a large bucket of water and bring it into the store. A large one, mind you."

Ophelia made a sour face at the two brothers seated with her. "Yes, Mashter Lamb. But you know I can't carry a big bucket by myshelf."

"Have your man bring it then," the voice called back. "Tell him to bring it inside the store, like I said."

It didn't matter that Master Williams didn't own Benjamin. Even a free black wouldn't dare disobey an order from a white man. With a resentful grimace, he rose and went outside.

A few minutes later, Benjamin passed by the open door of the shack, carrying a large canvas bucket. "I'll be back before you can spit."

But minutes passed while Moses and Ophelia sat and made small talk. Then the heavy blows of a hammer could be heard from somewhere in the village.

Ophelia looked worried. Moses, trying not to look concerned, began to wonder why the storekeeper had specifically ordered Benjamin to come inside. Except for Ophelia, who worked in the store, blacks weren't normally allowed inside. Moses tried to reassure her, but became concerned as more hammering came. "I'll go see what's keeping him."

When he got to the store, the pounding noise came from inside. He went up on the porch and looked inside the open door. His brother lay on his back, on the floor, wrists and ankles chained. Large staples had been driven into the pine floor holding the chains

222

down. An iron bar had been placed across his chest and Master Williams was stapling that to the floor also. Two other white men stood nearby.

"What are you doing?" he cried. "What has Benjamin done wrong?"

Master Williams looked up. "Oh, it's you, Moses. Sorry to do this, but I have no choice in the matter. Benjamin didn't do nothing wrong, but the sheriff sent word that his master's shipping business has failed and Benjamin will be sold to pay off debts." He placed another staple and began to drive it in.

Moses mind raced. There must be something he could do to get his brother out of this. But what? He could think of nothing. In the end he said, "But why do you have to pin him down like a hog? He wouldn't have run away."

"Go away, Moses," Benjamin said from the floor. "Don't get yourself into trouble, too."

Moses returned to Ophelia's shack and told her what had happened. The two of them spent that night on the porch of the store, talking to Benjamin through the wall.

Moses was concerned about how Mama would take the news of Benjamin being sold away. She had gone nearly blind over the last couple of years. Master James had no further use for her and she was living in a little hut in the woods, after the usual manner of old, worn- out slaves. She had a small garden and her children and friends took her food when they could. Moses agreed with his brother that Mama would be heartbroken, and wondered how he'd find the courage to tell her. *Give me strength, Lord.*

Shortly after dawn, the sheriff's deputies arrived, pried up the staples and took Benjamin away.

"...And Remember that I Am a Man."

"…And Remember that I Am a Man."

Chapter Twenty-nine

The Pharoah's Terms—1812 A.D.

I was now getting, as I have said, one dollar and fifty cents per day. I contracted for it; I earned it; it was paid to me; it was rightfully my own; yet, upon each returning Saturday night, I was compelled to deliver every cent of that money to Master Hugh. And why? Not because he earned it,--not because he had any hand in earning it,--not because I owed it to him,--nor because he possessed the slightest shadow of a right to it; but solely because he had the power to compel me to give it up. The right of the grim-visaged pirate upon the high seas is exactly the same.

About two months after this, I applied to Master Hugh for the privilege of hiring my time. He was not acquainted with the fact that I had applied to Master Thomas, and had been refused. He too, at first, seemed disposed to refuse; but, after some reflection, he granted me the privilege, and proposed the following terms: I was to be allowed all my time, make all contracts with those for whom I worked, and find my own employment; and, in return for this liberty, I was to pay him three dollars at the end of each week; find myself in calking tools, and in board and clothing. My board was two dollars and a half per week. This, with the wear and tear of clothing and calking tools, made my regular expenses about six dollars per week. This amount I was compelled to make up, or relinquish the privilege of hiring my time. Rain or shine, work or no work, at the end of each week the money must be forthcoming, or I must give up my privilege. This arrangement, it will be perceived, was decidedly in my master's

225

favor. It relieved him of all need of looking after me. His money was sure. He received all the benefits of slaveholding without its evils; while I endured all the evils of a slave, and suffered all the care and anxiety of a freeman. I found it a hard bargain. But, hard as it was, I thought it better than the old mode of getting along. It was a step towards freedom to be allowed to bear the responsibilities of a freeman, and I was determined to hold on upon it.

Life of an American Slave, Frederick Douglass, Boston: Anti-Slavery Office—1845 A.D."

"You're Moses, aren't you?" the white man asked. "James Grandy's slave?"

Moses looked him over from a sitting position on the edge of the dock. The man was tall and thin, with a long, dour face and a prominent Adam's apple. He wore a stylish suit and a broad-brimmed hat. He'd parked his shiny buggy up on the canal road, and walked out on the short pier to Moses. He looked somewhat familiar, but Moses couldn't place him.

"Yassuh," he said cautiously. "I'm Moses." He set down the rope he'd been splicing and got to his feet, respectfully taking his hat off. It was a cool February day and he felt moisture on his face. It wasn't quite raining but there was so much mist falling that there wasn't much difference. Vapor rose off the brown water of the canal to meet the moisture coming down.

The man looked Moses up and down. "They said I'd find you here. It's gotten around that you're a hard worker, know the waters, and can do sums. Is that so?"

Moses nodded.

The white man took his headcover off and wiped his brow with a sleeve. "I'm Grice. Let's get out of the weather; I need to talk to you."

Moses followed Master Grice off the pier and into the shade of a tree on the far side of the canal road. He now knew who the white man was. This man had married Master James's younger sister, Anna, a few years back. Moses had never met him, because he'd still been hired out when the wedding had occurred.

Master Grice got right to the point. "I need someone reliable to work for me. My wife says you might be that man."

"I'm always looking for work."

"So I've been told." Master Grice crossed his arms and appraised Moses, his head cocked to the side. "Richard Furley also speaks highly of you. So I've got a proposition for you."

"Yes, sir?"

"Word is that the damned British are setting up a blockade at the entrance to the Chesapeake Bay. If they do, goods can't be shipped up and down the coast by sea. Everything will have to go up and down the canal between Norfolk and the Albemarle. It's a damn nuisance, but there's money to be made."

Moses knew about the war. He kept his eyes and ears open. The British were blockading the mouth of the Chesapeake so the important ports of Norfolk and Baltimore would be strangled. The entrance to the large bay was a strategic location; not only did the blockade bottle up the Chesapeake, but any American ships traveling up and down the coast would be forced to veer far out to sea so they wouldn't be captured. The English, with their massive ships-of-the line, had the mightiest navy in the world, while America had a few small, fast frigates. It didn't take a genius to figure out how to make money out of the situation.

"Yes, sir," he said, reading Master Grime's expression. Was this a man he could trust? He'd dealt with many white men in the years since Master James had allowed him to hire himself out and now felt he was a pretty good judge of character. "I was sittin' here thinkin' how, if I was to have a boat or two, I'd go on up to Norfolk and let it be known I could take goods down this here canal—for a price, of course."

Master Grice nodded, smiling. "You've got the idea. I have half a dozen boats with shallow drafts. They could be poled up the canal, and then sailed to Norfolk. Load the boats there and bring them back down here, and then back again with some commodity that's going north. But I haven't been able to find anyone that can handle boats and also has the ability to conduct business." He gave Moses a keen eye. "There's some sharp traders in Norfolk."

"Yes, sir. I been there." Moses knew what Master Grice meant by not being able to find anyone for his scheme. He meant that, with a

227

war on, he couldn't find any *white* man to work for him.

"Moses, I'll be blunt," Master Grice said. "Most folks would think me a fool for even considering allowing a slave to handle cash money. But you've made quite a reputation for honest dealings. Can I trust you?"

"As God is my witness," Moses answered.

*

Moses stood behind Mister Grice, who sat facing Master James at his desk. For the past year, Moses had seldom spent time at home, if you could call a rented shack home. He had served Mister Grice faithfully and they both made money. Moses gave his benefactor—for he had become as much of a friend as Mister Furley—one-half of all he received for freight, being scrupulously honest. Out of the other half, he had hired blacks to man the boats and fed them. After those expenses, what was left went to Moses, who turned most of it over to Master James.

"I agree Moses should have a chance to buy his freedom, William," Master James said. "But I want eight hundred dollars."

"That's too much, James. Remember, you played with Moses when he was a boy. And his effort on the boats has made money for all of us. I ask you to be reasonable."

"Eight hundred *is* reasonable." Master James smiled agreeably. "I could get a thousand for him any minute." He took a sip of liquor from a glass on the desk. "He's quite valuable."

"And that's what worries me," Mister Grice said. He sat in the room's other chair. "What if something happened to you? Some jackass might buy him and put him to work in the fields. If he's a free Negro, that can't happen."

"Nothing's going to happen to me. I'm a young man."

Mister Grice sighed. "I'm not your father or your brother, but take some advice from an older man. You've been selling off slaves and land to pay off gambling debts and such, Anna says. You don't work the farm at all, anymore. If that keeps up, you'll go under and *everything* will be sold."

Master James bristled. "That's none of your business."

Moses, behind Mister Grice, was surprised. He hadn't known any of this, not living on the Grandy farm anymore.

228

"…And Remember that I Am a Man."

"No, it's not," Mister Grice admitted. "But Anna and I are making Moses our business. She's always been against keeping slaves, you know that; and she's convinced me that it's only a matter of time before the practice is ended. The Congress has already forbidden importing any more slaves. England may be abolishing slavery at any time, according to the London papers."

Master James leered and held up a hand. "If that's so, why should I let him go? Congress can make him free." He reached for his liquor again.

"And if they do?" Mister Grice raised his eyebrows. "You won't get a copper for him."

"Look here." Master James leaned forward, clasping the glass in both hands. "If you're so hot on setting Moses free, why don't you buy him and do it yourself?"

"Don't think I didn't offer. But what do you think Moses told me?"

"What?"

Mister Grice said, "Why don't *you* tell him, Moses."

Moses gulped. He'd gotten used to Mister Grice doing the talking during this meeting and hadn't expected to be called on. He'd already tried his best to convince Master James, several times, and it hadn't done much good. He'd managed to hoard three hundred dollars, most of it earned in the last year, but it would take years to come up with eight hundred. Even then, he wasn't sure he could trust Master James unless another white man witnessed his agreement.

"What I told Mister Grice," Moses said, "was what a wise old man told me. If I'm to be free in my heart, I have to earn my freedom." He didn't mention the other possibilities, fighting for his freedom or running north. Those options were more dangerous and he'd decided against them. For now.

Master James's eyes grew wide. "You were offered freedom and didn't take it?"

"Yes, sir. I'd owe Mister Grice money and that's not true freedom. I know I can do it for myself."

Mister Grice jumped in while Master James was off balance. "This is your old childhood friend we're talking about here, James. He'll still be making money for you while he saves up, remember. And he'll work all the harder if he sees hope."

Master James jerked to his feet, spilling his drink. "All right, you're on. I don't think any black man can do it; they can't keep from drinking up their money on Saturday night. But I'll set him free if he comes up with six hundred. And I want twenty dollars a year more than I've been getting."

Rising to his feet, Mister Grice confronted Moses' master. "That's not reasonable. You lower the price of his freedom but make it harder for him to save the money."

Master James gestured at the account book, open on his desk. "What am I to do? With the war on, I can't even sell my tobacco. I have no money coming in and I still have to feed the workers. The cash that Moses brings in keeps me afloat; he's more profitable than any other five of my Negroes."

Master James looked up at Moses and addressed him directly.

"That's the best I can do, Moses. Take it or leave it."

Thank you, Jesus, Moses prayed. "I'll take it, Master James," he said aloud.

"...And Remember that I Am a Man."

Chapter Thirty

Persimmon Beer—1813 A.D.

My mother was named Harriet Bailey. She was the daughter of Isaac and Betsey Bailey, both colored, and quite dark. My mother was of a darker complexion than either my grandmother or grandfather.

My father was a white man. He was admitted to be such by all I ever heard speak of my parentage.

The opinion was also whispered that my master was my father; but of the correctness of this opinion, I know nothing; the means of knowing was withheld from me.

Life of an American Slave, Frederick Douglass, Boston: Anti-Slavery Office—1845 A.D.

Moses hopped twice on his left foot, then put his right foot down behind him and threw the left into the air. The banjo player provided a lively melody, while the clickety-clack of the bones player kept up a quick rhythm. Moses had danced many a jig before, but this one was special. He danced with Naomi.

It was a pleasant summer evening, cool enough to keep the mosquitoes away. The smells of wood fires, cooking food and sweaty bodies filled the air. Around them, slaves from many plantations stomped and laughed and hooted. The corn-husking festival was being held on the Micheau farm this year and the slaves were allowed to revel in the knowledge that the long summer's labor was tapering off. Occasionally heard through the din, the sound of Atticus's lively fiddle-playing drifted down from the main house, where the whites held *their* celebration of the end of summer.

Moses couldn't take his eyes off his partner, wanting to savor every moment before some other man cut in to dance with her. Naomi's eyes sparkled and her skin glistened in the firelight. He'd never seen her so beautiful. She was as graceful as a yearling deer, and her movements betrayed how sensual her body was, something she seemed to downplay at other times. She held the hem of her skirt up to free her legs for the spirited dance, and her legs kicked high.

The masters had allowed the slaves to slaughter a lamb, a hog, and several roosters, so the blacks had feasted from washtubs of cooked meat, along with potatoes, collards and squash, before the dancing began. There was also corn whiskey, corn beer, hard cider, and persimmon beer to wash the food down, with fruit juices for the children and those who abstained from alcohol. A frolic like this was one of the few times drinking was allowed by the whites; normally slaves drank only on the sly.

As Moses had feared, a hand tapped his shoulder after a short while. He grudgingly nodded to the man cutting in and left the dance area. Rather than dance with some other pretty girl, he'd sit a couple of dances out, and then cut in to step lively with Naomi again.

To his delight, however, Naomi bowed out after the song ended and went to sit with other young girls on some log benches. He hurried over to the vat, filled two gourds, and then approached her.

"Would you like some persimmon beer?" He knew it was her favorite drink.

She smiled up at him, still breathing hard. "That would be nice, Moses. Thank you."

He handed her one of the gourds. The girl on her right smiled knowingly at Moses and slid over. He sat down next to Naomi, who took a deep drink.

"You're a wonderful dancer," he said, setting his gourd aside.

"Thank you," she repeated. "You're a good dancer, yourself."

"…And Remember that I Am a Man."

"How have you been?" He'd last seen her not a week ago, at prayer meeting, but didn't know how to begin what he wanted to say.

"I've been fine. How about you?"

"I'm good."

She smiled and waited for him to say more.

He gulped. "I - I want to talk to you about something. Could we take a walk away from the fire?"

Her smile disappeared and she started to object. He'd made a mistake. Pairs of young men and women had been drifting into the shadows all evening and none had returned to the dancing.

"Just over to that bench by the grain shed." He glanced at the young women sitting around them. "I want to talk to you in private."

Naomi closed her open mouth and regarded him closely. She looked over to the grain shed, which, by the full moon, was in clear view of the gathered slaves.

"All right, Moses. But just over there."

Finishing her beer, she stood and walked away with him. Several of the girls giggled and made remarks, assuming the couple was heading for the privacy of the woods.

They sat down by the shed. Naomi primly tucked her skirt beneath her. "What do you want to talk about?"

"Um, have you heard that Master James has agreed to let me buy my freedom?" He knew she hadn't. He hadn't told anyone about the deal, yet.

Her eyes went wider than a five-dollar piece. Her hand went to her upper chest and she took in a sharp breath. She cocked her head and regarded him as though trying to decide if he was joking. He nodded, smiling.

Finally, she said, "Why, that's wonderful Moses. I can hardly believe it. Congratulations."

Moses found he couldn't stop nodding. "Master Grice talked to Master James about it for me. When I've earned six hundred dollars, I'll be free. Six hundred above my usual hiring out, of course."

She pursed her lips and squinted her eyes. "Six hundred dollars! Why, that's more money than you could earn in a lifetime."

"Nope." He reached into his pants and took out a small cloth sack. He reached in and pulled out a handful of coins and paper money. "I sometimes make ten or twenty dollars for one trip up and down the canal. I figure I'll have enough money in two years."

Her face beamed with pride. "Why, Moses, you are amazin'. You must be the smartest man in the world."

"And now that I know I have prospects, so to speak," he took a deep breath. *Help me here, Jesus, if you would.* "I'm asking you to be my wife."

He might as well have hit her with a hammer. She stared at him in horror, as if regarding a poisonous snake. Tears leaked from her eyes. "Oh-oh-oh, Moses." She dropped her head into her hands and sobbed.

Now what? Moses knew that women sometimes cried when they were happy, but there had been no joy in her expression. He wanted to put his arms around her, but was afraid to. He sat rigid beside her, hope fading with every moment.

Finally she raised her head and regarded him, her face wet from crying. "I was afraid you'd ask me that, one day. I can't marry you."

He felt like he'd received a physical blow. "Why not? Won't Master Sawyer allow it?"

She shook her head. "That's not it. That white devil don't give a damn what goes on in slave quarters, as long as it don't cost him no money."

"Why then? Don't you like me?"

Naomi took a deep breath and regarded him with solemn eyes. "Moses, I've loved you for years. But I can't marry you. I kept hopin' you'd fall for some other girl, so I could get over you, but you keep comin' around."

Moses shook his head. "I don't understand. What's wrong?"

"It don't matter. I can't marry you."

She started to get up, but he grabbed her hand.

"Don't leave. Not until you've told me why you can't marry me."

"Moses, please." Her hand trembled in his grasp and her lower lip quivered.

"You kissed me once," he said harshly, hoping to get a rise out of her before she broke down in tears again. "You may not even remember that kiss, but it's kept my hope alive for years."

"Of course I remember." She took a deep, uneven breath. "I never should'a let down my guard. I didn't mean to give you no false hope."

"Why not?" Faces turned toward him from the folks standing around the dance area, and he realized he'd spoken loudly. "Why, in God's name, can't you marry me?" he asked in a whisper.

"Moses, I'm sorry." She looked down, unwilling to meet his demanding glare. "I don't deserve you. I'm not good enough. You'd be ashamed of me."

"What are you talking about?" He squeezed her hand in both of his. "Look at me."

When she'd raised her tearful eyes, he continued. "You're the most wonderful person I've ever known. I'd be proud to have you jump the broom with me."

"Moses, you don't know," she said in a quavering rush. "I've had to do things that would disgust you. Things that disgusted me. I don't know if I could ever do the things that a wife is s'posed to do for her man."

She pulled her hand away and again dropped her head and sobbed. "I can't lie with no man. I'm afraid."

Now he understood. Rage filled him. "Sawyer? He did things to you?"

She jolted upright, terror in her face. "No, not him. I'll never tell you who; I'll never tell anyone."

Moses didn't believe her. He could see it in her eyes. She wasn't afraid for herself; she was afraid for him, afraid he might go after a white man. His anger died and he gathered her in his arms. She collapsed against him and sobbed into his chest.

"I love you," he said, over and over. "I love you." He stroked her hair and took in her sweet scent.

They remained there until her crying abated. Her breathing became deep and regular and she pulled her face from his chest. He could see her looking up at him, but she was in shadow and he couldn't see her expression. Then her face came closer to his. Her fruity, warm breath washed over him. He lowered his face and kissed her.

Her kiss was hesitant at first, then she pulled away. "I love you," she said. Her lips returned and they feasted on him.

Moses lost track of time and place. His love was pure and he wanted to put every bit of devotion into his kiss, to lift her above the world's pain and affliction. He was a man, though, and purity of purpose wavered. His body reacted. The scintillating shiver from her soft lips ran through him like a fever and his kisses became more urgent. He became afraid she would feel his arousal, lying across him as she was, and tried to control himself. How could he show lust when she had confessed her terror of lovemaking?

When she stopped kissing him, however, she didn't try to pull away. "Do you still want me?" she asked. "Now that you know?"

He swallowed a lump that blossomed in his throat, and nodded. "I would never hurt you, though."

"I know that." She pecked him on the lips, then pulled herself free. Standing, she reached a hand out to him.

He took her hand and rose. "Now what?"

Her answer surprised him. "You wouldn't buy a pig in a poke, would you?"

"Er, I guess not."

She squeezed his hand and led him toward the darkness. "Somehow I don't think I could ever be afraid of anything when I'm with you, Moses. Let's go find out."

"…And Remember that I Am a Man."

Chapter Thirty-one

The Hawk and the Eagle—1813 A.D.

Negro marriages are neither recognized nor protected by law.

Does Slavery Christianize the Negro?, Rev. T. W. Higginson—1855 A.D.

They were forbidden to marry, in the strictest sense of the word. Marriage was a legal contract. Slaves had no legal standing in the commonwealth. Normally, a union between slaves consisted of "jumping the broom" with a slave who lived on the same plantation. These partnerships were encouraged by most plantation owners, and any children would remain the property of that master.

Naomi didn't have the permission of Master Sawyer, however, and didn't dare ask. But there were ways to get around this. Master Sawyer didn't spend much time taking care of his slaves and didn't have an overseer, either. He relied on fear to keep his slaves working. So he wouldn't notice which man Naomi took up with.

Since Moses had a pass to come and go anywhere between the Albemarle Sound and Norfolk, Virginia, he could bypass getting permission from Master James. If they were caught, Moses would be whipped for sure, and Naomi would suffer some similar punishment.

Yet, with the light of a crescent moon to guide him, Moses made his way through the woods, carrying a jug of wine in one hand and a rooster in the other. The bird's feet had been tied together and a small sack fastened over its head. He made his way toward a clearing where everyone would meet for the ceremony.

In keeping with the importance of the occasion, Moses wore a brand-spanking-new dark blue shirt and brown pants, along with a yellow bandana around his neck. A pair of new leather work shoes covered his feet.

His proudest purchase sat atop his head. In the months since he'd begun trading goods between the Chesapeake and the Albemarle, the men of his barge crews had begun calling him "Captain Grandy," and now he looked the part. Instead of the black stocking cap that marked most watermen, he wore a small, cocked, tricorner hat like those worn by officers on ocean-going vessels.

The fly in the ointment was that Moses hadn't been allowed inside the store to pick out his clothing. The storekeeper had brought different garments to the side door for Moses to choose from, commenting all the while how surprised he was that a slave could afford to buy such fine clothing. Judging from his tone, he suspected Moses had stolen the money.

The evening was warm for spring, but it was still too early in the season for the clouds of mosquitoes and deer flies that would come with the heat of summer. It had rained during the day, so male frogs peeped and croaked from the trees and hollows, calling out for mates. If a female responded, Moses knew, the male would climb on her back and lock his limbs around her, clinging to her and fertilizing the eggs she laid in some pond or puddle. His grip would be so tight that no other male could dislodge him before she was done laying her clutch.

He saw firelight winking through the underbrush and used it to guide him. The clearing was deep in the trees, far from any road or farm, so the fire would not be seen by any whites.

When he came into the open, several dozen people were gathered around a toothless old woman who sat on a stump that had been set for her. This was Uzoma, who had become too old to work, and been cast out by her master. She had rejected her slave name and reclaimed the Igbo name given her as a young girl in Africa. Too proud to accept the charity of other slaves, who had little themselves, she eked out a living as a fortune teller, reading the bones and entrails of small animals. She also performed ceremonies according to her early memories. Tonight, she would join Moses and Naomi together.

A murmur arose from the wedding guests as Moses made his way through them. All of them wore the finest, most colorful clothing. Many clapped his shoulder or grabbed his arm in friendship.

When he came to Uzoma, Moses knelt and placed the wine and the cock at her feet. "For you, mother."

Uzoma leaned forward and peered at him, her pupils a yellowish cloud. She had fashioned a hat from bright red cloth, somehow making it stand from her head like the sails of a ship. Carved bone hoops hung from her ears and a necklace of small seashells graced her long neck. She wore a bodice of red with white dots above a skirt of solid blue, revealing strings of more seashells wrapped around her bare midriff. Beside her was a beaded bag, held shut by a drawstring, and a broom leaned on the stump.

"Dat you, Moses?" she asked.

He nodded, then realized she might not be able to see well in the dim light of the fire and the moon. "Yes, mother, it's me."

"Where is de girl?"

"They're bringing her," someone said.

Moses knew that Naomi had been taken somewhere in the nearby woods, being kept out of his sight. It was bad luck for the groom to see his bride before the ceremony.

As he waited for her appearance, he couldn't help pacing nervously, despite the soreness caused by his new shoes. What if she lost her nerve at the last moment and went back to Sawyer's Ferry alone? She had mostly managed to get past her fears of intimacy with a man, but things were still touchy.

The crowd stirred as Naomi appeared, being led into the clearing by her female friends. Naomi wore a new yellow dress, purchased with money from Moses, and flowers in her hair, which had been braided in an African style. Her little sister, Betsy, followed behind with a bunch of flowers. After Betsy came Naomi's mother, Harriet, and Mama, who was being helped along by Tamar since she couldn't see well anymore.

They brought Naomi to stand beside Moses in front of Uzoma. Again the old woman peered. "Dat you, Naomi-girl?"

"Yes, Uzoma."

239

"…And Remember that I Am a Man."

"You two ready to get hitched as a pair?"

They both answered in the affirmative.

Uzoma looked out into the night and cocked her head. "Eberybody else ready?"

A murmur of agreement came from the crowd.

The old fortune-teller got off the stump, turned and rummaged in her bag. She came out with a length of braided leather. "Hold out your hands."

Uzoma tied Naomi's right hand to Moses' left and then went back into her bag. She removed two old battered cups, sealed with scraps of canvas cloth. She removed the coverings and put a cup into each of the couple's bound hands. "Drink from dis."

When Moses raised his hand to drink, he found the cord to be so short that he had to face Naomi and carefully raise his cup along with hers. She smiled at him and his heart seemed to stop. He could have gazed into her clear eyes forever.

"Drink," commanded Uzoma.

Moses put the cup to his lips and tilted it. Something thick and syrupy crawled down the inside of the cup and deposited sweetness into his mouth. Honey! But why was Naomi grimacing? Everyone liked honey.

In the background, Moses heard Tamar describing the events to Mama.

Then Uzoma's hands intruded and switched the cups between the two. "Drink again."

Moses again tilted a cup and something bitter oozed into his mouth. Molasses! No wonder his bride had made a face.

"Man and woman, dey got to take de bitter wit' de sweet," said Uzoma. She took the cups away and set them aside.

She went around and put the stump between her and the bridal pair, as if it were an altar. Moses had to turn his head to watch her. Again she reached into her bag. This time she brought out a smaller bag. She opened the drawstring and rolled a collection of bones onto the makeshift altar.

She leaned down and studied her castings, using a finger as a pointer to guide her eyes. When she looked up, Moses thought he caught a glimmer of sadness, but then the old woman's features brightened.

"You will be good for each udder as long as you are togedder," she intoned.

Then her voice changed to a command. "Hold your hands up, you two."

Moses and Naomi, still standing face-to-face, held their joined hands above them, so everyone could see they were bound together. Naomi's face was radiant and he was sure he looked the same. He'd never felt so happy before.

Uzoma raised her own hands in the air. " We pray to Jesus for happiness wit' you two. You will hab what is good for her and she will hab what is good for you. Let de hawk and de eagle perch togedder. If one is not good to the udder, let dat one's wing break."

Moses had to stifle laughter and saw Naomi doing the same. They hadn't expected the old woman to compare them to birds.

"You is joined," Uzoma finished.

The crowd, silent until now, broke into cheers and clapping. "Jump the broom," someone shouted and it soon became a chorus.

Naomi and Moses were shoved and jostled into position. They stood side-by-side, facing the fire. From the corner of his eye, Moses saw Tamar lean down and stretch the broom handle out behind them, about a foot off the ground.

Jonas appeared in front of them. "Don't look back," he warned. "That gets bad luck. You gots to try to clear the broom."

There was no need to explain. Both Moses and Naomi had seen this ceremony many times.

Jonas looked down and, apparently at some signal from Tamar, said, "Jump."

Moses jumped back and felt one heel hit the broom handle. He stumbled slightly. Beside him, his new bride, with her usual grace, cleared the broom handily. She had jumped higher. Cheers and laughter went up all around. Everyone knew Naomi would be the boss in this new family.

"…And Remember that I Am a Man."

"…And Remember that I Am a Man."

Chapter Thirty-two

A Dram of Money—1814 A.D.

"Is he so hard, then?"

*"Why, not a cruel man, exactly, but a man of leather, -- a man
alive to nothing but trade and profit, -- cool, and unhesitating, and
unrelenting, as death and the grave. He'd sell his own mother at a
good percentage -- not wishing the old woman any harm, either."*

<u>Uncle Tom's Cabin</u>, *Harriet Beecher Stowe—1852 A.D.*

Moses put a caulking tool into a pot of hot, acrid-smelling pitch and
began forcing the sticky mess between the boards of the barge. This
vessel had bumped another barge and begun leaking, so he had
ordered it pulled up on the bank for repairs. They would be late
getting underway to Norfolk, but it couldn't be helped.

As he sealed the leaks, Moses calculated how long it might be
until he came up with the six hundred dollars to buy his freedom. He
had paid Master James over four hundred already, so he guessed
maybe as much as two years. The war with the British had ended
and there wasn't as much freight going up and down the canal.
Before he'd gotten married, Moses had kept his money hidden away,
but Naomi had convinced him that it would be safer to pay Master
James a bit at a time, as long as he was sure to get a receipt for it. It
made sense to Moses; no one would steal a receipt, and he would

243

have proof of paying.

Smart woman, Naomi, not to mention hard-working and loving. He missed her already, even though he'd left her at home only the day before.

The tar was getting stiff, so he put the pot back on the fire and stretched, looking across the wide canal. A pier jutted out on the other side, where the three other barges owned by Mister Grice were tied up. A murmur of conversation reached Moses as his crew lolled about on the dock, unable to finish loading until he got the repairs finished. The delay was costing Moses money, not to mention it would be an extra day away from Naomi.

He heard the clop of horses' hooves and the squeak of wagon wheels drawing near, but paid it no mind. Then he heard the crack of a whip and turned to look. From the north, along the canal road, came a horse-drawn wagon, full of black women and children. Behind them walked a gang of male slaves, chained together. In addition to the white wagon driver, three other whites rode horseback, all armed. The horseman to the rear also carried a long whip, which must be what Moses had heard because he was coiling it as if he'd just used it on one of the walking slaves.

Moses recognized the rider on the left, nearest the canal. Mister Rogerson was a slave dealer who passed through the county a couple of times a year. Trade in slaves had increased lately, more blacks sold to plantations in the south where cotton had become king, as the white folks said, since the invention of the cotton gin. The gin couldn't pick cotton, however; it only removed the seeds from the cotton bolls. Slaves were needed to work the fields to provide fodder for the gin.

The sound of pitch bubbling in the pot reminded him he had a job to do and he turned back to his work. The faster he got this done, the sooner he would see his wife again.

Naomi had gotten over her fear of intimacy and they had a sensual, loving relationship. They had decided against children, however, though both wanted to start a family. It would be better to wait, Moses had convinced her, until he had bought his freedom and then hers. If there were children before then, they'd have to stay around until Moses could afford to buy his own children. Naomi had turned to Uzoma for herbal medicines that would prevent pregnancy.

"Moses," a woman's voice called. "Moses, my dear." Her tone conveyed despair.

He turned, a chill running through him and leaving numbness behind. It couldn't be.

Yet, it was. Naomi's tearful eyes looked out at him from the sea of black faces on the wagon. She wore the same dress she'd been wearing when she had kissed him goodbye. He ran toward her.

A horse came between Moses and his wife, ten feet from the wagon. He looked up into the hard, cold countenance of Mister Rogerson.

"Stay away from my wagon, nigger."

Moses stepped back to avoid the hooves of the prancing, nervous horse. "What's going on, Mister Rogerson?" he asked. "For God's sake, have you bought my wife?"

"Your wife?" Rogerson spat a dollop of tobacco juice at Moses' feet. "How in hell would I know who your wife is, boy?"

Moses tried to look around the horse, but his view remained blocked. "She's right there. On the wagon."

The slave dealer laughed. "Now don't that beat all. If you see her on my wagon, then I sure as hell have bought your so-called wife, you ninny."

"But why did he sell her? Did she do something wrong?"

Rogerson grinned. "Nope, she didn't do nothin' wrong. Sawyer just wanted the money for her, is all."

Moses started around the horse. "Let me go to her."

The white man blocked him with his mount. "I told you to stay back, nigger." He drew one of the two pistols from his belt and pointed it. A loud click sounded as he drew the hammer back.

The change in position had given Moses a view of the wagon again. Naomi's expression had changed from grief to alarm.

"Be careful, Moses," she cried.

Moses looked back up to Rogerson. "Please, if nothing else, let me take her hand and tell her goodbye."

"You want to say goodbye, you do it from here. I'll give you one minute, then we're moving on."

Moses looked at Naomi and gauged the distance. If she was to be lost from him, he might as well die holding her hand.

"…And Remember that I Am a Man."

"Don't get hurt, Moses," she pleaded. "It's too late for me. I am already gone."

"Don't worry," he called to her. "I'll come to find you, as soon as I can."

She smiled wistfully. "Forget about me. Take care of yourself."

Moses looked up at Rogerson. "Can I give her something? Some money?"

Rogerson's eyebrows rose and he smirked. "A nigger with money? Now don't that beat all?"

"Please, massuh."

Rogerson looked over to the man with the whip, who had pulled up nearby. "Mister Burgess, get down and take this man's money over to his woman. We're dealing with a high-class, moneyed nigger here, don't you know?"

"Sure thing, Guv'nor." Burgess swung down from his horse and walked over to Moses, grinning. "At your service, me fine fellow. I would be honored to serve you in such a fashion." He held out his left hand, but the whip remained coiled in his right.

Moses gave the man all the money he had, a few dollars he'd planned to use for feeding the men on the trip. Burgess, affecting a mincing manner, took the money and went to the wagon. "A dram for you, milady," he said, proffering it to her pretentiously.

Naomi took the money and tucked it away. She looked over at Moses.

"Thank you, dear."

"Fare well, my love."

"Goodbye." His voice broke. "I love you."

"I love you."

The driver clucked to his team and the wagon lurched away. Rogerson stayed where he was, watchful, as though expecting Moses might try to run after the wagon. After a few seconds, he eased the hammer down on the flintlock. He opened his mouth, about to speak, but then thought better of it and reined his horse after the wagon.

Moses watched until the slaver party passed from sight, feeling tears run down his cheeks. He'd done all he could, he told himself. At least she had some money, although the public display of passing it to her would probably ensure that the coins would be stolen from her. He'd done all he could. But how could God allow such a thing to happen? How much did Jesus think one man could bear? And then he felt shame for what he'd thought. It was Naomi who would have to suffer.

He looked down and saw the spreading tool, still full of pitch, atop his bare foot. He must have dropped it when he recognized Naomi on the wagon, but he hadn't felt anything as the hot tar burned into his flesh and stuck.

"…And Remember that I Am a Man."

"…And Remember that I Am a Man."

Chapter Thirty-three

Captain Grandy—1815 A.D.

From my earliest recollection, I date the entertainment of a deep conviction that slavery would not always be able to hold me within its foul embrace; and in the darkest hours of my career in slavery, this living word of faith and spirit of hope departed not from me, but remained like ministering angels to cheer me through the gloom. This good spirit was from God, and to him I offer thanksgiving and praise.

Life of an American Slave, Frederick Douglass, Boston: Anti-Slavery Office—1845 A.D.

Things were changing in Camden County. Although South Mills, the location of the southern locks, remained a small town with a store and a blacksmith shop, Camden, the county seat at the mouth of the Pasquotank was growing quickly. The docks bustled with activity as crops and lumber from the area were shipped out and merchandise arrived from Europe, England and northern United States ports.

There were more crops to be shipped. The Dismal Swamp Canal kept any of Lake Drummond's water from reaching the lower lands to the east, and the resulting dry land had been cleared. Tobacco prices had fallen off, so mules and slaves worked fields to produce cotton, corn, potatoes and more. Mister Kemp, Moses had heard, had gotten wealthy off the need for plows and plow animals and many slave dealers had surely gotten rich, too.

For several weeks after losing Naomi, Moses had remained in a stupor. Again, his faith in God was on shaky ground. He prayed but with little hope. He threw himself into the work of buying his freedom, so he could go looking for his lost wife. He worked as though possessed, helping pole barges along, pushing as strongly as any of his men, if not harder.

The men complained he was working them too hard. No matter how fast they poled the barges, or handled the cargo, it wasn't good enough. They didn't get enough time with their families, either; the captain wasted no time between trips. As soon as they'd unloaded their payload at one end of the canal, he arranged for a consignment of freight to carry the other way.

Since he no longer had a loving wife to welcome him home—or even a home, for that matter—he slept aboard one of the barges when either underway or tied up to the dock. Mama had died shortly after Naomi had been sold away, so the only times he went ashore were to pay Mister Grice his share, or to give money to Master James toward his freedom.

For all Moses knew, Naomi could have been sold to one of the farmers with holdings along the waterway he traveled. Even though she'd been going south when he'd last seen her, it was possible she hadn't gone far. Moses had given the problem of finding Naomi much thought. His solution was bribery. He'd keep working the barges for Mister Grice, even after he had his free papers. The next time he saw Mister Rogerson, the slaver who'd taken Naomi, Moses would pay him for information about her fate. Even if the slaver would only tell Moses what city or county she'd been sold in, it would narrow the search. He figured he could use the same tactic again, bribing the court clerk for records of the sale.

Today was different, though. Bringing a group of barges south, he carried the last of the six hundred dollars to buy himself free. First he planned to stop by the Grice's to pay Mister Grice his share, then he'd head straight to the Grandy place to settle with Master James.

He put his mind back on the business at hand when the barges reached the locks at South Mills. They were lowered into Joyce's

Creek, which would take them to the Pasquotank River. Once on the river, they passed Sawyer's Ferry, rekindling Moses' memories of Naomi as a girl.

At the Camden dock, they unloaded the barges and he paid off his crew, leaving instructions to beach the barges nearby. On the morrow, they'd be taking on a load of bananas and oranges, which had arrived from Florida, to Norfolk. Even though he would be a free man after today, this was no time to take a holiday. He needed money to begin his search.

On this crisp fall day with the leaves in high color, he walked three miles to the Grice home, a spring in his step for the first time since Naomi had been taken away. Mister Grice greeted him at the front door, and ushered him into his office.

"Well, Moses, how did you fare this time?" Mister Grice trusted Moses to make all the business arrangements for their partnership, and had no idea what went on from day to day. Moses told him the details, reciting the financial dealings from memory so they could be recorded in the ledger and then gave him his share.

"That leaves me seventeen dollars or so after paying off the crew," Moses said, "so I need those receipts you've been holding for me. Since I only owe Master James twelve dollars more, I'm on my way there next. I'll soon be a free man, and I have you to thank for that, Mister Grice. If you hadn't trusted me to be your captain, and persuaded Master James for me, I'd not be where I am today."

Mister Grice's eyebrows rose and he smiled. "Wonderful, Moses. I've been looking forward to this day. Let me call my wife." He went to the door and called into the hallway. "Anna, come here, please. I have wonderful news."

"What is it, my dear?" Anna Grice said as she came through the doorway, and then caught sight of Moses. "Why hello, Moses, I didn't hear you come in." She was a small woman, always smiling. She'd been that way even as a child, Moses remembered.

"Like I said, Anna," said Mister Grice. "I have wonderful news. Moses has earned the money to buy his freedom."

Miz Anna caught her breath, then smiled wider than ever. She stepped over to Moses and put her arms around him.

"Oh, Moses. I am so glad for you."

She was the only white woman who had ever touched Moses, so

he was taken aback. Her head came to his chest and he could smell the clean, fresh scent of her hair. At that moment, she embodied all that was good in Moses' world. He couldn't speak, so grateful was he that Miz Anna was so unlike her brother.

Releasing him, she turned to her husband. "Well, don't just stand there, William. Have the wagon brought 'round."

"Why?" Mister Grice asked.

"Why, to take Moses to my brother's house, of course."

"My dear, Moses is quite capable of handling his own affairs. I see no reason for accompanying him."

"Don't be silly," she replied. "I wouldn't miss it for the world."

Mister Grice drew himself up. "Anna, this is Moses' day. He is to be a free man and no longer needs us to intervene for him. Allow him the dignity of handling his own affairs."

"Oh." Miz Anna considered for a moment. "I suppose you're right, dear. Still, you know how my little brother is. He's likely to shilly-shally and bluster, and try to get out of it, like he always does."

"Nonsense. I am a witness that he agreed to free Moses. Now that Moses had paid the amount agreed upon, James has no choice."

"I suppose you're right, William. Still..."

"Hmm. Perhaps you're right, my dear. You know your brother best."

*

Master James wrote down the amounts of all the receipts Moses gave him, then added them up. He often glanced over at Mister Grice, and Moses was glad the Grices had come along. Master James would have tried to cheat him. Finally, after counting twice, Master James had to admit that the total had reached six hundred dollars.

"You'll soon be a free man, Moses," he said.

"Soon?" Mister Grice asked. "Why do you say soon?"

"What are you up to, James?" asked Miz Anna, her usual smile absent.

Master James chose to address her, rather than her husband. "Why, nothing at all, dear sister. Have you forgotten I can't file the papers until the circuit court judge comes around in a couple of weeks? I promised Moses his freedom, and he shall have it."

Miz Anna nodded and her smile returned. "Then that's that. I propose a toast to Moses' freedom."

"A toast?"

"Yes, a toast. Have a servant bring a bottle of wine and four glasses."

"Four?"

"Yes, dear brother, four."

Master James looked like he'd sucked an unripe prune, but called a house servant—a tiny, pretty young girl Moses had never seen before—and told her to fetch wine. In the meantime, Moses wondered what a toast could be. Toasted bread, perhaps, washed down with wine?

He was interrupted by the sound of paper being torn. "That's an end to it then," Master James said.

Moses turned and saw Master James tossing the receipts into the embers glowing in the fireplace. He felt his heart drop. Those receipts represented years of hard labor, not to mention holding all his dreams. "Why did you do that, Master James? Those were mine. You ought not to have done that."

Master James laughed. "You don't need them anymore. You have my word."

The wine appeared and Miz Anna took over. She poured the glasses half full, gave one to each person, and then raised her glass. When the two white men followed suit, Moses imitated them as they clinked glasses all around.

"To Moses' freedom," Miz Anna proposed.

"To Moses' freedom," her husband echoed.

Master James merely nodded and Moses didn't know what to say. While the Grices tossed back their wine, he took a hesitant sip. From the look he was getting from Master James, he had no doubt his glass would be thrown away afterward, unfit for use by whites.

"...And Remember that I Am a Man."

Chapter Thirty-four

Court Week—1815 A.D.

As the form of my manumission has something peculiar in it, and expresses the absolute power and dominion one man claims over his fellow, I shall beg leave to present it before my readers at full length:

Montserrat.—To all men unto whom these presents shall come: I Robert King, of the parish of St. Anthony in the said island, merchant, send greeting: Know ye, that I the aforesaid Robert King, for and in consideration of the sum of seventy pounds current money of the said island, to me in hand paid, and to the intent that a Negro man-slave, named Gustavus Vassa, shall and may become free, have manumitted, emancipated, enfranchised, and set free, and by these presents do manumit, emancipate, enfranchise, and set free, the aforesaid Negro man-slave, named Gustavus Vassa, for ever, hereby giving, granting, and releasing unto him, the said Gustavus Vassa, all right, title, dominion, sovereignty, and property, which, as lord and master over the aforesaid Gustavus Vassa, I had, or now I have, or by any means whatsoever I may or can hereafter possibly have over him the aforesaid Negro, for ever. In witness whereof I the abovesaid Robert King have unto these presents set my hand and seal, this tenth day of July, in the year of our Lord one thousand seven hundred and sixty-six.

ROBERT KING.

Signed, sealed, and delivered in the presence of Terrylegay, Montserrat.

255

"...And Remember that I Am a Man."

Registered the within manumission at full length, this eleventh day of July, 1766

<u>*The Interesting Narrative of the Life of Olaud Equiano, or Gustavus Vassa, the African, Written by Himself*</u>*—1789 A.D.*

Early on Monday of Court Week, Moses knocked on the back door of Master James' house. It took several tries, but he was finally answered by the small girl who had brought the wine to toast his freedom, the week before. She smelled of alcohol and hadn't bothered to put anything on to cover her skimpy nightdress.

"Yeah?"

"I'd like to talk to Master James."

"What about?" She looked him up and down, apparently unconcerned. One honey-colored breast hung mostly out of her gown. "You're Moses, ain't you?"

"Yes, I'm Moses. I'm here to remind Master James that he promised to go with me to Camden Courthouse today."

The girl laughed derisively. "Honey, I ain't gonna get Mas' James up at this hour for no reason. He's grumpy in the morning, that man is."

"But I need to talk to him. It's important."

She looked over her shoulder, as if to see if she was being watched, then slipped out and closed the door behind her, despite the cold weather and her skimpy clothing.

"This about him settin' you free?" she whispered, pulling up a strap to cover herself. He could smell her sour breath. "Like y'all was talking about?"

"Yes, he said..."

"Shh!" She glanced back at the door. "He really goin' to do that? Set you free?"

"Yes," Moses whispered. "I paid him six hundred dollars."

She forgot to whisper "Six hundred dollars!" She lowered her voice again. "Where'd you get that much money, nigger?"

Moses had had enough of the whispering. "That's none of your business," he said in a stern voice. "Tell your Master I want to talk to him."

"Ssh," she insisted. "You wake that man up now, he sure as hell

256

ain't goin' to do nothin' for you."

"But I need him to file my manumission papers."

She peered at him. "You really earn that much money?" She again pulled up the strap of her dress, which had begun to slip.

Moses nodded. "Took a while, but I did it."

She looked back at the door again and then her expression became conniving. "I'll tell you what. Mas' James normally wakes up late, but I know he's planning to stay in town, at Mister Woods' boarding house, for court week. There'll be a lot of white gentlemen there for the court and there's always gambling at card games or billiards. You wait 'til then, when he's in a better mood, to talk to him about goin' to court."

Moses considered. "You think that would be best?"

"Sure would. You really goin' to be free?" Her manner was changing again. She almost purred as she spoke.

He nodded. "I'll be getting my free papers today."

Again, she looked around to be sure they weren't overheard, and then stepped close. Her dress fell down low as she looked up into his face. "You gets to be a free man, you gonna need a woman to look out for you. You could buy me away from Mas' James and I'd take care of you, if you know what I mean."

Moses backed away. This girl, whose name he didn't even know, might reek of alcohol and sour breath, but she had a fine figure and was damn near naked, her nipples prominent in the chill air. Naomi had been gone for months and he missed the sexual satisfaction their marriage had brought. He felt shame for his quick arousal.

"I…I'll keep it in mind." He turned and fled, heading for the county seat, an hour's walk away.

Once there, he found a spot beneath a tree, across from the boardinghouse, and waited. He hadn't had breakfast, but wasn't hungry. The heat of the day increased. He didn't notice. His entire being was focused on getting free and going after Naomi.

In mid-afternoon, Master Grandy rode in on a chestnut gelding. Dismounting, he called for a nearby young slave child to take the horse to the nearby stable's paddock and turn it out. He threw the boy a half-cent, then disappeared inside the boarding house.

Moses waited for a while, in case Master Grandy was eating his dinner, and then went behind the establishment, where odors of

257

cooking food clashed with the stench coming from the outhouses. He knocked on the back door and, when an old black woman answered, asked to speak to Master Grandy. In a few moments, the woman returned and told Moses to go back around and wait on the front porch.

In due time, Master Grandy came out, a billiard cue in hand. "What is it, Moses? Do you want something?"

"W…why, court goes in session today, Master James." Could the man have forgotten? "You promised to file my papers."

Master James acted surprised. "Why, so it is. It had slipped my mind."

"Yes, sir." Moses nodded. "Today is the day."

"I'm afraid not, Moses. Not realizing what day it was, I left your manumission papers on my desk. You should have come by this morning and reminded me."

"I…I…" What could he say? *I did, but your fancy girl warned me against it?* He didn't want to get her in trouble. "I can run back and fetch the papers for you, Sir. Wouldn't take but a little while."

"No, don't bother. I don't have the time today and it's probably too late to get on the docket anyway. I'll draw up some new papers, stop by the courthouse in a bit and put my name down for tomorrow."

"But…Master Grandy…"

A male voice carried out onto the porch. "Grandy! It's your shot."

Master James glanced at the open front door. "Come back tomorrow at noon, Moses. Now, I have an important wager to win, so you be on your way."

Moses slunk away, trying to think of other words he might have used to convince Master James, but failing. He had never argued with a white man and didn't know how to start now. Besides, his master had a vile temper and might go back on his word if provoked.

Moses spent the night aboard a barge, just outside town. The next day brought a cold, drizzling rain. He soon became soaked on the way back to Camden. He had no way of telling time, with the sun obscured, but waited until mid-day and then knocked on the back door of the boardinghouse. Again he asked for Master James.

It took many minutes before the man appeared, bleary-eyed and hung over.

"What is it?"

"You told me to come today, sir."

"No need to remind me. I know what I said. But I didn't have time to file yesterday. I told you—I had an important bet to take care of. We'll take this up another day."

"Tomorrow, Sir?"

"I'll get to it when I get to it," Master James said loudly, his breath reeking of alcohol. "How is it that you can lollygag around town all day? Don't you have work to do?"

Moses had put off working since his manumission papers were more important. Yet if he spent his time hanging around the courthouse instead of working, it would take that much longer to earn the money he needed to search for Naomi.

"Of course I do. But…"

"Then go do it. Your pestering has thrown me off my game and I've lost a considerable amount of money."

Moses persisted. "Please, Master James. Can we go to court tomorrow?"

"Yes, yes, tomorrow. Be off with you now."

The next day, Master James sent word to go away. Moses considered for a moment then set off at a trot toward the Grice home, outside town. When he knocked on the front door—which he had been asked to use—Miz Anna answered.

She looked at his face and said, "Moses. What's wrong?"

"Is Mister Grice here?"

"Why no, Moses. He's away on business, but he should be home later today. Now, what in the world is wrong?"

Moses took a moment to compose himself. "It's your brother, Miz Anna. Three days in a row, I've asked him to file my manumission with the court, but he's put me off. I'm afraid he doesn't mean to give me my freedom."

Miz Anna's mouth set in a firm line. "And I fear you're right, Moses." She made an odd sound, almost a growl, and her shoulders quivered. "You go and tell him that I want to see him, this instant. No! That would only set him off." She turned and called into the house. "Milly! Come here, dear."

Milly was a middle-aged, gleaming, ebony woman who had been

259

"…And Remember that I Am a Man."

Miz Anna's nanny as a child, on the Grandy farm. She was the only slave owned by the Grices, since Miz Anna had freed the rest of the slaves left to her by her father, Master Billy. In truth, she would have freed Milly long ago, being fond of her. But Milly was afraid that, if the legal bonds were broken, she might somehow be taken away from her young mistress and had asked not to be freed. Now she acted as nanny for a new generation of white children.

When Milly came to the door, Miz Anna asked that she walk to the boardinghouse and tell her brother that she urgently needed to see him. As Milly waddled away, Miz Anna added, "Oh, and Milly, on your way back, please stop in the store and see if the fabric that I ordered has arrived yet."

"Yes'm. I'll surely do just that."

Miz Anna invited Moses inside. "Would you like some buttermilk, Moses? I've just churned some butter." Moses agreed readily. Buttermilk was a pleasantly sour treat he seldom enjoyed. She drained some from the churn, which sat out on the back porch while the butter separated, and gave him a large mug.

Moses sat down on the steps and sipped his drink. Miz Anna got a smaller mug for herself and sat beside him.

"That James," she said. "He's always been a poser. I remember how he used to act with you sometimes when you were both little. Whenever you'd show a bit of gumption, he'd put you in your place. That's all right, I suppose, seeing how things were, but sometimes he'd get downright petulant and Mama would have to set him straight."

"Yessum." He didn't want to think of all the petty things he'd endured.

"Well, Mama's gone now, so I reckon I'll have to take her place. When he gets here, you wait out in the shed—so he won't know what it's about at first—and I'll set him straight about keeping promises he's made in front of witnesses."

"Yessum. Thank you, ma'am."

When they heard the sound of an approaching horse, Miz Anna peeked out from the corner. "Here he comes. You go and get in the shed now."

Moses put down his mug, wiped his lip with the back of his hand and did as he was asked. At first, he could only hear a murmur of conversation through the open windows of the house, but then voices were raised.

"Damn you, Annie, who the hell do you think you are?"

"Don't you curse me, Jamie! I'm your sister and I'm looking out for your soul."

"I'll take care of my own soul, you meddling twit. Moses belongs to me and I'm not ready to set him free just yet."

"But you promised."

"I can't afford to keep that promise right now. The farm's losing money and I need the income from Moses to keep my head above water."

"The farm wouldn't be losing money if you weren't so busy drinking and gambling all the time. Papa would be appalled at you selling the farm off piece-meal like you've been doing."

"I'll thank you to mind your own business, dear sister. I'll be taking my leave now and, in the future, I'll expect you not to meddle in my Goddamn affairs."

A door slammed and Moses soon heard the sound of a departing horse, along with the mutterings of an angry Master James. He returned to the house, where he found Miz Anna seated at the table, her knuckles white and her lip quivering.

"That boy!" she said. "He acts just like father did."

"He ain't going to let me go, is he?" Moses' legs quivered and he wondered if he was going to fall down.

"Oh, Moses, of course you're going to get free. Jamie's merely letting off hot air. You have witnesses that you bought your freedom from him. We'll take him to court, dear boy."

They sat and talked for a time, until Mister Grice returned home. He became angrier and angrier as he heard how Master James had been treating Moses. When he heard that Master James had cursed Miz Anna, his face went livid.

"The cad! I'll thrash him."

"And what good will that do, William?" asked Miz Anna. "Oh, he can curse me day and night; he's beneath me and not worth my notice. But what he's doing to Moses is cruel, taking advantage of a man merely because he's black and helpless. Maybe we should buy Moses ourselves, then *we* can give him his papers."

"I wish we could, dear, but the I've just paid to stock the new store and I can't afford it. Besides, Moses has already paid. No, I'll go and talk to your brother myself. Moses has the law on his side, after all. But we have to settle it this week, we can't wait six months 'til the judge comes around again. Do you think James went back to the boardinghouse?"

"Where else?" Anna answered. "There's no other place to drink and gamble during the day."

Mister Grice stormed off and again Miz Anna sat and talked with Moses. He told her about how he planned to search for Naomi and even how he hoped somehow to operate his own ferry.

"I'm afraid that's probably not going to happen, dear Moses," she told him.

"Why not? Not even in the north? Is there a law about blacks not owning ferries?"

"No, that's not it. A ferry is part of the country's transportation system, like roads and bridges. To operate a ferry, you have to get a license from the government. It's a political thing."

Moses felt like all his dreams had been taken away.

When Mister Grice returned, he had good news. He had confronted Master James and told him he ought to give Moses his free papers. Moses had paid for himself, and it was court week, so there was no excuse. Master James had promised he would, and would wait for Moses at the boardinghouse.

Moses, his spirits restored, thanked Mister Grice and Miz Anna, then set off at a brisk walk. When he arrived at the boardinghouse, he walked boldly up onto the porch and knocked on the front door, which was answered by a Negro butler.

"Yes?"

"I'm Moses. I'm here to see Master Grandy."

"Master Grandy left here a little bit ago. I saw him riding out of town."

"…And Remember that I Am a Man."

Chapter Thirty-five

A Man to Do Business With—1816 A.D.

Bad as all slaveholders are, we seldom meet one destitute of every element of character commanding respect. My master was one of this rare sort. I do not know of one single noble act ever performed by him.

Life of an American Slave, Frederick Douglass, Boston: Anti-Slavery Office—1845 A.D.

Moses left Camden the next week. There had been no sign of Master James; apparently he had gone to Norfolk. Moses had no choice but to go back to work, since he had already signed on as first mate on a schooner owned and operated by a white man. Captain Minner ran the ship, but Moses exercised authority over the black crew. The ship spent several weeks sailing the Albemarle Sound, collecting and delivering lumber for various merchants, while Moses chafed at the delay in obtaining his freedom.

Moses learned a lot of seamanship from Captain Minner on that cruise, while the captain was impressed with Moses' business acumen and his skill with handling the crew. They became good friends.

At the end of the cruise, the schooner tied up to the docks at Elizabeth City, a new and growing community across the river from Camden. Moses was surprised to find a harborfront store with a large warehouse behind it. The sign proclaimed: Grice's Lumber and Trade. After he'd settled for his wages, he went to the front window of the store and looked in. Shelves and racks filled the space, piled with items like shovels, axes and sledges. Behind the counter, Moses recognized Mister Sutton, a man who worked for Mister Grice, writing in a ledger or some such.

He poked his head in the open door. "Mister Sutton?"

The man looked up. "Captain Grandy! I do declare. I'm glad to see you, Moses. Come on in."

Moses had never entered a white store in his life, but this was Mister Grice's place, and there were no white customers present, so he felt safe going in.

"Hello Mister Sutton," he said. "I see Mister Grice has found a new venture."

"Yes, indeed. We not only sell lumber from the swamp, we sell supplies and tools to the swampers who go in and bring it out. And that's why I'm happy to see you today."

"Why is that, sir?"

"I've got a large shipment of tools waiting on the Norfolk dock. Would you be willing to take a shipment of shingles up the canal on shares, and then bring the tools back?"

"I don't know, sir," Moses answered. "I need to get back to Camden and talk to Mister Grice. He said he'd take my case against Master James to court when I got back."

Mister Sutton nodded. "Yes, I know about that. It's all over the county how James Grandy did you. But Court Week is two weeks off. You can take a cargo to Norfolk with plenty of time to spare."

"Why is it so important?"

"Because if I don't get the tools down here soon, my customer will go elsewhere. We promised to have them two weeks ago."

Moses scratched his stubbly chin. "What would my share be?"

"Twenty—no thirty dollars." Sutton said. "And twenty percent of what you get for the shingles."

"I'll tell you what," Moses said. "You send word for Mister Grice to file my case to be heard at court week, and I'll take your shipment."

*

264

"…And Remember that I Am a Man."

"Do we have a deal, then, Captain Grandy?" asked Mister Moses Myers.

The two men with the same first name sat in the richly appointed office of Moses Myers' brick home in Norfolk.

Myers was a Jew with a long face and nose to match, whose droopy eyelids gave him a look of sadness. His close cropped hair was gray, but his bushy eyebrows remained black, accentuating his doleful eyes. He wore a frilly white shirt and a black, single-breasted suit. Myers had taken a liking to Moses over the years, as the two had sparred over prices for goods brought north on the canal and Moses had showed himself to be an astute businessman.

"Yes, sir," Moses answered. "If you'll arrange for transport to your warehouse, I'll get my crew unloading the shingles."

"Good man. Cypress shingles are in high demand just now."

"I wouldn't have guessed that from the price you first offered me," said Moses.

Mister Myers laughed. "But the point is proved by the high cost you extorted from me, now isn't it? Would you like a cup of tea, Captain Grandy?"

"Thank you, no. I want to get the barge unloaded so I can pick up a shipment of tools and get back down the canal."

"I certainly understand. You take care of your business, and then meet me at my store in an hour and we'll settle."

An hour or so later, Moses waited outside the store. Although Mister Myers was quite friendly when dealing with Moses in his own office, which could be entered by a side door, Moses felt he had to keep his proper place in public. Waiting inside the store would be unseemly, at best, and might tarnish the merchant's reputation.

Myers was one of the richest men in Norfolk, considered to be one of the gentility, despite his religion. He was also renowned as an honest and dependable businessman. His reputation extended around the world, from the Americas to Europe to Africa and the Caribbean. Yet he dealt with "Captain Grandy" personally, and always showed Moses the utmost in courtesy.

Mister Myers soon appeared, accompanied by another man. "Ah, here you are Moses. I'm sorry to be late. Here is your payment." Mister Myers handed Moses an envelope. "And I would like to present Mister Trewitt. Trewitt, this is Captain Grandy, whom I have

265

told you about."

Master Trewitt—Moses didn't dare think of him as "Mister," since that might cause him to say it out loud—was a gangly man with a chin like an axe blade. He had none of Moses Myers' grace and genteel demeanor, wearing musty ill-fitting clothing that gave him the look of a country bumpkin. His thin lips were set in a sneer as he looked Moses up and down.

Moses lowered his eyes and gave a slight nod. "I'm pleased to meet you, Master Trewitt."

"Captain Grandy," Mister Myers said. "I have told Trewitt that you're a man to do business with."

"Yes, I have some goods that need to be shipped south, and I need a reliable man," Master Trewitt said. "Mister Myers speaks highly of you, but I should like to know who has chartered these boats. Is it your master?"

Moses shook his head. "No, sir, Mister Sutton, who runs a store for Mister Grice in Elizabeth City, hired me for this trip. My master is James Grandy of Camden County, but I have bought myself from him and will soon be free."

"But you aren't a free Negro yet?"

"No, sir. Master James can't set me free just on his say-so. He has to file papers with the court."

Master Trewitt waved at the air as though shooing a fly. "Well, in that case, I shall consider buying you. I could use a man who knows the waterways."

"Ahem," Mister Myers broke in. "As Moses said, he has bought his freedom. It's just a matter of time, what with North Carolina courts meeting so seldom."

"Why, no matter. He's either free or he's not and he just told me he's not."

"Now listen here, Trewitt," Myers said. "Moses is one of our old war captains and he always delivers exactly as promised. He has never lost a single property entrusted to him. He is a hard-working and well-respected Negro, and I should not appreciate it if he were to be trifled with. Moses deserves his freedom."

Again Master Trewitt waved in dismissal. "Well, we shall see, Mister Myers. You're a J...an Englishman and you don't understand the way things work in this country. A slave doesn't become free merely because he says he's free. I'll look into the matter and see what's what. This boy is a valuable slave and he's exactly what I need for my business to prosper."

Mister Myers began to object, but Moses spoke first. "Master Trewitt, my freedom is between my master and me. It's all settled and the papers will be filed shortly after I return to Camden County. Let's get down to business. I'm only taking a partial load down the canal. What do you need shipped and what are you willing to pay?"

*

When he reached Elizabeth City, Moses had the barge offloaded and Master Trewitt's goods delivered to a rented warehouse. Next he hired a wagon and took the tools to Grice's Lumber and Trade, planning to settle with Mister Sutton. To his surprise, Mister Grice was there.

After the long-time partners had greeted each other, and Moses had paid Mister Grice his share of the profits from the trip, Moses asked after Miz Anna.

"She's well enough," Mister Grice said, "but she's still fit to be tied over how her brother treated you. She's been haranguing him at every opportunity and says she'll skin him alive if he doesn't file your manumission papers this session."

Moses grinned, remembering how Miz Anna had argued with Master James the last time. She was determined to "save his soul."

"Has the judge arrived yet?" There were only six judges in North Carolina, each with a different district. They were required to hold court in the county seats of their district twice a year.

"Checked into the boardinghouse yesterday," Mister Grice said. "Court begins Monday, two days from now."

"And Master James?"

"He's at the boardinghouse, too."

Moses sighed. This had been the longest six months of his life. His only consolation was that he had saved quite a bit of money for his search.

"How about Master Trewitt? He's the man who owes us for this last shipment, and he traveled down ahead of the barges. I need to settle with him, and then pay your share."

"If he's here, he'll be at the boardinghouse, I expect." Mister

"…And Remember that I Am a Man."

Grice got up from his stool and brushed the sawdust from the back of his pants. "Let me lock up and I'll go with you. I need some cash and we'll settle between us and be done with the matter."

This suited Moses. He could finish all his financial affairs, buy supplies over the weekend for his journey to find Naomi, and be off as soon as he had his papers on Monday.

They met Master Trewitt on the street across from the custom house. Moses introduced the two men, whereupon Master Trewitt said, "Well, Captain Grandy, I have bought you, as I said."

Moses didn't know what to say. *No, God, no! I can't go looking for my wife if I'm not free.*

"Nonsense," Mister Grice said. "Moses is not for sale. I am a witness to the fact that he purchased his freedom, and that's all there is to it."

"Well, James Grandy says otherwise."

"The hell he does. Not even my sorry brother-in-law would…" He broke off.

Moses knew what Mister Grice was thinking. He wouldn't put it past Master James to not only go back on his word, but to betray the very nature of their agreement.

"He belongs to me." Master Trewitt's sneer changed to a smirk.

"You'll be disappointed if you've made a deal with Grandy, Trewitt. Captain Grandy has bought his freedom and the court will uphold it."

"Why, no need to get nasty, sir," Trewitt said. "I'm simply stating a fact. I am this slave's new owner."

"You're a…" Mister Grice caught himself once again. He turned to Moses. "You know the figures, Moses. Let's go settle our bill with this man so we can be done with him."

"Why, by all means, let's settle our financial affairs," Master Trewitt agreed. "Then we'll take this other matter up. Follow me." He stalked off.

Mister Trewitt led them to a nearby house. "I've rented a room here for the week. The boardinghouse was full, with court week coming and all. If you'll be so kind as to wait on the porch, I'll be right back with your money."

When they were alone, Moses asked, "Do you think he's telling the truth, Mister Grice? About owning me?"

Mister Grice pursed his lips. "I wouldn't put anything past James Grandy, Moses. But I don't see how he could get away with it."

"But I don't have my free papers yet."

"It doesn't matter. My wife and I both witnessed his agreement with you, as I just told this Trewitt fellow."

"But…"

"Try not to worry, Moses. If James has been up to some sort of trickery, we'll soon set him straight."

Mister Grice put his hands behind his back and began to pace back and forth across the porch with his head down in contemplation. Despite what he'd said, Moses could see that his friend and protector was nervous.

Moses walked to a corner and stared down the road toward the south, the direction Naomi had gone when he'd last seen her. He imagined her looking north in hopes of his coming to get her. If Master Grandy had cheated him, he might never see her again.

Moses had done all he could do. He had earned his freedom with the fruits of his labor and the sweat from his brow. He hadn't asked God for help with that. Wasn't it time for Him to step in?

"Well, here you are, sir," came Master Trewitt's voice from behind. Moses turned to see the man hand a pile of bills to Mister Grice. "That puts us even."

Mister Grice didn't even glance at the money. "It certainly does. Good day, sir."

"Wait," said Master Trewitt. "I have something to show you." He held out a piece of paper in front of Mister Grice's eyes.

Moses saw the blood drain from his friend's face and knew what it must be, but he asked anyway. "What is it, Mister Grice?"

Mister Grice gulped, took a deep breath, and then turned to look at Moses with sorrow in his eyes. "It's a bill of sale. Grandy *has* sold you to this man."

God had let Moses down again.

"…And Remember that I Am a Man."

"...And Remember that I Am a Man."

Chapter Thirty-six

Your Honor—1816 A.D.

And The Lord said to Moses, "Pharaoh's heart is hardened, he refuses to let the people go."

Exodus 7:8,9

Moses felt the world crumble about him. This was even worse than when they'd taken Naomi away. It took all hope out of him. Numbly, he listened as the white men argued.

"Well, as you see, Mister Grice," said Master Trewitt. "I am a man of my word. This boy's owner says there was no agreement of any sort concerning his freedom."

Mister Grice's face went red with fury. "He's a liar. He agreed to give Moses his freedom."

Master Trewitt smirked. "Why, there are two things wrong with that statement, sir. One, Grandy is—or was, rather—the owner of this slave. He says there was talk about manumission, but no actual agreement. Two, even a slave's master cannot free him in the Commonwealth of North Carolina. That power is reserved by the courts."

"I know that," Mister Grice growled. "What kind of fool do you take me for?"

Master Trewitt's eyes flashed. "Why, I take you for an abolitionist and a nigger-lover, sir. What business is this of yours?

This is between me and Grandy."

"You...you..." Mister Grice sputtered.

"Good day, sir." Master Trewitt turned and re-entered the house.

Moses gulped. "What are we going to do, Mister Grice?" He knew he was powerless to act in his own defense. Without a champion, he was lost.

Mister Grice took a deep, shuddering breath and closed his eyes for a moment. "Lord, help me," he muttered, then looked at Moses. "I'll tell you what we're *not* going to do, Moses. We're not letting that scalawag win the day. This is all James Grandy's fault and my wife knows how to deal with him. You go and fetch her. I'll wait here."

"Yes, sir." Moses took off at a run.

When he neared the Grice home, Moses began shouting. "Miz Anna! Miz Anna!"

She met him on the porch, wearing an apron, a feather duster in hand. Her expression bespoke concern. "Moses, I thought you were still away. Whatever is the matter?"

Moses came to a halt, trying to catch his breath. "It's...it's awful, Miz Anna," he managed to gasp.

"What's awful, dear? Has something happened to the boats?"

He shook his head. "Miz Anna, you've got to come quick. Master James has sold me to a man from Virginia."

She gasped and dropped her duster. Her hand rose to her mouth, and her face went even paler than her husband's had turned earlier. "What...why...how?"

"Mister Grice says to come with me. He needs your help."

She gulped and nodded. Wringing both hands on her apron, she looked back into the house with consternation, then back at him. "But I was...let me get my...oh, never mind, it doesn't matter. Where are we going?"

"I don't know whose house it is, but it's right near the courthouse. Hurry, Miz Anna, we need to go."

He took her hand and led off. In minutes, they joined Mister Grice, who waited on the porch. Miz Anna went to him and took his hands.

"What's going on, William?" she asked. "Moses says James is up to his old tricks."

272

Grice nodded. "Worse than ever, I fear. But wait, I want you to see for yourself."

He knocked on the door and a white girl, who looked to be about twelve years of age, answered. She smiled but quickly turned serious when she saw the expressions of the Grices. "Yes?"

"Hello, Dorothy," Mister Grice said. "Will you please ask your guest, Mister Trewitt, to come out? And ask him to bring the paper he showed me a few minutes ago."

Master Trewitt soon appeared. "You again. What do you want now?"

"Mister Trewitt, this is my wife, Anna. She's the sister of James Grandy and I'd like you to show her that bill of sale."

Master Trewitt smiled affably. "By all means." He produced the paper and held it out. "Here you are, Mrs. Grice."

She accepted it with a trembling hand and held it up to read. Even though she'd been forewarned, she paled again. "Six hundred dollars," she said in disbelief. "Six hundred dollars." Her eyes filled with tears.

Moses felt himself begin to weep, also. He had come so close to freedom and it was being snatched away.

"Indeed," said Master Trewitt. "I was surprised to get such a prime nigra for so such a reasonable price."

Miz Anna looked up and glared at him through her tears. "No wonder! That's the same amount that Moses paid James for his freedom. Not only has he gone back on his word, he's doubled his profit while Moses remains a slave."

For the first time, Master Trewitt looked doubtful.

"You mean there really was such an agreement? Grandy told me it was all a sham, a story made up by abolitionists to discredit him."

"No, indeed," Miz Anna said through clenched teeth. "I saw the receipts for the money Moses paid. My brother promised to give him his freedom."

Master Trewitt squirmed under her stern gaze. "Why…er…I'm sorry. Grandy told me not to believe your husband, that he was…"

"An abolitionist and a nigger lover," supplied Mister Grice.

Master Trewitt used his comment as an excuse to take his eyes from Miz Anna. He looked at Mister Grice, his face flushed with embarrassment. "I'm sorry, sir. I'm afraid I was not aware of the true situation."

"And now that you know," asked Miz Anna, "what are you going to do about it?"

He regarded her again, and took a moment to draw himself up and gain his composure. "Why, I'll demand my money back, Madam, of course, and rescind the deal. I'm afraid I got carried away with the idea of having a slave who was so wise in the ways of commerce."

Moses leaned forward at the words. He felt a glimmer of hope.

"In that case," said Miz Anna, "I propose we take care of this matter on the instant. I'm sure I know exactly where my brother will be at this time of day."

She led the group toward Mister Woods' boarding house. Moses trailed behind the others, apparently forgotten in the heat of the moment, even though he was at the center of the matter. When they reached the boardinghouse, Moses held back on the porch, but Mister Grice pulled him inside. They came into a small foyer with a desk, behind which sat a small, bespectacled white man in an ancient, powdered wig. He looked up and frowned at the sight of Moses.

"You there, Grice. You can't bring..."

Mister Grice glared at him. "Hush, Woods. This is important."

Moses, unsure of himself, looked around. The boardinghouse was the fanciest building he'd ever been in. The walls were richly paneled, thick carpet covered the floor, and the stair railing leading to the second story was ornately carved. A painting on the wall depicted a group of white horsemen in red costumes, chasing dogs across a field. A buzz of conversation came from an arched entranceway and Moses glanced in.

Tables and chairs were scattered about below lighted candelabra that relieved the dimness of a large room with only one small window. Smoke filled the air, roiling up toward the ceiling. Along one side of the room ran a bar, where wildly gesticulating white men talked loudly to one another. At the far end of the space stood a billiards table, which Moses had heard of. Several men stood around the table, holding sticks, while another man leaned over to shoot. Even from behind, Moses recognized him by his spiky hair and wide buttocks. Master James.

Moses felt rage building inside him. He fought to quench the fire of his anger, as he always did, by recalling the day his mother had been whipped for nothing more than trying to protect one of her children. In this part of the world, it didn't matter if you were right or wrong, only if you were black or white. One false move against the white establishment, one "crime" that would be held against him, and everyone would "keep an eye" on him. The courts would never grant freedom to a troublesome nigger.

The Grices and Master Trewitt had apparently not realized their quarry was so near, because they were asking the boardinghouse owner to direct them to James Grandy. Moses found his feet carrying him toward the pool table. A hush came over the billiards room as he made his way across the space. Eyes went wide and mouths dropped at the unexpected sight of a black man among them, but no one tried to stop him. He came to a halt behind Master James just he struck a ball with the stick. That ball hit another, which rolled into a hole in the corner of the table.

"How's that for a shot, my boys?"

Master James rose and faced the players across the table, but quickly realized they watched something behind him. He turned, stick in hand, and went as white as if he'd seen a ghost. He swayed on his feet and Moses realized he was drunk. For only an instant did his eyes remain on Moses, and then they darted about, like those of a cornered animal.

Moses took a deep breath. "Master James, have you sold me?"

Master James eyes fluttered over Moses again, then resumed their quest for somewhere else—anywhere else—to be. Moses, who had never confronted a white person before, experienced a detached amazement. Where had this man's authority vanished to, when confronted with undeniable wrongdoing?

"Have you sold me?" he repeated.

"No!" Master James cried. His eyes locked on his accuser now, and they showed naked fear.

"Yes, you have," Moses insisted.

Master James looked slightly away and Moses realized that Miz Anna had come up to stand beside him. She remained silent, however.

"I…I…" Master James tried to speak, but then a sob burst from his lips. He turned, tossed the stick onto the table and stumbled toward a doorway into another room.

"You rotten scoundrel," Miz Anna whispered, so low that only Moses heard her. She stepped out after her brother, fury in her face.

Moses followed, but his way was impeded by curious white men who swarmed into his way. Moses didn't know them all by name, but most of their faces were familiar.

"What's going on?" one man asked.

"What's happening, Captain Grandy?" inquired Captain Minner, whom Moses hadn't known was in town.

"Master James has sold me to a man from Virginia," Moses told him.

"What? I thought he had made a deal with you," Captain Minner said. "Mrs. Grice has spread the word all around the county."

Moses was surprised by the amount of concern on the man's face? Why would he care what happened to a black man, even if they'd once sailed together? Glancing around, he saw the same worry on other white faces. What was going on?

Behind the men, Mister Grice and Master Trewitt had gone into the other room. Moses needed to get in there. He moved forward and the crowd parted to let him past, then followed him into what turned out to be a large sitting room, full of stuffed chairs and couches. Miz Anna confronted Master James, hands on her hips and chin out. Though she was half-a-head shorter, there was no doubt who was the master of this situation.

"You've shamed us," she told Master James.

"I…I'm sorry," he blubbered. Was he that drunk? Or was weakness a part of his character that Moses, his slave, had never seen?

Miz Anna said, "Don't you for an instant try to pretend you were too young to remember that Papa promised that Moses would never be sold, James Grandy."

The subject of her scorn sniffed and wiped his nose on a sleeve. She persisted. "So, why did you sell him?"

Master James gave his sister a pleading look. "You don't understand. No one understands. Everything's gone against me lately. I've had to mortgage what's left of the farm. It's like I don't have any luck at all."

276

"Have you ever thought about working for your luck, Grandy?" asked one of the men, billiards stick still in hand. "How do expect your farm to get along when you're in here, drinking all the time, while Captain Grandy is out working?"

That question brought a petulant, spoiled anger into Master James' eyes. "That's another reason I sold him," he said to the room at large. "I keep hearing about *Captain* Grandy, like he's something special. He's just another nigger, yet you all act like he's better than me, for God's sake."

Moses was astonished. Master James was whining like he had as a small child, and in front of all these people.

"Got more sense than you do, Grandy, that's for sure." Moses looked to see who'd spoken and was surprised it had been Mister Woods. Amazingly, though the owner had not wanted Moses in his boardinghouse, he now seemed to be on Moses' side.

"I want my money back," a voice demanded. Moses looked and saw that Master Trewitt had arrived. "I don't deal with those who go back on their word."

"Yes," insisted Miz Anna. "Give him his money back, on the instant."

"I…I can't." Master James had returned to his role of innocence betrayed.

"Why not?"

Master James wheezed air in through his nose and looked around the room like a dog expecting to be whipped.

"Yeah, why not, Grandy?" someone asked.

Lower lip trembling, Master James said, "I…I…I needed the money to pay off some debts. It's already gone."

"Tell you what," said Mister Woods. "I've had about enough of you, Grandy. Fetch your bags and get out of my establishment. You've worn out your welcome here, that's for sure."

Master James looked outraged. "What? Because I sold a nigger? He was mine to sell."

It was Master Trewitt who answered him. "Why, you don't get it, do you? You can sell your niggers, you can whip your niggers, you can starve your niggers, you can…" he paused and looked over at Miz Anna, "even mess with your nigger wenches. They're your property and you can do as you like. But you made a bargain with

277

this boy and he kept his half of it. And then you lied and, whether you tell a lie to a black man or a white, you lie before God, who sees all."

So maybe that was it, the reason for the consternation among the bar patrons. Was there some unwritten code the white men lived by? It seemed they were not so much sympathetic with his situation as concerned that Master James had been exposed as a liar by a black man.

Master James looked around, as though seeking a friendly face. "You…you don't…none of you understand!" he said, sobbing again, then bolted out of the room.

A silence fell. Men looked about at each other, and then made their way back to the billiards room. Soon, only Moses and the Grices remained. Even Master Trewitt had left. Then Moses realized someone else occupied the room.

In a corner sat a small, well-dressed man with a ring of white hair around a liver-spotted expanse of barren scalp. He had a large book on his lap and wore pince-nez spectacles with a chain leading to a vest pocket. The man had obviously been reading when James Grandy and the others had burst into the room. His eyebrows were quizzically cocked and his eyes bored into Moses.

Mister Grice also became aware of the distinguished man's presence and seemed taken aback. Then he nodded his head. "Good afternoon, Your Honor."

"…And Remember that I Am a Man."

Chapter Thirty-seven

Oyez, Oyez—1816 A.D.

The power of the master must be absolute, to render the submission of the slave perfect. I most freely confess my sense of the harshness of this proposition…But in the actual conditions of things, it must be so…[It] will be the imperative duty of the Judges to recognize the full dominion of the owner over the slave.

Thomas Carter Ruffin, Chief Justice, Supreme Court of North Carolina—1833-1852 A.D.
Writing in the case of State v. Mann—1829 A.D.

Moses sat on the ground outside the courthouse, beneath an open window. The judge, The Most Honorable Mister James Riddick, had agreed to hear Moses' case during this session, even though it had been filed late. Actually, it was Miz Anna's case; she had brought suit against her brother to force Moses' freedom. She said she was suing in Moses' name, but even that wasn't strictly true. Moses had no more legal standing than a mule, a fence, or a building. He was property, until the court said otherwise.

Not a breeze stirred. The day was blistering hot and Moses had been sitting there for hours, since he had no way of knowing when the judge would decide his fate. His only comfort came from being on the shady side of the building.

He spent a lot of time praying, but was often distracted by either

279

the action going on in the courtroom or the cawing of a large crow in a nearby tree.

Moses had already eavesdropped on a multitude of court actions that he'd never thought about before. It seemed as though nothing in the white man's world could be considered real until the judge had issued a marriage license, recorded a deed for land transactions, issued a birth or a death certificate, or performed some other legal function. Every significant event that had occurred in Camden County in the last six months, since the last session of the circuit court, had to be written in books that black men were not allowed to read.

The crow seemed just as interested in the goings-on as Moses. While court actions were being conducted, the bird would look toward the window and cock his head as though straining to hear. It often seemed to comment. Sometimes it let out a raucous, "Haw," as if it had expected the outcome of a case. Other times, it might softly say, "Uh-oh," as if disagreeing with the court proceedings. The crow probably knew about as much about what went on inside the courthouse as he did, Moses supposed, since much of the business seemed to be over his head.

He was nearly dozing when he heard, "…Mrs. Anna Grice versus Mister James Grandy." He got to his knees and put his ear close to the window, even though he'd had no trouble hearing from the ground. He did not raise his head above the sill, however, for it was likely he'd be chased away if he were noticed.

The clear, precise voice of someone called, "the bailiff," carried to Moses. "Mrs. Grice contends that her brother, Mister Grandy, entered into an agreement with a slave named Moses, who is the property of Mister Grandy. Mister Grandy agreed to set the slave free if the slave paid him the sum of six hundred dollars. According to Mrs. Grice, the slave, over a period of approximately four years, made payments to Mister Grandy, and the sum of these payments was six hundred dollars. Mister Grandy has refused to grant the slave freedom and Mrs. Grice begs the court to compel Mister Grandy to free the slave, Moses."

Judge Riddick, who had a low, deep, gravelly voice, spoke next. "Before we proceed, do any of the parties wish to have legal representation?"

"...And Remember that I Am a Man."

Moses had no idea what that meant, but he heard Miz Anna and Master James both say, "No, Your Honor."

"We'll hear from the plaintiff, first. Please swear her in."

All morning long, Moses had heard people sworn in, so he'd expected this. He waited while the bailiff recited the words.

When the oath had been completed, the judge said, "Mrs. Grice, please state the details of your case."

"Well, Your Honor..." Miz Anna went on to describe the situation, ending with, "But that scalawag of a brother of mine sold Moses anyway, after all he'd promised."

"You say that Mister Grandy agreed to sell the slave his freedom?" asked Judge Riddick.

"Yes, Your Honor."

"But you were not present when that agreement was reached?" the judge asked.

"No, I was not, Your Honor. My husband witnessed the agreement, though, and he is prepared to testify to that fact."

"But you *were* present when the final payment was rendered, you said."

"Yes, I was."

"And your brother agreed to free this slave?"

"Yes, Your Honor."

Someone cleared his throat; Moses figured it to be the judge, because he then asked, "Exactly what did he say?"

"Now let me think," Miz Anna said. "Something to the effect of, 'I promised Moses his freedom and he shall have it, as soon as I can file the papers.'"

"Hmm. And why do you suppose your brother mentioned filing papers?"

"Why, so he could record Moses' freedom, of course."

"I'll ask you to remember that point, Mrs. Grice," the judge said. Then, "And you say you saw receipts for money paid to Mister Grandy by his slave, Moses?"

"Yes, your honor."

"Did you read those receipts?"

Miz Anna took a moment to answer. "Well, no, Your Honor."

"So you do not actually know if the papers you saw *were* receipts, much less if they totaled six hundred dollars?"

"No, Your Honor." Miz Anna's voice sounded sheepish.

"Thank you, Mrs. Grice. Is Mister Grice present?"

"I am, Your Honor."

After Mister Grice had been sworn in, the judge continued.

"Mister Grice, you say you were present when Mister James Grandy entered into an agreement with the slave, Moses?"

"Yes, sir. James Grandy agreed to free Moses if he was paid six hundred dollars."

"And how was this sum arrived at? Why not eight hundred dollars or a thousand?"

"Well, sir, James,…um, Mister Grandy *did* originally ask for eight hundred, but I talked him down to six hundred."

"Hold on a moment," the judge said. "You say *you* talked him down?"

"Yes, Your Honor. I was…um, acting as his agent, so to speak."

Several seconds of silence followed, then Judge Riddick said., "This is very important. Your wife said her brother promised *the slave* his freedom. Was Mister Grandy's agreement with the slave or with you?"

"He promised Moses, Your Honor, like my wife said."

"And you witnessed this?"

"Yes, sir, Your Honor," Mister Grice said emphatically. "As God is my witness."

"Were you also present, when the slave presented his master with the last of his payments?"

"I was, Your Honor."

"And did you have occasion to read any of the alleged receipts given to the slave by Grandy?"

"I most certainly did, sir," Mister Grice replied with a firm voice. "Moses showed me several of them."

"Did you see all of them?"

"No, sir."

"And did you ever add them up to see what the total was?"

"No, sir. As I said, I didn't see all of them. But I was present when James Grandy added them up and said Moses had paid him the agreed price, so Grandy promised to free him."

"He promised the slave?"

"Yes, sir, Your Honor."

"…And Remember that I Am a Man."

"That's plain enough. Mister Grice, you may step down. Please swear in Mister James Grandy, bailiff."

Moses felt a surge of hope. It was clear that Judge Riddick accepted Mister Grice's word that there had been a promise of freedom in exchange for money.

"Uh-oh," said the crow from his branch.

Moses looked up and glared, "Shut up, bird. You don't know nothin'."

"Uh-oh," insisted the bird.

What was with that darned crow? Everything inside the courtroom was going in Moses' favor. And even though the bird's cawing had nothing to do with the proceedings of the court, Moses feared the crow might bring him bad luck.

Surprisingly, Mister Grice's voice came from the window again. "If you please, Your Honor, may I have a word?"

"Concerning?" asked the judge.

"I would like to comment on the character of the slave, Moses."

A moment's silence. Moses could just see that old judge staring at Mister Grice with his eyebrows cocked. "I can see no harm in it," Judge Riddick finally said.

"Your Honor, Captain Grandy…"

The judge interrupted. "You call the slave *'Captain'* Grandy, sir?"

"I do, Your Honor. Moses was the first black captain, back when the blockade was on during the war. He has been transporting goods in these waters for many years now, without ever losing a cargo. He has worked for me—as well as other merchants—on a percentage basis, for many years. In my case, I have given him authority to deal on my behalf in the selling of my products. Not once, in all those years, have his accounts been off so much as a half-penny. I urge the court to give him his freedom."

"I see. Thank you, Mr. Grice, I'll take that into consideration. Now we'll hear from Mister Grandy."

Moses felt pride that he could count a white man such as Mister Grice as a friend. But he couldn't help thinking of other whites who had seemed to be considerate. Master James had, as a child, been his friend. Mister Kemp had been nice, but then had abandoned him. Master Micheau had been touted as a kind master, but had beaten him with a fireplace shovel.

"...And Remember that I Am a Man."

But no, he told himself, there were others. Missy Hannah, Mister Furley, Captain Minner, Moses Myers up in Norfolk and, of course, the Grices. Mister Furley had once said, though, he did not believe black people to be anywhere near the equal of whites. How many of Moses' other white friends secretly felt that way?

Moses suddenly realized he'd not been paying attention when he heard Master James's voice coming from inside the courthouse. "Well, er, yes, Your Honor, I did talk with my slave Moses about him buying his freedom, in a manner of speaking. And I meant to go along with it, y'know, but then with expenses on the farm being so high, I..."

"Mister Grandy," the judge broke in. "I don't have a lot of time, seeing as how I added this case to the schedule. Let's cut to the chase. Mister Grice has testified to hearing you promise the Negro his freedom in exchange for six hundred dollars. Both Mister and Mrs. Grice were present when you accepted final payment from the Negro and they say you agreed the bargain had been kept. Is that true?"

"Well, er, yes, Your Honor, that was the gist of it."

"And, after you received that payment, you promised the slave his freedom. Is that true?"

"Well, I did, but..."

"Now this is very important," Judge Riddick said. "Did you make that promise to Mister or Mrs. Grice, or to your Negro?"

There was a short pause and Moses could guess that Master James's eyes were darting about, weasel-like, as they had done when he was a child when he wondered if he could get away with something. The silence was broken with a long sigh and then Master James said, "To Moses, my slave."

"And did you make the original agreement with the slave or with Mister Grice?"

Another sigh. "With the slave, Your Honor."

The judge said, "And do you both agree that this was the case?"

For a moment, Moses wondered who he was asking, but then Mister and Mrs. Grice both said, "Yes, Your Honor."

"In that case, the matter is clear and I'm ready to hand down my verdict."

"Uh-oh," said the crow.

"Shut up," Moses said. He didn't pay the bird much mind, though. The judge had got Master James to admit to their bargain, so the verdict was certain. *Thank you, Jesus.*

"Mister Grandy, a slave and all the fruits of that slave's labor belong to the master. The slave Moses, and all his earnings belong to you and you have the right to do as you please with your property. I find your behavior abominable, however. A man should always live up to his word."

Here it comes, thought Moses, taking a deep, unsteady breath. He was about to become a free man.

"That being said," continued Judge Riddick, "I must follow the law, which is clear concerning this case. In the Commonwealth of North Carolina, a slave has no legal status. Therefore, an agreement between a slave and his master has no legal standing, and is not binding. I find for the defendant, James Grandy."

Moses felt as if he'd been struck by the powerful hand of God Himself. Off in the distance, he heard Miz Anna cry out.

"But, Your Honor…"

"Silence in the court," the judge loudly said. Something banged down like a hammer hitting a board. Then the judge continued. "According to the law, a slave can not be freed by his master, no matter what the circumstances. Only the court can free a slave. The Negro in question will remain a slave until his legitimate master petitions this court for the freedom of this Negro, and he will not become legally free until he also spends a year and a day in a free, northern state to establish his residency."

Moses wasn't listening. Mister Grice and Miz Anna would soon be coming out of the courthouse, and he couldn't face them, much less have to look upon Master James. At the moment, he wished he never had to set eyes on another white man as long as he lived. He ran away from the courthouse.

"Haw," the crow cried. "Haw, haw."

"…And Remember that I Am a Man."

"…And Remember that I Am a Man."

Chapter Thirty-eight

Venom—1816 A.D.

I once heard Douglass in a speech in Rochester, in a strain of subdued yet powerful eloquence, say: 'I sometimes forget the color of my skin, and remember that I am a man. I sometimes forget that I am hated of men, and remember I am loved of God.

Frederick Douglass, the Colored Orator, by Frederic May Holland. 1895 A.D.

Moses headed deep into the swamp, his mind reeling, with no destination in his mind and no hope in his heart. His new master would probably put out a runaway notice on him, but he didn't care anymore. Just let them try to find him. He carried a long stick against snakes, as always. It would be better to have a gun, but being caught with any weapon, even a knife, could mean a whipping

The last time he'd run, after Master Micheau had beaten him, he hadn't known much about the swamp and had been running blind. Now, though, he knew where all the trails and railroads led. Besides, he was well known among the black laborers who harvested timber from the Great Dismal. He could hide out in here for years.

He gave no thought to running for the north, remembering what Mister Furley had said years ago. Even if he managed to get through Virginia, with its many wide rivers and bays, to a free state, he'd be brought back and whipped.

A loud hiss sounded and he started. Fear overtook him at the sound. A large, fat water moccasin lay in his path, coiled and ready to strike. If the snake hadn't hissed, he'd have walked right into it.

For the first time in his life, however, his terror of snakes was overcome by another emotion: rage. It seemed like something always stood in his way. Without consciously willing his arms to move, he took the walking stick in both hands and lashed out. The wooden staff struck the moccasin below the head and carried through. Part of the snake wound around the stick and the creature was pulled out of its coiled position.

Then Moses was on it. He struck again and again, crying and sobbing. The reptile was probably dead after the third blow, but he kept beating it.

"Take that. And that. And that," he cried mindlessly, until it became a litany. He didn't stop until he could no longer lift his arms. In the end, the once-terrifying creature was no more than a mass of blood, pulp and bone on the wet ground.

Moses had to lean on the stick to remain upright until his bawling ceased. His face ran wet with tears, his body soaked with sweat. He had never killed a snake before, having been too terrified to get near enough.

His mind cleared and he looked down on the gory mess at his feet, considering what he'd done. Finally, he said, "How'd you like them apples, *Master* James?"

Then he continued on, not bothering to walk around the dead snake, but stepping on the remains.

For the next three days, he wandered the swamp, killing snakes. The snakes all had names: Enoch Sawyer. Chadwick. Jemmy Coates. Wiley McPherson. Billy Grandy. Quentin Henholer. Judge James Riddick. William Trewitt. But many of the cold-blooded crawlers shared the same name: James Grandy.

*

Moses asked around and learned that Master Trewitt was now staying at Mister Woods' boarding house, which would not be over-crowded now that court week was over. He went to the front door of the establishment, knocked, and asked to see his new master.

288

"…And Remember that I Am a Man."

He waited on the porch, nodding obsequiously to white passersby like the most docile of slaves. The afternoon was chilly and cold, misty rain had been falling since the night before, so Moses was grateful for the shelter. He had been walking since the first light of dawn, determined not to let another day go by without hope.

"Well, if it isn't *Captain* Grandy, himself," Master Trewitt said as he appeared on the porch, in his usual shabby attire. "I thought I'd have to post fliers on you, *Captain.*"

Moses steeled himself. He'd have to walk a fine line between resolution and insolence.

"Yes, Master, I've returned," he said. "I'm sorry I lost my head and ran off, but I'll make it up to you, I promise."

Master Trewitt was obviously taken aback. "Why, why, yes, of course, boy," he said. "I'm a forgiving man. But you'll have to toe the line from here on in."

"What line is that, sir?" Moses could feel the firmness in his voice.

Again Master Trewitt seemed surprised. "The line between master and slave of course. The line between obedience and disobedience, respect and disrespect."

Moses looked the man dead in the eye. God had abandoned him, so it was all up to him. "Why did you buy me after Mister Grice and I both told you I'd bought my freedom?"

"Why…" Master Trewitt seemed at a loss for words, but didn't drop his gaze immediately. Then something went on deep within his eyes. Embarassment? "Why, I'm actually sorry about that, boy. I didn't believe someone would sell you your freedom for a measly six hundred dollars, so I went to James Grandy and inquired. He told me that, no matter what the common opinion in the county was, he had made no promises to you."

"He lied," Moses said.

Master Trewitt finally looked away. "I know that now. But what's done is done. You belong to me now."

"Yes, I'm your property," Moses agreed. "But what sort of a slave do you expect me to be?"

"Huh? Why, well, I already told you. An obedient slave."

"And a hard-working slave?"

A white man came out of the house, excusing himself. Moses and

"…And Remember that I Am a Man."

Master Trewitt stepped out of the way. The pause allowed time for Master Trewitt to regain his confidence now that Moses had agreed he was mere property.

"Yes, of course, a hard-working slave. Why else would I have been so interested in acquiring you, Moses?"

It was the first time Master Trewitt had called him by his true name and Moses hoped it was an indication he was softening.

"I assumed, Master Trewitt, it was because I was so profitable to my last owner and also to Mister Grice."

Master Trewitt nodded emphatically. "Exactly."

"Why do you suppose I earned them so much money, Master Trewitt?"

"Well, because you're a hard worker of course. But where is all this talk going, boy?"

"I worked so hard, sir, because I thought that work would mean my freedom."

Master Trewitt's eyes narrowed. "I should have guessed. We're back to that again, are we?"

Moses took a deep breath. "Master Trewitt, you said you're a forgiving and fair man, but you are foremost a business man, are you not?"

The white man nodded.

"You paid six hundred dollars for me, sir, and being somewhat of a business man myself, I realize that, to you this is purely a business investment, is it not?"

Master Trewitt nodded again and his look of suspicion deepened.

Moses plowed on. "I plan to make your investment profitable, and the best way to make that happen is for me to get something out of it. I will work as hard as possible and propose to make you a handsome profit. If you allow me, over time, to repay your six hundred dollar investment, you will have several years of profit from me and not have paid a cent for it. I, in turn, will have my freedom. What do you say to that, sir?"

Master Trewitt's eyes had flickered with interest every time Moses mentioned profit, but now his expression hardened again. Moses belatedly realized his final words had been uttered in a tone of challenge. He'd overstepped his bounds.

"...And Remember that I Am a Man."

"I say I'll have you whipped," Trewitt said, all the puffed-up slave master, "then put you to work. If you won't work, I'll sell you downriver. Now what do you say?"

"Sir, with all the respect in the world, if you were to whip me and then sell me, you'd lose money. No one would pay top dollar for a slave with a scarred back, a trouble maker."

"It might be worth it to shut up your sass, boy."

Moses summoned up all his will. "Sir, I have decided that, if you have me whipped, you'll not get a day's work out of me. But if you'll allow me to work for my manumission, I'll be the obedient, hard-working slave you desire, and you'll never hear another sassy word out of my mouth."

Trewitt shoved his face forward. His eyes narrowed and his cheeks sucked in. He looked so angry Moses half-expected smoke to come from the white man's ears and fully expected to be bloody-backed by nightfall.

Instead, what came from Trewitt surprised him. "You promise that?"

Moses gulped. He nodded.

"You've got a deal, then."

"...And Remember that I Am a Man."

Chapter Thirty-nine

A Suitable Person—1818 A.D.

In view of the failure to hear any thing of my wife, many of my best friends advised me to get married again, if I could find a suitable person. They regarded my former wife as dead to me, and all had been done that could be.

<u>*Narrative of the Life of Henry Bibb*</u>*—1849 A.D.*

Trewitt purchased two canal boats and Moses got pretty much the same deal he'd had with Grice. Moses worked hard and soon a third boat was added. It was taking longer than he'd expected however, to earn the extra six hundred dollars above and beyond expenses, because the economy was poor at present. It didn't help that hc had to pay higher wages because the county boasted fewer and fewer free blacks. Nowadays, it was quite common for a free Negro to disappear, often in the middle of the night. They were being sold south, of course, where cotton prices were high and labor forces low.

The dilemma of those free blacks was not unlike Moses' situation had been when Trewitt came on the scene. A black man might proclaim freedom so loudly God could hear him in heaven, but it did him no good without papers or the word of a white person to back him up. Even if one of these poor unfortunates had managed to hold onto his free-paper and produced it to someone in authority, the document would surely be torn to shreds.

Moses drifted like a canal boat, unable to leave its ordained path down the waterway. He had no one left. Mama was dead, Tamar had been sold away by the Grandy demon and Benjamin was long gone. Worst of all, as day piled upon dismal day, he found it harder and harder to call up Naomi's face. Every receipt toward freedom placed in his secret stash only helped to underscore his helplessness. He no longer prayed. At the court hearing, God had deserted him.

Then, one hot summer morning when the canal boats were passing by Sawyer's Ferry, he saw her. Slender and beautiful as ever, she was cleaning fish on the edge of the ferry dock, throwing guts and fishheads into the water. Another woman was with her and the two of them were laughing and carrying on as they worked.

"Naomi," he cried.

She turned toward him with a look of confused surprise. With the bright sun shining on her light-brown skin, her beauty seemed greater than ever.

He jumped into the river. He hadn't forgotten that he couldn't swim, but he *had* forgotten this wasn't the shallow canal, where he could wade. Even when he realized his predicament, however, he didn't turn back. Paddling, splashing, and trying to keep his head above water, he made his way toward the dock.

But he soon sucked in water and began sputtering. Panic overcame him. This was life or death. Movement became erratic, survival rather than purpose.

He took on more water and went under, arms and legs flailing, but he was unable to keep above the surface. There was no air in his lungs; his last breath had sucked in water. Within seconds, everything became dreamy. He could see nothing in the muddy brown water. His slowing struggles were soundless and his mouth and nose were deadened by tasteless fluid. The river was cool to his skin and he reflected how it felt quite pleasant after the blistering heat of the day. Maybe he should learn to swim one day, so he could beat the sweaty, dirty reality of life on the waterways. But for now, he'd relax and enjoy the quiet.

*

"…And Remember that I Am a Man."

He awakened to scorching fire, liquid flames searing his throat and nasal passages with ripping, tearing, scratching heat as he brought up water. Something slammed into his back—he was on his stomach, he realized, stretched out over something shaped like a mule's back—and another rush of sizzling, painful water went through and out of him. He gasped for air, but choked and vomited another torrent of water. Now his lungs also burned, deep inside. Through another bout of choking, gagging and coughing, he managed to snatch a breath of sweet, cool air.

Moses opened his eyes and they began burning, too. He could see nothing but a shimmering haze of colors, objects being too indistinct through the blur. What had cruelly yanked him from his cool respite in the river and tossed him into a fiery pit?

"I think he's breathing," a female voice said.

"Thank God," said another. "Let's get him off the barrel."

Hands tugged and pulled him down onto a hard surface and turned him on his back. A hand touched his face and the aroma of cooked crabs entered his nostrils. A thumb wrenched one of his eyelids wide open.

"He's coming around."

Moses' breath came easier now and the pain of fire receded. His vision cleared. A face appeared, looking down at him. As the features came into focus, he recognized Naomi. He brought a leaden hand up to touch her face, but she drew back.

Moses struggled. Although his muscles were painful and movements slow, he managed to rise onto his elbows and look for her.

There she was, kneeling beside him her deep brown eyes alarmed and concerned. For some reason, her thin dress was soaked. It clung to her body, nearly transparent.

She saw him looking.

"Whatcha gawkin' at? Aintcha never seen a girl before?"

There was annoyance in Naomi's words, but a smile graced her lips.

"I love you," he managed to say.

"What?" Wide-eyed, Naomi looked over to his other side and Moses realized there was a different girl there. He remembered everything then. It was the girl who had been cleaning fish with Naomi on the dock.

Naomi's eyes came back to him and now the annoyance showed in her face. "Are you crazy, mister? If you are, I jus' might throw you back in the river."

What was wrong with her? "Please," he said. "Don't—don't you recognize me?"

Naomi leaned closer and peered at his face. Recognition came into her eyes.

"Sure I do. You're Moses…"

His heart leapt with joy.

"…the man who married my sister."

*

Moses knew he should feel guilty about having feelings for a woman other than his wife, but he didn't. Betsy was *almost* Naomi and Betsy was *here*. Every time the boats were docked anywhere near Sawyer's Ferry, he went to see her.

It was almost as if he had gone back to when he'd been hired by Enoch Sawyer, and Naomi had always put him off. Betsy fussed and scolded and told Moses he should quit hanging around; she had several other admirers and they were all nearer to her own age. Besides, he was *married*, and to her sister. But she didn't chase him away.

There came a time when she stopped mentioning other young men, a time when they would take long walks and Moses would tell her of places he'd been and his hopes for eventual freedom. They even wistfully talked of Naomi and how much they both loved and missed her. Naomi became something Moses and Betsy shared, rather than a wife whose existence proscribed their own love.

When Betsy agreed to become his wife, Moses wanted more than the secret relationship he'd had with Naomi. He'd had enough of skulking around at night. He had nothing to be ashamed of and was doing nothing wrong.

*

And so, on a cool autumn morning, he knocked on the back door of Enoch Sawyer's house, identified himself, and asked to see the

296

master. He'd thought about going to the front door, since Sawyer didn't own him and he had nothing to fear from the man, but he didn't want to start off on a bad footing.

Enoch Sawyer soon appeared, wearing a smart-looking suit, but only stockings on his feet. He was smiling and didn't look nearly as much like a weasel as Moses remembered. He looked older, though, with his hair receding.

"Well, Captain Grandy," he said, standing in the doorway. "I'm surprised to see you here. Are you bringing me some consignment of goods, or is there something I can do for you?"

Moses was taken aback. He had introduced himself only as Moses, and was surprised Sawyer knew who he was. He'd had no personal contact with the man since he'd been hired away from the ferry.

"No, Master Sawyer, no goods. I came to ask something of you."

Sawyer chuckled, surprising Moses again. He had always thought of this man as a stern, uncaring bastard. "I'm not surprised. I've seen you hanging around young Betsy like an orphaned calf."

"You know about that?"

"I do. Not much happens with my slaves that I don't notice."

You don't seem to notice when they're starving in the winter, Moses thought. *You don't seem to notice they have no warm clothing.*

But Sawyer wasn't through speaking. "Not to mention I've been keeping an eye on you, Captain Grandy."

"On me, sir?"

Sawyer nodded. His smile was still wide, but he studied Moses' face as he said, "Ever since you set my boat adrift that time."

"Er, what boat sir?" Damn, he was stammering and he'd planned to be calm and confident, although still seeming subservient.

"Come now, Moses. I'm not a stupid man. I've had many a private laugh thinking about how you tricked me."

This wasn't going at all like Moses had planned. He hadn't thought Sawyer would recognize him, since they'd rarely seen each other and never spoken. He swallowed and wondered whether he should own up to his little act of piracy. But what if this white man was only trying to trick him into confessing?

Sawyer smiled even more broadly, as though he enjoyed watching Moses squirm. "Yes, ever since then I've paid attention to any gossip about you. News travels fast in this county, you know."

Moses nodded, wondering where all this was leading.

Sawyer continued. "No other slave has ever tricked me like that. You're one smart nigger, you know that?"

Moses didn't know how to reply. If he agreed, it would seem as though he had an inflated opinion of himself. And if he didn't, he'd be contradicting a white man he wanted a favor from.

But Sawyer wasn't through talking. "So I was pleased when you took up with my Naomi a few years back."

Holy Begeezus! Sawyer couldn't have surprised Moses more if he'd sprouted horns and a tail.

"Er, um, you knew about that, sir?"

"Like I told you, boy, I don't miss much. I was hoping for some right-smart whelps out of the two of you. Too bad I had to sell her off."

Did he dare ask? He had to.

"Why, sir? Why did you sell Naomi?"

Sawyer shrugged. "I had some debts coming due and someone offered me a good price for her."

"And did you…" Moses broke off. He wanted to ask if Sawyer had even considered how devastated Moses and Naomi would be. But, even as upset and befuddled as he was, he knew it would be the wrong thing to ask. Clearly, like most white men he'd known, Sawyer operated out of self-interest. It had been strictly business.

Sawyer's smile disappeared. As if he had been reading Moses' mind, he said, "But business is business and that's all water under the bridge. Now, boy, what brings you to my door, as if I didn't know?"

Moses had no doubt Sawyer knew. He'd already said he'd seen Moses courting Betsy. This was the most observant, intelligent man he'd ever come up against. Also the coldest. Moses realized now that Sawyer had been smiling because he planned to somehow get the best of this "smart nigger." Was he going to enjoy telling the black man who'd once tricked him to go jump off a pier?

"Um, it's about Betsy, sir. We want to…to…" To what? He couldn't say, "get married," because slaves weren't allowed to wed.

"…And Remember that I Am a Man."

And now Sawyer's smile reappeared. "Hell's fire, boy, go ahead and shack up with her, if that's what you want. Maybe I'll get those smart little nigger babies after all. Especially if you move in with her and hump her regular-like."

"…And Remember that I Am a Man."

"…And Remember that I Am a Man."

Chapter Forty

Christmas Gift—1819 A.D.

As a general thing, the great mass of slaves do not know or care any thing at all about freedom, and spend their money just as fast as they get it. A great many of them are even too indolent to strive to make any money for themselves, but spend their holidays sleeping, fishing, or playing like so many children; while the evenings are devoted almost wholly to dancing, banjo-playing, singing, chit-chatting, or to coon-hunting and night-fishing.

Social Relations in our Southern States, *Daniel Robinson Hundley—1860 A.D.*

On the day before Christmas, Moses and his crew tied the barges up at the dock Trewitt had rented, a bit north of Camden Courthouse. Once the cargo taken off and the lines secured, he headed for Trewitt's office with a spring in his step. He hoped his master had not gone home early because of the holiday. When the two had divided the money that Moses wore in a money-belt, Moses would have enough money to pay off the crew and also make the final payment for his freedom. It would take every cent he had, so he and Betsy might have lean times before he made any money as a free man, but lean times were no stranger to any slave household. But he and Betsy were determined their first child, due in a couple of months would be born to a free man. The infant would still be a slave, like his mother, though.

301

"...And Remember that I Am a Man."

Trewitt was not in the office, but Moses learned he could find the man at a nearby warehouse. He knew the place, where shippers sub-leased parts of the large building. Moses found him easily enough, in a corner of the warehouse, where several small offices were available for the use of clients. Trewitt seemed glad to see him, but not for any reason Moses expected.

"Why, Moses, I'm glad you're back," Trewitt said. "I have an urgent matter for you to attend to."

"On Christmas eve? I just got back from Norfolk and I want to go to my wife."

"Yes, yes, I know what day it is," Trewitt replied. "But I have a letter that must get to Mr. Mews, down on Newbegun Creek. He's leaving for Baltimore on the day after Christmas and he must have this information from me."

"Master Trewitt, I just got back from a long voyage and I have the last of the money for my free-paper." Moses pulled a stuffed envelope from his money belt. "Let's go to your office and settle up. I'd as soon not be carrying this much money over the holiday."

"My office is closed for the day." Trewitt reached out and took the envelope from Moses. "I'll hold on to this and we'll settle when you get back from Newbegun Creek."

Moses didn't want to take on an errand. Yes, he was Trewitt's slave, but not in the usual sense; they had more of a business relationship. Yet he couldn't refuse to do Trewitt's bidding. After they'd settled the last of the payments, it would be different, but until then...

"Sir, I'm very tired. I want to be with my wife on Christmas."

"Why, so you shall, my boy," Trewitt said. "Run this letter down to Mr. Mews this evening and you can come back on the morrow and spend Christmas with your wife. Tell you what," he pulled money from his pocket, "take care of this for me and I'll pay you two dollars. You can buy a Christmas gift for your woman."

Moses didn't bother to point out that the sole store in the area would be closed on Christmas day. "Sir, my wife is expecting me and..."

A man, who Moses recognized as Mr. Shaw from previous dealings, walked into the room. "Did I hear Captain Grandy's voice?" he asked, although he'd already seen Moses and had no need to ask. "I need your services, Captain."

Moses liked Shaw, who'd always treated him fairly and had once given him extra money for good service. "Hello, Mister Shaw," he said. "What do you need me for?"

"I've had a vessel loaded for two days," Shaw said, "because I have nobody I can trust to deliver them. It's urgent that I get the goods to the buyer. You'll need to leave right away."

"Why, hold on, Friend Shaw," Trewitt said. "I've already given Moses a letter to take to a client of mine, Mr. Mews."

"Mews?" Shaw frowned as if pondering. "Doesn't he live on Newbegun Creek?"

"Why, yes, that's right."

Shaw broke out in a smile. "Now that's a coincidence. My shipment must get to Mr. Knox. He also lives beside Newbegun."

Moses broke in. "Mister Shaw, I really don't want to take a trip downriver on Christmas Eve."

"I'll pay you five dollars," Shaw said. "That's decent money, considering the creek's so close."

"Why, that makes seven dollars, Moses," Trewitt said. "You can run down there this evening and come back in the morning."

Moses considered. "How big is your boat, Mister Shaw?"

"It's just a skiff. You can handle it yourself, if you don't mind the work of unloading the goods at Mr. Knox's dock. It's not that much and it's all in kegs, so it doesn't need to be put out of the weather."

Sighing, Moses realized the deal was too good to be refused. And it was an easy run up the creek, since a full moon would be rising early.

"I'll do it," he said. "If you'll pay me up front so I'll have something to show Betsy why I didn't come home tonight."

*

Moses anchored out in the river, off the mouth of Newbegun Creek on the western side of the sound, a few miles south of Elizabeth City. The night was cold and breezy, but Moses was inured to all types of weather by his years as a waterman. He slouched down beneath a gunwale, out of the wind, and waited for the moon.

303

"…And Remember that I Am a Man."

Seven dollars was a lot for one night's work, and a bit of money *would* be welcomed by Betsy. She'd been scrimping by all this time, so he could get his freedom as soon as possible.

Moses and Betsy had decided he would stay in Camden County, once he got his free-paper, even though it would have been safer for him to go north and earn the money to buy her free. After all, how would he get back down here to bring her north, along with the baby who would be arriving in short while?

Besides, it had taken him nearly three years to get the money for buying himself, and he wasn't about to leave Betsy alone for that long. He'd already lost one wife; he didn't want to lose this one, too. Sawyer might sell her off, along with the baby, before he could get back. Moses had been paying Sawyer, a little at a time, so the white man would be seeing a profit off Betsy. That was how most white men thought, in terms of profit. Especially Master Sawyer, who squeezed every penny.

Betsy had laughed when Moses told her how smart her master seemed to be, not letting anything get by him.

"Moses, darling," she had said, "he's not all that smart. He's cunning, though. He's got spies that let him know what's going on."

"You mean he's got slaves telling on other slaves?"

"You've got it," Betsy said. "He gives extra food to those who'll spy for him."

Moses remembered the time he'd been duped by a fellow slave and locked in a shed overnight. Betsy was right. Sawyer was devious and tricky.

When the full moon rose, Moses put his oars into the locks and headed up the wide creek. His muscles were stiff from the cold, but soon warmed up. There wasn't much current so he made good time.

He tied up to Knox's wharf and, one-by-one, lifted the heavy kegs to shoulder height and slid them onto the dock. Then he climbed up and stacked them neatly. By the time he had finished, dawn was about to break.

He continued his journey up the creek until it narrowed and jogged to the right. Now that it was light, the landing was easy to find. He pulled the skiff up onto dry land so it wouldn't float off when the tide rose, then trudged two miles up a narrow path to Weeksville Road, eating a piece of corned herring as he went along.

304

"…And Remember that I Am a Man."

Mister Shaw had given him directions, so he had no trouble finding his way.

The two-story, shingled house sat well back from the road. Smoke curled from the fireplace and Moses hoped Mews might invite him in to warm up. He knocked on the door.

Moses was surprised when Mews appeared at the door still in his nightshirt. It was two hours past daybreak and most people were hard at work by this time of morning. Then he remembered what day it was.

"Happy Christmas, Mister Mews," he said.

"And Happy Christmas to you, boy," Mews answered. He was a short, thin, balding man with a heavy mustache. Moses remembered him because he'd been one of those who supported him when Master James had back-stabbed him.

"I have a letter here from Mister Trewitt, sir," Moses said.

Mews's eyebrows rose and he frowned. "On Christmas Day?"

"Yes, sir."

"Well, come in and warm up by the fire, Moses. Let me see what this is all about."

Moses entered gratefully. The room was richly appointed with dark wood furniture and brocade curtains. A fireplace stood in one wall. He went over and held his hands out to bask in the heat.

"I sure do appreciate letting me warm up, Mister Mews."

Mews, intent on the letter he had opened, did not answer. Moses studied a long rifle that hung over the fireplace. It was a fancy piece, dark wood with silver fittings and fancy engravings. Mews must be worth a lot of money. Moses figured the gun to be valued at more than he was.

"Well, you belong to me now, Moses."

Moses whirled around. "What?"

"I said 'you belong to me'." He brandished the letter. "Trewitt has failed."

"But how, sir?"

"He's gone under, lock, stock and barrel," Mews said. "He's been in financial trouble for quite some time, but I thought he'd come out of it."

Moses took a deep breath. "I understand 'failed,' sir. But how does that make you my master?"

"Do you recollect when Trewitt chartered Wilson Sawyer's brig to the West Indies?"

"Yes, sir, I do."

"Well, Trewitt came to me to borrow money, but I wouldn't loan him anything without collateral. The only thing he hadn't already mortgaged was you."

"He...he mortgaged *me*?" *The bastard.* He—and Shaw, too, apparently—had tricked Moses into coming here and had even made him carry the letter that betrayed him. "How long ago did he take out the mortgage?"

Mews pursed his lips. "Hmm, let me think. I don't know the exact date, but it was around harvest time."

Moses fingered the seven dollars in his pocket. He would have been tricked out of even that paltry sum if he hadn't insisted on advance payment. Trewitt had been taking money from Moses the last few months with the knowledge that freedom was out of the question. Was there nothing that white men would not stoop to doing for a few dollars? Then he remembered Judas. Even Jesus had been tricked for a few dollars.

"I'm sorry, Moses," Mews was saying. "I thought he'd buy the mortgage back, but then the brig hit a reef and Trewitt couldn't pay me. I still had hopes, but now he's said he can't pay."

"But, please sir, didn't you support Mister Grice and Miz Anna when they tried to get my freedom from the court?"

"I did and I still think you should have been freed." Mews sighed. "I would not have taken the mortgage on you, but I thought Trewitt was sure to make a profit on that voyage."

Trewitt had wanted Moses to captain that brig to the Indies, but Wilson Sawyer had insisted on his own captain. Now Moses wished he'd gone on that ship; he'd have been better off going down with her.

"…And Remember that I Am a Man."

Chapter Forty-one

Blackmail—1819 A.D.

"Joe," said a master, "if you will work well for me, you shall be buried in my grave." The slave said nothing, in reply; but thought, Massa is a bad man, and that he would not like to be buried near him. The slave thought he had been too near his master, all his life, and had rather be away from him, when he died. Seeing the slave idling, "Joe," shouted his master, "have you forgotten what I promised you, if you work well?" "No, Massa, me bemember; but me don't want." "What for, Joe?" "Because de debbil might some day come, and steal me away, in mistake for you, Massa." His master was silent on this subject ever afterwards

Slave Life in Virginia and Kentucky, or, Fifty Years of Slavery in the Southern States of America, Francis Fedric—1863 A.D.

Moses didn't remember crossing the room and opening the door, but the cold air outside made him aware of his surroundings, although still numb with shock. All he could think of was getting home to Betsy, to the only place in the world where he was truly welcome. He was halfway back to the creek when he heard someone coming up behind him. Expecting it would be Mews, he quickened his pace.

"Wait, hold up there, you."

"...And Remember that I Am a Man."

It didn't sound like Mews. Moses stopped and turned. An old man with a fringe of white hair around his shiny black scalp was walking quickly, despite a severe limp in his left leg. He wore livery that marked him as a house servant.

"What do you want?" Moses asked.

The man came to a halt ten feet away, huffing and puffing. "Massah...Massah..." He took a deep breath. "Master Mews says you come back. He says you needs to talk."

Moses shook his head. "I have nothing to say to the man."

The old man looked concerned. "Don't you be sayin' nothin' like that. White man says you come, you come."

"To hell with white men. I've had enough of them."

"Why you actin' like that, boy?" The oldster was obviously horrified by such talk. "Somethin' got you riled?"

Moses set his mouth in a firm line and shook his head, afraid he'd burst into tears if he mentioned how he'd been duped again.

The old man peered carefully at him. "You know what you're doin', boy? Master Mews is purty easy to get along with, but he don't take kindly to being disobeyed. He'll send the pattyrollers after you."

Moses wasn't afraid of the patrollers, but only because he didn't think they'd be able to find him. He would head up the river and into the swamp, where the patrol wouldn't follow. This time he'd stay there, find a group of maroons to join.

Then he realized things had changed since he'd run away before. There was Betsy to consider. The swamp was no place to give birth to a baby. If he left her at Sawyer's Ferry, she'd be safe, but would he ever see his son or daughter? Once Moses got into the swamp, he'd be a wanted man, unable to come back out.

"What does your master want to talk to me about?" he asked.

"Now how in tarnation would I know, boy? I don't know what you was talkin' about in the first place. All I knows is Master Mews says, 'Clarence, you go after that boy. Get him back here; I weren't done talkin' to him yet.'"

Moses sighed and tried to stiffen his spine. "All right. I'll come with you."

Mews had changed out of his nightshirt when they got back.

"Where the hell did you think you were going?" he asked. "I told you. You belong to me now and I'll not have one of my nigras being disrespectful."

Moses swallowed. In the past, when a white man got angry, he'd have used submissive "Massah" language to mollify the white, but he was done with that. He must keep a firm tone and still seem respectful.

"I'm sorry, Mister Mews," he said. "I wasn't thinking straight."

"Hmmph." Mews went around a small desk near the fireplace and sat behind it. He didn't ask Moses to sit and Moses didn't expect it.

Mews put his elbows on the desk and rested his chin on his thumbs, tenting his fingers in front of his lips, muffling his words slightly. "Look, boy, I'm sorry what Trewitt did to you. I'm sorry that Grandy treated you so poorly, too. But *I'm* not the man who promised you anything; I'm a simple business man trying to eke out a profit. I can't afford to take a six hundred dollar loss."

Moses looked at the expensive rifle on the wall, but kept his thoughts to himself.

Mews continued. "Not to mention the interest that I'll probably never get out of that dammed Virginian. I mean to get my money back one way or the other."

"That's what Mr. Trewitt said when he bought me," Moses said, "that he couldn't afford to take a loss."

Mews dropped his hands and glared at Moses. "Don't you dare compare me to that Virginian scoundrel. I pride myself on being a man of my word and, if I had made an agreement with you, I'd have honored it. I have no intention of making such a deal with you, however. I need my money back now, not have it dribbling back to me over time."

"So what do you propose, sir?" Moses asked. He hadn't planned on asking to buy his freedom. He'd already lost twelve hundred dollars.

"I don't know, boy," Mews said. "You're a valuable nigra and I think I can work something out. You get on out of here, now, and come back in three days. I should know by then."

*

309

"...And Remember that I Am a Man."

The worst part was telling Betsy. She had joined him in his quest for freedom, hoping that, one day, their son or daughter would be free of slavery. But, to Moses' surprise, her concern was for him. She watched his face carefully as he told her what had happened. Then she took him in her arms.

"Don't be like this, darling," she said. "Don't be defeated; they'd love to think they've beaten the fight out of you. You've always been the strong one. Everyone in the county respects you."

"I'm beaten," said Moses. "I've paid all that money and I've not one thing to show for it. I could pay a million dollars and it wouldn't matter. The white devils have no honor and God has deserted me."

Betsy sighed and he felt her chest move against him. "I know, Moses. But I also know you, and I know you'll figure out the best thing to do. If you decide we should run north, I'll follow you. If you decide to go into the swamp, I'll hide with you. I love you, Moses."

Over the next few days, they talked incessantly, trying to reconstruct their shattered dream. Moses could still dream of living beside a stream and operating a ferry as a free man. Betsy could envision her children running free in the northern states, never to be bought or sold. The only thing they couldn't imagine was the bridge that would take them there. It had been taken away from them by Trewitt.

Despite that, Betsy and Moses affirmed their loyalty to one another. Moses had lost his faith in God, though.

"I'm selling you to Enoch Sawyer," Mews said.

Moses felt fear to his bones. "What? You what?"

Mews had once again retreated behind the steeple of his joined fingers. His eyes studied Moses carefully. "Hear me out, Captain Grandy. Sawyer needs an overseer for his swamp operations. You're the man for job. We both agreed that you got a raw deal and he's agreed to allow you to buy your freedom."

"Agreed?" Moses fought hard to keep from sneering. "I've learned the value of an agreement between a slave and a master, Mister Mews, and I'll have none of it. They've already got twelve hundred dollars out of me, they'll not get a cent more."

"I know, Moses. I remember what the judge said, but Sawyer's agreement is with me, and he's put it in writing. All according to the law."

"The law, sir? No, thank you."

"You really don't have much choice in the matter, boy." A note of severity entered Mews's voice.

Moses set his lips. "I have to go to Sawyer. I have no choice. But I'll not enter into any agreement with him."

Mews came out from behind his desk as he slammed a fist down on it. "Damn you, boy, I've already made the arrangement with Sawyer. You'll abide by it."

"And how will I earn money towards my freedom if I'm stuck in the Swamp, working for Sawyer?" Moses heard anger in his voice, but couldn't stop it. "A slave isn't paid when he works for his master; slaves are only paid for hiring out."

Mews's tone was calm. He seemed to have vented his anger on the desktop. "Sawyer will pay you by how much you produce. He'll pay a bounty on every barge-load of shingles or boards you bring out of the swamp. You hire the men you need, provision them, and keep what's left."

"I have no choice in working for Sawyer," Moses said, passion in his words. "But I'll work as a common slave. If Enoch Sawyer needs an overseer, he can hire a white man to order his slaves around."

Mews smiled and Moses realized the man had not calmed down. He'd gone cold. "Sawyer thought you might say that. Don't forget he also owns your wife. He'll put you to work in the swamp, all right, and you'll not be allowed to see her. If you so much as show up at the ferry, you'll be flogged, or even shot."

Moses fought his rage. His very soul wanted to go across the desk and strangle the little man. Slavery held him in its grip, no matter which way he turned. If he ran, Betsy and her unborn child were lost to him. If he defied Sawyer's wishes, the same result would occur. If he attacked Mews, he would die.

"Very well, Mister Mews," he said. "It seems I have no choice."

Mews broke out in a genuine smile. "There. You see, my boy, it's as I said. I get my money back and you are none the worse for it. Sawyer will see you get your freedom."

"…And Remember that I Am a Man."

Chapter Forty-two

Snake—1821 A.D.

FIVE HUNDRED NEGROES WANTED.

*We will pay the highest cash prices for all good Negroes offered.
We invite all those having Negroes for sale to call on us at our mart,
opposite the lower steam-boat landing. We will also have a large lot
of Virginia Negroes for sale in the fall. We have as safe a gaol as
any in the country, where we can keep Negroes safe for those that
wish them kept.*

'BOLTON, DICKINS, and Co.'

Memphis Eagle and Inquirer, November 13th, 1852 A.D.

It didn't take Moses long to figure out the best way to bring out the
lumber. He proposed to Sawyer that they hire enough men to dig a
ditch, so they could use lighters—flat-bottomed boats with square
bows and sterns—to transport the lumber to the canal, where it
could be loaded on large barges. He managed to convince his new
master that the cost of the narrow waterway would be much more
efficient than the present method of using mules to drag the felled
trees and shingles to the canal. Moses also argued that selling the
mules would offset some of the cost and then there would be no
need for costly animal fodder. Finally, Sawyer agreed and talked to
the other men, who had shares in the operation into the project.

"...And Remember that I Am a Man."

It took nearly a year to dig the ditch. Moses was glad to be back working with mules, even though he was too high in position to drive them himself. He often paused to watch them work, and thought back to the good times when he'd been on the Kemp farm. When the ditch was finished, he decided to keep two pairs of mules on, since there was often a need for more brute strength than even a gang of slaves could produce.

Once he had the operation underway and running smoothly, Moses went home to Betsy nearly every night, riding a full barge down to Sawyer's Ferry and riding an empty one back to the swamp next morning. He couldn't get enough of his son, Elijah, a chubby little boy with bright eyes and a smile for anyone who came near. The baby, Catherine, was cute as a button with bright brown eyes and a wide smile. Betsy plaited ribbons into her short hair, making her look like a doll when asleep in the cradle. Moses wondered if their next child would be a boy or girl, but it would be several months before they'd find out.

Although the situation was the best he'd known for some time, Moses remained resentful. The slaves' lot at Sawyer's Ferry hadn't improved. Although Sawyer sent food in for the swampers, who toiled from dawn to dusk and had no time to grow or forage food, the slaves living at the ferry had to get by on their own. Moses was paid well enough to take care of his own family, even after Sawyer had deducted money toward Moses' freedom, but there was little extra to help the others.

Betsy worked in the Sawyer home, cooking and cleaning for Mrs. Sawyer, who was a demanding taskmistress but very kind in other ways. She often sent treats home with Betsy for the children.

Sawyer, who considered himself a good Christian, allowed his slaves to hold prayer meetings in a grove near the ferry. Moses had taken to attending Sunday gatherings, now and then, but his interest was half-hearted. He went more for his wife's and children's sakes than for any other reason. Betsy was a firm believer.

On a morning in early summer, a cool blanket of fog covered the earth, giving no hint of the scorching sunlight that would soon burn it away. Moses and his wife paused in the doorway of their shack and said their goodbyes before parting to go to their work. She held out Elijah and Moses kissed the boy.

314

"Bye-bye, Lijie." He opened and closed his hand several times in farewell.

The baby, who was only beginning to walk, smiled at the familiar gesture and repeated it, cooing happily.

"Be a good boy for Auntie Jessie," Moses said. Auntie Jessie was an old woman they paid to watch Elijah and Catherine while Betsy worked. They were fortunate to have enough money to pay for someone to care for their little boy.

As Moses approached the dock to board his transportation into the swamp, he was surprised to see a solitary figure waiting, indistinct in the haze. Usually there were several men bustling about, getting the barge ready. He was even more astonished when he got close enough to recognize Enoch Sawyer.

Moses put on his good-nigger face. "Good morning, Master Sawyer. You're up mighty early this morning."

Enoch Sawyer's face looked grim. "Morning, Moses. Right foggy this morning, isn't it?"

Moses nodded. It always astonished him that the whites treated slaves courteously most of the time. Why would they show courtesy to animals they could buy, sell, or whip? Sometimes whites seemed to grow fond of some particular slave, treating them like a favorite horse or dog. No, that wasn't quite true. An owner might pat a horse or pet a dog, but they seldom laid a hand on their male slaves, unless it was a fist. There was a distance that had to be maintained to preserve the lie that Negros were not human. Yet even that aloofness disappeared when a white man desired a slave woman.

"Where is everybody, Master?" Moses asked. "Is something wrong?"

Sawyer grimaced. "Those two worthless bastards who married my daughters, that's what's wrong."

"How so, sir?"

"They wanted to go into business in Norfolk and I backed them," Sawyer explained. "I should have known better."

Moses felt his throat constrict. Every time some white man's business failed, blacks were likely to suffer. He wanted to ask what was going to happen because of Sawyer's bad fortune, but couldn't muster the courage.

Sawyer continued. "I've had to sell my share of the swamp operation and two of my largest fields…"

Moses had heard that Enoch Sawyer's holdings had grown vast in the last few years, but he had no personal knowledge of anything but the ferry and the swamp crews. He hadn't known Sawyer worked any fields.

"…and I'm probably going to have to sell off a passel of niggers."

"S-sell niggers?" Moses parroted. His insides twisted into knots.

Sawyer waved dismissively. "Not you, Moses. Not your wife or child, either. My wife relies on Betsy."

Moses breathed deeply, suddenly aware he'd been holding his breath. He sighed. "Thank you, Master,"

Sawyer nodded and smiled graciously. "But there's going to be some changes made. You're going to have to work in the fields, temporarily."

"But…but what about the money I've paid you?" Moses had two hundred and thirty dollars in receipts stashed away. That would all be for nothing. Field niggers weren't paid anything.

Sawyer continued to smile. "I can see where you'd be worried. But, like I said, this is only temporary. I'll be back on my feet in no time. Of course, there's no lumber coming out of the swamp, so I can't pay you out of profits. Best I can do is eight dollars a month. I'm going through some hard times right now."

Hard times. Moses would bet that the man had never felt the emptiness of true hunger in his life. He slept on a mattress and never did physical labor.

"Thank you, sir," he said.

Sawyer went on. "Now, I know you won't be able to afford to pay me much toward your freedom on eight dollars a month, so I won't take any out, you'll get every penny of it. You pay me some when you can afford it, if you want."

Moses knew he wouldn't be able to make any payments, now that his income had been drastically chopped. But this was not the time to argue.

"You head on over to the large cornfield on Lamb's Road, near the Ferebee place." Sawyer pointed into the distance. "You know the one I'm talking about?"

Moses nodded.

Sawyer spread his hands as if he was helpless in the whole affair. "Don't worry, boy, once I've sold the crop in the fall, I'll get back into the lumbering business and put you back on full salary. For now, you report to Mister Brooks, the overseer over on Lamb's Road."

Moses went rigid. He'd heard of Brooks.

*

Every morning after that, Moses left his family's shack well before sunrise to walk to a nearby farm. There, he joined the slaves of that farm in marching to whatever field needed work while the overseer rode along behind them.

He was a bad one, this Brooks, on his large, dun gelding. He was a short, portly man with a full black beard, speckled with gray. His eyes were narrow and mean beneath eyebrows like wooly caterpillars. His face, what you could see of it for the beard, was leathery and wrinkled. Moses had never seen a smile on the man's lips. He was quicker to use the whip than McPherson had been on the Micheau farm, so many summers ago. His coiled whip hung on the right side of his saddle, close to hand. On the other side hung a battered horn.

"Okay, move out," Brooks shouted. "Put your legs to it."

The gang of slaves increased their pace slightly. Brooks couldn't even wait until they got to the field to begin harassing his workers. The dirt beneath their bare feet was damp and morning dew glistened on the weeds beside the path. They walked quietly; there would be no banter under the watchful eyes of Brooks. None of them had any idea how far they'd need to walk to get to the day's chosen field; only the overseer knew. The woman walking beside Moses had taken down one strap of her dress and suckled an infant at her ebony breast. The babies in the group would be the only ones to get breakfast.

After a mile or so, Brooks turned the horse off the road. A mule-driven cart awaited them, an old colored man in the driver's seat. In the cart were hoes, more than enough for each slave to have one.

The women separated from the men, going to the grassy strip at the edge of the field that would be in shade all morning. There the infants were set down in threadbare blankets. Toddlers were given

317

straws, pinecones, dry corncobs, anything that might amuse them. Older girls were reminded to keep order and not let crawlers and toddlers wander off.

In the meantime, men selected their hoes. It had become tradition for them to choose the oldest implements, leaving the newer tools, with smoother handles, for the women. Moses picked his hoe and ran a finger over the edge. The old man who tended the cart was supposed to keep the tools sharp, but it was wise to check. An extra moment to hone down a metal burr with a whetstone would make the work a bit easier.

Once all had taken tools to hand, they set to work. Each slave selected a row, the women going near the edge of the field where they had left their children. Men, women, and older children alike moved into the corn, hilling it. At each step, the slave would chop up a foot or so of soil to loosen and kill any weeds that might have taken root. Then the blade of the hoe would be used to move loose soil up on either side to bury the roots that rose from the soil as the corn plant grew. At this stage of growth, the rows of corn sat half a foot above the ground between.

Brooks never went into the field with them. He sat astride his gelding and watched for laggards, as always. His job would be easy today. The corn was only waist high and he'd have a clear view. Later in the season, when the plants stood higher than a man, a slave could take a quick breather if he were careful, but not now.

Moses kept a steady pace, as always. He was a strong man and the work wasn't hard for him. Besides they were required to work in line abreast and they couldn't go faster than the slowest woman or boy. But that slowest slave dare not hinder the pace overmuch or Brooks would send in his "field-boss," a slave who would lay a paddle on the offender's back. The field boss couldn't hold back on the punishment either, or he'd feel the lash of Brooks' whip when he came back out of the corn.

The paddle was a stiff, thick piece of leather, bound to a wooden handle. Holes were drilled in the leather, allowing air to pass through so the paddle could move faster when striking. It left welts for every hole.

The sun went higher and beat down on Moses' bare back. He never wore a shirt to the fields. Even on cool days he needed to

318

sweat off the worst of the heat built up in toiling muscles. When they reached the end of the field, Brooks waited for them, having ridden around the field so his horse wouldn't crush any crops. It was too early in the day for Moses to expect a drink of water and he was right. They moved over and commenced moving back up the field.

Moses' muscles became sore, but he ignored them. In time, they'd loosen up under the accustomed labor and remain pain-free until he went to bed and allowed them to rest. After a bit, they reached the end of their rows and were turned about again.

Once they'd made the third passage through the corn, Brooks allowed them to drink. They pushed through the hedgerow and went down in one of the ditches that kept the cornfields from swamping in heavy rains.

Moses swished his hand over the surface of the water to clear it of scum, then cupped his hand and drank. His insides were used to the dirty water. When he'd first become a field hand, it hadn't been so. For days he had worked in wet, stinking britches; shitty pants was not an excuse Brooks would accept for malingering.

They returned to their labor. After a bit, the woman in the row beside Moses began to moan softly and he glanced over. She'd been the one suckling her infant on the walk to the fields. Like most women, she'd stripped to the waist for relief from the heat and her ebony skin shined with a coating of sweat. Her large, distended breasts hung pendant, swaying in time with her hoeing motions. Drops of sweat ran down and dripped from her nipples. She needed to feed her baby, Moses knew, and would moan until the noontime break, when she could ease the milk-swelling of her breasts.

In time, Brooks blew the horn and they left the field, hoes in hand. The women went straight to their children and the men went to where trays of food had been set on the ground, having been brought from the farm. They flopped to the ground beside the trays and waved their hands over the food to keep the flies away until the women and children joined them.

The food was the same as every other day. Large loaves of bread and boiled hominy. Hominy was what some called, "Indian corn." It was ground in the watermill, unless the creek ran low, then the field slaves were obliged to use hand mills to grind their food each night for the next day. There were two corned herrings apiece for those working the fields and one fish per child. These fish had been preserved by "corning," or soaking them in brine and then drying them in the sun. They were quite salty and the workers would be thirsty in the afternoon, no matter how much they drank during their dinner hour. Boys had fetched buckets of water from the ditches to drink from ladles while they ate.

Moses went to the other side of the hedgerow to relieve himself, but had only got his pants unfastened when a woman screamed. He re-tied the knot and leapt through the hedgerow as the screaming continued. A woman stood with one hand at her mouth and the other pointing at the ground. Other women were screaming as Moses, the first man to arrive, came up.

On the ground lay an infant, apparently asleep despite all the ruckus. Around the baby's neck and face a large, non-poisonous, black snake had coiled. The snake wasn't large enough to crush the child, and black snakes didn't kill by constricting anyway, but it was possible the child could have suffocated to death with the serpent on its face.

Then the baby's eyes opened and Moses breathed a sigh of relief. He squatted down and grabbed the snake behind its head. With his other hand, he gently unwound the creature's body from the infant and stood up with the snake in his hands. The mother immediately snatched her child up and held it to her bare breast, weeping and crying, "Thank you, Jesus."

Moses ignored the commotion around him and walked away with the snake held firmly, though it squirmed. A black snake in corn was a good thing, devouring rats and other rodents that scavenged the crop. He would take it to the far end of the field and turn it loose.

He passed near Brooks, who had dismounted and sat in the shade of a tree, eating the bag lunch that had been brought for him. By his side was a bottle of ale. Brooks took a swig as the commotion died down, then took his pocket watch out and checked it. Snake or no snake, live baby or dead baby, dinner break would last exactly one hour, to the second.

"...And Remember that I Am a Man."

Chapter Forty-three

Promises and Money—1822 A.D.

If at any one time of my life more than another, I was made to drink the bitterest dregs of slavery, that time was during the first six months of my stay with Mr. Covey. We were worked in all weathers. It was never too hot or too cold; it could never rain, blow, hail, or snow, too hard for us to work in the field. Work, work, work, was scarcely more the order of the day than of the night. The longest days were too short for him, and the shortest nights too long for him. I was somewhat unmanageable when I first went there, but a few months of this discipline tamed me. Mr. Covey succeeded in breaking me. I was broken in body, soul, and spirit. My natural elasticity was crushed, my intellect languished, the disposition to read departed, the cheerful spark that lingered about my eye died; the dark night of slavery closed in upon me; and behold a man transformed into a brute!

Life of an American Slave, Frederick Douglass, Boston: Anti-Slavery Office—1845 A.D.

Sawyer did not make good on his promise to liberate Moses from field work after the harvest, which was no surprise to Moses. Whites were quick to say how true they were to their words, but their actions often belied their assertions. Although, truth be told, most blacks were not much better. It seemed human nature to forget

321

promises when circumstances changed or the passage of time dimmed their memories.

Moses bided his time, however, because Sawyer continued to promise to take him out of the fields as soon as possible. But then he heard through the gossip mill that Sawyer planned to sell his share of the lumber ditch. That would be Sawyer's last tie to the swamp and its sale would make it unlikely Moses would get out of the fields.

Not that the hard work was beyond Moses; he had toiled just as hard on the waters. It was certainly easier for him to hoe a row than for a woman or oldster. Nor was it the monotony of day after day without any break in Brooks' routine, although he missed the relative freedom he'd enjoyed as a waterman. What he couldn't bear was that the overseer had pregnant women paddled or had old women whipped for not keeping up the pace. It just didn't seem right to hit a woman.

During the Christmas holidays, Moses got the opportunity to complain—politely—to Sawyer. Sawyer happened upon him near the slaves' quarters and asked how he was getting on. For some reason, this man seemed willing to talk to Moses though he seldom came near any of his other slaves.

"Well, to tell you the truth, sir," Moses said, "I don't think I can stand it much longer." Not that he had any choice in the matter; it was all up to his master. But he'd noticed the smell of liquor on the white man's breath and hoped he was in a good mood because of it. Alcohol was a touchy thing, it could go either way.

"Why not?" Sawyer asked. "You're young and strong."

"It's not the work, Master Sawyer," Moses replied with a calculated smile. "Though, Lord knows, I'm not used to such severe labor. But I'm starved near to death, most of the time."

Sawyer laughed. "You're just used to eating high on the hog, boy."

Moses shook his head. "No, sir. It ain't just me. Sometimes one of the workers will up and faint in the field for lack of food. It ain't easy to work until noon without a bite to eat when you ain't had nothin' since the night before."

"Brooks needs to get an early start, Moses. Surely you can see that."

322

"Yassuh." Moses nodded agreeably. "But if we could get a dab of extra meal or corn every evening, we could bake our own bread and eat it while we walk to the fields."

Sawyer raised an eyebrow. "Extra? I feed my niggers pretty well already, if I do say so myself."

The hell you do, thought Moses. "Yassuh, you do, Master Sawyer. But it's like that ditch we built last year. It's easier to float lumber than drag it. That little bit of extra meal will help the workers keep goin' strong from morning to dinner. You'll get more work done." Moses knew the comparison was a bit of a stretch, but he was hoping logic and an extra helping of subservience would go a long way toward bridging the gap.

And sure enough, Sawyer, who had taken a flask from a pocket while Moses spoke, was nodding in agreement. "All right, Moses. We'll give it a try. But you let everyone know they have to do their baking on their own time, you hear?" He put the liquor to his mouth.

Moses made sure his smile was wide as he said, "Yassuh. Thank you, suh."

Sawyer gulped down a swallow of liquor, then smacked his lips. "You're welcome, boy. Don't want anyone saying old Enoch Sawyer don't take care of his niggers." His smile matched Moses' as he held up the flask in a mock toast. "Anything else on your mind, Captain Grandy?"

Moses considered before answering. There was another matter, but it was more touchy than food. But there *had* been that time he'd gotten McPherson fired.

"Well, to tell you the truth, Mister Brooks is a mighty hard man, sir." He paused and searched Sawyer's face before he continued. "He uses the whip pretty often, even on the women."

Sawyer had continued to smile, weaving slightly. "Moses, you're one shm... smart nigger, but you're not used to the fields. Field hands are dumb creatures, or they'd be put to other tasks. Brooks is doing what he has to do if I'm to get a good crop. He hasn't whipped you, has he?"

"No, sir, he hasn't."

"That's because you're a hard worker. You're the only black I would ever trust to keep working without supervision. Most niggers are like mules. They'll only work when someone is driving them."

323

"…And Remember that I Am a Man."

*

It was a cool Sunday morning in the late spring and Moses was trying to repair his boots with twine and a sturdy needle. A heavy rain had fallen during the night, so the frogs were still chirping in chorus. On the Sabbath, except during harvest time, the field hands were given the day off and he was using the time to try to salvage his footwear. He was the only field hand who could afford such a luxury; the other hands went barefoot, even in the occasional snow that fell in Camden County. And, if Moses couldn't make his repairs, he'd be in the same shape.

Betsy was at the nearby Sawyer house, cooking for the master's family. Slaves who didn't work the fields—house niggers and ferry keepers and such—didn't get the entire day off because, "They don't do *real* work," in the words of Enoch Sawyer.

Elijah played around his father, dragging a stick through the dirt for some reason known only to little boys, while little Catherine played with a corncob doll next to the crude wooden cradle holding little Betsy, the baby. Moses rocked the cradle gently while he worked.

He heard the sound of a door opening and turned to see Enoch Sawyer step out on his front porch. The master sat down in his rocking chair and began tamping tobacco into his pipe. Mrs. Sawyer couldn't abide the smell of pipe tobacco, so he often sat on the porch to smoke.

"Elijah," Moses said. "Come rock your sister and keep an eye on her for a moment."

The little boy stopped what he was doing and came over to tend his little sister, a serious expression on his face. He was used to such duties, as were all slave children with younger siblings. Moses knew he could rely on Elijah, especially since he'd be within eyesight.

Moses walked over to the master. It wasn't far, because Mrs. Sawyer had insisted that Betsy always be available, and had ordered a shack built for Moses and Betsy.

"Good morning, Master Sawyer."

The white man looked off into the distance for a moment, then nodded affably, blowing a cloud of smoke from his mouth. "Mornin', Moses. Something on your mind?"

324

"…And Remember that I Am a Man."

Sawyer was reminding Moses that it was not normal for a slave to speak to a white man unless the white initiated the conversation.

Moses took a deep breath. "Yes, sir. It's about me buying my freedom."

Sawyer smiled. "That again?"

"Yes, that again. Master Sawyer, I can't stand working the fields anymore."

The smile became a grin. "And what do you propose to do about it, Captain Grandy?"

"Sir, I've already paid you two hundred and thirty dollars. I'll let you have that as profit if you'll let me free for another six hundred—the six hundred you paid for me."

Sawyer grew serious. "No, no, Moses. We have a deal. Besides, it would take you years to come up with another six hundred dollars. Why would you propose such a ridiculous thing?"

"No, sir, I mean if I pay you six hundred dollars now—this very week."

Sawyer sighed and shook his head. "Moses, you don't have six hundred dollars. You know that and I know that."

"But what if I could get it?" Moses persisted.

"That's enough, Moses." The master rocked forward and planted his feet on the porch, pointing the stem of his pipe. "I came out here to enjoy the silence and you pester me with fantasies about money that you don't have and could never come up with. You go away, now, and leave me in peace."

"But…"

"No buts. You go away." Sawyer stood up, knocked the dottle from his pipe and went inside.

Moses turned and went away, feeling like a dog with his tail between his legs. He was a proud man, and probably a bit stubborn too, but he was through trying to go it alone. Several times, white, abolitionist acquaintances had offered to loan him money toward his freedom and he'd refused, since owing *any* white man money would be another hold on him. But he'd had enough. At least he'd be free of the hated fields, able to work on the waters again.

He went back to rocking little Betsy, seething inside. If he borrowed money, he'd have to stay in Camden County until he could repay it, instead of going north, where wages were higher and freedom safer. But at least he'd be near his family.

When Sawyer returned to his rocking chair, with a drink in hand, Moses approached him again.

"I'm serious, Master Sawyer. I can get six hundred dollars, I'm sure of it."

Sawyer lowered the newspaper he was reading and frowned at Moses. Then he turned and called for his wife to come outside.

Mrs. Sawyer appeared, a thin, hatchet-faced woman with a smile that relieved her severe looks. She stood in the doorway, glanced down at Moses, and then looked quizzically at her husband.

"What is it, Enoch?"

Sawyer puffed himself up and then spoke loudly, like an actor on a stage instead of a white master on his own porch. "Moses, here, is acting quite strange today. Do you think he has taken to drink?"

Mrs. Sawyer frowned and stared at Moses like a hawk regarding a squirrel. Her large nose added to the hawk-like image. "Moses, have you been drinking?"

Moses shook his head. "No, ma'am."

She looked at her husband and sighed. "Enoch, is this another of your silly jokes?"

Sawyer laughed. "Not a joke, my dear. Moses has offered to pay me six hundred dollars, cash-money, for his freedom. If he's not been drinking, he must have lost his mind, reminding me that he's worth that much money when cash is in short supply. Do you think I should sell him off?"

"You're the one who's been drinking, Enoch," she said.

Sawyer turned to Moses. "How about that, Moses? Should I sell you to someone who really *does* have cash money?"

Moses began to reply, but Mrs. Sawyer cut him off, apparently not realizing her husband was joking.

"Don't be silly, dear," she said. "Captain Cormack put a thousand dollars on the supper table for Moses last Friday and you wouldn't take it." She turned to Moses. "Captain Cormack wants to buy you, but Mr. Sawyer would not touch the money. He wants you to be overseer in the Dismal Swamp again, when he gets back in the lumber business."

326

"…And Remember that I Am a Man."

Captain Cormack, Moses knew, was an evil old man who got about on crutches. His wife had died the year before and he had been coming around to the Sawyer house lately.

"I'd cut my throat before I'd go to that old bastard," Moses blurted, angry at the teasing from Sawyer. When anger appeared on Mrs. Sawyer's face, he realized he'd gone too far. He had to say something quick, to take her mind off his words. "But I know why Captain Cormack said he'd buy me. He's trying to make himself look big, because he's courting Miss Patsey and knows he's nothing in his pants to offer but money."

Mrs. Sawyer's eyes went wide and her hand flew to her mouth, but not so quickly that Moses couldn't see she was beginning to laugh. She turned and, with a smothered guffaw, slammed the door shut behind her.

"Get out of here, Moses," Sawyer said, raising his newspaper to hide his amusement, though the paper shook with his laughter. "'Old bastard'," he murmured as Moses went away, "got that right."

Moses didn't sleep at all that night. On Monday morning, when Brooks blew the horn, Moses decided not to join the others. He went to the Sawyer house and knocked at the back door.

Betsy came out of the kitchen, a small brick building situated a few yards from the main house, her eyes wide and worry on her face.

"Moses," she cried. "What in the world do you think you're doing?"

"I'm not going back into the fields," he said. "No matter what."

"They'll whip you." Her eyes filled with tears. "They'll whip you."

"I don't care if they do." He had come to the realization, during the long night, that he had reached his breaking point.

"What the hell are you doing here, Moses?" came Enoch Sawyer's voice from behind him. "Is it more of your freedom crap?"

Moses whirled. "With respect, Master Sawyer, it's not crap. If I go out in that field one more day, I'll never get free."

Sawyer crooked an eyebrow. "Oh? And how do you figure that, boy?"

Moses took a breath. "I can't bear it any more. If I see one more woman or child whipped because of Brooks, I'll try to kill him.

327

Either way, if I succeed or not, I'll be a dead man." Moses had played his trump card. A dead slave was a considerable financial loss.

Sawyer peered at him. "Are you serious? It's that bad?"

"Yes, sir. I've been trying to tell you. I can't take any more of it."

Sawyer grimaced. "Grandy should never have taken you into his house when you were a child. You learned white ways. Just what we need, a sensitive nigger."

"Please Master Sawyer." Moses put out his palms in supplication. "Give me a traveling paper, so I can go to Norfolk. I swear, I'll raise six hundred dollars for you and, like I said, you can have what I've already paid, too."

Sawyer regarded him. Behind Moses, Betsy sobbed.

Finally, the white man sighed. "Moses, you're more trouble than you're worth. And there's something else. You go around talking about freedom all the time and it's making my other slaves restless. I don't think you can come up with that much money, but I'll give you a paper and let you try."

Moses' heart leaped. "Thank you, Master, thank you."

Sawyer set his lips in a thin line. "I'd rather have six hundred dollars than a scar-back troublesome nigger. But, if you don't get the money, you'll go back into the fields."

Suspicion crept into Moses. "And will you put on that paper that you've agreed to set me free?" Even though Moses couldn't read, he knew that putting words on paper made them more important.

"Don't push me," Sawyer warned. He stood glaring at Moses, sucking on his lower lip. Then he nodded. "All right. Since you've been tricked before, I suppose that's reasonable."

Moses, trying to hide his smile, decided to risk one more request. "And will you rent me a horse?"

"...And Remember that I Am a Man."

Chapter Forty-four

Champions—1822 A.D.

Sometimes standing on the Ohio River bluff, looking over on a free State, and as far north as my eyes could see, I have eagerly gazed upon the blue sky of the free North, which at times constrained me to cry out from the depths of my soul, Oh! Canada, sweet land of rest--Oh! when shall I get there? Oh, that I had the wings of a dove, that I might soar away to where there is no slavery; no clanking of chains, no captives, no lacerating of backs, no parting of husbands and wives; and where man ceases to be the property of his fellow man. These thoughts have revolved in my mind a thousand times. I have stood upon the lofty banks of the river Ohio, gazing upon the splendid steamboats, wafted with all their magnificence up and down the river, and I thought of the fishes of the water, the fowls of the air, the wild beasts of the forest, all appeared to be free, to go just where they pleased, and I was an unhappy slave!

Narrative of the Life of Henry Bibb—1849 A.D.

The village of Deep Creek, which had grown up around the locks at the northern end of the canal, wasn't much to speak of, a general store and a few dozen houses. Canal traffic seldom stopped at this Virginia hamlet; all cargo went on to Norfolk and points north. Once past this point, it was an easy trip down the southern branch of the Elizabeth River to the Chesapeake Bay.

"…And Remember that I Am a Man."

Moses rode the rented nag to the house of Captain Minner, who he had sailed with in the past. He hoped the captain would be able to find him passage to Norfolk for a reasonable price. And even if Captain Minner was off on a voyage, his wife was a friendly woman who always gave Moses something to eat when he stopped by.

The captain was at home, however, and he greeted Moses heartily, putting out his hand. "Captain Grandy, what a pleasant surprise. What has it been since we last spoke, two years?"

"Yes, sir, Captain Minner, that sounds about right."

They shook hands, then Minner said, "Word came up the canal that Sawyer's lumbering operation closed down and you'd been put in the fields." He shook his head. "Damn shame, that."

"Yes, sir, Captain, it was rough. A cur dog has a better life than a field nigger." Moses wouldn't have voiced that thought to most white men, but he knew Captain Minner to be a good man, and an abolitionist who made no bones about his dislike of slavery.

"That's an apt description." Minner grunted and shook his head. "Yet here you stand at my door. Have you been put back on the waters, then?"

"No," Moses said. "I'm on my way to Norfolk. Master Sawyer has agreed to give me my freedom, if I can come up with the cash. I'm hoping some of the Norfolk merchants will chip in to loan me the money."

"How much do you need?" asked Minner.

"Six hundred dollars."

Minner snorted. "Six hundred dollars! Sounds like the same old ruse, all over again."

Moses shrugged. "I know. But this time, instead of handing the money over in advance, I won't pay up until Sawyer gives me my freedom paper, in front of witnesses."

Captain Minner pursed his lips and nodded. "That sounds like it should work. But what's changed your mind about borrowing money? You've always been dead set against it."

Moses sighed. "It's a long story."

"Well, come on in and tell your story then, my boy." Minner stood aside and gestured Moses in. "I'll have my wife get some vittles for you."

"…And Remember that I Am a Man."

As Moses stepped through the door, Mrs. Minner called from the back of the house. "I'm already fixing something for Moses, dear. Hello, Captain Grandy."

"Hello, Miz Minner," Moses replied. "How are you?"

"I'm fine, Moses. I'll be out in a moment."

Captain Minner led Moses to the dining room. "Now, Moses," he said, after they'd both taken a seat, "tell me what's on your mind."

Moses began by describing how horrible the fields were, especially when working for a cruel overseer. Minner nodded sympathetically, asking questions now and then. Before Moses knew it, he was telling this kindly man all his troubles, dreams and hopes, even his fear that he would be unable to control his temper and attack a white man if provoked. He barely noticed when Mrs. Minner joined them at the table, bearing a mug of hard cider for each of them.

Moses took a drink, then continued. When he had finished, he was embarrassed, for tears filled his eyes. He reached into a pocket and wiped the moisture away with a soiled piece of cloth. "I'm sorry, Captain, Miz Minner," he said, "I don't mean to burden you."

Captain Minner looked over at his wife, whose eyes were also moist, then turned back to Moses. "What have I always said to you?" he asked. "How many times have I told you I was willing to help?"

Moses nodded. "Yes, sir, but six hundred dollars is a lot of money for one man to put up. I'll go to Norfolk and see if some of the merchants will buy shares toward my freedom, like they might go into a joint business venture."

Minner slammed a fist down on the table. "Moses, I'm an old sea-dog and I've set aside my share of dollars. There's no use letting them sit around and rust. Allow me to help you and we'll make sure no man ever calls you a slave again."

Moses noticed Mrs. Minner give her husband an anxious glance. He shook his head. "No, sir. I know you put up that money for your old age."

"I don't care, son. Don't give Sawyer time to change his mind. If you don't hoist your sail now, when the winds are with you, you may never be free."

"…And Remember that I Am a Man."

Moses set his teeth and sighed. The captain was right. "Only if you'll allow me to pay you back. I want papers drawn up that it's to be a loan."

"If we do that, you won't be free until you've paid me back, according to the law."

"I know, Captain," Moses said. "But that's the only way I'll take your money."

"If that's the way you feel, all right," Captain Minner replied. "But we'll draw up the papers later. You stay with us tonight and, in the morning I'll go with you to see Enoch Sawyer, as your witness."

*

The next morning, a thin blanket of fog hung over the canal as Captains Minner and Grandy rode south along the tow path. The fog wouldn't last long, Moses knew. It would begin to dissolve as soon as the bright sun heralded another scorching day. Great blue herons and the smaller white egrets fed in ponds and puddles, seeking their breakfasts in water shallow enough to wade.

For a while, the two men rode in silence, then Minner asked. "What are your plans, Moses? Once I've given Sawyer the money, I mean."

"I don't rightly know, Captain. How am I to get my papers from the court without being tricked again?"

"Hmm, that's a poser," Minner said. "Let me think on it."

After a while, Minner spoke again. "Moses, I think what you need is a champion, someone who can speak to the court on your behalf. Do you trust me?"

Moses considered. This captain had a reputation for honest dealing and had always treated Moses fairly and well. And he was right. Sawyer had tricked him often in the past. But what could he do? Buying his freedom was the only way he'd be able to get Betsy and the children free, once he was free of his own chains.

"Whoa." Moses reined in his horse.

Looking startled, Minner also stopped, concern on his face.

Moses turned and confronted him. "Captain Minner, to tell you God's truth, I don't think I can ever truly trust a white man. I trusted James Grandy because he'd been my childhood friend and he betrayed me. I trusted Mister Trewitt because he was a smooth talker and he seemed real sorry I'd got such a bad deal already. But now I have to deal with Enoch Sawyer and I don't trust him at all. Do you know who I do trust, though?"

Minner nodded gravely. "I think I do."

Moses matched his nod. "That's right. I trust in The Lord. I know that, if I keep trying, The Lord will set me free in one way or the other." He raised his voice. "But only by getting my freedom in a righteous manner, by the white man's rules, will I be able to set my wife and children free. I'm going to borrow your money, like you offered, but I'm not going to rest until I've paid you back."

He had taken time to think things over on the ride to Deep Creek from Sawyer's Ferry. In the end, he'd decided not to doubt God any more. Maybe it was his doubts that held him back. God would see him through. He ignored the nagging little voice that told him he wasn't quite true to his conviction

Putting up his hands, Minner began to protest Moses' refusal of his offer.

"Hear me out," Moses insisted. "If I go up north owing money to a white man, the first slave dealer who learns about it will bring me back south again. Until I'm free and clear of every obligation, I'm a fugitive according to the law. So what, in God's name, do you suggest I do?"

Minner stared at him, slack-jawed, and Moses realized that, for the first time in his life, he had spoken harshly to a white man. It made him feel small, because Captain Minner had always been good to him and was not to blame for his troubles. There was no reason for him to distrust this kindly sea-captain, who had never owned a slave in his life.

"I'm sorry, Captain," he said, "I didn't mean to speak rudely to you. I will put my life in your hands. What do you propose?"

*

They didn't have to ride all the way to Sawyer's ferry. Moses knew this was the day Sawyer would be selling his shares in the lumber ditch, so all the investors would be meeting at the home of a man named Farrance, who lived near the ditch, a bit below the state line. Moses knew Farrance's place, a two story frame house across the tow path from the canal, surrounded by vast fields reclaimed from the swamp. When they arrived, several white men sat at a table beneath a large oak, obviously driven outdoors to seek a breeze. They had apparently finished their business, because all held tankards of ale, presumably drawn from a keg upon the table.

Along with Sawyer, Moses recognized Mr. Farrance, a tall bean-pole of a man with a dour face, along with a Mr. Ferebee and his son-in-law, Mr. Lamb, who also held shares in the enterprise. There was also another partner, Mr. Davis, from Pasquotank County and a man who always evoked a tight knot of fear and hatred in Moses' belly: Wiley McPherson, the overseer who Moses had gotten fired, all those years ago. The other partners, Moses knew, had hired McPherson to run their lumbering operation after Sawyer had dropped out. McPherson peered intently at Moses, who wondered if he'd been recognized.

"Good day, gentlemen," Captain Minner said as he and Moses halted their horses at the edge of the road.

The half-dozen men returned Minner's greeting as the pair dismounted.

As soon as Moses' foot reached the ground, Sawyer said, "Moses, you might as well climb back on that nag and light out for home. I've decided not to sell you."

Moses turned slowly to face his master. His insides felt sick and twisted. He opened his mouth to speak, but then went witless as McPherson regarded him with a cynical smile, fingering his short mustache.

Captain Minner, who had come up to stand at Moses' elbow, was not at a loss for words, however. "What are you talking about, Sawyer?"

Sawyer shrugged. "I was merely pulling the boy's leg, Captain. I wanted to see if he could come up with enough cash money by himself, but Mrs. Sawyer wasn't amused. Why, the last thing she said to me this morning was to send him home if I should run across him. She's fond of this boy, you know, as well as his wife, who keeps house for us."

Captain Minner nudged Moses. "Hand me that paper."

Numb, Moses reached into a pocket and produced it. Then the captain stepped close to Enoch Sawyer, unfolded the paper and showed it to him.

"…And Remember that I Am a Man."

"Is this not your handwriting, Mister Sawyer?"

"Of course it is," Sawyer said irritably. "But I told you, my wife doesn't want me to sell him."

Captain Minner looked around. "Gentlemen, this paper—signed by Mr. Sawyer—says that he will sell Moses his freedom for six hundred dollars." He waved the paper in front of Sawyer. "Will you not live up to your word, Mr. Sawyer?"

"It's not all that simple, Captain Minner. I never should have given the boy that paper. If I let him free, all my other niggers are going to want to be paid for their work. Besides, my wife is worried that, if he goes north, he'll arrange for his wife and children to escape in order to join him. She prizes his wife and needs her in the house."

"Ah, I see your point, Mr. Sawyer," cried Minner, seizing the moment he and Moses had expected. "I propose you sell Moses to me."

Minner produced a bag, which he shook to demonstrate it held coins, and addressed the other whites present. "Mind you, gentlemen, I do not want him for a slave; I want to buy him for freedom. He will repay me the money, and I shall not charge him a cent of interest for it. I would not have a coloured person to drag *me* down to hell, for all the money in the world, despite the affairs of Camden County." He looked directly at Enoch Sawyer when he mentioned hell. "Moses will repay me the money in time and I'll be sure to free him in the Virginia courts. Nobody down here in Camden County, will be the wiser and you won't have to worry that someone might say you boys are too easy on your niggers. What say you?"

The men looked around at one another. Moses was astounded how easily Minner had bypassed Sawyer's ownership and made Moses' status a concern of the entire county.

Ferebee cleared his throat. "You know, it *is* a shame how Captain Grandy has been treated. Young James Grandy started a mudslide when he reneged on his word, and that mud is carrying this boy along on a sea of broken promises. It's about time we in Camden County live up to our promises, if they take note in Virginia of how we mistreat our slaves, for God's sake."

"...And Remember that I Am a Man."

"Easy for you to say, Ferebee," Sawyer said. "I paid six hundred for the boy and now he wants to be set free for the same amount."

Moses' courage had returned. "Not so, Mister Sawyer. I've already paid you two hundred and thirty dollars. You'll be getting eight hundred and thirty. And I've paid a whole lot more than that, over the years."

Mr. Davis, a slight, balding man, laughed. "He's got you there, Sawyer. That boy's made more money for white men in Camden County than a coon can eat corn."

"Well said, sir," cried Captain Minner. "What say we have the boy sit down over by the tree and we'll discuss this over a mug of ale, if you'd be so kind to invite me to partake after my morning on the road."

Moses retired to the tree, where he took a drink of water from a small flask on his belt. He wouldn't be asked to share the white men's ale; that went without saying. He listened.

Moses and Captain Minner had discussed how to handle any perfidy on behalf of Enoch Sawyer. Since Sawyer was within his rights to treat Moses as callously as he wished, Minner had pointed out that public opinion was their only weapon. After all, he had said, it was only the southern attitude toward slavery that kept the Negro race down. In the northern states, slavery had been abolished when public opinion demanded it. In England, outrage over slavery had reached the point where abolition was inevitable in the British colonies.

Captain Minner was given a drink and he began persuading the North Carolinians they should support Moses' bid for freedom. Rather than arguing for Moses' rights, of which he legally had none, Minner pleaded for sympathy. When Ferebee's young son-in-law, Mr. Lamb, admitted he didn't know the history of the affair, Captain Minner seized upon the opportunity to relate, in detail, how Moses had been misused.

Once informed, Lamb weighed in on Moses' side. He and his father-in-law joined Captain Minner in trying to sway Enoch Sawyer into doing the right thing. Sawyer, supported by Davis, argued that, although it was true Moses had been cruelly tricked by two former owners, it was not the responsibility of his present owner to correct the injustices.

As Moses watched and listened, ignored by the whites, Sawyer remained adamant, his arguments becoming more befuddled as he consumed more alcohol. Six hundred was not enough, he maintained, for a nigger as smart as Moses. When Minner countered that the amount was actually more than eight hundred, Sawyer argued that he could get more than a thousand if he put Moses on the open market.

Minner then wondered why, if Moses was so valuable, was he working in the fields as a common laborer? Surely field hands weren't selling for anywhere near eight hundred. Sawyer contended that he would probably get back into the lumbering business and then he'd use Moses as an overseer again. Besides, Sawyer's wife didn't want to lose her cook and housemaid, Betsy.

Ferebee reminded Sawyer that Moses would be staying in the area until he'd paid back the borrowed money, so Betsy would remain right where she was. Instead of answering this charge, Sawyer offered to sell Moses to Ferebee on the spot for a thousand dollars, saying he'd be valuable as an overseer since he was already familiar with the operation that Sawyer was abandoning. To Moses' surprise, McPherson spoke.

"Seems to me," he said, "that the position of overseer is filled."

Minner jumped back in. "Mister Sawyer, I agree that you have many valid arguments against letting Moses go, but you haven't addressed the main bone of contention, here. Selling Moses his freedom, after he's been tricked out of his money twice already, is the right thing to do. Can you deny that?"

Sawyer sneered. "It's not my responsibility."

"Seems to me that it is your responsibility, Mister Sawyer." Again, surprisingly, it was McPherson offering his opinion. "If you didn't think so, why did you write that paper and give it to the nigger?"

Moses remembered something. Interrupting a conversation between white men was dangerous, but he had to do it.

"Master Sawyer?" he said, loudly enough to be heard from where he sat.

Sawyer whirled to look over to Moses, fury on his face. Moses had been right to worry about interrupting.

Quickly, he said. "You gave Mister Mews a paper, too, Master. Mister Mews said it was all legal like."

"Why, why, I…" Sawyer sputtered.

"There, you see," McPherson said. "Puttin' your mark on a piece of paper is a serious thing."

Master Sawyer spun around to confront McPherson.

McPherson wasn't a "landed gentleman," like the others, being a wage-earner; he wasn't considered to be in the same class as them. The overseer, however, was a stern man who commanded an imposing presence. Moses wondered if, even though McPherson posed no obvious threat to them, Sawyer and his former partners sensed the menace that blacks felt in the presence of this hard man.

"In fact," continued McPherson, "I don't believe in mollycoddling niggers. But white men should live up to their word and this boy has been bamboozled too damned many times. You signed a paper. You should let him go."

Moses could hardly believe his ears. This man was infamous for his treatment of slaves. From what Moses had heard, McPherson showed no mercy to his slaves, sometimes in the bog to their necks, setting a grueling pace. He would tie up a slave and flog him in the morning, merely because the black had been unable to finish the previous day's task. After the slave was flogged, pork or beef brine was put on his bleeding back to increase the pain. McPherson would then have the suffering slave tied up all day, his feet barely touching the ground, his legs tied and a block of wood put between his legs. Yellow flies and mosquitoes added to the extreme torture. McPherson had even flogged slaves to death on a few occasions, according to some. He'd never been called to account in any way for it, as far as Moses knew.

From the way Sawyer's eyes darted about, Moses could tell he was wavering, now that McPherson had championed Moses' cause. Sawyer couldn't dismiss the overseer as a "nigger-lover," as he might others.

Moses had no idea why McPherson would come over to his side. Unless the man had some grudge against Sawyer, Moses could only think that The Lord must have opened McPherson's heart to say what he had. And then he remembered. He had re-affirmed his faith in God aloud on the ride down the canal trail. God must have been listening.

"He's right, Sawyer," said Davis, who had been Sawyer's last ally. "You promised the boy his freedom if he could come up with the money."

"All right, all right," Sawyer said. "I can see the right of what you say. I never should have written that damned note. But I want *seven* hundred, so I can give my wife something extra and keep her off my back."

Captain Minner pounced. "Jiminy, Sawyer, do you think I'm made of money? Your note said *six* hundred. But I'll give you six-fifty in gold coins, here and now, on the spot." He looked over to Moses by the trunk of the tree. "Is that all right with you, Captain Grandy?"

Moses nodded, amazed at the turn of events. He would have accepted any amount rather than go back to the fields.

Sawyer also glanced in Moses' direction and shook his head. "Damn, I never should have bought him in the first place," he said to the world at large. Then he returned his attention to Captain Minner and stuck out his hand. "It's a deal, Captain. Six-fifty and Moses is *your* headache from now on."

Captain Minner shook Sawyer's hand. "You're a good man, Mister Sawyer. A good man."

Even through his astonishment and rising elation, Moses noted the hypocrisy.

"...And Remember that I Am a Man."

Chapter Forty-five

The Pattyrollers—1824 A.D.

RULE 3rd.

If any slave shall violate the foregoing Rules, the Patrol shall have power and it shall be their duty (any two of their number being present) to whip the said slave, either at the time of the offence being committed or at any time within three months thereafter, the number of stripes not to exceed fifteen, unless the said slave shall be guilty of insolent behaviour, or make his escape from the Patrol, in either of which cases the number of stripes shall not exceed thirty-nine.

PATROL REGULATIONS FOR THE TOWN OF TARBOROUGH, (N.C.)—18--? A.D.

Moses put the last of the lumber he'd cut that day on top of the stack and stretched, arching his back. He put both arms straight out and curled his fingers into fists, feeling the tightness and pain of the rheumatism he'd gotten from so much time out on the open water in all sorts of weather.

Captain Minner had been true to his word and the court had issued manumission papers for Moses. When the circuit judge had come to the Norfolk County courthouse in the town of Great Bridge, the captain had petitioned for Moses' freedom. Virginia's laws were nearly identical to those of North Carolina and the judge agreed to allow manumission, and issued papers to that effect, but there were two stipulations. The first was that Moses must repay his benefactor in full. Secondly, Moses would be required to spend a year and a day in one of the northern states. Moses wasn't sure why all judges seemed to tack this on, but figured they didn't want freed slaves around to remind other blacks they were *not* free.

So Moses had gone back to the canal boats to earn the required money. In a way, he was buying his freedom for a fourth time. This time, however, there were other factors. Captain Minner, unlike the first three scoundrels, was not a slave holder, but an abolitionist. The main thing buoying Moses' hope, though, was God. The Lord had given a sign when he'd inspired Wiley McPherson, a nigger-hater to the core, to speak up for Moses.

But now the "rheumatiz" had taken hold of him, and he couldn't take the freezing days and nights out on the water. Old Uzoma, the woman who had performed the wedding ceremony for Naomi and Moses, had prescribed a trip into the dismal swamp as a cure, along with a bag of herbs for medicinal tea.

Moses had enlisted a friend to take him into Lake Drummond on the cross-canal—the canal that fed the main canal with run-off from the circular lake's underground springs. There, he'd constructed a swamper's hut on the west bank. For the past few months, he'd lived here, felling trees and cutting cooper's timber, which would be split into staves by coopers and used for barrel-making. Every ten days, Moses' friend returned in a lighter with provisions and carted out the lumber—for a share of course. So at least Moses was putting *some* money toward the day of his freedom.

He walked back to his hut and stirred up the fire, adding a few sticks. Barefoot, he waded into the lake and used a metal pot to dip brown water from the lake. He set it on the fire to boil for Uzoma's tea, which seemed to help his aches and pains.

By the time he'd gone into the woods, relieved himself, and returned, the water was ready. He put in a measure of Uzoma's dried leaves, berries, and whatever, into the water. He'd grown fond on the stuff and really didn't want to know the ingredients. He sat on a log and watched the sunset, sipping tea directly from the pot, after it had cooled. He remembered the first time he'd tasted swamp water, hiding out with his family.

"…And Remember that I Am a Man."

Moses had quite a family of his own, now, two boys, two girls and another child on the way. They'd been blessed with a child every year they'd been together. He hadn't seen Betsy, Elijah, Catherine, Betsy and Ben for quite some time and missed them terribly. He consoled himself with the fact that they were mere miles away and he could decide to leave the swamp at any time to see them. At least he hadn't gone north, yet. It would be hard on him, being that far from his family for so long. But he had to do it.

Captain Minner held his manumission paper, the two of them having decided it was too risky for Moses to carry the document. Instead, Moses used "traveling" papers, written by the captain. These gave him permission to wander nearly anywhere in Virginia and the Carolinas, although he had to adhere to any local regulations about blacks being out at night and such.

The late autumn sun was going down, casting a red sheen over the glassy waters of the lake, a perfect mirror. Every juniper out in the open water stood above an upside-down image of itself. Each cloud in the sky had a counterpart below. A great blue heron flew majestically, legs trailing behind and long neck tucked into a crook, and an identical heron flew, upside-down, through the waters below. In the nearby shallows, a white egret stalked warily, moving its long, stick-like yellow legs in slow motion, careful not to make ripples that might conceal tasty minnows or frogs. Its reflection imitated every movement. Moses looked upon the beauty of nature and wondered how he had ever doubted God, who had created this world.

He had been alone for a long time. He'd not taken orders from any white man, not had his papers checked. He toiled only for wages instead of by force. He should have felt free, he supposed, but he didn't. In Captain Minner's lockbox were papers that said Moses was free, but they'd need to be stamped by the court before becoming law.

White men didn't need papers to be free; they were born into it. Why did such a paper mean so much to black people? If he'd been born in Africa, he'd have been his own man, without papers. But here, he still wondered what it felt like to hold his head high.

When he'd finished his tea, he added wood to the fire and lay down in his shack. The temperature was dropping fast, now the sun had gone down. Besides being out of the north winds, having a fire was another reason his time in the swamp was beneficial. Out on the water, in wooden craft, there was no respite from the cold, even at night. Here, hard labor warmed his muscles during the day and his hut remained cozy at night.

Like all of its kind, the shelter remained open on one side, where the fire was maintained at all times, reduced to glowing coals during the day. Moses kept his feet to the fire at night and felt comfortable, although he sometimes needed to get up and add fuel. Unless the breeze came from the wrong direction, wood smoke was not a problem.

As every night, he offered God prayers for Betsy, his children, and the Minners. He always added a plea that nothing tragic would befall the captain before Moses obtained his freedom, although he felt selfish for thinking such a thing. He closed his eyes.

*

A warm, wet, smelly puff of air in his face awakened him. The hut was in total blackness. The fire had burned down and the night was moonless. Something—something large—was smelling his face, snuffling loudly. Whatever it was, bear or panther, its breath had the reek of a carnivore. Before he could give any thought as to how to react, a damp, cold muzzle touched his cheek.

Yelling at the top of his lungs, he thrust up with his hands. They came into contact with a heavy, furry body. It seemed to be the size of a large calf and weighed much more. The thing burst into a flurry of activity, buffeting him about, and then it was gone. It crashed out of his camp, and he heard it going off through the swamp.

Moses didn't sleep the rest of the night, keeping the fire blazing so high he had to stay at the far end of the hut. He prayed for protection. But he also kept his axe beside him.

The next day, as he worked, he often glanced about, nervous. What if it returned? He had no gun, of course. Only whites carried guns. He made up his mind to leave the swamp on the next boat.

That night, though, when he said his prayers, God changed his mind. He needed to get well so he could finish getting free and then begin saving his family. God would protect him. Without getting up to add extra wood to the fire, he closed his eyes and slept soundly.

Moses stayed in the swamp until the first breath of spring. When he came out, he sold his lumbering tools, since he'd be going back to the boats. He used the money to buy a shirt, trousers and a pair of shoes, then set off for Sawyer's Ferry, planning to spend a week with his family before going back to work.

At dusk, when passing close by a house at the side of the road, Sawyer's nearest neighbors, the Murfrees, he heard a voice call out.

"Hey, you, boy. Come here."

Moses peered into the darkness and made out several shapes beneath the canopy of a large tree. "Yassuh," he said quickly and moved into the gloom. A match flared, a lantern was lit and four men were revealed, each carrying a rifle in one hand and a saddle in the crook of the other arm except the one with the lantern, who had set his gear down to light the lamp. The one on the right was Mister Murfree, a thick-bodied, muscular man with a large paunch and full beard. Moses didn't know any of the others.

"Step inta the light, boy," Murfree said, "an' drop your bag."

Moses stepped forward and set down his duffle, which contained all his belongings. "Yes, sir, Mister Murfree, sir."

Murfree set down his saddle, took the lantern from the man beside him and held it up. "I recognize you. You're Moses, ain't you? Used ta belong to Enoch Sawyer?"

"That's right, Mister Murfree."

"That's *Sheriff* Murfree, boy. Ya been gone so long ya don't know who the county sheriff is?"

Moses nodded. "I reckon so, Sheriff. Sorry, sir, no disrespect intended."

"Ain't this the Grandy nigger?" one of the other men asked. "The one always tryin' to buy hisself and callin' hisself 'captain'?"

"That's the one." Murfree turned his head aside and spat out a gob of tobacco. "Where you off to, boy?"

"Just up the road to the ferry, Sheriff." Moses replied with a nod. "Going to see my wife and family."

"Nothin' wrong with that," the sheriff said. "Let's see ya paper."

"It's in my bag, sir." Moses knelt. "I'll get it out." He bent and began untying the drawstring.

"Hold the light, Jethro." Murfree passed off the lantern and took something from his shirt pocket. Out of the corner of his eye, Moses saw him take a bite of it. Plug tobacco.

Moses stood and took out the paper from Captain Miller. He held it out to the sheriff.

Murfree took the paper and unfolded it. It was torn and tattered, thin at the creases. He held it to the light.

"This heah paypa's two yeahs old. This Minna' fella, he owns ya now?"

"Yes sir, Sheriff."

"How come ya carryin' two yeah old papers?"

"I've been away, working in the swamp. The paper's still good, though, sir."

Murfree snorted and a spittle of tobacco juice moistened Moses' face. "I'll be the judge o' that, boy. I'm the sheriff and the captain of the duly appointed patrol."

"Yes sir." Moses had already figured these men to be "pattyrollers." The tune of a song he'd heard sung by a black waterman last year ran through his head, a take-off on a white song.

Run, nigger run, or the pattyroller catch you.
Run ,nigger run, well you better get away.
Run, run, or the pattyroller catch you.
Run, nigger, run, well you better get away.

Nigger run, nigger flew.
Nigger tore his shirt in two.
Run, run, or the pattyroller catch you
Run, nigger, run, well you better get away.

Nigger run, run so fast,
stove his head in a hornets' nest.
Run, run, or the pattyroller catch you.
Run, nigger, run, well you better get away.

Hey, mister pattyroller don't catch me,
catch the nigger behind that tree.
Run, run, or the pattyroller catch you.

"…And Remember that I Am a Man."

Run, nigger, run, well you better get away.

"This heah, Minner, he live way up in Deep Crick?" Murfree continued to study the paper, which was now speckled with brown.

"Yes, sir, Sheriff," Moses said.

"What you doin' way down heah, then?"

"I work the canal boats."

The sheriff looked up and glared at Moses. "Thought you said you was workin' in the swamp."

"Yes, sir, I did," Moses replied. "I work different places. Sometimes the swamp, sometimes the canals, sometimes I sign on to a schooner or some other boat."

"Sign on?" asked one of the white men, a youth with a sparse beard. "I thought you said you was a *captain*."

Moses turned. "No, sir, Master. That was just something they called me, way back in the war. I'm just a reg'lar ol' nigger."

Murfree snorted again. "Uppity nigger, if'n you ask me." He folded the paper and handed it back to Moses. "Get on your way, boy."

"Yes, sir, Sheriff Murfree, sir." Moses bent and carefully put the paper in his bag. As he began to pull the string shut, a boot hit his rear end and sent him sprawling.

"Sheriff said to get on your way, nigger," said Jethro. "Now get."

"Yassuh." Moses scrambled to his feet, still holding his bundle, and jogged away. Glancing back, he saw the four men walking away with their gear, one balancing the lantern with a rifle in the same hand.

"…And Remember that I Am a Man."

"…And Remember that I Am a Man."

Part Four

Diaspora

Chapter Forty-six

Hard Scrabble—1825 A.D.

When, at length, I had repaid Captain Minner, and had got my free papers, so that my freedom was quite secure, my feelings were greatly excited. I felt to myself so light, that I almost thought I could fly, and in my sleep I was always dreaming of flying over woods and rivers. My gait was so altered by my gladness, that people often stopped me, saying, "Grandy, what is the matter?" I excused myself as well as I could; but many perceived the reason, and said, "Oh ! he is so pleased with having got his freedom."

The Life of Moses Grandy—1843 A.D.

Moses stood at the rail of the schooner Brilliant as sailors brought her safely alongside the wharf. It seemed odd to sit and watch other men work without taking part himself. On every other voyage he'd taken, he'd been a member of the crew—if not captain—and he wasn't sure if he liked being a mere passenger. He had enjoyed his first ocean voyage, however, even though he had chafed at being idle. He'd never been out on the open sea; none of his masters had been willing to risk such a voyage, where escape might have become a possibility.

The Minners had bought him new clothing and a suitcase, using their own funds, and Moses wore a blue, double-breasted wool suit with bone buttons, which he found quite comfortable on this cold, early spring day with a stiff breeze blowing in off the Narragansett Bay. At his side, he held his high-topped, wide-brimmed hat, since it was a bit too large for him and would have sailed away on the wind. The hat wasn't new; it had formerly belonged to Mrs. Minner's uncle, who had recently passed away. Although his hair had begun to recede in front and his close-cropped beard had a few gray speckles, Moses was sure he looked quite the gentleman, especially with the red bow-tie he wore.

The day he'd repaid Captain Minner and been given his manumission paper had been the proudest of his life. He'd run nearly all the way home, almost thirty miles, to show the paper to Betsy. He didn't dare tell any of the six children about his freedom, though, since they might tell someone. If word of Moses' freedom got out, there might be whites who would take it out on his family, since he'd gotten so "uppity." Or, they might kidnap him, take his papers and sell him down the river. It would be best for him to keep mum until he'd completed the final requirement for freedom and had it recorded by the court.

So Captain Minner had arranged passage for Moses on the Brilliant, which was commanded by an old friend of Minner's, Captain Howard. There'd been a bit of muttering among the white crewmen of the ship about "the nigger who rates a cabin," but no one had dared make open remarks with Howard as Moses' patron.

And now the ship had arrived in Providence, Rhode Island. Captain Minner had given Moses a letter of introduction to a Reverend William Hodgson, of the Universalist Church, who had been recommended as an abolitionist who had helped refugee slaves in the past. Captain Howard had agreed to locate the reverend on Moses' behalf.

Captain Howard would be busy for a while. Moses remembered how *he* had always made sure the cargo was safely ashore. So, once the ship was tied up, he sat out of the way and watched. A crew of burly stevedores swarmed up the gangway from the dock and headed down into the holds. Ship's crewmen pulled back the canvas sheets that covered the hatches leading down into the storage areas. Booms swung out over the ship, ropes were lowered into the holds and soon barrels, crates and bales began rising from the depths. Wagons waited on the wharf and the goods were lowered directly into them.

Moses had watched for at least an hour when someone appeared beside him.

"Captain Grandy?"

Moses jumped to his feet. "Yes, sir, Captain."

"Get your things," Captain Howard said. "I'd like to get your business done forthwith, so that I might not be delayed in my own affairs."

When Moses had fetched his baggage from his stateroom, Howard led him onto the wharf. Moses paused for the briefest of moments to thank God for this moment. Then, striding through the hustle and bustle, the two men soon came to a wide cobblestone street, where the captain waved down a carriage. This wasn't like the wagons back home in the Carolinas; it was a grand affair with high, steel-rimmed wheels. It had been painted shiny black with red trim and wheel spokes.

"Where to, Guv'nor?" asked the driver, turning around in his seat.

"Do you know the Universalist Church on Westminster Street?" asked Captain Howard.

"Sure do. That be where you want to go?"

"Please," replied the captain.

The driver grinned. "Can't take ye there, Guv'nor."

Captain Howard looked annoyed. "This carriage is for hire, isn't it?"

The driver put his palms out to imply helplessness. "Oh, I can take ye to Westminster Street, thet I can. But the church ain't there anymore."

Moses wondered how anyone could move a church. And where had they taken it?

"What do you mean?" asked Howard.

"It burnt down two days ago, along wit' most o' the buildings around it, Guv'nor."

"…And Remember that I Am a Man."

Howard threw Moses a look of dismay. Moses quickly realized the captain wanted to be rid of his black charge, and this news was a setback. The captain recovered his composure, however, and turned again to the driver.

"Was anyone killed?" he asked. "I mean… the minister, is he all right?"

"Oh, no one died. Most folks was at the t'eatre, it bein' 'bout eleven in the evenin' or so."

"Do you know where the minister…?" Howard pulled a paper from his pocket and looked at it. "Reverend William Hodgson. Do you know where he lives?"

"Argh, that I do."

Howard smiled thinly. "Take us there, then."

"As you wish, Guv'nor. Sean Sweeney, at your service." Sweeney turned and pulled some sort of handle next to the seat, shook the reins and clucked. The horse, one of the sorriest old nags Moses had ever seen, stepped out.

The horses' iron-shod hooves clattered on the cobblestones and the carriage bounced with a slight, regular rhythm that was soothing, rather than jarring. They'd had a few cobblestone streets in Norfolk, but Moses had never ridden over them. Whites rode. Blacks walked.

There was a lot of traffic on the street, mostly heavy wagons drawn by four horses. At first they went by large, squat, brick buildings with high windows: warehouses, the same the world over. Every building had several tall, thick chimneys with smoke coming out in clouds. When the wind happened to bring a draft smoke down to the street, Moses gasped. He'd never smelled anything so foul. It was worse than a hog wallow.

Moses hadn't been speaking at all, because it was all he could do to keep up with Sweeney's accent. But when he'd caught his breath from the smoke, he asked, "Why do they have fires lit at this time of year? It must be hot as all get out in those buildings."

Captain Howard looked at him in puzzlement and then laughed. "Those fires aren't for heat. They're smelting metals in those factories. They make a lot of machinery in this city, besides all the shipping that goes in and out of here."

"Don't ye forget textiles, that's our biggest concern," Sweeney said above the din of traffic. "And silver. Some of the fines' silverware in the country."

They soon left the factory district and traveled along a wide thoroughfare, lined with small, wood-shingled homes, which seemed to have been built before the revolution and had seen better days. And then they were in the city proper. Homes were larger here, crowding the side of the lots they sat upon, with only narrow spaces between structures. Many of them were businesses, as well as residences. Moses, although he couldn't read, recognized jewelry and furniture stores, haberdasheries, butchers, grocers and all the goods needed by city folks. This place appeared to be quite a city, maybe even bigger than Norfolk, back in Virginia.

"How'd the fire start?" asked Captain Howard.

"Nobody knows for sure," the driver said over his shoulder. "Like I said, near ever'body was at the t'eatre. Somebody saw flames 'tween Mr. Rhodes' house and Mr. Allen's furn'ture man'factory. Sounded the alarm, they did, but, like I said, near ever'body was at the t'eatre. By the time they got the pumper wagon there, it was what ye call a roarin' inferno, what wit' all the varnish and turp'ntine and what not."

"Quite a blaze, eh?" Captain Howard commented.

"Warn't so bad yet, Guv'nor." Sweeney spat on the horse's rump. "Thing's really lit up when the church caught on."

Howard raised an eyebrow. "Why is that?"

"Some o' the members had stored over a hun'red bales o' cotton in the basement, along wit' dozens o' barrels o' whiskey."

What in the world was a basement? Moses wondered, but after showing his ignorance about factories, he decided to keep quiet.

"In a church?" Howard asked.

"Why not, Guv'nor?" Sweeney shrugged. "Per'aps they figgered it to be the safest place o' all."

Or maybe God didn't appreciated hard spirits being stored in his house, Moses thought.

I don't know 'bout the whiskey," Sweeney said, "but a lot o' them universallers has got shares in textile mills, like everybody what's anybody in this town."

At the word, "shares," Moses took an interest. He understood business.

"That seems odd." Captain Howard ran a hand through his hair. "Why would abolitionists be dealing in cotton?"

The driver laughed. "Lip service, Guv'nor. They all talk 'bout bein' against slavery and what not, but a dollar's a dollar, in a textile town, right?"

Moses had never thought about it, but this wise-cracking Yankee was right. Cotton fueled slavery. Why, he had brought cotton north himself, as cargo on the canal and never thought about what he was doing. He'd just thought of it as "business," as these so-called abolitionists appeared to be doing.

"Speakin' o' abolitionists, this darkie your man-servant, Guv'nor?" Sweeney spat on his horse again.

"Er, no, he's not," Howard replied. "We're merely traveling together."

"Well, you might want to keep a sharp eye on 'im, anyway," Sweeney said. He turned and fixed Moses with a hard gaze. "Darkies ain't too pop'lar 'round here, right 'bout now."

Moses found himself growing angry. He'd come all this way to be treated as poorly as he had been in Camden County. "Why not?" he asked.

"Had us a bit o' riot here last October," Sweeney said, turning his attention back to the road. "Darkies kicked up a bit o' ruckus down in Hard Scrabble."

Howard frowned. "Hard Scrabble?"

Sweeney nodded. "That's where all the Darkies live."

"Are there many, er, darkies in Providence?" Moses asked.

"Wha'd he say, Guv'nor?" Sweeney asked. "He talks too funny for me to make out."

Howard repeated Moses' question.

Sweeney spat on the horse. "Must be over a t'ousand o' the rascals."

Moses felt a little better about having come here. At least he wouldn't be the only negro in town.

The carriage stopped in front of an elegant, two-story stone home. Moses noticed the smoky odor of recently burned wood in the air.

"...And Remember that I Am a Man."

"Here we go, Guv'nor. Rev'rend Hodgson's place."

Captain Howard leaned forward. "Can you wait and take me back, Sweeney? I shouldn't be more than a few minutes."

"Sure 'nuff, Guv'nor."

Howard shepherded Moses out of the carriage, through a wrought iron gate and up onto the porch of the house. He reached out and dropped the door clapper three times.

He turned and smiled at Moses. "Well, Captain Grandy, you are about to become the resident of a free state. Congratulations."

"Thank you, Captain." Moses knew he should feel excitement, but the thought of a year away from his family was hard to bear. Captain Minner had promised to get money to Betsy now and then, but there was more to it than that. Moses knew Betsy and the children could be lost to him on a white man's whim. Why, for all he knew...

The door swung inward. "Good morning, sir. May I be of assistance?"

The voice was female and the accent was southern. Were the Hodgsons from his part of the world? He strained to see over the tall captain's shoulder.

"Please," said Howard. "We're here to see Mr. Hodgson."

The captain moved aside slightly and Moses was surprised to see a black woman standing inside the doorway. She looked to be about ten years younger than Moses, maybe thirty, wearing a dark blue, muslin dress, long-sleeved and full-skirted, with a white apron and a frilly white cap. Her eyes were a deep brown, above a wide, generous nose and thick red lips that were accented by her skin tone. Tiny in stature, her skin was a rich, shiny black.

"The reverend isn't in at the moment." She talked to Howard but her eyes bored into Moses. "Would you like to leave a message?"

Her speech was cultured, like a southern white person putting on airs.

Moses sensed Howard stiffen beside him. He looked over. The captain twice began to reply, but caught himself. He glanced back at the waiting carriage.

"I'm afraid that won't do, young lady...er, ma'am. I have a letter for the reverend, introducing this man and... how soon do you expect the reverend to return?"

To Moses' relief, the woman had stopped staring at him and turned her attention to his companion.

"It will be at least mid-afternoon before Reverend Hodgson returns. He's dealing with his insurance solicitor. Have you heard about the fire, sir?"

Howard nodded nervously. "Yes." He glanced back at the waiting Sweeney again. "I guess I'll have to return..."

The woman cut him off. "You can leave the letter with me." She pointed a thumb at Moses. "Him, too."

"Well..." Howard's eyes couldn't seem to light anywhere, flying from the woman to Moses to the carriage and back again. "...I do have business elsewhere."

"Leave him," the woman said. "I'll see he gets to the reverend, and I know what to do with him until then."

Howard thought for a second, and then turned to Moses. His eyes held the assurance of a career officer who had made a command decision. "Well, that's it then. I've fulfilled my duty." He stuck out his hand. "Goodbye, Captain Grandy."

"Yes, you've done your duty, Captain." He took Howard's hand and shook it. "Thank you, sir."

"You're welcome." Howard released his grip. "Good luck to you."

"Fair seas and a following wind to you, Captain Howard."

Howard turned and went down the steps, walked to the carriage without looking back, and climbed in. As Sweeney's horse clopped away down the street, the small woman regarded Moses with apparent indifference.

"Another runaway, huh?" She looked down at the luggage in his hand. "Got more than most, I see."

"I'm not a runaway, I'm..."

She cut him off. "Don't matter. Get in off the porch before some white trash gets a look at you."

"White Trash?" Moses had never heard the term.

The woman gestured for him to hurry. "You know, them whites that work in the factories or on the wharves. Or don't work at all." She gave him a shove as he passed her, then closed the door. "They see another darkie on the reverend's porch and, next thing you know, a committee shows up and tells the reverend not to bring any more

new ones in." Her formally proper speech had changed, Moses
noticed, now there were no whites present.

Moses turned and looked down at her. "Why's that? I thought
former slaves were welcome in the north."

"Used to be that way with most folks," she replied. "Not so many
are welcoming now, leastways here in Providence."

Her voice was hard enough to make him wonder if she belonged
to the "not so welcoming" crowd, but why would a fellow black feel
that way? More likely, she was establishing her position of authority
in the house, putting him in his place.

"What's your name?" he asked.

She hesitated, then said, "Lenora."

"Pleased to meet you, Lenora," he said. "I'm Moses Grandy."

"That white man called you 'Captain Grandy.'"

Was that her reason for her near-hostility? He said, "That's just
the way sailors talk. I'm nothin' but plain old Moses. But, tell me
something. Why don't the white workers like the blacks?"

She sighed, her attitude visibly softening. "It's all about jobs. The
blacks want factory jobs and the owners would like to hire them as
laborers, but the white trash don't want it. They're afraid they'll end
up working for lower wages."

So that's why Moses hadn't seen any blacks working as
stevedores, or as dock laborers.

He asked, "So where do blacks find work?"

Lorena indicated the ornate foyer they stood in. "The women
work in white folks' houses. The men…" She shrugged. "The men
get jobs sweeping floors or any work they can find."

Moses, reminded of his surroundings, turned in a full circle and
whistled. The home was ornately furnished, putting every white
home in Camden County to shame.

Lorena smiled for the first time. "You ain't seen nothin', yet.
There's homes around here that makes this place look like a
sharecropper's shack. Listen, I'll put in a good word with Mrs.
Hodgson. The reverend's charity sometimes runs a bit on the lean
side."

*

"...And Remember that I Am a Man."

By the time Mr. Hodges returned home, Lenora had installed Moses in a small room at the back of the house. Moses would have preferred to wait for the reverend's arrival, but she assured him this was normal procedure. At least he had a chance to wash his face and use the outhouse. Once out in the back yard, he could see the charred timbers and rubble of many structures that had once stood nearby. This house had been spared only because of its stone construction, more than likely.

Hodgson turned out to be a small, mousy man in his forties, whose eyes seemed unable to meet a direct gaze. His wife, a younger woman who stood a couple of inches taller, was attractive despite being a bit chubby. She stood at her husband's side and read Captain Minner's letter along with him.

When he'd finished, the reverend folded the paper and put it away. He looked at Moses with a genuine smile, or at least a very good imitation.

"This is a remarkable story, Moses. Most of the refugees who come to us have slunk through the night, from safe-house to safe-house. You travel openly, as a paid passenger, with a letter of recommendation stating that you have purchased your freedom, not once, but three times."

Moses nodded. "Yes, sir, that's right."

"And it says here, you're an experienced sailor."

"Yes, sir."

"Well, welcome to Providence, Moses."

"Thank you, sir."

Hodson's wife nudged him.

The reverend cleared his throat. "Harumph. Well, er, let me tell you how we do things here, Moses. Normally we would put you up in one of the church outbuildings, but I'm afraid that's out of the question. You've heard about the fire?"

Moses nodded again.

"Because of that fire," said the reverend, "all we have now is the room Lorena put you up in, which we normally don't use. It's a bit small, I'm afraid."

His wife nudged him again.

"Yes, er, how it works, we normally employ a new man or a woman until we can place them somewhere. Nothing difficult, just

358

light cleaning of the church and such. That's usually for a month or so, and then…"

Another nudge from the wife. He glanced at her and read something in her eyes, then turned back to Moses.

"Of course, at the moment, there *is* no meeting house to clean and church funds are low, due to the fire, but I'm sure we can put you up for two weeks, or so, until we can find work for you. Then you can find an inexpensive place to stay…"

"That's all right, sir," Moses interrupted, annoyed. From what he could gather, the good Reverend Hodgson used the church for commercial purposes, putting a good deal of money in his pocket. "Church funds" came from Sunday collections or charity drive and this money was used for humanitarian purposes—after he took a salary of course.

"I have my own money," Moses said, "and I'm certain I can find accommodations by tomorrow, so your room will be available for others."

Moses figured the man for a blustering, pompous ass, a "man of God" who used the church to perform good deeds so he could feel superior to others—as long as it didn't put him out, personally. Moses wasn't about to accept condescension just to get charity he didn't need.

Mrs. Hodgson stepped forward. "Oh, there's no need to be hasty, young man," she said, although she was probably younger than Moses. Again, she nudged her husband.

"Yes, yes, of course," the reverend said. "You've just finished a long sea voyage. At least stay the night, boy. You are in the hands of friends."

*

The next morning, Lenora brought a plate of food to Moses' room. She seemed friendlier, but it was hard to be sure. After eating, he took a walking tour of the city feeling a dry, crisp quality in the air, and a bite to the wind. He appreciated the salt tang coming off the Narragansett Bay as only a sailor can, his mind refreshed.

In the more affluent parts of the city, he marveled at the size and splendor of the houses and the precision of their surrounding wrought-iron or white picket fences. The homes huddled close together, and the yards were small, but neat. Several times, he came across black men who trimmed shrubbery with clippers or cut grass with some contraption that whirled and clanked as it was pushed along, leaving a green, level carpet of grass behind it. Occasionally, he saw black women hanging fashionable garments on clotheslines. He waved at the workers, but most seemed not to see him.

On the cobblestone streets, fashionable women rode in fashionable carriages, the ribbons and feathers on their fashionable hats fluttering. Uniformed black men drove. Occasionally, on the sidewalk, he would encounter a fashionable mother, pushing a fashionable baby pram with an attached parasol to protect the infant passenger. He saw no white men. Presumably, the men of the houses were absent on unfashionable, but profitable, business affairs. Running businesses using cotton picked by slaves, but not allowing black men to work for a decent wage..

In the working-class areas, the houses, packed together, were small with faded, board exteriors. There were no lawns, no fences, and no sidewalks. There were clotheslines, but white women tended them, hanging faded cotton or muslin dresses, men's work clothes, and diapers. Unfashionable women walked along the edge of dirt streets, but they pushed no prams. Instead, infants rode in slings and toddlers trudged along. Gangs of older children raced about the neighborhoods, yelling as they kicked balls along or rolled hoops with sticks. Again, men were absent during the day.

One similarity between the disparate neighborhoods presented itself to Moses. Fashionable women pushing prams, working-class women carrying babies or buckets or bundles of laundry, playful children, all steered clear of Moses. They would cross the street, turn a corner, even reverse course to avoid proximity to this strange black man in their midst. Moses tried to be understanding, since there had recently been a riot. Fear and racial tension ran high. Still, it hurt to be shunned.

When he reached the area known as Hard Scrabble, the homes weren't much better than the shacks of slave quarters. The only improvement over the southern slave shack was the presence of stone fireplaces with chimneys. Here, in the north, a fire on a brick slab and a hole in the ceiling wouldn't keep out the harsh winters. Other than poorer dwellings, Hard Scrabble was pretty much the same as the white working class neighborhoods. Men were present here, though, sitting on front stoops or loitering on street corners.

They didn't avoid Moses here, and greeted him when he passed. But their hellos were neutral and their eyes suspicious. They were all considered "black," from tan skins to ebony, but Moses was a stranger in a strange land. His rolling seafarer's gait, his different clothing with his handsome hat, and his southern accent set him apart. He didn't fit in here, either.

It didn't take long to find a place to stay, though. Just a one-room shack

When he asked around, there were plenty of cheap places to rent. He settled on a one room shack with a stone fireplace that looked like it might be able to keep the place warm on cold winter nights. That night, after buying a cheap, used mattress to lie on, Moses blew out the candle and yearned for his family, by the light of the moon coming through his small window. How could he bear a year's separation? After a while, visions of white sails on the Albemarle blocked out his conscious thought and he fell asleep.

"…And Remember that I Am a Man."

"…And Remember that I Am a Man."

Chapter Forty-seven

Fancy Hat—1825 A.D.

During the 1820s, as Providence became more densely populated, as its older houses became less habitable, and as its factories darkened the landscape, tensions increased between the white working class and the black community. The fact that Negroes were stripped of the right to vote in 1822 and were segregated by the Providence School Law of 1828 intensified their resentment.

Most blacks lived in an area called Hard-Scrabble (where a) minor race riot occurred in October 1824. Although it resulted in no deaths and only moderate damage, it shocked the citizenry and kindled debate not only on the issues of race but also on those of law and order and governmental reform. The old town meeting system, said some, was no longer adequate for the administration and security of a community harboring nearly 17,000 socially and racially antagonistic residents.

Three and One Half Centuries at a Glance, ProvidenceRI.com

Moses' search for employment began on the docks. With what he'd heard about race relations in Providence, he figured he'd better settle for handling cargo. Yet the employers he approached pointed out, even if they *would* hire blacks, Moses wouldn't qualify. He'd never done enough heavy lifting to build up the needed muscles, so why would they hire an older darkie when there were plenty of strong, young men around.

At factories, the only job given to blacks was floor-sweeper, and all those positions were filled.

Next, he applied to various businesses around town. Most were family enterprises with no outsiders needed, white or black. Larger businesses only hired blacks as floor sweepers or delivery boys. Again, every position was filled.

He tried the livery stables, since he had considerable experience tending for horses and mules, but every barn already employed whites. There *were* jobs for blacks, mucking stalls and shoveling manure, but, once again, every job was spoken for.

"Do you know of any whites who might need a driver for their carriage?" he always asked, to no avail.

Each evening, he returned to his rented, twenty-five-cents-a-week, hovel. He cooked beans, which had been soaking in a pot of water all day, over a small fire. Sometimes he allowed himself the luxury of adding a bit of salt pork.

This was his only meal of the day other than a penny's worth of bread for breakfast, purchased from an old woman who'd set up on the side of the street. It would hold him until evening, although he'd be ravenous when he returned "home."

He'd exhausted the possibilities in town, so he turned to the countryside, hoping for farm work. He could see, from the fields he passed, that there was plenty of work to be done. But the white farmers had heard about the fall riots, and their faces hardened when Moses approached.

His money was being spent at an alarming rate. His neighbors in Hard Scrabble still hadn't accepted him. The men remained wary of anyone who might compete for work. The women held the age-old fear of a single man in their midst.

Even though shunned, Moses felt the tension gripping the black community, their animosity against whites. He was not included in conversations, but groups on the street corners did not stop talking when he came within earshot. Although illiterate, the inhabitants of Hard Scrabble weren't stupid. They knew that, without training, they were destined for menial, low-paying jobs. At least when enslaved in the south, they'd been fed. Here, joblessness meant hunger. The recent riots had increased the friction between races.

A third of the black men stayed in Hard Scrabble during the work day with nothing to do. They were as uneasy as injured snakes, ready to strike at the first thing to come within range. There'd be more violence between the races; he was sure of it.

As for Moses' joblessness, he had a hole card. He was a sailor, experienced in a skilled profession. Ship captains were always on the lookout for anyone who knew how to reef a mains'l, set a jib, or keep the wheel steady in a gale, whether black or white. Moses was sure he could hire onto one of the dozens of vessels that put into Providence every week.

There *was* a flaw in this strategy, however. Moses needed to establish residency in a northern state for a year. Serving on a ship at sea wouldn't qualify.

Nevertheless, he set out for the harbor one morning, munching bread from the old woman's stand. During the night, he'd come up with a solution for the residency issue. If he used all the money he had left, he could rent his shack for an entire year. Even though he wouldn't be physically present, maybe he'd be considered a resident. It sounded reasonable, but he couldn't be sure. He'd never had to deal with legal issues.

Once at the docks, Moses asked for work at each of the four ships in port. The captains were satisfied with his qualifications, but had no berths available.

These results were not all that discouraging. Ships came and went all the time, Eventually one would need a crewman, and Moses would be signed on. Unless, of course, the captain was set on not hiring blacks. There was no shortage of racist captains.

After leaving the last of the ships, Moses chanced upon two black men idling about the docks, sailors by the cut of their jibs. He stopped to chat.

One of the men hailed from Edenton, North Carolina, a port on the Chowan River. As a slave, he'd hired out on fishing boats. When his master died and freed him, he'd signed on for a transatlantic journey and not gone back south since. The other came from New Orleans, Louisiana, which might as well be on the moon, for all Moses knew about it.

But it didn't matter where they came from, all shared the lot of a seafarer. Since the visiting sailors had nothing to do until their ship went to sea again, they sat around and talked for hours. Finally, as the sun slipped below the horizon, Moses said his goodbyes and headed back toward Hard Scrabble.

He passed into the shadow of a twelve-foot high stack of cotton bales, protected from the rain by a canvas tarpaulin. As he was about to come back out into the light, two white men stepped in front of him, one very large and muscular.

"What you doin' down heah on the dock, niggah?" asked the smaller of the two. "Lookin' for somethin' to steal, you and your fancy hat?"

Moses was about to answer, but the man produced a truncheon and began smacking it against his palm. There was no answer to appease these men. They must have been watching him for some time, since it was too dark now for them to see his hat.

The pair moved toward Moses. The steady beat of the truncheon gave the promise of a beating to come.

"Speak up, niggah. What you doin' heah?"

Moses backed away. His only hope was to get deeper into the gloom, then turn and make a break for it. His assailants followed. Once they'd entered the shadows, they became neither white or black, but seemed to be wraiths, silhouetted by the meager light behind them.

It was time to make his move, Moses decided. Before he could turn, however, someone grabbed him from behind, pinning his arms.

"I got 'em, boys."

Moses stepped on his captor's instep and ripped his arms free. His eyes had adjusted to the gloom and he saw the first two were upon him. He dodged sideways, but the big man moved with lightning speed and a ham-sized hand grabbed Moses' arm and hoisted him. He flew through the air and slammed face-first into the cotton. Something hard—the truncheon—smashed into the back of his head and fists began to pummel his lower back. The truncheon worked over Moses' head and shoulders while someone else battered his kidneys. Moses doubted this was the giant or he'd have a broken spine by now.

"You niggahs have to learn to stay off the docks," said the original speaker, breathlessly. He'd paused in his beating but fists still punched his back. The truncheon struck again, hitting the base of his skull and he felt himself slipping away.

"You take the word back to all them other Hard Scrabble niggahs."

A huge hand wrapped around the back of Moses' neck, digging cruelly into the already-bruised flesh. He was lifted and turned around. The giant, a blurred phantom, held his prey at eye level. He cocked his arm and a ghostly fist raced toward Moses' face. It hit like a musket ball striking a squirrel.

*

Moses awoke to the light of a three-quarter moon, which he could barely see through swollen eyes. Although he ached all over, his face was the worst. He reached up and assessed the damage. His nose screamed in pain when he touched it, but his mouth and teeth seemed all right. Apparently, the big man's fist had hit him straight on, one time. His assailants had apparently quit once he passed out.

The night was cool and he welcomed the breeze as he took in air through his mouth, since his nose didn't seem to be working at all. For a while, he lay there gathering his strength, and then struggled to his feet, leaning against the cotton bales. He noticed his hat on the ground, battered and worthless, while he waited for his dizziness to subside. When he began to walk, he staggered and lurched from side to side. He finally got himself headed in the general direction of Hard Scrabble.

Moses met no one on the slow journey back to his shack. He guessed it to be two or three in the morning. When he arrived, he lit the one precious candle he possessed and washed his face in the bucket of water he collected every day from the common well. There didn't seem to be much blood, so he hoped his nose wasn't too badly broken. He felt the back of his head and didn't feel much blood there, either, merely a collection of extremely sore lumps. He went to the narrow cot—the only furniture other than a rude table and stool—and eased into bed on his belly, turning his head to the side to avoid more pain.

"...And Remember that I Am a Man."

He awoke again in the late afternoon. A full bladder had awakened him. He went to the earthenware pot that served as his toilet, and braced one hand against the wall. When he began to urinate, he screamed at the unexpected pain. The urine burned like hell and was tinged red with blood. He took a small swig of water from the pot where he soaked beans all day, since his normal drinking water had been soiled by washing in it. He was careful not to drink too much, since it would only make him urinate, and then went back to bed. He prayed to get well, since it was out of his control and surely a matter for The Lord.

On the second day—or was it the third?—someone knocked on his door, waking him and called out in the cracked voice of an oldster. "Hello. You in there. You all right?"

"Aagh," he croaked, struggling to find his voice.

The door opened and the face of the bread lady peeked in. "I haven't seen you for a couple of days." Her eyes grew wide as she got a glimpse of Moses' face. "What in the world happened to you?"

He tried to grin. "I met...met the Providence welcoming committee." His voice came out in a hoarse rasp.

"I should say so." The old woman rushed in and leaned over him. "You look a sight."

"I'll be all right," he said.

"In a pig's eye, you will." She reached down and gently touched his face. "How long ago did this happen?"

"Two days, I think."

"I ain't seen you in three mornings; that's why I came by. Have you had anything to eat?"

"It hurts too much, here." He touched the side of his stomach.

"Let me see." She went around behind him and lifted his shirt to expose his back. "Oh, my. They worked you over pretty good, sonny."

"There were three of them."

She stood. "You wait. I'll be right back." She began to leave the shack but then looked down at his chamber pot and turned to him, concerned. "You're passing blood?"

Moses was too far gone to be embarrassed. He nodded and she shuffled quickly out the door.

Moses dozed off until he realized she was back. She had already built a fire and put on a pot. Idly, he wondered if she was cooking the beans that had been soaking for all this time; he was getting very hungry. But then he caught the aroma of herbs. When the old woman realized he had awakened, she said, "I'm making a poultice for your back. We'll fix you right up."

No beans, then.

The old woman, whose name was Zilla, took care of him for over a week. She left him alone at night, apparently going home to bake her bread and then selling it at her stand before showing up mid-morning. Her poultice worked; he was soon able to urinate without passing blood and the pain eased shortly thereafter. She fed him clear broth, at first, and then more substantial food.

She didn't talk much and never asked him exactly what had happened. When she pronounced him well, he offered to pay her for taking care of him. She accepted and he didn't blame her for taking any money she could get.

When the schooner Brilliant tied up at the Providence docks two weeks later, Moses went aboard. When he found the ship would be putting in to Elizabeth City as a port of call, he arranged with Captain Howard to work as a crewmember, in exchange for passage home.

"…And Remember that I Am a Man."

"…And Remember that I Am a Man."

Chapter Forty-eight

Packet Rat—1825 A.D.

The Flash Packet

It's of a flash packet, a ship of great fame
In the western Atlantic she bears a hard name
With crews of ill usage, of every degree
All slaves of the galley they plough the salt sea.

All thoughts of tobacco you must leave behind;
If you spit upon deck your death warrant is signed
If you spit on the gangway or out over the stern
You're sure of six dozen, by the way of no harm.

At four in the morning, our work it began
For brooms and for buckets cries every man
And fore- and main-top, O they loudly do bawl
For sand and holystone, both great and small.

And now me brave heroes, comes the best of our fun
When you have to reef tops'ls and tack ship as one
With the boys up aloft and the helm run down
"Stand by, tops'l halliards when the main boom swings round."

"Stand by, tops'l halliards, for bowline and all
Then slack away tops'ls and let the wind haul

"…And Remember that I Am a Man."

Aloft and way out and take two reefs in one."
For all in a moment this work must be done.

When he arrived in Elizabeth City, Moses walked north along the western shore of the Pasquotank until he came to Sawyer's Ferry at dusk. He paid his six pence to take the last trip of the day, cautioning the ferrymen not to let Enoch Sawyer know of his return. He soon slipped into Betsy's quarters and held her in his arms. Elijah, nearly seven now, and the other children danced around their parents as they kissed, awaiting their turns to be picked up by their father.

Later, when all the commotion had subsided and Betsy had put the children to bed, she added sticks to the fire and warmed some leftover cornbread for Moses. She served it with thick clabber and a sprinkle of syrup, then sat back to watch him eat.

"Eat it all," she said. "You're getting skinny."

He grinned at her, feeling juice run from the side of his mouth. "I missed your cooking."

"Hmmph!" she said, "I'll bet you tell that to all your wives."

"All eight of them." He heard a giggle from Elijah's bed and then Catherine joined in. He looked over at their beds and saw their eyes reflected in the firelight. They were too excited to sleep. The little ones seemed to have dozed off.

"What happened to your nose?" Betsy asked.

"A labor dispute," he answered. "Seems the Yankees aren't all that eager to have blacks come north, after all."

"I'll bet." She looked him up and down. "Your new clothes is all torn and ragged."

Moses put down his spoon and met her eyes. "It was a mistake to go north. There's no work there for the likes of us, even if we are free. I'll never make enough money to get you and the children away from Sawyer if I'm up there."

She nodded, her expression concerned. "So what are you goin' to do?"

"I'm going to talk to Captain Minner. I need to find work that

372

pays a decent wage, then we'll all go north together."

Her eyes grew wide. "That could take years and you'll be in danger of bein' kidnapped the whole time. Go back north and get yourself set. Me and the chil'ren'll be all right 'til you can send for us."

"No." He shook his head. "I have a plan."

Her eyes grew wide. "You always has a plan. But for now, sit back down and eat. The chil'ren will go to sleep soon, then we can talk."

From the look in Betsy's eyes, Moses knew she had more than conversation in mind.

*

Moses walked north to Deep Creek the following day. Captain Minner and his wife were glad to see Moses, but also concerned that he'd come home early. Once Mrs. Minner had fed them a meal of baked chicken and all the fixings, heaping food on Moses' plate, they all retired to the sitting room for a glass of wine. The captain lit his pipe, filling the room with sweet tobacco smoke, and the Minners listened to Moses' account of his time in the north, Mrs. Minner occasionally clucking in disapproval. Captain Minner often shook his head. "I had no idea the situation was that bad up north."

When he'd finished, Captain Minner said, "I believe you were right to get away from there, Moses. You had no chance of earning a decent living, much less saving to rescue your wife and family, but what are you going to do now?"

"Now, Captain," Mrs. Minner said. "Let's not worry about that for a bit. Moses has had a hard time in the north and a long voyage home. He needs a few days to rest."

Moses leaned forward in his chair, holding his wine in both hands. "No, Ma'am. The captain's right. I've been feverish to get back to work, but there must be some way I can finalize my freedom and still earn a decent wage."

The captain blew a smoke ring and watched it float away. "Well, we could try a different city. You just had a bit of bad luck. If Reverend Hodgson's church hadn't burned down, I'm sure he'd have found a good job for you."

Moses turned toward him and raised an eyebrow. "A good job?

Only if you consider unskilled labor, which is all he believes blacks can do. Hard Scrabble wasn't much better than the slave quarters around here. The only difference between being free and being a slave is getting a wage, and if the wage can't buy a proper place to live and food for the table, it's the same thing."

"So, what do you propose?" The captain blew another ring of tobacco smoke. Moses was reassured, because Captain Minner always said he did his best thinking when his pipe was in use. "No fire in the bowl, no ideas in the skull," was one of his many mottos.

"Well, sir, I had the idea that I could sign onto a ship and make enough to get by, especially because my food and lodging wouldn't cost me anything. One or two good voyages and I might earn enough on shares to approach Master Sawyer about buying my family. If I could just put something down and get a paper, it would greatly relieve my mind that Betsy won't be sold away while I'm getting the rest of the money."

"That sounds like a good idea, Moses," said Mrs. Minner. "Don't you think so, Captain?"

"I agree, my dear. But there's a problem in that, isn't there, my boy?"

Moses nodded. "Yes, sir. I can't get my residency that way."

The captain eyed him while taking a deep draught of tobacco. He held the smoke for several seconds and then blew two columns from his nostrils, grinning all the while. "I've got an idea how we can finalize your freedom for the court and still keep you at sea, Moses."

"What's that, Captain?"

"Reef your mains'l, mate." The captain's grin grew even wider. "I've got something in mind, but it'll take a few weeks to see if I'm on the right tack. You go back and visit your wife for a few days, then come back up here and we'll find something to keep you in vittles until I can firm things up."

The next day, on the long walk home to Sawyer's Ferry, Moses' heart was lighter. He trusted Captain Minner more than he'd trusted anyone since Missy Hannah Kemp, so many years before. He had trusted her because of her abiding faith in God, which she had passed along to him. The captain, on the other hand, represented a more worldly faith. He and Moses shared the brotherhood of the sea and had gone through some rough storms together.

374

He spent the next two weeks with his family, the longest period of inactivity he'd ever known. Surprisingly, he didn't chafe at the unaccustomed leisure, but found he enjoyed taking part in the lives of his children. He learned how much he had been missing because of his frequent, prolonged absences.

And how much they were missing due to his absences. It weighed on him. But it was in the children's best interest that he worked so hard to buy their freedom wasn't it? He would rather miss most of their childhood than have them be enslaved all their lives.

He began teaching the older children how to count and do simple sums. To his delight, they took to it readily, good-naturedly competing with each other.

His leaving for Deep Creek was more heart-wrenching than any previous departure. He'd had a taste of what married life *could* be. Not only white men, but those male slaves who lived on the same plantation as their spouses, could go home every night after work. Someday, perhaps, Moses could do the same. He prayed for their safety while he was gone.

When Moses arrived at the Minner home, the captain could barely contain his enthusiasm.

"I've found just the job for you, my boy," he said. "I think you'll like my solution."

Moses smiled. "I knew I could count on you, sir. What did you come up with?"

The captain held up a hand. "Not yet. Let me explain first. I've been up to Norfolk and consulted with the circuit judge. He agrees that, as long as you spend a year and a day in the north, it doesn't have to be in a single state."

Moses wrinkled his brow. "So I'll be traveling between states? How can I hold a job if I'm doing that?"

Captain Minner grinned. "Ah, but what if traveling *is* your job?"

"How could that be? I'm no tinker."

"I've arranged for you to join the crew of the packet ship, Tuscarora. An old friend of mine, Captain Stead, has agreed to take you on."

Moses frowned. "But if I'm…?"

Again the captain put up a hand. "Wait. Are you familiar with packet ships?"

"Yes, sir. They carry the mail back and forth across the Atlantic."

The captain shook his head. "Not the Tuscarora. It sails only between Philadelphia and New York City. So you'd never leave the northern part of the country."

Moses felt a surge of excitement, but checked himself. "That could be a dangerous situation, Captain. Both those ports deal with English ships. They send press crews out on the docks to shanghai any poor soul they can find. I could end up in a different sort of slavery, where I'd never see my family again."

"You're absolutely right." The captain nodded somberly. "I'd suggest you stay aboard when the ship is in port, especially at night. Only go ashore with a gang of your crewmates. You can handle that for a year, can't you?"

Moses nodded. He'd do whatever it took.

*

When Moses reported aboard the Tuscarora in Philadelphia, he was taken to the captain's stateroom, which surprised him. A new crewman would have normally reported to the first mate. Captain Stead must have a high regard for Captain Minner to take such an interest in a common sailor. But he almost fell over when his new commanding officer told what his position would be.

"A steward's mate?" He shook his head. "Captain, I'm a first rate sailor. I'm not even sure what a steward's mate does." There'd been a steward's mate to serve the officers aboard Captain Howard's Brilliant, but Moses had eaten his meals in his cabin on his first trip on that ship and in the crew's mess on the second.

The captain shrugged. "I know, Grandy, but I don't need any topside hands at the moment. I only took you on as a favor to an old friend."

"Captain, I'm…," Moses began, then saw a hard glint come into Stead's eyes. "I understand, and I'm very grateful, sir."

"You're welcome." The captain smiled and his eyes became friendly again. "Don't worry. I'll have the steward instruct you in your new duties." He called out, "Simmons."

The cabin door opened and a rated sailor poked his head in. "Aye, Captain?"

"Take this boy to Mister Wright." The captain turned his attention to the papers on his desk as if Moses had never existed.

As Simmons guided him aft, Moses noticed sailors on their knees with buckets of soapy water and holystones, abrasive rocks that were used to smooth and polish wooden decks. The sails were neatly reefed, all unused line was coiled in perfect circles, and every bit of brass glittered in the sunlight. He'd never sailed on such a well-kept ship.

Moses was led to a storage hold, where a short, portly man with snow white hair was supervising a gang of sailors loading supplies. "New man for you, Mr. Wright," Simmons said, then disappeared through a hatchway.

The ship's steward wore a blue jacket over a pristine white shirt, along with an officer's cap. His hair and beard were meticulously kept and his shoes were highly polished. He barely glanced at Moses. "Lend a hand here, lad. Those bags of 'taters need to go in the bin, and mind not to bruise 'em."

"Aye, aye, sir." Moses hopped to his duties. In all his time at sea, he'd never used such formal language, but sensed the steward would expect it.

In the coming weeks, Moses learned a packet was nothing like the cargo and fishing vessels he had crewed on. In addition to carrying the mail and some light cargo, the Tuscarora boasted half a dozen staterooms for people traveling between the two cities. For those who could afford it, sea travel was far more comfortable and luxurious than traveling overland by horse or coach.

Mr. Wright was in charge of the care and feeding of passengers, officers and crew, including ship's stores. Beneath him was the chief cook, who prepared the food for the saloon, where officers and guests dined, and the mess cook, who cooked for the crew. Below them were Moses and the other two steward's mates. Alonzo, a Spanish-speaking ex-slave from the Caribbean, was the messman. Willie, a black senior steward's mate who had been born free, served as the cabin steward. Moses' job, as the junior man, was to assist the chief cook and tend to diners in the saloon. He worked twenty hours a day while at sea, catching up on his sleep when they were in port.

Noting that all the non-whites occupied menial positions of servitude, Moses figured Captain Stead had not put him with the topside crew because of the color his skin. But Moses didn't let that bother him. There weren't as many black watermen in the north, so Stead probably wasn't comfortable with the idea of a black being an able seaman.

So, instead of dealing with wind and wave and weather, Moses concerned himself with waiting tables, and the whims of high-society diners. Instead of a pea jacket and sailor's cap, he wore a white jacket, black pants and shiny black shoes. Mr. Wright expected his juniors to keep up appearances.

On a passenger ship such as this, even common sailors were required to have manners. They were forbidden to smoke, spit, curse or perform any other act that might offend a sensitive, high-society lady. And, as Moses had noticed right away, the ship was kept spotless at all times. Maybe Moses was better off being a steward, since it beat holystoning a deck. Although the hours were long, his duties weren't hard. In fact, he was bored.

He was reminded of the time he'd been a "butler" with Master Micheau, although the Micheau home had been slovenly compared to the Tuscarora. Moses had hated waiting on whites then, and his attitude hadn't changed much. But now, as an adult, Moses shrugged it off. He was a free man now, and could always quit his job if he chose.

For months Moses did as told and kept his mouth shut. He stayed aboard in port, saving his pay and the coins he was sometimes given as tips. His pay remained "on the books," for when his year was done. Then, one day, after arriving in Philadelphia, he was ordered to report to the captain's cabin.

Moses checked his uniform for cleanliness, wiped his shoes with a cloth and soon knocked on the captain's door.

"Come in."

Moses entered and walked to stand in front of the captain's desk. "You sent for me, Captain?"

"Yes, Grandy, I did." The captain reached across his desk and picked up two envelopes, one opened and one still sealed. "I've received a letter from Mrs. Minner of Deep Creek."

Moses felt an immediate sense of dread. "*M-Mrs.* Minner, sir?"

Captain Stead looked up at him, his expression grim. "Yes, I'm afraid so. Captain Minner is dead."

"Dead, sir?" Moses felt his knees go weak.

"Yes," the captain replied. He kept his eyes on Moses' face. "Two weeks ago last Friday. According to his wife, he was set upon by bandits, while traveling near his home. They beat him pretty badly and he died two days later."

Moses raised his eyes and looked over the captain's head, out of the small window piercing the transom at the back of the stateroom, which doubled as Stead's office. He took a deep breath and swallowed, willing his legs not to buckle. Had Captain Minner been beaten for his abolitionist stand? It was possible.

"Do you need to sit down, Grandy?" Concern had entered the captain's voice.

"No, sir," he said. "I'll be all right."

"As you prefer, Grandy." Stead held up the other letter, catching Moses' attention. "This one's also from the captain's widow. Addressed to you."

Moses stared at it blankly. No one had ever sent him a letter. "Would you tell me what it says?"

Captain Stead looked puzzled for a moment, then his expression cleared. "Oh, of course. I should have known. Here, let me open it."

Captain Stead took a single page from the envelope and shook it open, holding it to the light streaming in through the transom window. He cleared his throat.

"Dear Captain Grandy. As Captain Stead has no doubt told you by now, my husband has passed on. He spoke of you before he died and asked me to write to you. He was concerned that, upon hearing of his death, you might decide to return to Deep Creek or Camden County." Stead paused and looked up. "That where you're from?"

When Moses nodded, Stead went back to reading. "He urged you, on his deathbed, to remain in the service of Captain Stead for at least one more month. At that time, when the year and a day requirement has been met, the good captain will send me a letter attesting that you have met the court's conditions for your freedom and I will file it with the court. I implore you not to return until that time. Your wife and family are fine, and I will do all I can to ensure their safety and well-being until you return for them. Sincerely, Mrs. Edward Minner."

Edward. Moses had known Captain Minner for many years without once learning the man's first name and now he was dead.

379

"…And Remember that I Am a Man."

Moses would never be able to thank him for all he'd done.

He felt his eyes begin to water. "Thank you, Captain Stead," he said. "Will that be all?"

Stead stuffed the letter back into the envelope and thrust it into Moses' hand. "Here, this belongs to you. I take it you'll be staying aboard?"

Moses nodded.

"That's all then. Dismissed."

"…And Remember that I Am a Man."

Chapter Forty-nine

Freedom—1826 A.D.

When we mounted her decks we found her full of slaves. She was called the Feloz, commanded by Captain Jose' Barbosa, bound to Bahia. She was a very broad-decked ship, with a mainmast, schooner rigged, and behind her foremast was that large, formidable gun, which turned on a broad circle of iron, on deck, and which enabled her to act as a pirate if her slaving speculation failed. She had taken in, on the coast of Africa, 336 males and 226 females, making in all 562, and had been out seventeen days, during which she had thrown overboard 55. The slaves were all inclosed (sic) under grated hatchways between decks. The space was so low that they sat between each other's legs and [were] stowed so close together that there was no possibility of their lying down or at all changing their position by night or day. As they belonged to and were shipped on account of different individuals, they were all branded like sheep with the owner's marks of different forms. These were impressed under their breasts or on their arms, and, as the mate informed me with perfect indifference 'burnt with the red-hot iron.'

Notices of Brazil in 1828 and 1829, Reverend Robert Walsh— 1831 A.D.

Moses' manumission documents, with the official seal of the Commonwealth of Virginia, finally arrived and he was called to

"...And Remember that I Am a Man."

Captain Stead's cabin shortly after they cleared the Philadelphia harbor and set off down the Delaware River. When he left the stateroom with Stead's congratulations ringing his ears, papers in hand, Moses felt powerful and capable. The feeling reminded him of the first time he'd taken command of a vessel and known that the fortunes of ship and crew rested upon his decisions. Now it was his own fate that depended upon his judgment, and he felt confident that he'd soon be able to bring his family to join him.

One thing took some of the wind out of his sails, however. Captain Stead had read aloud the conditions spelled out by the court. Moses didn't dare go back to Norfolk, or Deep Creek, or Dare County now, not even to visit. He had always known that freed slaves were encouraged to stay away from their home states after serving their residencies in the north, but hadn't expected it to be tacked on as a condition of his manumission.

He'd already known that returning to Camden County would be dangerous. The North Carolinians of his home territory held bitter feelings against Virginians, who tended to feel themselves superior to their neighbors on the south. They considered themselves to be somewhat noble, calling themselves cavaliers while using the insulting nickname "tar heels" for the Carolinians. The implication was that the latter were barefoot country bumpkins with dirty feet from swamp mud and field soil. The whites of Camden County— some of them, at least—would like nothing better than to rip Moses' Virginia-issued freedom papers into shreds and sell him into servitude in the Deep South, where he'd have no way of petitioning Virginia courts for help.

In Virginia, returning could be even more hazardous, now that Captain Minner wasn't there to protect him. The authorities, if they found him in the state, were ordered by law to throw him in jail, revoke his freedom, then auction him off to the highest bidder. He'd have to stay in the north, away from the family he'd not seen in well over a year. He had never seen his youngest child, who had been born after he left.

Moses was due in the dining salon, to set the tables for supper, but he had something to do. He went below to where his hammock hung in a small compartment located in steerage, on the lower decks. This was where the cables ran between the ship's steering

wheel and the rudder ran under grating, a space which was often
awash when the Tuscarora encountered heavy seas. Moses and the
other steward's mates shared this small area, apart from the deck
crew.

Once there, he took his sea bag down from a peg and rummaged
around for his empty money belt, an oilskin bag attached to a cloth
strap, which could be tied around his waist, beneath his clothing. He
hadn't bothered wearing it on this ship, since his back pay was kept
in the captain's safe, but he considered his freedom papers too
important for such treatment. Not that Captain Stead wasn't a good
man as far as whites went, but there had only been two people in
Moses' life that he would have trusted deeply enough to entrust with
his papers. Captain Minner was dead and he had long ago lost track
of Missy Hannah, who'd sailed away to attend school in the north.
She'd never returned, as far as Moses knew.

He took out his paper and looked at it in the dim light of the
single lantern. Captain Stead had shown him where his name was
written on the paper, in the looping whorls of whatever clerk had
drawn them up. "Moses Grandy." He had always been called that,
since a slave was given his or her first name by the master and
further identified by the last name of the master. Now it was his
legal name. He had never thought about it before, but now he
wondered if, had he been allowed, he would have chosen a different
last name.

A single bell sounded, loud enough to be heard even this far
belowdecks. It was the first bell of the first dogwatch, four-thirty in
the afternoon, by landlubber time. Moses should have been on duty
by now. He folded his freedom paper into his pouch, tied it on, then
headed up the ladders to his duty station.

Mister Wright waited for him, looking pointedly at the pocket
watch that timed the day for the steward's mates. "Y'are behind
schedule, boy. Have y' an excuse?"

Moses nodded as he began pulling pewter plates from a
cupboard, turning his back to hide his smile. Wright knew damn
well where Moses had been; there were no secrets aboard ship,
especially among the few officers. "Yes, sir. Sorry, sir. The captain
called me to his cabin."

The Ship's Steward looked at him skeptically, crooking an

eyebrow. "Oh, did he, now? And, if I may be so bold as to enquire, did he offer ye a promotion t' Ship's Steward?"

"No, sir, Mister Wright." Moses began piling eating utensils atop a stack of plates and napkins. "My freedom paper just arrived by post from Virginia, and the captain gave it to me. I'm a free man, now, sir."

Wright grinned wryly. "Oh, are ye, now? And, since y'are free, I suppose ye think ye don't have to keep up with yer duties, do ye, boy?"

"No, sir. Sorry, sir. It won't happen again."

"See that it doesn't." A hand suddenly clasped Moses shoulder and he nearly dropped the tableware in surprise.

"Congrad'lations on gettin' yer papers, boy," Wright said. "Good luck t' ye."

*

For the next two days, Moses lived in a daze. Every few minutes, he reached inside his shirt to be sure the paper was truly there, that he wasn't dreaming. Word about his good fortune got to the crew, of course, and most of the men took the time to congratulate him. There were some who didn't take any notice of his new status, and a couple of men who glared for some reason, but it didn't bother him. They were the same ones who had never taken notice of him anyway. A few of the passengers noticed his elation and he was proud to tell them how he had bought his freedom. They smiled and congratulated him, but like most northern whites, they seemed uncomfortable acknowledging slavery, even in such an abstract fashion. Only Alonzo, who had once been a slave himself, seemed to appreciate how important freedom was to Moses.

Mr. Wright called him aside on the second day.

"Boy, I know y'are happy to have got yer freedom papers, but don't let it go t' yer head. Y'are not paying attention to yer job. Y'are off in yer own little world and the diners sometimes have t' wave and holler t' get service from ye."

"Yes, sir, Mr. Wright," Moses said automatically. "I'm sorry, sir."

But as the steward walked away, Moses felt hurt, then humiliated and then angry. What good was freedom if you still had to work for whites and wait on them hand and foot?

384

Maybe he should quit. Free people could do such a thing. It would be his first act of independence. But what was the use of that? He had a good job on the Tuscarora. True, he didn't make much money other than the pennies and five-cent pieces some of the passengers tipped him with, but it was a job where he got his meals and lodging as part of his employment.

That evening, a white businessman named Gallagher offered Moses a job working in a Boston shipyard. He took Gallagher's card and promised to travel to Boston as soon as possible.

First, however, he had to be sure Betsy and the children were taken care of. On his last day, Captain Stead was kind enough to take him ashore in New York and introduce him to a banker. At the bank, Stead paid Moses his back wages, which he immediately turned over to the bank, saving only a little for himself.

Moses wasn't exactly sure how it worked, but the banker would send papers to another bank, in Virginia, which would turn over the money, a hundred and twenty dollars, to Mrs. Minner. The banker also wrote a letter on Moses' behalf, requesting Mrs. Minner to pay Enoch Sawyer a hundred dollars—the banker called it a retainer—to keep Sawyer from selling Moses' wife and children. Also, Mrs. Minner was asked to deliver twenty dollars to Betsy.

When he arrived, Mister Gallagher had forgotten offering Moses a job, since he had been full of wine at the time, but still took him on. Moses' work, however, depended on how busy the small shipyard was. The Gallagher yard didn't build ships, only repaired them. In between jobs, the yard crew was laid off. So the "generous" salary didn't go far.

Living in Boston was expensive, even though Moses shared a room with three other men. He made do by working on the docks, in the coal yards, or wherever a strong back was needed, but it wasn't enough. He soon became aware it would take many years to earn the money he needed.

He fell back on the sea, which had always sustained him, and got a berth as an able-bodied seaman on the schooner-rigged New Packet, which made regular runs from Boston to the Caribbean. Captain Cobb, who was also the ship's owner, made no bones about hiring black seamen and paid them the same wages as whites. In addition, he paid shares to the crew when they made voyages in good time, which was important when carrying the mail.

Moses heart lifted as the ship cleared the harbor, navigated the channel, then turned south around Cape Cod. Even though the late spring breeze blew warm by New England standards, he looked forward to warmer weather and air that didn't stink of smoke. He'd never been to the Caribbean, but it had to be better than New England.

He didn't have time for sight-seeing, though. The first mate kept shouting Captain Cobb's orders, keeping the sailors busy at trimming sails to take advantage of the brisk, northerly breeze. Although Moses wasn't familiar with the New Packet's rigging, he didn't have trouble identifying which gear needed to be adjusted, since all ships used the same nomenclature for sails, lines and tackle.

"Ahoy, lend a hand wi' le jib, here, mon."

Moses turned and saw a small, bare-footed, coal-black man wearing a tattered blue monkey jacket, with sleeves coming to just below his elbows, and short pants, despite the cold. This was the usual garb of a sailor who worked the rigging, keeping a man's arms and legs free to move when aloft. This man, who looked to be in his late twenties, struggled to haul in a line against the pressure of the ballooning jib, the foremost sail on a schooner. His calf muscles strained as his feet tried to gain purchase on the wet, slick deck, but he was being pulled forward.

Moses leapt over and grasped the line behind him. Now that two men pulled, the sail came under control. "Haul, mon," the other sailor said, "Le skipper say to take le luff out of le sail."

The sail was luffing, or shaking, because it wasn't properly trimmed for the prevailing wind. They struggled backward, but slid forward every time a gust filled the sail. If not for the block and tackle, which added force to their efforts, two men wouldn't have had a prayer. When they finally got the line tied off, it sang with tension as the captain brought the ship onto a broad reach, running with the wind but allowing enough leeway to stay well clear of rocks along the shore.

"Zat is good," the sailor said. "We get outta le wind, now." He ducked down beneath the gunwale and Moses joined him.

"You le new mon, yes?"

"Yes, I'm Moses."

"I am name Lucius."

Moses looked Lucius over. A good six inches shorter than Moses, he probably didn't weigh half as much, which explained why he'd had such trouble getting the sail hauled in. The wrists poking from his too-small jacket were thin, but the hands were larger and more powerful-looking than would be expected on a small man. Lucius' eyes were narrow beneath thick brows and above high cheekbones. His protruding lips were thick, his nose long and narrow, flaring to wide nostrils.

"Where are you from?" Moses asked. Lucius' accent was one he'd never heard before.

"I from Haiti, mon."

Moses knew of Haiti, of course, even though he'd never been to the Caribbean. The slaves there had revolted at the turn of the century and thrown out the French. It was the only black-ruled country in the world, outside of Africa.

Moses had encountered a few Frenchmen in his travels and he could recognize the accent, along with Caribbean accents he couldn't place.

"What brings you to the United States?" he asked.

Lucius shrugged. "Nozzing brings me to zis country. I am le sailor. I go where le ship goes."

"I mean, why did you leave Haiti? It must be wonderful there."

The Haitian nodded proudly. "Eet eez a beyootiful place. I am very proud of eet. But zair ees no work."

"No work?" What do you mean?" But Moses had an inkling of what he would hear, after learning how hard it was for blacks to get work in the northern states.

"When les Franchayz leave, so do most of le plantation owners. And zen le Americains make les trade embargoes against Haiti. Now zair eez leetle work, you see."

Moses gave a curt nod.

"Hey, you two in the bow," came a shout. "Lay 'midships and lend a hand with the mains'l."

The little Haitian sprang to his feet and made his way along deck, easily changing his gait and balance to offset the pitch and roll of the vessel. Moses followed close behind, a bit more slowly since he hadn't regained his sea legs yet.

"...And Remember that I Am a Man."

*

On the trip south, as the weather grew hotter day by day, Moses and Lucius shared the same watch. The New Packet sailed with a crew of six, including the captain. Two men at a time stood four hour watches, one at the helm, or ship's wheel, and one acting as lookout and trimming the sails if necessary. They also kept a close eye on the ship's clock and rang the bell every half hour. The watches were stood in addition to their regular duties. Sailors couldn't expect much sleep when at sea.

Moses wasn't sure if Captain Cobb had assigned them together because they were the only blacks aboard, but he didn't mind. He relished talking with a black man who'd had such different experiences. In turn, Lucius seemed to enjoy his company.

Lucius was amazed that Moses had worked for so many masters. On Haiti, so his mother had told him, slaves almost always died under their first master. To him, the southern American system of slavery seemed mild.

"In le Caribbean, a slave from Afreeca eez sent to work in sugar field in le very hot sun," he once said. "Zey work one, two years and zey die. White master, he geets another slave, zen works zat one 'til he die. In America, slaves are more, how you say, loocky?

"Lucky? Not hardly," Moses replied. "My mother was whipped when they sold my brother. When she got old, the master put her out in the woods to starve."

Lucius, who tended to gesticulate when talking, put out his hands, palms out. "I understand, mes ami. But, in les islands—not in Haiti anymore, merci à Dieu —le négrier not survive to grow old. Les children, if zey unlucky enough to be born in such a place, die before zey grow up."

Moses was fascinated that this young black man from Haiti had been born free. Lucius said his mother had been a child when his hero, Toussaint L'ouverture, had rebelled against the French. Lucius had been born after Haiti had been declared a republic, years after L'ouverture had been killed by the French.

Moses gradually became aware Lucius resented not having the opportunity to participate in the Haitian revolution. Even though Lucius had been too young, he somehow felt that he was less of a man for not fighting as other blacks had done. Or maybe he felt guilt for reaping the benefits of freedom without earning it. Perhaps he also felt he had to prove himself because of his small stature.

Moses learned, however, that Lucius had very little experience with slavery at any level. He had been found by Captain Cobb several years back, a teen-aged lad trying to sail to the Bahamas, where he had heard there were still a few small-time privateers that resorted to minor acts of piracy. Lucius had hoped some pirate captain would take him on as a ship's boy, since his mother had died and he had no hope for the future in Haiti. Instead, he now worked for Captain Cobb.

Lucius was not impressed that Moses had bought himself free. "Why you not fight for your freedom? That ees how L'ouverture would have won heez freedom."

Moses considered how to answer. "You said that on your island… What did you call it?"

"Hispaniola."

"You said that on Hispaniola, one white family might employ hundreds of slaves on their plantation?"

"Oui, zat is true."

"Where I come from, there are many more whites than blacks. Besides, the whites have guns and horses. They put down any insurrection before it has a chance to spread."

"But you said escaped slaves live in les swamps. You could have killed your master and gone zere."

Moses sighed. "That's not freedom. You said that your people hid in the mountains while they fought the French, right? And they were called maroons, like our runaways?"

"Oui."

"Well, consider this. Your maroons outnumbered the whites. They were isolated by the ocean, thousands of miles from the French army. The slaves in this country are badly outnumbered, and are surrounded by whites with guns. That makes all the difference."

Moses' logic meant nothing to Lucius, however. The young uneducated Haitian seemed convinced that bravado would convince everyone of his bravery and heroism. Yet he often showed how he put his own interests first.

For one thing, Lucius thought Moses a fool for his passion to return to North Carolina and buy his wife and family free.

"You are already free, non? You are no longer in le south, so you are safe from l' esclavage. How you say? Le slavery. Zere are many woomon to choose from. Why put yourself in danger again?"

Lucius also took Moses to task for his religious beliefs. Christianity, he said, was a "white" religion, teaching slaves to passively accept their lot in life. "Een Haiti, we believe een les old gods, from Africa. Black people should have black gods, not some old white god far away in heaven, who do not answer prayers from blacks."

Once they'd cleared the southern point of Florida, the ship swung west to avoid the many small cays of the Bahamas, until they came within sight of a large island. Lucius identified it with an offhand wave. "Hispaniola."

Beyond the pale blue of the shallows and the white of the beaches was lush undergrowth, punctuated by tall, stately palm trees. Past that, dark green fields of sugar cane dominated the landscape until the land rose in a rugged peak covered with even darker green vegetation. "That's where you're from? Haiti?"

Lucius shrugged. "Ozzair side. Zees is Domeenica."

"Doesn't it make you homesick to be so close?" Moses was thinking of how he'd felt when they'd passed the mouth of the Chesapeake Bay and then the Outer Banks.

"Pah! Zair ees nozzing for me in Haiti."

Still, after they'd filled wooden bowls with the mid-day meal, the pair sat on deck and watched the beautiful scenery slide by. Moses had never seen such a majestic land.

"Ship ho!" someone cried. "Off the starboard bow."

A schooner-rigged ship had cleared a headland, coming into view. Moses paid it scant attention. They had passed many ships since passing the Bahamas, bound into or out of the Caribbean, where all commerce was done by sea.

When they'd finished eating and turned to take their bowls and spoons back to the galley, the other ship had drawn near, passing close down the port side. She was unusually wide in the beam. Schooners tended to be long and lean, built for speed. His eyes went to the top of the ship's mast, where he saw a flag with two red stripes on a field of yellow: a Spanish merchant. The breeze carried a faint stench across to the New Packet, reminding Moses of a hog sty. The smell was different, though, more acrid.

He glanced over at Lucius. To his surprise, the Haitian glared at the other ship with undisguised hatred.

"What's the matter?" Moses asked.

"Don't you know? Zat ees a slavair."

"Really?" Moses looked more closely, but could see nothing that marked the ship as different. "How do you know?"

"Can't you smell eet? Her hold is full of les Afreecans, jammed een like logs in le woodpile, lying in zair own sheet. Zat ees why she ees so wide, to hold more slaves."

Moses had heard how slaves were transported from Africa in the past, but the laws had been changed. Transporting slaves to America was illegal; he had assumed slave ships were a thing of the past.

"Where is she headed?" he asked.

Lucius snorted. "Cuba, maybe. She must have ducked eento a cove when she saw us, een case we wair Amereecan warsheep. Her Capeetan ees vairy fooleesh to come so far nort', where he might be captured. Most Slavairs go to Brazeel."

Moses couldn't take his eyes from the ship until her sails dropped below the northern horizon. He was descended from someone who had survived a long journey on such a ship.

The next day, after they'd docked in San Juan, in Puerto Rico, Lucius talked Moses into going ashore, saying it would be a celebration of his freedom. Deciding it would be foolish to miss his first, and perhaps only, chance to visit another land, Moses drew a portion of his first-voyage pay from Captain Cobb. An hour later, the two black sailors occupied a table in a dockside tavern, where Lucius ordered tankards of rum.

The tavern was a small dingy, smoky room and the bar was merely rough planks set across two large barrels. The heat was oppressive, despite the two windows which had been opened to catch any stray breeze, but only admitted the stench of the harbor, which mingled with the smell of unwashed bodies, sour vomit and other odors Moses couldn't, and didn't want to, identify.

They had nearly finished their drinks when the door burst open and a large woman bustled in, shouting, "Donde esta? Donde esta? Whar ees mi pequeño sailor mon? Whar ees Lucius, mi amor?"

Lucius stood with a broad grin. "Here, Juanita. Here I am, ma cherie."

The Puerto Rican woman rushed to their table and swept Lucius up in a bear hug, smothering his face with kisses. Moses was forced to pull his chair away to avoid being knocked over. The woman, who must have been twice the size of Lucius, reeked of cheap perfume, which Moses appreciated, since it overpowered the other barroom odors. Juanita wore a frilly blouse, cut low to reveal abundant breasts, over a voluminous full-length skirt. She wasn't fat, so much as large, but even this skirt could not disguise her large rear end. Moses noticed that she was also barefoot, which made him glad for his shoes, which kept his feet from touching the filthy floor.

"Mi Querido," she said between kisses, "I come as soon as I hear your sheep has come in. I have meessed you so much."

Lucius mumbled something, then pulled away from his over-sized paramour. His beaming face was covered with marks from the woman's heavily rouged lips. "Julio," he shouted toward the barkeeper. "Another round of rum, por favor. And a cerveza for my woomon."

Juanita, flushed and beaming, sat down with a flounce, causing Moses to fear the chair would collapse. Her face was round, with sweat dripping from a double chin and jowls that had begun to sag. Now that he had a clear view of her face, Moses realized she wasn't of Spanish origin, but African, at least mostly. She might once have been pretty, but now only her eyes were attractive, dark brown and expressive. She looked Moses up and down, then turned to Lucius.

"So, mi querido, who ees thees handsome mon you have brought weeth you? I have not seen heem before, I think."

"Juanita," Lucius gestured with a wave of his hand. "S'il te plaît, allow me to eentroduce my friend, Capitan Moses Grandy. He ees from les Carolinas, een Los Estados Unidos. Moses, this is ma épouse, my wife, Juaneeta."

Moses hardly knew what to do. Lucius had introduced him so formally—in three languages—that some ceremony seemed to be required. But what? He felt like a fish out of water, especially since he'd been introduced as "captain." Nodding, he stuck out his hand. "Pleased to make your acquaintance, er, señorita."

Juanita took his hand and pulled it to her soft, pillowy breast. A great many cheap, gaudy rings adorned her fingers. She leaned forward and said, "Eet is a great honor, Capitan. What ees the name of your sheep?" Her breath smelled of cinnamon and carrion.

"Er, I don't have a ship, not anymore. I sail with Lucius, on the New Packet. I'm not a captain now."

What was going on here? Lucius had occasionally talked about his wife in Boston, and now he'd introduced Juanita as his wife.

The bartender brought their drinks. As he set them out, he and Juanita bantered back and forth in Spanish, while Juanita occasionally glanced at Moses and smiled. After a grinning glance at Moses, the waiter left.

For the next few minutes, Moses was left out of the conversation between Lucius and Juanita. They didn't purposely leave him out; they often made comments to him. He couldn't understand much, however, from the rapid fire conversation that only occasionally included English.

As he sipped his rum, his attention wandered until his eyes were drawn to a woman entering the dingy room. He wasn't the only one to notice her, either, every man in the room, including Lucius, turned toward her.

Her skin was the color of roasted coffee beans. She had high cheek bones, a square jaw and pointed chin. Her eyes, although he couldn't see them well in the dim light, seemed unusually narrow, with large upper lids. She was looking around the room, obviously seeking someone or something but couldn't make anything out until her vision adjusted to the gloom.

She wore a lacy, shoulderless colorful dress that accentuated her full hips, and displayed the tops of her full breasts. Bare toes peeked from beneath her skirt. On her head was a turban-like headdress. Curly, black locks cascaded down over her ears, from which dangled large hoop earrings.

Moses' ears were suddenly assaulted as Juanita, sitting next to him screeched, "Evalisse! Evalisse! Acqui, Evalisse."

The woman at the door peered in their direction. Juanita wave, then she smiled and yelled to the newcomer in excited, rapid-fire Spanish, which was no improvement, even though Moses only had to attempt to understand one language at a time, for a change.

But it soon became clear he was being introduced to this woman,

Evalisse, so he held out his hand and said, "How do you do?"

She ignored his hand, but smiled, showing sparkling teeth behind her ruby lips. "You Americain, yes?"

He nodded and began to answer, but she quickly pulled; an empty chair from a nearby table and sat close to him. Bracelets jangling, she put a hand on his arm. "I love Americain sailor-mon. You buy me drink, yes?"

Moses looked over to Lucius.

Lucius grinned and shrugged. "Ease off, mon. You have leeved a hard life. Enjoy yourself por une fois."

Moses had no idea what a prunefwah was, but he caught the drift. And what could it hurt to buy a pretty woman a drink? It wouldn't go any further than that.

*

The next morning, Moses woke with a hammering headache. Aware of someone lying beside him, he turned over to say good morning to Betsy, but it wasn't his wife. It took a moment, but he quickly remembered meeting Evalisse the evening before, even though he had no recollection of how he ended up in bed with her. Remorse struck him with a blow that made his headache insignificant.

He raised his head and looked around. Moses and the harlot—and he had no illusions that she might be anything else—reposed in a crude bed beneath a tented screen. Surrounding them was a one-room shack not much different than slave quarters in Camden County, except for a large window in each wall. There was no glass in the windows, and the wooden shutters hung open. The door also stood wide open. There was no fireplace, so the room didn't have the familiar odor of old smoke that he was used to inhaling when indoors. Instead, a floral perfume came in through the windows on a warm breath of air. He also caught the scent of straw and realized the structure had a thatched roof.

Moses was naked beneath a thin sheet and Evalisse was also unclothed, apparently. Her breasts were exposed above the bed covering. He had no appreciation for their beauty, however; he was too disgusted with himself. As for her face, the splendor of the night had been belied by smudged make-up and clear-eyed vision not besotted with rum.

The sunlight streaming through the window told him it was mid-morning, which was a relief. The New Packet would sail on the afternoon tide and Captain Cobb would sail on schedule, whether Moses was aboard or not. And the captain wouldn't hire him back aboard when the schooner returned to San Juan next trip, not after he'd missed the ship's departure.

He looked around for his clothing and found it scattered about the floor. Along with it, he spied his money pouch. Quickly, he leaped out of bed and swatted the mosquito netting aside, and grabbed the bag up. Looking inside, he saw all his money was gone, not that there had been that much of it, but his freedom paper was still there.

"Que pasa?" came Evalisse's voice behind him. "Por que esta despierto?"

Moses had no idea what she was saying. Other than, "I love sailor," and "Buy me drink, yes?" Evalisse spoke no English. It hadn't seemed to make any difference last evening, however. He debated asking her where the rest of his money was, since he should have at least *some* left over after paying for drinks. He decided not to. It didn't seem to matter, not with the throbbing in his temples. He tied the pouch around his waist and began pulling on his clothing.

Evalisse sat up and began asking more questions, but he ignored her. He went out the open door, pulling his shirt on.

"…And Remember that I Am a Man."

"…And Remember that I Am a Man."

Chapter Fifty

The Devil to Pay—1826 A.D.

Chestertown and Baltimore, PACKET-BOAT
The Subscribers respectfully inform the public, that they continue
running a Packet-Boat, which is now in excellent order. The Cabin
is large and commodious, well calculated for the Accomodation of
Passengers. Merchandise, Produce, &c. carried on the lowest terms.
From experience they can assuredly say, that the Packet is safe, and
sails remarkably well. –Will regularly leave Chestertown, every
MONDAY at nine o'clock, A.M. and set out for Baltimore every
THURSDAY at Nine o'clock, A.M.

John Constable,
Master of said Boat, and one of the proprietors, will use all
possible Diligence to Accommodate Passengers, as well as be
prepared to execute, with punctuality, every trust committed to his
charge.

John Constable,
James Piper.
Chestertown, May, 17, 1793

1793 ad for a packet schooner, Chestertown, MD.—1793 A.D.

On the voyage north, Moses avoided Lucius, who seemed amused
that his overtly religious friend had consorted with Evalisse. He

397

made lewd comments, such as, "Oh, mon, that Evalisse, she eez one hot-blooded woman, ees she not?"

Moses spent most of his time off-watch sitting alone on deck, especially at night. As the miles slipped away beneath the keel, the autumn winds blew cooler and the moon grew fuller. After they rounded Cape Hatteras and ran offshore of the Outer Banks, he became increasingly aware his family waited for him there. If he could somehow be put ashore, he could walk less than a mile across the sand barrier. Then only a short sail across the sound would take him to Camden County.

How could he have betrayed his wife, who stayed home in their shack, tending his children? How could he have betrayed God? This time, it hadn't been an unavoidable sexual encounter. And he couldn't even blame it on the rum. He had drunk willingly

Staring up at the stars, he looked back on his life and pondered his future. Now that he was free, he would have to make all his own decisions and live with the consequences. The Kemps, although he hadn't realized it at the time, had instilled values in him that had set his course in life. This had allowed him to escape the fate of most slaves, who were completely dominated by their masters. Missy Hannah had given him his faith in God, which had sustained him through many difficult times. Mister Kemp, in addition to giving Moses a valuable skill, had shown him that any task was worth doing well and that persistence would prevail. And he mustn't forget Keentoon. The old warrior with the whipping scars on his back had counseled Moses to value his African heritage and not be ashamed of the color of his skin.

He had learned from his other masters, too, if only not to blindly trust anyone, such as Master James, the childhood friend who had betrayed him. There had been bad masters and good masters, cruel whites and sympathetic whites who tried to help end slavery. And then there were those who straddled the fence, who openly professed anti-slavery sentiments, but would only lift a black man so far, to menial positions in society. Now, even though he was no longer a slave, his life depended on whites.

As a slave, he had thought release from bondage would make him truly free, but he wasn't. He couldn't, as he'd youthfully dreamed, run his own ferry. But he could run his own life and fight for what he believed and desired: true freedom.

He would keep his faith in God. He would conduct himself as an "African warrior," as Keentoon had advised. He would be respectful to whites, but only so far as they deserved it. All the while, he would strive to earn the respect of the whites, while fighting for true freedom—equality.

Moses was practical, however. He couldn't change the world. But he'd do his best, because the alternative would be to allow himself to be dominated. He had let himself, Betsy, and God down. Now it was time to beg God's forgiveness and ask for his help in freeing his wife and family.

When the faint light of dawn showed in the eastern sky, he went below to his hammock. His spirits were lower than they'd ever been. As bad as he'd sometimes felt during his struggle for freedom, at least he'd had family nearby.

The next evening, as they neared Cape May, New Jersey, dark clouds began to gather in the south and the winds shifted from southerly to easterly. The captain decided to try to outrun the storm and make it to port, so the crew was sent aloft to put on sail. During the night and the next day, the ship rolled more and more as the waves hammered them. The gusting winds added to the ship's motion and the ship often heeled over dangerously.

Shortly before morning, Captain Cobb ordered the crew to reef sails and began tacking into the gale, the safest way to ride out a storm. The two strongest men aboard, Hans and Paolo, manned the helm, struggling to keep the rudder steady enough to hold course.

They were fighting a particularly strong Nor'easter, which would drive the waves and the tides into the coast, hammering it. This northeasterly course also took them away from the shore, which would keep the ship from being driven onto coastal rocks or shallows.

Even though the day was warm, the driving rain and waves that washed over the deck soon soaked Moses, chilling him. His hands and bare feet became numb as he moved about the ship with the other sailors, making adjustments to the rigging as Captain Cobb directed.

Disaster struck two bells into the forenoon watch, while Moses and Lucius huddled in the scant shelter of the foremast trying to stay out of the worst of it. Moses nibbled on a piece of hardtack and watched the crew on the quarterdeck. A large wave washed over the ship and he saw Paolo lose his footing and stumble into Hans, knocking him off the helm. The large wheel spun out of control and the New Packet went broadside to the wind and waves, then broached.

"She's going over," Lucius cried, wrapping his arms around the mast.

Moses grabbed hold of a jib cleat as the ship careened over to starboard. Lines and stays popped as they broke, loosing the sails. The spars slewed and the boom of the foremast dipped into the water, which pulled the ship further over. Moses was sure she was going to turn turtle. Then, with a crack like cannon fire, the mast broke in two, not a yard above where Lucius clutched it. It knocked him loose and he slid down the topsy-turvy deck, screaming. He went into the water, where a tangled web of wood, canvas and rope awaited him.

The ship seemed to stabilize when the weight of the mast broke free, and she might have recovered if the rigging hadn't held her down. Moses could see Lucius struggling below, but there was no way of reaching him without a long drop into the wreckage.

The captain's voice boomed above the commotion. "Cut her loose, boys. Cut her loose or we're goners."

Moses looked about and saw several lines nearby, close enough to reach if he could keep from falling on a deck that was nearly straight up and down. He drew the knife from his belt, cut the nearest line holding the ship to the mast, then put the blade between his teeth and swung to another position.

The ship didn't toss as badly as before, since the water-logged rigging kept her from rolling. The fury of the storm expended itself on her underside, exposed by her position, so wind and rain didn't slow Moses as he worked. He was dimly aware of other sailors working nearby. Though worried about Lucius, he had to devote his every bit of his attention to keep from falling.

Finally the last attachment to the mast had been severed, and the ship began to roll back upright. Moses immediately looked back down to his fallen crewmate. Lucius had grabbed a rope and held on, despite the pull of the waves. But now that the ship was going up, he was being stretched to the limit because one ankle was trapped in the floating cordage. He wouldn't be able to maintain his grip.

Moses sheathed his knife, let go of his hold on the ship, and slid down the wet deck. He crashed into rope railing, as he'd intended, and grabbed for the single line that kept him from going overboard. He missed. His life hung in the balance for a moment, his top half on the ship, his hips and legs overboard, then slid off.

At the last instant, his fingers clutched on the inch-wide gap between the topmost board of the ship's side and the edge of the decking lumber. Caulking this gap, which was very difficult to waterproof, was a dangerous job that often meant hanging partly over the side. Because of the peril, this fissure had become known as "the devil," and the job of filling it was often assigned as a punishment, as in, "You'll have the devil to pay if you run afoul of the skipper."

Moses was, in nautical terms, between the devil and the deep blue sea.

Nevertheless, he wasn't sunk yet, so he grabbed with the other hand and began creeping down the side of the ship toward Lucius, hand over hand like a squirrel on a branch.

Lucius saw him coming. "Dépêchez-vous!" he cried. "Help me, camarade."

Moses was quickly at his side. But now what? To free his shipmate, he'd have to go into the water. He couldn't swim. Quickly sizing up the situation, he let go with one hand to draw his knife.

"Hold tight to the line," he warned Lucius. "I'm going to cut it."

"Are you a fool? What are you sayeeng? Eet ees crazy..."

Moses ignored the Haitian's babbling and sliced through the rope. Lucius dropped into the water and Moses let go, falling with him. A moment later, they floated, the ship's deck above them, out of reach.

"Do you still have the line?" Moses asked.

"Oui, but..."

"Don't let go, no matter what." Moses took a breath, put the knife between his teeth again, and went under. He made his way, by touch, down Lucius body until he came to the ankles. Holding on with one hand, he felt around with the other. He found a piece of rigging, tightly looped around one foot. Taking the knife, he cut the cord and freed it from his friend's foot.

A moment later, he resurfaced, still holding onto Lucius for fear of sinking beneath the waves. He took a gasping breath, then asked, "Do you still have the rope?"

"Oui. I have eet."

"Good." Moses grabbed the same line. "It's still attached to the rail at the other end. Hold on until the ship rolls down toward us, then take in every bit of slack and hang on. When the ship goes back up, climb for your life."

Lucius grinned. "I see. You are breeliant, my friend. But what about you?"

"You go first. Then me."

The Haitian did as he was instructed and it worked perfectly. When the ship pulled him up, his momentum allowed him to scramble back aboard. In the meantime, Moses simply held on to the slack end of the line, awaiting his turn.

In no time, they were both back aboard the New Packet. Helping each other, they crawled to the edge of a hatch and grabbed hold of the raised edge, or coaming, to keep from slipping back overboard on the slippery deck.

"Merci beaucoup," Lucius whispered after he'd caught his breath. "I zought I was, how you say? A goner."

"So did I," said Moses. "Both of us. Thank The Lord we're alive."

"Oui. Grâce à Dieu."

They weren't safe yet, Moses knew. They were on a crippled ship in a terrific storm and he could still lose his life, but now he had time to make his peace with God.

Suddenly, Moses was hammered by an overwhelming feeling of horror. His hands went to his waist and felt for his pouch. It was there. Relief washed over him. His paper, hopefully, hadn't gotten wet inside the oilskin. Even if it had, he could dry it. But if it had washed away on the storm-tossed waves, he would be at the mercy of any unscrupulous white man who wanted to make a few dollars by selling him as a slave."

"Moses?" Lucius asked with a hint of timidity in his voice. "Can I tell you something?"

"Of course."

"I am sorry that I made joke weeth you about Evalisse."

Moses swallowed, the deadly taste of salt water still in his mouth. "It's all right, Lucius. I deserved it."

"No, that ees what ees so funny." Lucius looked him in the eyes grinned. "You deed nozzeeng to zat womon. You were too drunk."

Moses felt as if a weight had been lifted. Could it be that he *hadn't* been unfaithful to his wife—and his God? "Too drunk?"

"Oui. Too drunk for l'amour. Zat Evalisse, she was mad as hell wit' you, mon."

"…And Remember that I Am a Man."

"…And Remember that I Am a Man."

Chapter Fifty-one

Voyages—1827, 1830 A.D.

"I did not at all find it unpleasant. This was a perfect opportunity for me to tell him that we could not only not indulge in such demands, but that I also considered him to be my prisoner from that moment on."

Attributed to Dutch General H. Merkus de Kock—18?? A.D.

When the storm blew the New Packet into the shallows off Cape Cod, she once again heeled over. The crew could do nothing but wedge themselves behind deckboard equipment. Going below was out of the question; the danger of being trapped was too great.

When the storm had abated, they dropped down into the sea and waded ashore. Only then did Moses realize Hans had not made it. No one had seen him since the ship had broached, but everyone had assumed him to be somewhere else on the ship, riding out the storm. Paolo was inconsolable. He and Hans had been close friends.

Captain Cobb insisted they try to right the ship, though it would be near impossible with her keel pointing away from shore. At his direction, two of the men waded back out and tied ropes to strong points. When the tide came in, they pulled for all they were worth, but couldn't budge her. The tide merely pushed her further aground. The crew spent a miserable night on the beach until being rescued the next day.

"…And Remember that I Am a Man."

Penniless, with only the clothes on his back, Moses threw himself on the mercy of the Boston Presbyterian Church and the Reverend A. A. Phelps, who was strongly against slavery. Not only did the reverend feed and clothe Moses until he could find employment, Phelps took down a letter to Betsy and sent it in care of Mrs. Minner. Moses had no idea how or when the letter would reach his wife, or who would read it to her, but it made him feel better about his near miss with unfaithfulness.

Word on the docks was that Captain Cobb had recovered the New Packet and was refitting her in a nearby shipyard, but Moses needed to be making money and couldn't wait for her to sail again. He got a berth on a large brigantine, the Spirit of Weymouth, with a complement of twenty-eight.

Although he wasn't accustomed to square sails, he soon became skillful with this type of rigging on the voyage to Europe. The Spirit of Weymouth made regular runs to the Mediterranean Sea, carrying textile machinery and returning with wine or olive oil. Moses was the only black on board.

The ship traveled to the port of Naples, in the Kingdom of Two Sicilies. They tied up to a stone wharf that looked as though it had been built in Biblical times, if not before. The stone buildings looked just as old.

It was as though Moses had traveled to another world. In the afternoon, small, brightly colored fishing boats pulled up on the beach. The pier soon bustled with activity, a city unto itself, with vendors hawking fresh fish and shellfish, while goat's meat, wine and other wares were sold at the landward end of the dock. There were also women who could only be prostitutes, who not only solicited business on the wharf, but called out to sailors on the vessels, pantomiming their expertise.

Moses stayed aboard as the sun set and the dockside turned into a carnival, with lively, lilting music, laughter and dancing. The Italians of the waterfront seemed to be as poor as dirt, but as unrestrained as the clouds. He wondered what it might be like to feel so carefree. He doubted it was only the wine.

When the Spirit of Weymouth left port, she turned toward the south, rather than head east toward the Straits of Gibraltar as Moses had expected. Two days later, they came in sight of a desolate coast, where the sandy beach stretched out into the far distance. The shoreline was unbroken by vegetation or habitation.

"Africa," a sailor told him.

The Spirit turned back north until the land had dropped below the horizon, then sailed back and forth, east and west. Moses was ordered to a lookout post. Even though it was early spring, the day was blistering hot, so Moses kept in the shade as much as possible. Even so, he was soon covered in sweat. Everyone on the crew seemed nervous, for some reason. Shortly before dawn, the first mate handed out muskets to a few of the men.

"What's going on?" he asked a passing crewman.

"We're off the Barbary Coast," the sailor said. "There are pirates in these waters."

They anchored offshore at dusk and all lights were extinguished. The captain appeared on deck, pacing nervously. An hour after dark, he lit a lantern and swung it for a few seconds, then snuffed it out. After a while, a light appeared onshore, and grew brighter. Moses realized someone was coming out to meet the ship.

As it drew near, the light revealed three men in a row boat. They were dressed in white, flowing robes and their heads were turbaned. One rowed, while the other two stood, rifles at the ready. If it hadn't been so obvious the captain was waiting for them, Moses might have thought them to be pirates.

Lines were thrown and the boat tied up close alongside. In the light of the lantern, Moses could see the dark, bearded faces of the two gunmen, who glared suspiciously at the sailors above them. The rower shipped his oars and hoisted two small casks up to the deck of the schooner. The captain handed a small, water-proofed package to the mate, who passed it down to the rower. Lines were set free and the boat turned back toward shore while two sailors took the casks below, followed by the captain. Not a word had been spoken.

The mate barked out an order to raise anchor and Moses sprang forward to take his place at the capstain with three other sailors. "What was that all about?" he asked the sailor on the opposite spoke of the windlass.

The man turned his head and glared. "Don't ask."

*

407

When the ship returned to Boston, Moses turned most of his pay over to Reverend Phelps for safekeeping. He'd hoped for a letter from Betsy, but nothing had arrived. A few days later, he was on the way back to the Mediterranean aboard the Spirit.

The voyage was almost identical to his first, except that he had become accepted by some of the crew now. Others still wouldn't have anything to do with him, of course. When the ship again made its brief visit to the coast of Africa, he found out what the casks contained. Opium.

And, this time, the pirates found them. At dawn, two sets of sails appeared in the west, running before the wind. Soon, they topped the horizon and showed themselves to be medium-sized sloops, square rigged, with a gaff sail off the single mast. The Spirit, which had been sailing close hauled to windward, turned and raised every bit of canvas to put on speed. By this time the pirates were only a few hundred yards away.

Moses could see men swarming over the decks of the two sloops, a much larger crew than required. There must have been forty or fifty men aboard each, most of them fighting men. From what he could see, each craft had two small cannons mounted on swivels, fore and aft. Since the Spirit was unarmed, she would have to surrender if the pirates got within firing range.

But the Spirit of Weymouth was a well-built American brigantine, designed for quick transits across the Atlantic. Sloops, on the other hand, were designed for the short haul, highly maneuverable in shallow waters. Best of all, the pirate ships were in poor shape with ragged sails and hulls probably fouled with barnacles. It was nip and tuck for a while, but the Spirit finally showed the brigands her heels and they gave up the chase. They were "hit-and-run" ships, not designed for the open seas.

When the Spirit returned to Boston, Moses took leave of her. He had no idea if the owners of the ship knew their Captain was engaged in the opium trade, but it made no difference. Although she paid fairly well, money wouldn't do his wife and family any good if he was killed or enslaved in Africa by the Moors.

Again, there was no word from Betsy. Since it would be extremely difficult for her to get a letter to him, it didn't bother him badly. What *was* worrisome was that money for his family's manumission was so slow in coming. It was much harder to earn money as a sailor in the north than as a white man's business representative in the south. And he couldn't earn more by working ashore; he wasn't a skilled laborer. No, the sea was a better way to go, and safer, since there was no chance of being kidnapped and sold south, which was not all that uncommon.

For the next two years, he sailed up and down the east coast on one ship or another, putting into Boston now and then to leave money with Reverend Phelps. Each time, the reverend opened an envelope and showed Moses all his money was safe.

Once, there was a message from Betsy, written down by Mrs. Enoch Sawyer, and sent on to Mrs. Minner, who had mailed it. Betsy and the children were fine. Elijah had been put to work in the fields and Catherine looked out for the younger children during the day, a regular little mother, according to Betsy. She hoped Moses was well and she would pray for him every night.

Time dragged on. Moses had been free for nearly four years, but it seemed he might never get a chance to earn enough money, but then he heard that a full-rigged ship, the three-masted, square-rigged James Murray, commanded by Captain Woodbury, would be leaving on a voyage to the East Indies. Since most sailors weren't fond of such long absences, crewmen for such a large vessel would be hard to find. The owners were offering top wages. He signed on for the voyage. It wasn't until the ship was underway that he learned of another reason for the good pay. She was a gunrunner.

The ship's bos'n, a man who liked to seem even more important than he was, filled Moses in. The James Murray's cargo was a collection of left-over muskets from the Napoleonic wars, along with a few rifles and cannons. She also carried a large amount of gunpowder. The whole lot was to be delivered to a native prince who was fighting against the Dutch rulers of Java, an island in the far Pacific.

It made no difference to Moses, cargo was cargo. If the voyage was to help dark-skinned people throw off white overlords, all the better. He imagined it must be like the Haitian insurrection. He did feel a bit uneasy sitting on top of tons of explosives, at first, but he got used to the situation as the days went on without incident.

"...And Remember that I Am a Man."

They crossed the Atlantic, went down the west coast of Africa, and sailed around the horn. Moses had guessed that their journey was nearly over, but he was wrong. They had to sail across the Indian Ocean and cross the equator for the second time to reach the East Indies.

When they neared the large island of Java, two large, heavily-gunned ships came from shore and raced to intercept them. The Murray turned and ran, but she was outclassed. Soon a cannon fired and a shot went over the ship, splashing into the sea a hundred yards ahead.

Moses expected the captain to break out arms for the crew to use in repelling the pirates, but instead, he hauled down the ship's flag and surrendered. Now what? If these pirates were anything like the pirates of the Barbary Coast, he could expect to be enslaved?

"Why didn't we fight?" he asked the talkative Bos'n.

"Are you crazy?" the sailor cried. "If one cannonball hits the gunpowder, we're all dead."

Better dead than a slave, Moses thought.

But when the two warships came near, Moses saw they flew Dutch flags. A boat was put into the water and sailors rowed an official, wearing a uniform that rivaled a peacock in splendor, over to the Murray.

Soon word went around the ship. The insurrection was over. The Dutch had defeated the Muslim forces of Prince Dipo Negro, then tricked him into a truce talk and captured him. They escorted the Murray into the port of Surabaya and confiscated her cargo.

Since the captain had expected to replenish supplies on Java, the return voyage across the Indian Ocean was a harrowing time of hunger and thirst. The ship made an unexpected stop at the British port of Cape Town for food and fresh water, then went on to Boston. Since the cargo had been lost, Moses was paid only a tenth of what he'd been promised.

This time, when he went to see the reverend, a letter awaited him. But it wasn't from Betsy. Mrs. Minner had bad news. Enoch Sawyer had sold all Moses' children.

"...And Remember that I Am a Man."

Chapter Fifty-two

Dirty Jews—1831, 1835 A.D.

Q. How did Jesus Christ die?
A. He was nailed to a cross of wood, by the wicked Jews.
Q. In what way did they nail Him to the cross?
A. They drove nails through His hands and feet, and fastened
Him to the cross.
Q. How long did He hang on the cross?
A. Till He was dead.
Q. What did they do, to see if He was dead?
A. They thrust a spear into His side.
Q. Who put Jesus Christ to death?
A. The wicked Jews.

Protestant Episcopal Church in the Confederate States of America
A Catechism to Be Taught Orally To Those Who Cannot Read;
Designed Especially for the Instruction of the Slaves.
Raleigh: Office of "The Church Intelligencer", 1862.

Enoch Sawyer had not sold Betsy, only the children. He had
instructed Mrs. Minner to write that he was willing to sell her
freedom for four hundred dollars. Moses had saved only three
hundred dollars, but he had Reverend Phelps send it on to Sawyer
with a letter explaining that Moses had already paid Sawyer a
hundred dollars not to sell Moses' children, so three hundred should
be sufficient.

Moses took a job ashore. He couldn't risk being at sea when he might have to go south to fetch Betsy. A few weeks later, a reply came. Sawyer, via Mrs. Minner, agreed to accept the offer.

Mrs. Minner advised Moses not to come to Virginia, though. There had been some sort of slave rebellion in nearby Southhampton County. Dozens of whites had been murdered, led by a slave called Nat Turner. Whites were suspicious of all blacks, now, and it would be too dangerous for even a free black man to travel about.

Moses smiled inwardly when he heard this. Not only had he once met Nat Turner, he knew that the insurrection might have been partially instigated by a black Bostoner, another former Tar Heel. David Walker, who had been born free in Wilmington, North Carolina about the same time as Moses, had migrated north in the 'twenties. He was now one of the leading abolitionists in New England and had written a circular called "Appeal to the Colored Citizens of the World," advocating armed revolution. Unknown to most white abolitionists, black sailors had been smuggling copies of this document throughout the south. Moses had not circulated this paper, himself, as he hadn't been sailing to southern ports, but he knew of it.

The next paragraph, as read by Reverend Phelps, pleased and astonished Moses.

"I met a Quaker woman a few weeks ago. She is originally from Camden County and has recently returned from Ohio. She now lives in Suffolk. Her name is Hannah Herndon, but you knew her as Hannah Kemp. She is active in some sort of organization which helps escaped slaves, which prompted me to mention your name, dearest Moses. I was astonished to learn she knew you well.

"Mrs. Herndon sends her regards and bade me to tell you that she and her friends will do everything in their power to locate your missing children, where ever they may be. I have given her Reverend Phelps' address and she will let you know if she is successful.

"Mrs. Herndon and her Quaker friends have donated funds to pay passage for your wife to Boston on the regular packet from Norfolk, as well as for traveling expenses. She will be arriving on Wednesday, October 21."

"…And Remember that I Am a Man."

*

Moses saw Betsy for the first time in six years as she waved from the railing of a packet ship putting into the Boston docks on a bitterly cold day. The first thing he noticed was that her coat was thin and ragged. Then, as the ship drew near, he saw the tears in her eyes.

He knew what she had to be feeling, because he felt it, too. The joy of their reunion had been crushed under the weight of their childrens' fates.

*

Three long years passed without word of their children. Betsy took a job as a nanny for a rich white family and Moses made a living on ships that plied the waters off New England.

Moses remembered how he had been unable to locate his first wife, Naomi, after she'd been sold. It would be difficult to find their children, but at least he had allies in the south.

They weren't looking for children with the last name of Grandy. Betsy and the children had been listed in North Carolina records as having the name Sawyer. And now that they'd been sold, their surnames would have been changed. If Elijah had been sold to a man named John Smith in North Carolina, he would now be Elijah Smith. If little Charlotte had been sold to a Georgian man named John Jones, she would be listed as Jones in the Georgia census. And none of the southern states was likely to open their records to abolitionists or Quakers.

But finally Missy Hannah, as Moses still thought of her, sent word she had located Elijah, who was now fifteen years old. He had been sold twice more and now belonged to a man in Norfolk. When Missy Hannah had approached him about buying Elijah's freedom, the man, Daniel Tuttle, had demanded a price of four hundred and fifty dollars.

"I'm going to Norfolk," Moses said as soon as Reverend Phelps had finished reading the letter.

Betsy gasped. "No, Moses. No."

"I have to get Elijah."

"Why can't you just send the money?" asked the reverend.

413

Moses shook his head. "We don't have it. Betsy and I have been setting aside every penny we can and it's still only a little more than three hundred."

"We'll send that," Betsy said. "Maybe your friend can raise some money from her fellow Quakers."

"No. It would take too long," Moses answered. "You know how white men are when it comes to business. If someone else makes an offer, we could lose track of Elijah again. But if I can show this Tuttle cash money, he'll probably take three hundred."

"It's too dangerous for you," the reverend said.

"Don't go," Betsy whispered, tears in her eyes.

Moses took her in his arms. "Betsy, he's our son. I have to go."

*

"You can't get off the ship, boy," said the man blocking the foot of the gangway. He had a pistol in his belt and a star on his shirt. Moses peered at the letters on the badge, wishing he could read.

"Who are you?" he asked.

"Deputy Sheriff." The man turned his head and spat over the edge of the pier. "Mayor says no northern niggers in Norfolk."

Moses felt his jaw drop. He was dumbfounded. "But why? I'm here on business."

The deputy smiled, but with malice instead of friendliness. "Don't matter. You set one foot on this pier, you go to jail." He spat again, this time at Moses' feet. "Northern niggers ain't allowed anywhere in the south. It's the law. It was posted in all the Yankee papers."

"How the hell would I know that?" Moses asked passionately. "I can't read."

"You gettin' sassy with me, boy?" The deputy put a hand on the pistol butt.

Moses took a step back, holding up his hands in surrender. "No. Sorry. No offense intended, sir."

With a snort, the deputy said, "This what the Goddamn Yankees teach you, nigger? Sassin' your betters? Get back on that ship. Now!"

Moses retreated up the gangway and stood at the top. The deputy glared at him for a while, daring Moses to try something. After a minute or so, he left.

414

"…And Remember that I Am a Man."

It was a hot, moist day, like most summer days in this part of the country. For a few minutes, Moses stood wondering what to do. Maybe he could get word of his predicament to Mrs. Minner or Missy Hannah, but they were several hours travel away. He didn't dare leave the ship, not even for the short time it would take to reach any of his old business acquaintances, some of whom were important figures in Norfolk. He should have looked for a spot of shade, but he barely noticed the sweat that running down his face.

"Appuulls. Who wanna buy some appuulls?" A young black boy, no older than six, was walking alongside the ship, holding up a shiny red apple. "Three foah a penny." At his hip was a bag bulging with more apples. Moses grinned, thinking the apples had likely been stolen from some white man's orchard.

"Hey, young man."

The lad glanced up, then looked behind him to see if Moses could possibly be calling *him*. He'd probably never been addressed as anything but boy or hey, you. He put a finger to his chest, then cocked his head as though saying, "Who, me?"

"Yes, you." Moses nodded encouragingly. "Come over here."

The boy's wide mouth opened in a delighted smile. He broke into a run, the bag of fruit slapping his upper leg.

He skidded to a stop opposite Moses. "You wanna buy some appuls, mister?"

Moses nodded. "Sure, I'll buy some. But there's something I want you to do for me, first."

The youngster's smile disappeared. His eyes narrowed. "Like what?"

"Do you know a man named Moses Myers?"

"Suppose I do?"

Moses tried to look as friendly as possible. "Do you know where he lives?"

The boy pointed behind him. "Big brick house on Olney Road?"

Moses nodded. "That's it. You're a smart boy. What's your name?"

"Henry."

"Henry, you go give Mr. Myers a message from me, and I'll buy your whole bag of apples and give you a five-cent piece besides."

"Really?" The youngster's eyes were wide.

"Really," Moses said soothingly. "I'll pay you for the apples right now and pay you the nickel when you get back. How many apples do you have in your bag?"

Henry shuffled his feet, looking down at the bag. "I got a bagful."

"But how many?" Moses asked again, then quickly realized he'd never get an answer. The boy probably didn't know how to count.

"I tol' you. A bagful."

Moses eyed the bag. "Seven cents?" He actually *was* interested in the apples. He could have some for lunch and save the rest for later.

"You gots a deal, mister."

They met at the end of the gangway and changed money for fruit. Moses told Henry the message, made sure the boy had it right, and then sent him off. Henry streaked away, his pennies clutched in a fist.

Twenty minutes later, he returned. "Mistah Myers, he say hol' tight, he comin' to see you right quick."

"Good job." Moses handed over a shiny nickel. "Here you go."

Henry put the nickel with the other coins, still in his fist, and looked at them proudly. "Mama ain't gonna believe I made this much money in one day."

Moses laughed. "You go on home and show her, then. Just don't let anyone know you're carrying so much money."

The lad looked up at Moses as though he'd been insulted. "You think I'm stupid or somethin,' mister?"

Before Moses could answer, the boy streaked away, coins once more clenched tightly. A good day's wages for a six-year-old.

Mr. Myers' two-seater carriage showed up within the hour, carrying Myer and two men who Moses knew from previous business ventures. All three came striding confidently aboard, as if they owned the ship. The black driver remained with the vehicle.

Myers, other than his hair perhaps turning a shade more gray, hadn't changed a bit. He greeted Moses like an old friend, clapping him on a shoulder. "Captain Grandy, what a pleasant surprise. I never expected to see you again, at least not here in Virginia."

"It's good to see you, Mr. Myers," Moses replied. "I never expected to see Norfolk again, but I have pressing business."

Myers gestured toward his companions. "Moses, you remember Mr. Gold and Mr. Weimer."

"I do. Good to see you, gentlemen." Both these men, Jews, were against slavery, and had treated Moses well in the past.

"So, Moses," said Mr. Myers. "The boy said you're not allowed to come ashore?"

"That's right, sir," Moses said. "A lawman stopped me and said it was the Mayor's orders that no northern blacks are allowed anymore."

Myers nodded. "That's true. Everyone is upset after the troubles a couple of years ago, and there have been restrictions enacted to curb black travel. Especially northerners and especially sailors. They've been distributing anti-slavery literature, you see."

Moses was glad he wasn't carrying any of David Walker's circulars. He'd decided it wasn't wise in the current racial tension and, besides, the appeal had been well-distributed over the last couple of years.

"Yes, sir, I understand. But I'm here on business." He explained about his mission.

"That seems reasonable." Myers turned to his companions. "I think we need to speak to the Mayor, gentlemen. He's on his high horse again."

"As for the *"mare,"* Weimer said. "He's as bad as the horse he rode in on."

Gold laughed. "We should have sent that horse back to the stable. Damned goy Nullifier."

"Watch yourself, Mr. Gold." Mr. Myers looked around as though to see if anyone was near enough to hear. "There's no need for such language."

Moses didn't understand the joke, and didn't know what "goy" meant, but he had heard of the Nullifier Party. They were southerners who advocated a state's right to "nullify" any federal laws they didn't agree with. Something to do with taxes on British goods that hurt the southern states. Moses took a lot more interest in politics now that he knew so many northern abolitionists, who supposed nullification would apply to national slavery laws, too. But that was neither here nor there, at the moment.

"Can you help me, Mr. Myers?" Moses asked.

Mr. Myers puffed himself up. "I should say so. Are you with me, Gentlemen?"

"…And Remember that I Am a Man."

Within minutes, the three Jewish men had taken Moses ashore and they walked to the nearby mayor's office, leaving the carriage behind. They stormed in and confronted the mayor.

It was obvious that the men had differences and that Moses was merely an excuse to argue, but the results were satisfying. The mayor allowed Moses a nine-day stay in Norfolk to conduct his business, since his ship wouldn't be leaving until then.

"But you'd better be back on that ship when she sails," said the mayor. "We don't need northern niggers running around and stirring things up. If you're not gone on the tenth day, I'll have you locked up and sold for the good of the commonwealth."

*

The next day, Moses walked out into the county, looking for the farm of Daniel Tuttle, the man who owned Elijah. Another hot, bright day had come and he soon worked up a sweat. He'd gotten good directions from Mr. Weimer, though, so the place wasn't hard to find. He knocked on the front door, since the house was too small to rate a rear door, probably only a great room downstairs and a loft for sleeping. A middle-aged woman with a florid face answered.

She looked him up and down and before he had a chance to utter a word, said, "The mister's out in the barn." She closed the door.

When Moses reached the barn, he stopped for a moment to let his eyes adjust to the gloom inside. The pleasant, grassy smell of fresh horse manure filled the place. Tuttle was working on a horse collar he'd put over a cross-rail, re-nailing a metal ring that had come loose from the wooden hames. He was a big man, with a big gut to match. His hair was nearly gone in front, so he combed it forward in an attempt to cover his scalp. A thick mustache hid his upper lip; the rest of his face was covered in three days worth of bristles. Sweat ran down his face, carving white rivulets in his grimy skin.

Tuttle turned when he realized someone stood in the doorway. He squinted, unable to make out Moses' features with the sun behind.

"Elijah? Why ain't you in the field, where you belong?"

"Mr. Tuttle?" Moses approached slowly. "I'm Moses. Moses Grandy. From Boston?"

"Boston?" Tuttle took a step forward, eyes still narrowed, hammer in hand. "I don't know no one in Boston, boy. What you doin' sneakin' up on me?"

Moses held up his hands to show he meant no harm. "Mrs. Herndon spoke to you about me. About buying my son, Elijah."

"Your son...?" The farmer's expression cleared. "Oh, yeah, I recollect now. The Quaker woman."

"Yes, sir. I came to talk to you about buying my son's freedom."

Tuttle pursed his lips, what could be seen of them for the mustache. "Hmmph. I knowed I never should'a talked to that lady." Then his face cleared and he smiled. "You got the money?"

"We need to talk," Moses said.

The smile disappeared. "Talk? What's there to talk about? Either you got the money or you ain't."

"I've got the money," said Moses quickly. "Most of it, at least."

"How much you got?"

Moses hesitated, regretting he'd come to the farm without notice. He should have made an appointment, set up a meeting where pleasantries could have been exchanged before business, such small courtesies as were allowed between a black and a white, anyway. Instead, this meeting had started with suspicion and wasn't likely to go anywhere useful.

"Hell," Tuttle said, "You're wastin' my time. I got stuff to do." He wiped his brow, turned back to his work and began fussing. "Get on your way, boy."

"I can give you three hundred dollars," Moses blurted. "Cash money."

The farmer turned and glared at Moses, hands at hips, hammer poking out on one side. "I don't give a damn if you got goldamn gold, boy. If I was to sell Elijah, to you or anyone else, I'm goin' to have to buy another nigger to replace him. Three hundred dollars! I never should'a talked to that pushy!—damn!—Quaker!—woman!" He spat the last words out in one-word bursts.

Even though he knew his cause was lost, Moses begged. "Please, Mr. Tuttle. Elijah is my son. We lost track of him and I haven't seen him for nearly ten years."

Tuttle didn't look up. "That ain't my fault. An' I didn't ask for no uppity-dressed nigger to come on my place and bother me about

419

sellin' a slave I had no intention of sellin' before that Quaker woman came 'round. "

Moses had to force himself to stand in place, not to shuffle his feet. At the same time, he fought to control his anger. What had he done to offend this man? Nothing, of course. Nothing but being black.

"Please, Mr. Tuttle. Three hundred is all I have."

"Ain't my fault, neither. Carry your ass, nigger." He held a nail in place and lifted the hammer.

"At least let me see Elijah, Master Tuttle. Let me talk to my…"

"Son-of-a-bitch," Tuttle shouted. He'd hit his finger with the hammer. He whirled on Moses. "You light outta here, boy. I let you talk to Elijah and you'll find a way to steal him away. Get outta here, like I say."

"But…"

"One more word and I go get me my shotgun. Now Git!"

It was no idle threat, Moses knew. He left.

Once out on the road, he walked slowly. His heart told him to do what Tuttle feared, wait until nightfall, steal Elijah away and run for Norfolk. But if Tuttle found Moses on his farm, he'd shoot him. And the ship wasn't' sailing for days. There was no way they could get away with it. Elijah would be whipped and sent back to the fields. Moses would be enslaved again and surely whipped, if not hanged.

Though it went against his very grain, Moses slunk away. He had to stay free to help Elijah. But maybe David Walker was right. If Moses had a shotgun, himself, wouldn't that make him the equal of Tuttle? And if all blacks possessed firearms, could slavery long stand?

There was no use dreaming of and army of slaves with guns, though. Instead, Moses wondered what he'd tell Betsy when he arrived back in Boston without her first-born son.

*

Moses had seven days until the ship sailed north again. He would have liked to travel to Deep Creek and Suffolk, but didn't dare set foot out of Norfolk, where the mayor had jurisdiction. Even if the mayor had given him permission to conduct his business, it would be risky to spend time ashore. He'd offend whites by his manner of walking, dressing and speaking, which had changed since living in the north. And he remembered the thugs who'd beaten him in Providence. If a group of white men were to subdue Moses and ship him south, he'd just be one more frog in a swamp full of frogs.

Finally, the ship left port on a clear, breezy morning. She sailed out of the mouth of the Elizabeth River, past Fort Norfolk, into the Chesapeake Bay. A starboard turn lined them up with the wide gap between Cape Henry and Cape Charles, their route to the Atlantic. But now that they were in open waters, a strong wind blew from the north-east. The captain began tacking the ship toward the sea, but the wind pushed them toward the south on every port tack.

The crew kept busy, swinging the jib from side to side as the helmsman changed course. Every time they sailed directly into the wind, the jib luffed for an instant as the ship briefly went in irons, but then recovered with the sailors' deft ship handling. Even so, they were drifting south. The opening to the sea was ten miles wide, but had only a narrow channel at the south end. In a wind like this, the shoals on either side of the channel were unpredictable; sand was often driven by the churning sea onto the shoals, leaving less keel-way. The wind put them at hazard of running aground. Moses began to worry, wishing he could help the others, but this was not his ship.

Moses was relieved when the ship turned about and ran before the wind, racing back to port. They might have anchored in Hampton Roads, one of the biggest anchorages in the world, but the captain chose to return to the Elizabeth River, where the ship would ride easier. Since they had no need to handle cargo, they anchored off the waterfront rather than tie up to a pier, which would have required the ship to pay docking fees.

The wind died down later in the morning, but they were stuck for a day, at least, since they'd missed the tide. The heat and humidity became oppressive again. There was nothing for Moses, a passenger, to do but stay topside, changing position occasionally to keep out of the sun. There was an unusual amount of human traffic around the courthouse throughout the day and Moses surmised it to be court week.

In late afternoon, a crowd began to appear at the jail, identified by the bars on the windows, as well as the stocks and whipping posts in the yard. It soon became apparent what was about to happen when a line of perhaps a dozen Negro men were led from the courthouse to the jail, in handcuffs and leg-irons. Moses recognized one of the guards as the deputy who had prevented him from leaving the ship.

The blacks waited along the southeast wall of the jail, in the strong sunlight, and Moses guessed they must be dripping sweat, although he was too far away to see. They didn't have long to wait. A white man came out of the jail through a side door and walked to the whipping posts. The deputies knelt and began unlocking prisoners from their leg-irons. Two blacks were released.

The men were led to the posts and the chains of their manacles attached to rings set high on the poles. One of the deputies stepped forward and read something from a paper in his hand. Moses couldn't hear the words, but he knew what the meaning was. On cue, the whipping commenced. The black on Moses' right was flogged first. Every blow was clearly audible out on the river, as was the shouted count from the deputy Moses had recognized. "One." "Two." Three." The count went to twenty, interspersed with screams from the man being thrashed.

Moses couldn't watch any more. He went below decks, despite the sweltering heat. Still, he heard the counting and the slapping of leather against flesh as he remembered how Mama had been whipped long ago.

The next morning, the ship left port again. But the winds were still gusting, and they were forced to turn back. For the second day in a row, Moses listened to his fellow blacks being whipped.

On the third day, they were again forced back into Norfolk. As the ship made her way back across the bay, Moses noticed a pair of ships coming from the north, with the wind. From their course, he reckoned they were sailing from the eastern shore of Virginia, or maybe down from Delaware. An hour after Moses' ship had anchored, the two ships sailed up the Elizabeth behind her.

They were unwieldy ships, not much better than scows, certainly not capable of sailing the open seas. As they neared, Moses could hear cows lowing and he soon smelled fresh cow shit. When they anchored a short distance seaward of Moses' ship, he saw a group of black men, women and children clustered astern on each ship, guarded by men with whips. Slaves and cows were both being

422

brought to Norfolk for auction. The breeze carried the sound of women and children crying. One child bawled and a guard shouted, "Shut that whelp up, or you'll be sorry."

A while later, a boat pulled out from the Norfolk waterfront, heading directly toward his ship. On board was the deputy Moses remembered from his first day in Norfolk. He suddenly realized he'd been in the city for longer than the allowed time. What a fool he'd been. The deputy was coming to arrest him. He should have stayed out of sight from shore.

Moses ducked back and went to the seaward side of the ship, watching from behind a stack of cargo. After all the abuse of blacks he'd seen since returning south, he panicked, thinking he'd rather die than return to slavery. He had about decided to jump overboard when the rowboat swerved around and went to the two newly arrived ships. The deputy went aboard each, in turn, and then returned to shore.

Next day, the winds had died down some. Moses' ship cleared the mouth of the Chesapeake, and turned north. Although the winds still blew against them, they pushed on until the following morning when, as if on a divine schedule, a nor'easter blew in, the worst yet. The ship put into Delaware Bay and sailed into the sheltering mouth of the Maurice River, a stream too small to be navigable by anything bigger than a rowboat.

Moses heard the captain say they'd spend the night and then put to sea again. He began to worry. If a nor'easter blew them south again, he'd have to worry about being taken back into slavery. Finally, he convinced himself it wasn't worth the chance. He should have listened to Betsy in the first place, and stayed in Boston.

He went to the captain.

"Captain, we're in New Jersey here, aren't we?"

The captain, a short, stout man, white of hair and beard, confirmed they were.

"Then have your men take me ashore in a boat," Moses said. "Set me on free land once more. I'll travel home overland, rather than risk going back to Virginia."

The captain waved at the air. "Nonsense, boy. We're nearly halfway home to Boston. We'll be there in a couple of days."

"…And Remember that I Am a Man."

"No, captain, no. I can't risk it. I have to put my feet on free land again, where I'll be safe from everything I've seen over the last few days."

An hour later, he was ashore. He spent a miserable night in the open, then asked directions and set out for Philadelphia. He'd make his way back to Boston by land. Once there, he'd find some way to raise the money to free Elijah and send it south. He'd fight slavery with every bit of his strength, but he'd never return to the land of the white masters.

"…And Remember that I Am a Man."

Chapter Fifty-three

The Red Sea—1842 A.D.

Then Moses stretched out his hand over the sea, and all that night The Lord drove the sea back with a strong east wind and turned it into dry land. The waters were divided, and the Israelites went through the sea on dry ground, with a wall of water on their right and on their left.

Exodus 14:21

Shortly before dawn on a warm summer morning, Moses stood on the deck of a rolling ship, as he had so often done before. There were differences this time. For one, he was headed to Great Britain. Also, the ship was powered by steam, which powered two side-mounted paddle wheels. She had two masts, which could be used when winds were favorable, or if the steam engine should break down, but she hadn't hoisted a square foot of canvas since Moses had come aboard. Even if he wasn't a passenger, the ship would have little use for a sailor who could interpret the whispering winds, read the map of the stars, and hear the language spoken by the thrumming lines of a ship's rigging. As far as he was concerned, the sailors manning this ship might as well have been factory workers.

He hadn't wanted to leave Elijah, Betsy, and two of his other daughters, Catherine and Charlotte. These two, inspired by their father had both bought themselves out of freedom and managed to find their parents in the strange land of the north. Catherine, their second child, had been sold three times, finally to a Frenchman in Louisiana, who had purchased her out of the cotton fields to tend for his sick wife, who suffered from consumption. After the woman died, Catherine's master offered her the chance to buy her freedom and she took the opportunity.

Charlotte, their youngest child, had also ended up in Louisiana, and had also bought her way free. The two had gotten together and learned of their parents' whereabouts. They had sailed to Boston and the whole family now worked to buy Charlotte's children, left behind in New Orleans.

About that same time, Moses had located Betsy. Missy Hannah had found her near Norfolk, in Surry County. Her master, a Mr. William Dixon, wanted five hundred dollars for her.

Moses hadn't seen any way to earn enough money to save his child and grandchildren in a reasonable time, but then this trip had come about. It had begun last year, when Reverend Phelps, who had become a steadfast friend, had introduced Moses to George Thompson, an English abolitionist traveling through the United States.

Thompson had thought Moses' life story so fascinating, he had written it down. The Englishman believed that it would be worthy of publication in his home country, where anti-slavery sentiment ran swift and deep. To that end, he had written an introduction to a publisher friend in England and purchased a round-trip ticket for Moses. As Thompson said, "If it comes to naught, you're not out a farthing. But if your story is published—Ah, if it should be published in my country—you are likely to earn the sum you need to redeem your family. You'll be in demand for public speaking."

Ahead, on the horizon, the top of the sun peeked over the featureless horizon. Within seconds, the surface of the ocean turned a sparkling red. The prow of the steamer, unstoppable in her power, threw a wave to either side, slicing through the sea.

"…And Remember that I Am a Man."

Part Five
The Promised Land

Chapter Fifty-four

Beyond the Land of Moab—1863 A.D.

"This is the land which I swore to Abraham, Isaac and Jacob. I will give it to your offspring. I have let you see it with your own eyes, but you shall not cross there"

Deuteronomy 34:4

"Gran'pappy, Gran'pappy, wake up, Gran'pappy."

Moses opened his eyes. "Betsy?"

"No, Gran'pappy. Grammaw's gone, you know that."

"Gone where?"

"Oh, Gran'pappy, you've forgotten again. No matter, I'll explain it all later. I want you to hear the great news."

He opened his eyes. A child stood there. She looked like she could be one of his daughters, but they were all grown up, he remembered. "What news?"

"The packet schooner has just arrived from Washington, D.C. The president, on the First of January, signed a law that frees all the slaves in the south."

"Jefferson?"

"...And Remember that I Am a Man."

"No, Gran'pappy, President Lincoln. Once the war is over, there'll be no more slavery."

"The war? Are the British still blockading?"

"*Gran'pappy!* Pay attention; this is important. Can you understand this much? There is to be no more slavery."

No more slavery. Moses could understand that. There would be no more slavery for those children and grandchildren he had been unable to find. He wondered if Naomi still lived to enjoy a short time of freedom in her old age.

He remembered now that Abraham Lincoln, a Yankee, was president, and a horrible war raged across the south. And the spilled blood would not be black or white, but red. Freedom came at a cost, as he well knew. Many northern soldiers would pay a higher price than Moses Grandy had paid and most would pay that steepest of prices for people they had never met.

He drifted off.

*

Moses stood on the shore of a wide river. Unlike the brown hue of the Pasquotank, The Dismal Swamp Canal and other waterways of his youth, this stream was light blue with ribbons of silver as it danced with current and wind. Although he stood on a wooded shore, where the shallows grew weeds and water flowers, the other side seemed barren, like some of the desert lands he'd seen on his voyages to the Mediterranean Sea. Sand dunes went on into the distance like the backs of whales swimming on the surface.

He looked into the sky, where a fat, summer sun looked down, and saw the skies to be a darker blue than the river. He smiled. There was a name for that particular shade. Carolina Blue. Oddly, he could look directly into the sun without hurting his eyes and he felt no heat upon his face. Or perhaps it was that a breeze, as fresh as the showers of spring, washed over him. The moving air made him aware he wore no clothing, but it seemed natural and he felt no shame. He looked down and saw his body was still that of an old man, sagging muscles and wrinkled skin, but he felt no pain in any of his joints as he'd done for several years.

Raising his eyes, he could see a pier of some sort, almost too small to make out, even though his eyes had regained the clarity of youth. Something was moving away from that dock, apparently a boat. He looked up and down the banks on his side, but saw no landing here.

Other than that, it was eerily like some of the dreams of his younger days, when he'd been naïve enough to think the whites might give him a ferry license. He'd dreamed of sharing it with Naomi, who he'd never seen again after that horrible day on the side of the canal.

The boat, for that's what it was, grew larger. He'd never seen anything like it. There were no sails. At bow and stern, it rose in graceful curves, as though huge swans paddled on either ends, their long curved necks in the air. On both sides, banks of long oars came up and flashed in unison as the sun caught them, and then fell to sweep through the water.

It came on fast and soon he could see a small, dark-skinned figure at the bow, peering across the water at him. He soon realized she was naked, but that didn't surprise him. He had figured the place out by now, and his heart soared. Soon he was certain of recognizing his first wife and remembered when Betsy had stripped naked and saved him from drowning. This wasn't Betsy, however. Naomi looked as young and beautiful as the day he'd last seen her and he wondered briefly why he remained old and withered—in appearance at least.

Naomi stood alone on the deck. The rowers, if there were any, could not be seen inside the dark ports from which the oars protruded. Moses sort of hoped the oars were manned; he could think of a few people he'd like to see rowing for eternity, never to step ashore on the far side. A fitting atonement, perhaps.

The oars stopped their graceful sweep. Without a sound, the boat stopped only a few feet off the shore.

Naomi looked down. "Hello, my darling. I've been waiting for you."

He found himself speechless.

"Come aboard, Moses." His long-ago wife dropped a rope, knotted every foot or so, down into the water.

Moses waded out into the water and, like one of those fakirs in the bazaars of northern Africa, climbed the rope with the effortless strength and grace of a young man. Without surprise, he noted that his feet and legs had not gotten wet. When he reached the deck, he took Naomi into his arms and gazed into her eyes, afraid that she might vanish if he kissed her.

"I love you," he said, as the boat set out into the river.

"And I love you," Naomi said. "Betsy told me to come on ahead. She's waiting for you."

He looked across the water at the sand dunes. "Over there?"

"Over there." She brought her face forward and kissed him. Their nude bodies pressed together and his skin drank in her spirit. Yet there was no sexuality to their nakedness. After a time, he said, "You look as young as the day I last saw you. I hoped for word of you for years."

She smiled wistfully. "I wasn't there. I came here shortly after we parted."

He started to tell her how sorry he was, but then realized the time for sorrow was long past. They kissed again.

Eventually, she pulled her lips away. "We're almost there."

He looked and saw the dock, made of the finest juniper logs. There stood an oldster with pure white hair and beard. This man wasn't unclothed, though. He wore a roughly-woven, brown robe and carried a walking staff. He looked vaguely familiar.

"Who's that?" he asked.

"He's been waiting for you," Naomi said, "for a long time. His name is Moses, too."

Moses felt his knees go weak. "Moses? You mean the Moses that. . .?"

"Yes, darling. That Moses. He's taking you to meet The Master.

End.

"…And Remember that I Am a Man."

Author's Notes:

This novel was written for several purposes. It is intended to be a tribute to a remarkable man, Moses Grandy. It is also an attempt to bring about a greater awareness of this historic figure and the significance of the Great Dismal Swamp, which was a hiding place for refugees, called "maroons" and later an important part of the Underground Railroad. In addition, it attempts to portray culture, religion, politics and other aspects of life in the new nation of the United States of America, which proclaimed that all men are created equal, yet allowed slavery. I urge you to read Moses Grandy's life story, and other slave narratives at the University of North Carolina site, Documenting the American South. This site was the main focus of my research. http://docsouth.unc.edu

Since I have no personal knowledge of Moses Grandy's life, nor any way to validate his version of history, which was written by another man. I must assert that my depictions are of events that <u>might</u> have occurred. The characters in the novel are also fictional, even those who I have named after persons mentioned in The Life of Moses Grandy. Also, I cannot verify that Moses Grandy was a religious man, but use him as an example of religious views of the time. I presume this man must have had a great deal of faith and determination.

A great deal of research has gone into this novel, and I took great care to attribute quotes applicably. Some of the words of Moses Grandy were used in narrative and dialogue without attribution, since it would have broken the flow. I acknowledge that any words or phrases matching words or phrases in The Life of Moses Grandy are quotes, as his narrative was the basis of this novel.

I came across the story of Moses Grandy while researching the history of the Great Dismal Swamp, which I hope to chronicle in future novels, concerning subjects such as the Culpepper Rebellion, the underground railroad, the digging of the Dismal Swamp Canal, and the building of a railroad into the swamp during World War II. I began with Grandy's story since it is the most fascinating to me.

"…And Remember that I Am a Man."

About the author:

John Bushore, who lives on the edge of the Great Dismal Swamp, has had dozens of stories and poems in both e-book and print magazines and anthologies, blending horror, paranormal, science fiction and romance. He is a three-time recipient of the independently judged James Award and two of his stories are included in a university course on Gothic and horror literature.

He also writes for children as MonkeyJohn, whose SpaceMonkey Adventures are a regular feature in Beyond Centauri, a science fiction magazine for children.

Books:

What's Under the Bed? (Children's fantasy poetry)

Friends in Dark Places (Speculative horror) 2003

The Prisoners of Gender (Paranormal romance) 2009

Wolfwraith (Paranormal horror) 2010

Websites

http://www.johnbushore.com

http://monkeyjohnstore.homestead.com

Made in the USA
Charleston, SC
21 March 2012